The Little White Cat
&
The Dog Who Wasn't

CASTLE IN KILKENNY: ROMANTIC FAIRY TALES

CHRISTY MATHESON

To those who keep fighting for freedom
(for everyone)
Even when the path is fading as quickly as dew in the morning sun.

Reader's Notes

Ailbe = Ava

You do not have to keep all the dogs straight.

Chapter One

Being a prisoner in the Castle of a Thousand Doors wouldn't be so bad if it weren't for the dogs. Dozens of them, as tall as my chest, black as fate. Everywhere I go, they watch me. They follow.

I am not pleased to be trapped here, but my days are not terrible. There are extensive gardens surrounding the castle where I may wander as I desire. I have my own room, with a clear glass window that I can open to listen to the birdsong and leave crumbs for the squirrels. The faceless servants are odd, but they bring everything I need and treat me with quiet respect. Every evening, Lord Trencoss points out that I have everything to make me happy and therefore I must be happy.

But the dogs. So many dogs. Dozens of them, as tall as my chest, all black as fate. They all look the same, and I shudder whenever I see them, which is always. Everywhere I go, they watch. They follow.

Tonight, they stand watching me in the back courtyard, sewing in the fading light. When they pace closer, the rabbits dart into the shrubbery, but I cannot escape. The dogs circle round like a shadowy nightmare of collie-dogs, lowering their heavy heads to snap at the air. I am the errant sheep, and they must control.

"I am going," I tell them, as haughty as a princess. "Just let me put my needle away."

One of them growls, and I shiver. I glance behind me, wanting to take note of which dog loses his patience so quickly, but already he has crossed paths with another and I can't keep track of which is which. I can't tell!

Keeping my head high and my back straight, I let them chivvy me into the castle. Several dogs pace behind me, their nails clicking on the stone. One leads the way, looking back to check if I am following obediently enough. Something about him gives me pause, and I rush forward a few steps in order to see him closely—but no. This dog has a notch on his left ear.

They all look the eerily the same, but they are not the same dog—impossible to tell apart without close examination, quickly lost in the crowd. One has gray in his muzzle. One has eyes too close together. Some have slight limps, or scars making a pattern in their wiry curls. They are real dogs, but there is something sorcerous about having so many of them, so much the same, all together. Real wolfhounds come in all sorts of colors and patterns, and even two black parents will produce brindles and white spots. I don't understand, so I measure my strides and keep the column of my spine angled just right.

We turn a corner into a broad corridor, pointed windows lining one side and huge doors along the other.

"No," I tell them. "I don't want to go into the ball room."

The dog to my left flickers his teeth. Not a growl, just a warning. Lord Trencoss has ordered me to call it the throne room, and the dogs obey Trencoss.

I stop, my heart beating fast at the flash of tooth. My birth father was the dog-master for a king wealthy enough to keep an entire pack of wolfhounds, and I know in my head the beasts will not hurt me. But when they rear onto their hind feet these dogs are taller than a man—and I am much smaller. They keep records of their success on the battlefield, and I've seen them take down an elk. It is hard not to feel helpless when there are so many of them, all around me.

The dogs in the back pad closer. The one to my left shows all his teeth, and the one on my right fixes me with a stare. The leader moves towards the doors, checking me over his shoulder.

"I do not want to go in," I repeat. Wolfhounds will not hurt a human, I remind myself.

Not unless it's war, and their master told them to. What did Trencoss tell them?

They crowd closer. A growl—so deep that it seems to come from the stones—rattles into my bones.

Fine. I lift my chin and go where they tell me. I am not afraid, I am—very well, I am afraid. There are so many of them, and they are so much the same.

The carven doors swing open as we approach; yet another unsettling element in this castle-that-is-not-right. Trencoss is seated on the far side of the vast room, blue and gold tiles set in a pattern that radiates like a sunburst around him, while a hundred candles flicker in lanterns arranged in tiers towards the ceiling, invisible in the dark above us. The whole effect is so absurdly over-done. Knowing he is seeking my attention, I avert my eyes. A small, polite, rebellion.

Instead, I look for the dogs.

There are two lines of six by the walls, each sitting at attention. They are half in shadow and I see nothing beyond what I already know—black curly hair falling over their deep-set eyes, powerful shoulders, strong muzzle. They each wear the same collar with spikes all around, Trencoss's symbol forged in the iron with his magic fastening them closed. My own six-dog escort crowds me forward, and I yank back my fingers before they brush the closest shoulder.

"Come and sit at my table." Trencoss smiles, a thin line on his ghostly face. He is one of the White People, born with magic in his blood. "Delighted you could join me for dinner, Princess Ailbe."

I do not sit down. I am not a princess, but I am tired of repeating myself. He can think what he wants.

"Don't you wish to dine?" Trencoss raises his eyebrows. "Princess. Sit."

He gestures to the dogs—it would be less awful if he could control me directly—and one bumps my ribs with his great head while another paws my chair into position. My heart hammers with sheer horror, and I jump away from the solid pressure behind and try not to cringe away from the mouthful of teeth that is far too near.

Resigned, I sit at Trencoss's table, but I fold my hands in my lap and fix my gaze on my gold-rimmed plate. He cannot make me smile, and he cannot make me eat.

But Trencoss just smiles, leaning back in his chair as though we were old friends. "So, Princess, how was your day? I see that you ventured to the fountains in the west gardens. I hope you found them to your liking?"

I hate how he knows where I have been. I don't know if he uses magic to watch me, or if the dogs tell him.

"Do you like the clothes I have prepared for you? Yes, you do, for you are wearing the crimson dress with gold trim. It complements your dark hair, my lady. And did you have a pleasant time sewing in the garden, with the finest silk that I have dyed in the most vivid colors for your enjoyment? Yes, you did. The weather was perfect. I make you very happy here, Princess Ailbe."

It is never any use to argue with powerful men, but I am truly tired of these one-sided conversations. "I thank you for your gifts, but they do not bring me joy while I am trapped within these walls. Give me my freedom, Lord Trencoss, and you will make me happy."

He chuckles. "Will it, my lady? What if I open these gates tomorrow, and let you leave...alone?"

I do not reply. We have had some variation of this conversation at every dinner since I arrived, and he knows I want to leave as I arrived—with my companion.

"But my poor darling!" Trencoss tut-tuts, his face contorted into a parody of concern. "Once you leave my protection, there will be dangers! You might encounter monsters..." He leaves these pauses, as though

I am speaking. "or brigands intent on ravishing a beautiful girl like yourself—or—wolves!" He breaks into cackling laughter.

All around us, the wolfhounds rustle and stare.

I would bring them all if I could.

"Much better to stay with me." Trencoss grins, worse than any wolf. "Therefore, I am delighted to share the good news with you."

I stare down, stiff and silent. I doubt his definition of good news matches mine.

"Since I have defeated your guardian and carried you here." —Trencoss's tone is mocking, and naturally he speaks of the battle between males, with myself the mere prize—"I am within my rights to keep you, as…" He taps a narrow finger on his sinuous smile, drawing it out, letting me imagine the worst.

But that takes no imagination. I have been the head Lady for two different castles, from the time I became an adult at fifteen until my queen was stolen a year ago. I know the things that men do to women under power; it is my job to nurse those women through their recoveries.

It was my job. In this castle, I am the captured.

At my continued silence, Trencoss is disappointed with my lack of reaction, so he clears his throat and shakes back his hair, swinging his arm so his silken sleeves sway and his gold bangles and jeweled rings catch the candlelight. He always wears a léine either dyed black or bleached white, both of which only make more work for the women who must weave and wash for him, and aren't even pretty. Tonight it is white léine and black cloak.

"I will marry you," he announces, pitching his voice so it carries through the entire hall, echoing off the marble and making the dogs prick their ears and shift their feet. "In three days time, you and I will wed, Princess Ailbe of Dún Allaine."

I rearrange my hands in my lap, as quiet and subservient as possible. "But my lord, I do not wish to marry you."

Trencoss scoffs. "That hardly matters."

I do not even glance up at the glare I am sure he is leveling at me.

"My lord," I say softly, "I am a full adult with no father to speak for me. My consent is required for the marriage ceremony."

"Would you rather—" Trencoss abruptly cuts off his snarl. He pauses, then laughs lightly. "Let me tell you a story, Princess Ailbe."

I have told him a dozen times that I am not a princess. My parents were servants at Dún Allaine, both Fir Bolg, and I have the typical look of our race—medium-dark skin, thick black hair that half-curls, dark eyes with a distinctive slant. Only someone as disconnected from reality as Trencoss could persist in imagining that a tall, blond, Celtic king could have possibly produced a child like me. King Bodhbh Dearg let me use his name in honor of my service, not my blood.

Trencoss stands with a flourish and paces back and forth, making his anklets flash and his léine flutter around his knees.

"I begin," he announces. "This is my tale."

Despite myself, the traditional words settle me for the story. My shoulders touch the back of my chair; my hands loosen in my lap.

"One year past, I received a message in the form of a dove. It was sent from Fionn mac Cumhaill. Prior to this, I never bothered to meet the man, for despite the legends around his youth, he was the mere leader of a band of fianna, like dozens of others across Ireland. But some ten years ago, he became powerful enough to build a castle for his warriors."

Trencoss pauses to check my reaction, which is none. Of course I know about Fionn, but I am curious what Trencoss believes—and what Fionn promised him. I keep my eyes on Trencoss and my expression blank.

He clears his throat. "By this time, Fionn had begun to style himself a king. When he married the eldest daughter of the King of Leister, the other kings and lords began to murmur among themselves that his place was now fixed. The question is only how high he will ascend."

The King of Leister is the most powerful seat in all of southern Ireland, but Saba is his only child—not his eldest daughter. As for the elder between us—that is, if Trencoss thinks I am a princess too—she and I were born the same day, the same hour; not even the midwife, running between the queen's bedroom and my mother, knows which of us entered the world first.

"I sent my messengers out to other kings in the mortal realm after the dove arrived." Trencoss glances at me again. "It turned out that Fionn's wife had just been kidnapped to the Fae realm and declared lost. In the light of losing the connection with the King of Leister, Fionn wished to strengthen his position now that his wife was dead."

Saba is not dead! She is hiding in the Peaceful Valley, where she always goes when she is frightened. Fionn gave up after three days, but I have spent the last year searching for her. The moment I escape these gates, I will continue looking still. She needs me. I allow no words to escape, but can't stop emotion from flickering across my face.

Trencoss is pleased to note my reaction. "You wish to know who my messengers are, of course. They are birds. That's how Fionn could use a dove—it's my magic."

I wasn't thinking anything of the sort, but I have been in this castle long enough to notice the importance of the animals. I settle back into polite disdain.

"The reports from my messengers were that Fionn had become even more important than I had imagined, so I performed a divination. I determined that his star is still rising. Therefore, I resolved to attend his banquet and enter into an alliance with him. I made quite the impression, for although I do not have armed men, I arrived with half a dozen wolfhounds. Everyone was very impressed! I was given the most honored seat at the table, above all the ordinary lords."

I did not see the delegation arrive, but I know his wolfhounds then were not all black. I made a poultice for his fawn bitch after she was injured on a boar-hunt, and I am distracted with wondering what happened to her while Trencoss natters on about his grand entrance and the favors Fionn bestowed on him.

"Since Fionn was gaining so much power, I was braced for his offer to be disadvantageous to myself." Trencoss taps his be-jeweled chest. "Imagine my surprise when it was quite the opposite—he was making alliances by marriage, offering up his lovely ladies-in-waiting in exchange for our loyalty. We went over the contracts in the afternoon, and then Fionn prepared a feast to celebrate."

It was I who prepared that feast; or rather, I coordinated the dozens of servants necessary to provide feasts and lodging to a number of kings and lords who all descended upon us without warning.

"If we wished to enter a contract with Fionn, we had only to select our bride from the ladies who arrived for dinner," Trencoss continues. "I had no difficulty, for as soon as you walked through the door,...I knew I must have you."

I wonder why, but I will not gratify him with asking. The other women were all genuine daughters of noblemen and kings.

"Fionn agreed to my request, and the more I watched you"—Trencoss swoops a hand onto his heart—"the more passionately I fell in love. Fionn arranged the wedding feast for the following night. But alas and alack, just before the druids arrived to lead us to the ceremony, a cloud descended and a foul miasma overtook the entire hall."

Or rather, it overtook everyone who had drunk the wine. I am amused by his lofty phrasing; the men who drank it vomited their guts out. The only miasma was the stench, which perhaps was so vile that it did form its own cloud. I didn't stay to find out.

"By the time we came to ourselves, the ladies had all vanished into the night. No one knew where they had gone." Trencoss raises an eyebrow at me, as though I might have known where they went.

Of course I do. I was the senior Lady, and I wouldn't have poisoned the wine if I didn't have a plan.

I say nothing.

Trencoss beats his breast. "For an entire year, I have searched for you! My beloved, my betrothed! I have cast every divination in my power, I have traveled by foot and by spell. Many times, I have arrived in a place only to find you had just departed—your footsteps damp upon the earth, your campfire yet smoldering."

Not true! We never left a fire burning.

"I have followed you to the Fae realms and back into mortal villages." Trencoss glances at me, clearly curious how a non-magical being like myself manages that.

I look away, still insulted that he would say that I endanger the forests by not putting out my campfire. My companion and I always took the time to do it properly, even when we could tell Trencoss was close.

"The other kings gave up," Trencoss tells me. "Some of them even went so far as to say that the engagements were invalidated by the brides running away. Most of the women returned to their fathers, who refused to uphold the contract that Fionn negotiated honorably. Disgusting traitors!"

Finally I speak, because this is in defense of Saba. "The bridal negotiations were Queen Saba's to manage, not Fionn's. I am sorry that he deceived you, and perhaps he meant no harm by it, but the truth—"

Trencoss throws his arms wide, interrupting me. "Finally! We are together again, and our wedding draws apace!"

"I will not marry you."

Trencoss narrows his eyes. "You have promised. You cannot go back on your word."

"Fionn promised, but—"

"Fionn had the right to negotiate your marriage."

He did not. Saba did. But there is no point in arguing. I have one point to make, and only one.

"No," I say.

Trencoss raises his eyebrows. "You think to refuse my offer of marriage?"

Visions flash through my head—the battered women under my care, what he would do if I am his mere prisoner—but my heart is already broken twice over, and he can trap my body but I will make no promises of the soul.

"I refuse," I repeat, holding myself close and tight.

Trencoss smiles, slow and thin. "Let us try this again. Ailbe of Dún Allaine, will you marry me?"

"I will not." The law is clear. No matter who negotiated my engagement, I myself must consent.

Trencoss glances around the room, crooking one finger.

Three dogs stand—another—two more. They circle our table, shoulders rolling under their fur with every step. One flickers his teeth, but the others do not look at me.

From my earliest days at my father's knee, I have always loved animals. In some horrible ironic way, it makes sense that I would meet my end by tooth and claw.

Trencoss crooks his finger again. "Ailbe of Dún Allaine, will you marry me?"

Four more dogs join the others. Others creep towards the wall, panting with nervousness.

"I will not." I clasp my fingers tightly, taking deep breaths to brace myself for the pain.

Trencoss laughs. "Ailbe of Dún Allaine, will you marry me?"

I would rather die by any other animal. A bear, a stampede of elk. Anything but a black wolfhound.

"I will not," I say, my voice steady.

"Very well then." Trencoss lifts his hand.

A few feet in front of me, huge black paws lift off the ground, and I can't help but wince as I prepare for his body hitting mine.

But the paws swing higher, until the whole dog hovers in the air. The dog's breath rasps in his throat as he bats at his collar, back feet windmilling for purchase.

Trencoss is watching me, a faint smile on his pale face, clearly pleased at the display of his own power.

The dog shakes, like a puppy caught by the ruff of its neck to remind him of his manners. But this dog is hanging from his collar, giant limbs flailing. Unwitting, my hands go to my own throat—

As suddenly as he rose, the dog drops to the floor. He rolls onto his belly and shakes out his head, ears flying, and coughs. Clearly he is not gravely injured, but grown dogs aren't meant to be shaken like that. I am horrified, shivers going down my spine.

Trencoss flicks his finger and another dog yanks into the air.

"No!" I cry, but the word sticks in my throat.

The second dog shakes in the air, flopping like a fish.

I find myself on my feet as the second dog drops to the floor. He lays on his side, chest heaving, breath rasping, and I step towards him.

"Princess Ailbe..." Trencoss speaks in a sing-song.

I spin towards the sorcerer as he lifts the next dog. This one gives a strangled bark, thrashing wildly just before his feet are snatched off the ground.

"Stop!" I cry.

I can feel two dozen canine gazes boring into me. They do not draw closer, but their eyes are intent, their hackles raised. I must stop him.

"No! Put him down!" I stumble towards Trencoss, hands outstretched.

"Like this?" Trencoss smiles, and the dog crashes to the floor with a yelp of pain. "What do you want, Princess?"

Without moving more than his pinky, Trencoss throws another dog to the side. The great beast tumbles like he was hit by a boulder.

"This?" Trencoss throws another dog aside, skittering across the marble. "This?"

The dog yelps. Along the wall, other dogs whine in fear.

I grab Trencoss's wrists, half-blinded with tears, knowing I am too small to have any effect on a grown man. "Stop!" I shake him desperately. "Don't hurt them, please! Stop!"

Trencoss jerks his hands out of my grasp, sending me stumbling backwards.

Despite the violence surrounding them, the dogs stay in their natural positions, sprawled on the floor or facing our tableau. They are all staring at me, even the ones he just knocked over.

Trencoss smiles, slow and predatory. His tongue darts out and whets his lips.

"Ailbe of Dún Allaine," he says, enunciating every syllable, "will you marry me?"

I swallow a sob. "If you don't hurt the dogs."

He spreads a hand, indicating the room around us. "Use your eyes, woman. You control this scene."

My own gasping breath pulls at my throat, my heart hammering. I can't bear to hurt them. I can't.

"Right now, everyone is fine, are they not?" he taunts. "No one is hurt, little princess."

The dogs stare at me with steady gazes that I cannot interpret, do not understand. I turn in a circle, checking that every single one is safe.

"So...Ailbe of Dún Allaine...will you marry me?"

"Yes." My answer is immediate.

Trencoss smiles. "Of your own free will, you agree?"

"I will marry you." I keep my voice steady, my eyes on the ground.

"Very well then!" Trencoss throws up his hand and all the candles flare high. "Our engagement is final. A woman of your standing would not go back on her word. Goodnight."

He spins and strides back to his throne, his back to me as if to emphasize how powerless I am.

I pause for a beat, and then skitter towards the distant door. I do not know how much longer I can hold in my foolish sobs, as though I were the one who suffered, instead of me being the one to cause pain.

"I'm sorry," I mumble to the dogs as I pass. "And to you. And you. I'm sorry."

"Escort her to her room," Trencoss calls, pouring himself a glass of wine.

Several of the dogs fall in behind and beside me, but even without touching them I can tell something has changed. They are my guardians, not my jailers. Our steps tap all the way across the long, grand floor, and when I finally reach the door it swings open on its own.

"Princess Ailbe!" Trencoss calls.

Although I want to run, I don't dare. I turn to the sorcerer, my heart pounding.

"Remember, Princess..." Trencoss raises his goblet, as though he is toasting me. "You may have the power of the animals, but so do I. You cannot use them against me."

The power of animals? I don't understand. I wait for three heartbeats, but he says nothing more. I jerk a curtsey and flee.

***

I rush down the corridors and up the stairs, and of course the giant dogs keep pace with me easily. I must hold myself together until I'm alone. I've lost Saba, and after that I lost my home, and now I've even lost—

I skid to a stop in the hallway by my bedroom, chest heaving. Did I see—was that...

I plunge backwards into the milling dogs, grabbing wiry fur as I trip over my own skirts. I catch myself against a muscular shoulder, my knees hitting the stone floor, and turn his muzzle to face me. The dog's eyes blink in surprise.

No. He wasn't the one I saw.

The other dogs crowd around, and I pull another face closer. No, not this one either. I seize a pair of ears, pulling this dog to look at me. Another. He drops his head and licks his nose, apologetically. Curly fur and midnight eyes waver out of focus and my breath stabs at my lungs, and I realize I'm sobbing.

"Acushla!" I cry. "Where are you? Is it you? You?" I can hardly see, hardly breathe. My desperate hands meet warm shoulders and ribs, but no one responds to my call.

A heavy head pushes through the others. I already know he's not right and turn away, but he shoves closer and licks my face. I gasp at the huge tongue, and then another lick catches the back of my neck. I would laugh—some part of me wants to laugh.

But I just sink to the floor, subsumed in a wave of black wolfhounds, all of whom look almost the same and yet none are him. None are my beloved.

"My Acushla," I say, my face in my hands. "Where are you? Where are you?"

One of the dogs barks. Another drops to the floor beside me. A third licks his nose. I pull myself up to my knees, clutching my cheeks and trying to breathe.

"What monstrosity is this," I demand, "that you all look like him? Everywhere I turn, I think I see his face, but it is never right!"

They pace, turn, pant. Almost as though they're as agitated as me.

"I didn't want much," I tell them, the words hot in my throat. "I just want my place in the world—to save Saba, and to work together." I thought I had found someone to be my partner again. "I only wanted to find her, and now look what trouble that brought me. And now I have lost the only one who would help me..."

But the pattern of speaking aloud to a dog is so familiar, so comfortable, that I can't bear it. I can't be comfortable while my Acushla is lost in this awful castle—imprisoned somewhere, beaten daily, who knows. It's huge, and Trencoss has shown his casual cruelty. Every day, I search somewhere different, and there are dogs I haven't met, and but none are him. Not yet.

"Go away!" I flail my hands at the not-right dogs, knowing they won't leave, but my palm snags on something sharp—the spikes on a collar. I turn my hand to check it in the lantern-light. No blood. Odd, but I should know better by now. Nothing here is as it should be, and I don't have the energy for any more mysteries tonight.

I push myself to my feet, slowly, one limb at a time, and wade through the sea of dogs, refusing to look at any of them. It's not their fault, but I hate them for not being him.

They never follow me into my room. I pass the threshold to my room, and they stop. They never follow me inside. Some of them will spend the night on guard, sprawled in the hallway just in case I ever wanted to leave.

I close my door, but it doesn't help. Being alone no longer feels like sanctuary.

It's torture.

Chapter Two

This bed is more luxurious than any I have ever known, with smooth fabrics made from fibers that I do not know, and a blanket that is thick and yet as light as feathers. But physical comfort does not make the mind content—although I'm sure I am more content than if Trencoss threw me in the dungeon.

My mind races ahead to the things that Trencoss might do to me, were he to send me alone to a dungeon. It was one thing to act brave when I was wearing a fine dress and dining upon silver and gold, but now—in the dark, in my nightgown—my stomach curls in fear. I don't know if I have made my situation better or worse by agreeing to marry him. He might enjoy making a fuss over a wife and I would live a life of luxury—but I will be bound to him even more tightly.

In ordinary places, a woman can apply to divorce her husband. This is no ordinary town. There is no magistrate; no over-lord to whom I can appeal.

I am more alone than I have ever been in my life.

I stare towards the tall rectangle of window. It is covered by a curtain and hidden from the sky by an oak tree, so the window is neither pale nor bright, but it is less dark than the rest of the room. As long as I can see that shape, I know I am not in a dungeon.

What a macabre turn of thought. This isn't doing anyone any good.

I leap out of bed, pull back the curtain, and open the window mechanism. At home, windows are made of sheets of bone or oiled hide, and one must push the whole frame aside in order to see out. In the Castle of a Thousand Doors, the windows are pure glass, and there is a small pane set at the base of the large one. As soon as I lift it, I am bathed in the chirping of crickets, the sweet scent of grass, the chill of dew against my skin.

There.

I am alive, I am human. I am trapped, but not wholly a prisoner. I shiver and slide back into my bed, leaving the window open.

When Saba was taken from me at Dún Allaine, I slept in the room we had shared and used her tools and keys. It was not only practical, as I needed them to perform her duties, but it gave me great comfort. Now I wish I had one thing to hold, to remember my Acushla the same way. Trencoss's story keeps playing in my mind—the story of myself, created by Trencoss and Fionn.

I wonder what he meant about the power of the animals. If we count the furry and winged ones, then I am not so alone. I get out of bed, wrap a soft blanket around my shoulders, and light the candle to go searching in the corners. Up here, the walls are made of wood, and there are always cracks in the wood. Here, behind the wardrobe. Or at the edge of the fireplace.

"Good evening, little mice," I call. "Hail. Is anyone there?"

I find a bun and a pat of butter on the little hutch and workspace beside the fire; the place where the maids mix my cosmetics and arrange my breakfast tray. I crumble it and sprinkle it on the floor.

Then I sit and wait, leaning my back against the warm stone of the hearth. Any so-called power of the animals would involve a lot of patience, that is what I think. It is the first thing I would tell my apprentice.

That's a joke, and just as my smile sneaks along, my heart comes crashing back down. I used to amuse myself with such thoughts, but lately I have had Acushla to share them with.

That's the story I want to tell, of my time with Acushla—and just then, I catch a twitter of movement. The little creature scurries from crumb to crumb, then sits up on her hind legs to examine me.

I greet her in the formal way, giving my name and asking how she slept.

She just twitches her nose.

"Mistress Mouse, would you like to hear a story?" I ask. "For I have tales to tell, if you have ears to listen."

She drops down to all fours, and I hold out my hand so she could come closer.

Instead, she turns and runs back into the crack in the wall—and I am devastated. I let my head drop onto my knees, crumping into myself. Foolish me, joking about having an apprentice. Maybe I was born with the power of the animals, but I have lost it. Look at me, being fearful and jumpy around dogs—dogs, of all things!—and scaring the mice away. I am trapped, and don't have any power at all.

Just then, a squeaking startles me into raising my head. It is not just one mouse, but a dozen, racing around the crumbs and then settling in. They like to curl up beneath some object, tucked away, but tonight they are all watching me, unconcealed

"So you do have ears to listen, don't you?" I half-laugh, my mind whirling faster than their little feet. Maybe I know more about animals than I think I do. Maybe I need patience with myself.

Tomorrow, I will do something about the dogs. Meanwhile, I promised the mice a story. I gather pillows and blankets from the chairs by the hearth, moving slowly and explaining my actions so not to startle my guests. I get the sense that they approve of me building myself a nest.

A short-eared owl calls in the distance, and the oak leaves rustle in a jasmine-scented breeze.

I flip through my memories of traveling with Acushla like they are a pile of tablecloths. The early days when both the wolfhound and I tried to use our best manners. Learning to build a camp together. Our first village. The first time he nudged me through a Door, and I was so afraid—it was perfectly fine, but we did not find Saba. Me building a harness for him, sewing and adjusting each strap. The night of the storm, when we worked together so desperately we forgot to be polite.

That evening in Lochan Uaine. This is the one I have been looking for; the moment when everything changed.

"I begin..." I say it out loud. "This is my tale."

We came to Lochan Uaine about three months after we escaped from Fionn mac Cumhaill. It was a human town, ordinary enough with its round thatched houses, grazing pens, and central well. The lake the town was named for had gone marshy then grown in, creating a serpentine sort of swamp. You could walk through it well enough in the day, keeping your feet to the path and occasionally leaping from one tussock to the next, catching glimpses of the strangely green water through the reeds. It was, of course, a place on the edge of Between, but the people there never spoke of the Good Neighbors. They did not even tell warning stories nor sing the songs, but they left out plates of milk and kept their children close. Acushla and I were looking for the door to the Peaceful Valley, so we sought out the places like this. We were not afraid.

One of the mouselings chitters, cocking his head.

"You wanted to know why we were searching for the Peaceful Valley?"

He squeals, waving his little paws.

Saba is the sister of my heart, but she was born under a curse. The Dark Man pursues her, but she is one of the White People, and she has a deer form. In her deer form, she can always escape to the Peaceful Valley. She can take someone with her, and we have gone together many times. I hoped that my familiarity with the place would allow me to cross the Veil, even though I am not magical. So we kept moving and looking, my Acushla and I, and this day, we found the village of Lochan Uaine.

From the lake, the villagers gathered plants to make the vibrant green dye. Up and down the kingdoms of Ireland, we are united by our love of bright colors. The town of Lochan Uaine bought plain linen and sold bright green linen, and from that they were wealthy.

Wealthy enough to hire us—or so we had heard. We had our pattern by then. I stashed our cart in the forest and put on my fine dress, and we walked in together, my Acushla and I. By the time we reached the central square, we always had gathered a crowd.

Only kings and their highest lords keep wolf-hounds. I do not know if this is the law; in practice, they cost a fortune and eat another fortune each year. Wolfhounds dine with royalty, who award them jewels after feats of bravery, like the warriors they are. Once glance at Acushla was enough to know that he was of the finest breeding, training, and pride.

As for myself, I am small like a songbird. My eyes are large and my chin delicate, which has a predictable effect on men. I made Acushla look more rugged, and he made me look more vulnerable, which improved our bargaining power significantly.

On this particular day, the headman of Lochan Uaine greeted me with a goblet of mead, and the town's guard and merchants and magistrate gathered around. My Acushla lay at my feet, front paws crossed, head held high. The headman took the first sip and I took the second, and we started in bargaining.

He did, indeed, want to hire my Acushla to go out with their hunting parties. It was autumn, and they had a few trained dogs but none who were so strong or bold as mine. At first, the headman declined any services that I might offer, but one of the women whispered in his ear, and we bargained that while my Acushla hunted I would teach the women embroidery patterns. Usually, I bargained for foodstuffs—oats and oil and salt and dried meat—and clothing. Today, I wanted to earn the large sheets of heavy, oiled linen to use for a tent, and had guessed this town would be rich enough to offer it.

Over the next few days, we turned out to be luckier than I had even imagined. They gave me the oilcloth straight away, extending trust that Acushla would do his part, and then while the younger men were away, my host's father spent the afternoons helping me stitch it into a tent. I had spent my life in a castle, working as hard as any servant, but in the same physical comfort as Saba, so this was all unfamiliar to me. This gentleman spent hours showing me how to tie knots, pack stores efficiently, and which type of trees would best support my new tent. Meanwhile, I found easy friendship among the women of Lochan Uaine.

The second and third day, the hunters did not find their game. The fourth, they took down a pair of boar, but Acushla was injured slightly. This happened regularly on his hunts but was still my greatest fear, although I never let it show. I kept on hand the salves Saba had shown me how to make, and scissors and bandages and a needle that could sew flesh. That day, I did not need the latter. I cut his fur away around the wound, so I could clean very thoroughly—boar hunting is filthy work—but the cut wasn't deep. Acushla panted with the pain, but when I paused, he nudged me with his nose or caught my ear with a reassuring lick.

I laughed. "You would think it is me that is hurt, not you."

He nudged my arm, his dark eyes warm and gentle.

"I am perfectly fine," I told him. "I am just worried about—"

Even I could hear the fearful crack in my voice. I was always worried about the warriors getting hurt, but I hadn't realized how much I worried about *this* warrior. Him.

Acushla cocked his head, pinning me with his stare, meaning: See, you are not fine. You are worried.

"Maybe you shouldn't go hunting tomorrow," I said.

Acushla gave a gusty sigh and laid his head on my knee. It meant that he was going, and I shouldn't be anxious.

The next day, they were to hunt deer. Before they left, Acushla assured me, with nudges and wags, that deer were not too taxing, and he would be back safely, but his gestures were—I wouldn't say apologetic, but they were restrained. He understood that I was truly on edge. He was not dismissing my fears, but acknowledging them.

I worked with the women all day. In the afternoon, a messenger returned, and told us that the hunt had been very successful. Now they had so much meat to dress that they would be home later than expected. The women cheered, and several left to prepare the smokehouses.

"Your dog is incredible!" The messenger turned to me, bright-eyed. "He understands so much! It's almost like he—"

The boy cut himself off in the same moment that one matron cleared her throat and another dropped a spoon.

I was disappointed the boy had stopped; I was curious what he thought Acushla truly was. I didn't know then, and I still don't know now. He might have some kind of Fae—blood or bargain or curse—but I was certainly not going to mention any such thing to the people of Lochan Uaine.

It occurs to me now, looking at the mice, that it might be me who was different. It might be a Fae blessing—or curse—that can only be realized by the two of us together.

I must find him.

The mice blink up at me.

"Thank you," I replied to the hunter, as though I had not heard the women's distress. "My father, the dog-master, always said that the best dogs can simply look in your eyes and understand your thoughts."

Everyone relaxed, nodding and mentioning good dogs they had known, which was my intention.

The statement, of course, was nonsense. My father never said any such thing, because he actually trained dogs. If left to their own devices, dogs would rather go eat something disgusting and take a nap. I love them dearly, but not because they read minds.

Once the women resumed preparing for the meat, I was only in the way, so I slipped away and took a moment to enjoy the quiet. As the sun set, I stood at the edge of the woods, stretching my back and hands after a long day of sewing. A fox darted out from the underbrush and paused, staring at me.

"Good evening, little lady," I said.

She darted back again, and I was thinking that I ought to go check my camping supplies, when she came back with three kits tottering after her.

I cooed. "What lovely babies! Aren't they so pretty? Look at this shiny fur."

I squatted on my haunches, reaching out a hand. I wouldn't approach a wild animal, but it thrills me when they choose to come to me. I ran one finger down each tiny silky back as they toddled up to me, showering them with praise the whole time. They grabbed at my fingers, and I laughed at their antics but kept my hands away. I dangled the end of my crios belt instead, which wraps several times around the waist and then drapes to the knee. I giggled as the kits jumped and batted the fringe, which was longer and fluffier by the time they were done.

The mother fox pricked her ears at a rustling, then yipped to her kits and darted away.

"Thank you for visiting!" I called after them—very softly, so it didn't disturb her hunt.

I was retying my crios, smiling to myself, when something caught my eye.

White. Tall. Half-glowing.

My eyes flew up, and looked straight into a cervine face. Long muzzle, big ears.

I gasped, but before I could gather my thoughts the white deer had already turned and leapt into the forest. I burst forward, but tangled in the bushes.

"Saba!" I cried, broken-hearted with frustration. "Saba!"

I caught sight of her again—another dozen paces farther, looking back at me.

A path! Just to the right! I pushed through the branches and followed.

I almost made it to her, but had to dodge to the side. We reached a meadow, and I ran until I had a stitch in my belly. "Wait, Saba!" I cried out. Then later, "Are you hurt?" And later... "Is something chasing you?"

I paused, hand pressed against my side, and opened my mouth to call, "Why do you need me?"

But my own question gave me pause. Saba had never run from me, never. Something else must be chasing her...I looked around, holding my breath and straining my ears. There was nothing else and the forest was full dark. Actually, we were not in the forest; the sky was too open.

No one was chasing her.

Or me.

"Saba?" I called. "Is it really..." You, I was about to say, but if it was not her then I should not alert whoever-it-was that I knew what was going on. "...dark already?" I finished. "You're taking me to the Peaceful Valley, right? Right, Saba?"

The deer form appeared again, closer this time, and seemed to nod its head.

I knew it wasn't her, had never been her. I didn't know where I was and couldn't think of anything else, so I obeyed and followed the creature. I could no longer see the lights and smell the village fires, so we had come a long way.

Saba has an animal form, a white deer, but she is still always herself. She cannot vanish into the air, and maintains her human understanding. She knows that I am safe in the village, and would never have led me away.

Even though I knew better than to follow something into the marsh at sunset, I had yearned for her so deeply that I could not think. I can't afford that, not ever. I am always the careful one.

That night, I failed.

I stopped, and the white deer appeared on one side and the other, tossing her head and twitching her ears. I did not argue, but I didn't go any closer. All I could feel was the pain in my heart—Saba was still lost to me.

The white deer appeared again, and stamped its foot. It vanished in an explosion of white sparks, and then it was a little white human-ish shape, still stamping its foot, and before I could look closely or run away the Fae sank into the ground, stamping and stamping all the while.

I was alone in the dark and needed to get back to the human village. I took a step, but the damp earth squashed beneath my foot.

I tested around in a slow circle before finding a safe place to walk. A clump of birch trees forced me to turn, and I mis-stepped and splashed again.

More careful now, I found the path. Step by step, reaching out each toe before I put down my weight. I must be in the marsh, where even the villagers who work here dare not travel at night.

When I first started back, I knew I was going back the way I came, but I had to turn again and again to avoid obstacles. Which way around these reeds? Or these? I knocked into an old stump and lost my balance. I caught myself before I fell, but knew I could have tumbled straight into the bright-green water, which could be deeper than a man at this point.

Something called in the distance. I was too terrified even to identify what creature it was.

Even though I was lost, I couldn't just stand here in the muck. I turned, jerky, staring into the dark, trying to find where I was. Anything.

I decided to go back to the clump of birches and wait. I couldn't tell if they were the same ones I had passed or new ones. But once I was thinking about the trees, I stepped too boldly—it felt like dirt until my foot sank and sank.

I windmilled my arms, flailing back. I grabbed an old dead branch, which was just enough to keep my balance, but my foot wouldn't come out.

I pulled and wiggled, inching my fingers up the branch to try to find something solid. It wasn't a whole tree, just something low and scrubby. I couldn't put any weight on it.

I was so stupid! I had been too cavalier, thinking that I knew better than the villagers. Always stay in the village at night. Always stay together. Beware the lake.

My foot popped out, and I almost fell the other way. But I took a deep breath, for I had learned long ago not to give into hysteria. Saba is wrapped around in stories and curses, and I am the one who keeps things working. I kept her father's castle running smoothly when she was gone for three years. She has the worse of it, and I do my part. We are two halves of the same.

And I had lost her—that night, and she is still lost today.

I crept back to the trees, concentrated fiercely on every step. Not allowing myself think about Saba.

The dark grew thicker and the ground solid, once I had made it to the clump of trees. The birch's roots made a steep tussock, and their trunks a narrow vase. I propped myself among them and spread out my skirts so they would dry a little, trying to be sensible.

Clearly I couldn't make it through the marsh with no light, and the villagers wouldn't come for me. They were frightened to death of the marsh at night. I debated calling out, but Fae were more likely than humans to hear me.

Dear mice, in that moment, shame wrapped heavy and stinking around me.

I decided that my best option would be to spend the night among the birches. It wasn't safe, but drowning in the marsh sounded worse than the other ways of dying. I heard freezing wasn't that bad; you just went to sleep. And the Fae might—

Then, suddenly, there were lights.

I went absolutely still, clutching my cloak around me. It was dark, and might hide me.

Bobbing lights. An odd, slinking rattling sound.

Dark again.

Bangity-bangity-bang! Metallic clattering—what sort of monster makes that sound? Is it coming from above?

The light again. So they were coming around trees and bushes, like I did myself—but so did the White Fae, leading me forward. Which one was this? How many? I racked my brains, remembering every story, every warning—

A deep bellow rent the night. It seemed to pull all the air inward, then split the marsh, bellowing through the earth and reverberating off the hills.

"Here!" I cried. "I am here! I am here!" And I slid down the tussock, wrapping my arms around my knees and swallowing a sob.

If this were but a story, my mouselings, my Ascushla would have been there instantly, and perhaps able to speak in human tongue.

But this was just my ordinary, foolish life. It took another quarter hour for my him to lead the small band of villagers through the strange and eerie marsh. I watched through blurry eyes. They banged their pots and shook their rattles and tested every step, and it took forever.

When they were close enough to speak, I let myself cry. I was frightened enough, and it might change their anger to pity. Especially the men.

"I'm sorry," I called out. "I was such a fool. I'm sorry. I'm sorry."

The light bobbed closer, footsteps squelching and low voices speaking to each other.

"Are you well?" called a woman.

"She's here!" said the headman.

"I'm sorry," I repeated, and buried my head in my knees.

Here was my Acushla, nudging my knee, pressing up against me. His wiry coat was damp, but I buried my hand in his fur anyways.

"Don't apologize," said the woman, wrapping a blanket around me. "They've caught many of us."

"Myself, I was lured into the marsh," added a man.

"I lost a daughter, well old enough to know the tales," someone else said.

"Tricky ones—"

"Shh!"

I allowed myself to be pulled to my feet. Two women had their arms around me, solid, and I leaned into them. I did not want to die, and I wanted to go to the Fae world on my own terms. Not theirs. Their bargains were always terrible.

"We're just glad that we were able to get out here tonight." The matron squeezed me.

"It's because of your dog," the head-man said, and the others chorused agreement. "We knew he would keep us safe from any *creatures* that might threaten us."

The way he said the word, I knew he meant the Fae would not tangle with a giant dog. Maybe they were small Fae, here; I did not know.

"And he followed your trail," added another man. I could place him now; the head of the hunt. "I gave the word, and he did not hesitate. Some of 'un can only follow game, but yours is right smart."

"You can just look at a good dog and he knows what you want! Her father, the dog-master of Dún Allaine, said so!"

This was not even the messenger boy, so my false story had spread quickly. The others murmured their agreement, and I took the excuse to sink to my knees and embrace my Acushla.

He lowered his head, and I leaned my forehead against his, letting my hands tangle in the fur below his shoulders. His breath was hot on my chest, his heartbeat slow and strong under my hands. He smelled like mud and fresh air and the sweet spice of slightly damp clean dog fur, so I knew he had gone swimming after the hunt. He didn't like coming home with blood on him; I think he worried it bothered me.

I wished that I could lean against his shoulder, but he wore the spiked iron collar. Most wolf-hounds wear a spiked collar when they hunt, which protects their neck from the killing bite, but I could not unlock the one Trencoss put on Acushla. I had learned to cuddle and groom and play with him without touching it, but I couldn't ever throw my arms around his neck or lean against him. That night I so longed to forget myself and just sink into the comfort of him.

"Thank you," I whispered against his muzzle. "I was frightened."

Acushla made a small, reassuring noise in his chest.

"You will always come to me?" I translated his intention, pulling back to look at him. "Unless you're hurt. Or trapped. Or something stands between us." I tried to laugh.

He pulled his head back, and this low noise was a little growl. He tossed his head, then nudged me. Firmly.

I *thought* that meant that he would always come, no matter what dangers stood in the way. Always. But that was far too large to assume; too big to put into words on his behalf. I just rested my face against the back of his jaw—before the shoulder, before the collar, but still almost comfortable.

"Are you ready?" said the motherly woman.

"Good boy," said the head hunts-man. "Good dog. Home. Let's go!"

The women helped me to my feet, and Acushla turned towards the village, checking that we were all together. We set off, chatting softly to make the night seem less deep, but not boldly enough to draw the attention of another Fae. The others kept close to me, offering me support on any tricky footing.

I could not keep my hand on Acushla's shoulder as we walked, for we moved in a slow wobbly group, always trading places and balancing and twisting. But all through that long, terrible walk, I knew we were together—and would remain that way. He would protect me at any cost, and I him.

Never fear, my mouselings—I never stopped loving Saba with every breath of my soul. We were born on the same minute, slept in the same bed, learned the same lessons, took the same punishments. Our fates are intertwined and we are closer than friends, closer than sisters. I will search for Saba my whole life, if that is what it takes, and I will love her forever even if I never see her again.

But that night, something began to shift. Loving Saba in exile didn't mean that my heart was frozen; I am not divided between one kind of love and another. In this moment, in this world, Acushla is here with me. I don't care if he is part-Fae, I don't care if he can't escape his collar. We work together and understand each other and trust each other, and there was a joy that was growing in it.

That was the first night that we slept curled together, my Acushla and I. I left my palette to join him by the fire, but my hostess caught us and shooed us both away. Acushla was the hero of the house, and she pulled my bedding down from the loft so that he might sleep in comfort with me.

It took me a while to find a comfortable position, out of the way of his paws and his sharp collar. Eventually, I fell asleep with my head pillowed between his forequarters and his chest, my body curled up to his. He kept me warm, and his heart beat low and steady into my soul.

Chapter Three

The song of the turtle dove wakes me, sunlight streaming through the glass pane and onto my pillow. I thought I was dreaming about the Fae swamp, or…mice. I have a strong feeling about mice.

I roll onto my back and listen to the dove. Nothing ever seems so hard in the morning. So, maybe Trencoss has captured me. Maybe I will even have to marry him—I shiver despite the sunlight. Maybe…

Enough moping about, Ailbe. I will make one thing better. One thing today, one tomorrow.

I slide out of bed, lean out the window to thank the doves for their song, and move towards my wash basin. A half-dozen blue tits flutter in, heading for the last of the—the crumbs. There really were mice! They listened to me, and I could see their thoughts in their faces. One blue tit perches on the top of the mirror and washing bowl, and a chaffinch hops across my floor. I set down my hairbrush and hold out one finger, but get nothing but a peck for my trouble.

"I'll bring seed tomorrow," I tell them, smiling. So this isn't just a coincidence, hm? Trencoss told me I have the power of the animals, as though it were something I already knew. I was raised almost entirely upstairs, with Saba, but perhaps my birth father gave me something after all.

Or perhaps he was skilled in handling dogs and loved them, but what I have is different. He never talked about having one-sided conversations with the foxes and badgers, but then again, we did not talk very often.

The faceless maids arrive to help me with my hair and dress, then a younger maid brings the breakfast tray and I settle at the little table by the window. Perhaps I should explore more of the castle today and I will find my Acushla to guarding one of the doors that I have not yet encountered. It is, after all, called the Castle of a Thousand Doors, although I have not wasted my time counting them.

I spread the preserved fruit on toast and pour the rich brown tisane. I do like the food here—I should figure out how to send my compliments to the cook. It's basic household management to be on good terms with the cook, and polite besides. Because there are so many unusual foods—light and fluffy breads, as much sweetener as I want—I assume that we are in one of the Fae realms, but I'm not really sure. It could be that the servants are ordinary, and it is just Trencoss's sorcery that makes them appear faceless. Or maybe his magic fetches things from other places or times.

I am not particularly interested in that puzzle. I have things to do today. I catch the last of the preserved fruit on my finger and tuck the waxed cloth around the cheese, considering my options. I tidy my room, don my headdress, and head out.

As soon as I open the door, a half-dozen dogs scramble to their feet. I clap my hands.

"That is enough of this!" I declare.

One of the wolfhounds cocks his head.

"See what I mean? I don't even remember which one you are. If you always look at me like that, you might be a funny one. If you're the one who licked his lips, you're apologetic. None of us can get along with each other like this, can we?"

They all watch me. Dogs are always good listeners, but I suspect these ones understand.

"I don't know how many of you there are in this palace, but all of you who want to work with me—meet me in an hour. I will find a room. And anyone who wishes to follow me personally?" I waggle my finger at them. "My own guard must attend the meeting, so that means all of you. Attendance is optional for the dogs who only work the stable and gates."

With that, I lift my chin and soar past the giant beasts, my skirt fluttering behind me.

***

I spend a while opening and closing doors (all different colors and patterns, highly ostentatious) to find a room that suits my purposes. The palace itself forms two half-finished squares. The front courtyard has a broad paved area, appropriate for mustering troops, sorting a delivery caravan, or hosting a party—not that I have seen anyone human to invite. Small gardens with walls or hedges spread on the far sides of the open area, and I have not had time to explore them all yet. I assume the kitchen wing is at the far side, but I need to go and check. The cook seems to manage without me, but I must find the stillroom.

The back of the castle cradles the nicest gardens. Right out the back steps is a little paved sitting area, shaded by trees and scented with roses. It is my favorite place to sew—and I have to admit, Trencoss has given me a good sewing box. If I wander farther, there are flower gardens and herb gardens, and even several statues that shoot water into the air, each sitting in their own little pond. I have heard of these "fountains" in far-away places like Rome, but never thought I would see one. I wasn't even sure they were real, although come to think of it, they might be magic. I am suspicious of everything now

Beyond that, there are orchards on this side of the castle with the lake in the distance. On the other side, there are meadows with the mountains in the distance. But between me and the lake and the mountains, Trencoss has a high wall. When I tried to examine it closely, the dogs pushed me away and bared their teeth.

The castle is four stories tall and it takes several minutes to walk from one end to the other, and it seems to me that none of it matches properly. The rooms are different, some of them small and dark while others could hold entire barracks. Some are filled with looms like the workrooms in the castles where I lived with Saba, and others have furniture and tools that I do not recognize in the slightest.

I end up choosing a large, pretty room on the ground floor, with wide glass doors leading into the back gardens. So much glass! I have to admit, I am impressed by all the glass. I like seeing nature when I am snug inside. Based on the nature of the tools on the shelves and the subjects of the paintings, I suspect this room was used for teaching. I push the few items of furniture out of the way and lay out the rugs and mats instead, for a gathering that will be canine instead of human.

I examine the items on the shelves, searching for anything useful, my mind busy the whole time. I do not wish to marry Trencoss, but he considers that I am already bound to him. I have attended many meetings in other castles, available to pour drinks and demonstrate the importance of my lord—Saba's father, and then her husband. I always stand quietly, but I know how to listen, so I know about the terms of bargaining.

In order to escape the marriage that Trencoss expects, I have to adjust the bargain that he has laid out, or propose something he cannot resist.

So far, the only bargain he has offered was that I could leave, if I am willing to leave alone.

No. I will marry my worst enemy and lay with that slime for the rest of my life, rather than leave the only companion that I have left.

The black wolfhounds begin to arrive. I hold out my hand and each one sniffs it, solemnly. A few them turn for me to rub their ears, and others pull back with their heads held high. Some wander about the room, sniffing and pawing, others sit and watch by the windows or doors. It is raining lightly, and some of their coats are damp. The cheerful, airy, room becomes crowded and smells very much like dog. After several minutes with no new arrivals, I figure this is everyone who chose to attend.

My Acushla is not here. Never mind. That simply tells me he is not free like the others, for I know he would come if he could.

I clap my hands again. All the big, shaggy heads swing towards me, and I still have to fight down panic. It's the natural reaction to their predator forms—and also, it is uncanny, so many and so much the same. I never cared for sorcery.

"My friends!" I speak clearly, but do not yell. After all, dogs have excellent hearing. "I apologize for taking liberties, but I must organize you in some way. So first of all, we need names." Actually, it's rude to not present myself properly. "I am Ailbe. I am—I was—" I stumble under their steady gazes, unused to talking about myself. I draw breath and try again. "I was born to a serving woman in the castle of Bodhbh Dearg, King of Leinster, on the same day that his first child was born. The queen called my mother to keep her company, and the two women became fast friends. Therefore, I was raised with the Princess Saba from the moment of birth. We were, I suppose you could say, littermates..."

That sounds a little silly to say out loud. One of the dogs sneezes, which is a dog's way of laughing.

"Or not," I agree. "At any rate, I trained with her, and when she married I followed her to the castle of Fionn mac Cumhaill. And now...here I am." There, done with that part. I brush off my hands and smile. "Now, as for all of you! Wait—how many are there?"

It takes a couple of circuits around the room, for some of them *will* keep milling about, but I point very clearly where they must stand and one of them growls for the others to pay attention. Lined up, they aren't so overwhelming.

There are twenty-four, which is a good proper number. Two dozens, or a set of six for each of the four cardinal directions. But they are already moving around again, trying to sniff me or look out the window. I clap my hands for their attention.

"You all need names!" I declare.

Some perk their ears, but others turn away.

"I'm terribly sorry," I say. "I'm sure you already have names of your own, and it's disrespectful to give you new ones. But you cannot speak, and I must have something to call you. Then I can remember who you are." And once I know each dog, I won't be afraid of them any more, but I am not about to say that out loud.

I glance around the room again, and my eyes catch. When I was learning Greek with Saba, we had a painting like that. The symbols are something called the alphabet, and there were twenty-four of them. The Greeks could paint them on parchment, which then recite their message for them. I'm not clear on the details, for we only had a Greek tutor for a year, but I memorized the letters. Aha, there it is—they have a box of tiles, like we had in our own schoolroom, each painted with a symbol.

"Here we go!" I sweep my arms. "I shall call you each by a letter. Then it's not a real name, so it doesn't take the place of who you already are."

The dogs like this. The lighter-hearted ones give an open-mouth pant and a little prance, and even the more solemn dogs pad out of my way, watching me with ears pricked.

"This is why I called my companion dog Acushla," I explain, as I sort out the rugs and tiles. "And he called me Mavourneen. Or I mean—rather"—it all sounds silly when I have to explain—"I called myself Mavourneen when I was speaking out loud. From him, that is."

It means "my heartbeat," that's all, and "my little joy." I'm not sure when they turned from just words tripping lightly off my tongue to something like names, that I no longer said a stór or cuisle mo chroidhe. He became my Acushla, and I was his Mavourneen.

When I saw my own mother, she was more concerned about teaching me manners than calling me endearments, but Saba's mother called me Mavourneen when she kissed me goodnight. May she rest with the goddess.

"Alpha," I recite, pointing at the tile in front of a little rug. "Beta, gamma, delta, epsilon. Come, stand by them, my friends. Each of you choose one. Zeta, eta, theta—no, you can't sit on two. You, put down that tile!"

The bossy dog growls again and the other one drops the tile. I put it back on the mat after iota.

The bossy dog chooses Theta, still managing to imply that he is suspicious of my idea. I memorize the tiny details that make him unique. I will be sure to watch out for Theta.

The dogs grow terribly intent on choosing their names. A couple drop casually next to Pi and Tau, heads on their front paws. Two others get into a scrap over Alpha. I think the one with the intense gaze picks Rho not because he cares about the name, but because when he's standing there, he can see out the window. The others pace back and forth, sniffing the tiles carefully, nudging me so that I say the names again.

I add the sounds, and when I *ooo* for Omikron, one of the dogs howls along and eagerly pushes his way to the proper mat. Mu and Nu choose their letters together, settling down back-to-back. The dog for Xi picks up his tile and moves both it and himself to the far side of the room. The dog who didn't get Alpha feels very strongly about Upsilon, pushing a more even-tempered dog onto Phi, since he—Upsilon—is the largest one. Someone barks, someone skids on a mat, and someone whines and knocks over a chair.

As for me, I'm laughing. Imagine that! Actually laughing! One sleeper sighs and turns around so his tail is on Tau and his head is under a shelf, and I laugh more.

"Lambda!" I call. "Do we have a Lambda in the house?"

Two of them race over, which makes an entire avalanche of dog, and I laugh harder.

"You can be Sigma," I suggest to the slower one, who hangs his head. "We really need a Sigma. It's one of my favorites."

At that, he perks up and makes his claim. I ruffle his fur and he wipes me with a giant tongue.

I circle the room, taking time to speak with each one. I find where they like to be petted, noticing their slight physical differences. Their personalities, it turns out, are vastly different. Some sniff me all over, some wag their tails, some give me one regal tap of their nose. Their personalities emerge more honestly than humans, without so many words getting in the way. I have names to think of them now, instead of a constant barrage of not-Acushla, not-Acushla everywhere.

"There!" I put my hands on my hips, beaming around the room. "I think we begin to know each other now. If you—"

I hear a deep rumble, then more until it's a harmony of warning. They are growling at me! My stomach plunges. What have I done—

"Well, well, well."

The voice comes from behind me, and I spin around, my heart clattering.

My fiancé has found us.

Chapter Four

"Go," Trencoss tells the dogs, flicking his fingers. "I wish to speak to my beloved."

My skin crawls, but I merely clasp my hands and bow my head. The door on the far side of the room opens of its own accord, and most of the dogs leave—some slinking, some bounding, most pretending something very interesting just occurred outside. Tau yawns, padding behind.

I do not look over, but I can hear several sets of breathing still behind me. Feel their solid protection at my back.

"I said go!" Trencoss raises his arm, and my eyes follow where he points.

Sigma is hauled upwards, drooping from his collar like a puppy. His eyes widen in shock as his body rattles back and forth, front paws swinging in the air. They catch on two tiles, clattering into a hundred pieces. Then the collar releases Sigma and he drops, coughing.

Rho nudges him, worried. Sigma shakes his head and stands. These big dogs are tough but I can't stand to see this.

"Go," I whisper, as Trencoss lifts his hand. "I will be fine."

I will make one thing better, I think as the last dogs file away. I can't do much, but I will make one thing better.

My eyes fall on my headdress, set aside while I was stooping and working. The shimmering jewels and fine veils remind me of Trencoss's bragging the night before. While I was busy, I felt satisfied for the first time in days—and I have it. A tiny chink in the bargain.

"My lord." I sweep a deep curtsey. "You said I would remain with you, for you had made me happy."

"Ye-es." Trencoss narrows his eyes, suspicious. "I have given you everything to make you happy, therefore you are happy."

"Of course, my lord." I curtsey again, and can feel him relax. "Naturally, I will be happy once you have given me everything I need."

He sweeps his cloak, drawing it around him as he crosses his arms. "Princess Ailbe, your every need has been cared for!"

"Every need of my body…" I glance up at him through my lashes. I have never tried flirting before, but I have watched the other ladies. "But not my mind. My lord, I am bored, and therefore I am not happy."

As soon as I say it, I see the flaws and my heart drops. I just wanted something useful to do, or some sort of delay, but Trencoss could twist my words a thousand ways to make sure I am not bored, but I am more miserable yet.

He presses his mouth.

Who am I, to dare to make bargains with someone so powerful? Saba spent years under her father's tutelage, suggesting her ideas and having him tear them apart so she learned to make them strong. I just sat in the corner with my needle. This is my first time attempting such a thing, and the stakes are so high!

"Come with me," Trencoss snaps, and strides out of the room.

I hurry behind, trying not to guess where he is taking me. Down the long hallway, up dark stone stairs, down another hall. Two dogs follow in the far distance, but the corridors Trencoss chooses are empty. I glance around, looking for mice.

Trencoss waves his hand and a door swings open. He gestures that I precede him.

I enter the dim room slowly, wary of what I will find. With another wave of his hand, Trencoss opens the velvet curtains. It is still raining, but the windows are tall and soft daylight fills the room.

It does not seem so terrible. I spin, slowly, seeing tall shelves filled with shallow boxes, chairs so deep and puffy that they might be beds. With another wave, Trencoss sets a fire blazing in the granite hearth.

"You like stories, Princess Ailbe?"

I do not understand. I was waiting for work, and I see nothing to do in this room. No looms, no mops and rags, no nuts to shell or servants to organize.

He gestures to the shelves, impatient. "You are supposed to explore this room. Take a box down."

I obey.

"Open it."

I do, and a voice lilts into the room, making me jump.

"I begin. Many years ago, there was a farmer, and do you know what he did? He took his cows down to the sea…"

I search around, startled, looking for the gentle man speaking the words. I close the cover, the voice stops, and I immediately am curious about the cows. That's a good story.

Trencoss shrugs. "The story is in the box. Each of them, they have a story."

"And there are…" I lean back, craning my neck to examine the shelves reaching towards the shadowy ceiling. Hundreds. Thousands?

"The ones down there are full of music." Trencoss gestures. "You may take any of them wherever you like. Out in the garden with your sewing, to your room at night, while you eat. I don't care. Listen as much as you want."

"Thank you." I don't know what else to say.

"The rest is in your solar," Trencoss says, and sweeps out the door and away.

I pull my arms close to myself, buffeted with conflicting emotions. I am thrilled about the stories. I love stories as much as the next person, and I haven't heard many new ones since I left Fionn's castle. And I'm terribly relieved that Trencoss's way of entertaining me is so—well, entertaining. Telling stories is a perfectly ordinary thing to do when someone is bored, although ordinary people don't keep stories trapped in boxes in a room with chairs like featherbeds.

On the other hand, he has just solved my problem. By my own bargain, I have agreed to marry him.

***

Well seasoned in obedience, I stay to explore the room—library, he said—long after Trencoss has left. I test all the chairs, climb up and down a ladder, open the cupboards, and select three boxes of stories and two with music to take with me. This is what Trencoss expected me to do, so I do it, though I am wracked with guilt whenever I feel my fingers tap to the music or my mouth smile at a story-teller's joke.

It is still raining, so I will go to the solar to work. I am relieved that several of my dogs are lounging in the hallway, ready to accompany me through the castle, which is better than traveling these strange cold hallways alone.

"Hello, Omikron," I say, tucking the boxes beneath my arm.

Omikron gives a little dance and yips his greeting.

"You are a talker, aren't you?" I turn to the other dogs. "Good day, Theta and Delta and Psi."

Theta stalks ahead, and Omikron puts back his ears and pants with a big smile. Today, I let my hand rest on his withers as we walk. I think we are friends, now.

In the solar, I discover that Trencoss has left me not only lunch, but also fine linen and silk léinte. It is dyed but undecorated, with piles of ribbons and beads and colored thread. Before, it was just a box for occasional sewing, but this unlocks a rich world of creative work. I sort through the materials; I have none of the simple spinning and weaving to do (what a relief!) but several types of lap looms for decorative work. My mind is full of patterns and color, and I can't resist fingering the vivid colors and sliding the needles between my fingers. So smooth and perfect!

Look—I am smiling again. So perhaps Trencoss is right, and he has made me happy. That doesn't sound right, but I can't figure out why.

Restless, I set the ribbons down and go to the window. I lean against the cool glass, watching the leaves twitch and dance under the raindrops. A rabbit emerges, nibbling the clovers in the grass, flicking his ears when the wind blows. He pauses, meeting my eyes through the glass.

Maybe this is all I deserve. Trencoss is right, Fionn did promise me to him. What grounds do I have to complain? If I had lived the life that I was born to, I would have been married years ago. Perhaps I would have had some say in the matter, or perhaps the winter would have been hard and I would have taken whatever man could feed me. He would have likely been twice my age, like Trencoss, for poor women die even younger than sheltered ones.

Instead, I have an entire castle, and hundreds of stories in boxes. I have fine meals and warm fires, and no one expects me to scrub the floor or even supervise the servants. Trencoss must be right, and he has made me happy.

Except for my Acushla.

And Saba.

So perhaps I am not happy after all, and that is why tears tickle my cheeks.

CHAPTER FIVE

I close my bedroom door as Delta and Sigma drop onto the hall floor with matching sighs. My bubbling joy of the morning has faded into muddy, oily, sludge. I tried to make a bargain, and Trencoss bested me in five minutes. I wish I could just bury myself in blankets and drift into unconsciousness, but I am not the kind of woman who goes to bed in the middle of the day. I must hold onto who I am, even if no one who knows me is here.

There isn't even anything that I am supposed to do. I toss my headdress and shoes aside and sink onto the window seat, sagging onto the wide stone sill. The chill sinks through my linen sleeves.

I catch a snippet of birdsong, but the window dims the sound. I lift my head, shivering, searching for the thrush. I open the pane to look around. Fine droplets blow onto my face, along with the scents of greenery and rain. The oak branches obscure everything but the few yards around my window, soft grass dusted with wildflowers several stories below.

I find this more comforting than the fine views from other rooms in this vast palace. It's cozy. With oak leaves rustling around me, I can close my eyes and imagine that Saba and I have escaped from our lessons to explore the forest.

Acushla and my favorite camps were beneath a tree, too. Our last camp was beneath an old mother willow, a winding river just through the berry bushes. It was so beautiful we thought we might build a house and stay through the winter, but it turned out that we were in the same valley with

Trencoss's castle, and he— I would rather remember last autumn, when I went harvesting in the forest while Acushla hunted partridge, and we had flour and cheese that I had traded in the village before. Well provisioned, we wandered the hills, pausing often to admire the view. We slept together in the sunshine, my head pillowed on his chest, and it did not seem like laziness. It was treasure, each golden moment.

I startle at a squawk and flutter of wings. The branch above my window shakes and spatters, and while I brush the droplets away something thumps on the windowsill.

I leap to my feet, my heart pounding...but it is just a cat.

A white cat, exceptionally fluffy, that is vigorously washing its face.

"Terribly wet out," it complains. "Makes my fur stick together. Terrible stuff, rain. Terrible!" With that, it licks its chest.

Automatically, I retrieve a small towel from the washstand, but pause just before rubbing the little beast.

"What are you waiting for?" it snaps. "Make yourself useful!"

Those are definitely words. Real words, out loud. I speak to animals all the time, but they do not speak back.

This is not normal.

Nevertheless, I stroke the cat with the towel, rubbing each foot as he raises them. If talking cats are unexpected, that is all the more reason to be polite.

"I have a hearth, Sir Cat..." I offer, gesturing vaguely. "If you would like to warm yourself...?"

"Don't mind if I do," the cat replies, hopping down from the windowsill in a sinuous gesture. "Shut the window, now, before any more of that water can blow in!"

Quietly, I close the window and build up the fire, which I had not cared enough to tend for my own sake. I bundle a pillow and blanket on one of the chairs and offer it to my guest, perching on the chair opposite while he makes himself comfortable. I half-bow and offer my formal name, but I am too shy to add all the explanations I gave the dogs this morning.

The cat blinks his wide green eyes. He has a small black patch on his ear, and a larger one on his hind leg, and his fur has dried into a halo of white fluff.

"My name is Bob," he announces.

"Bob?" I test out the sounds, short and sharp on my tongue. "Bodhbh—badhbh—"

"No, no." He cocks his head, amused. "Not bay-vuh. Make it simple. Bob."

I try again, but it feels cut off and rude. "Is that all? So short?"

"Well...." The cat licks his paw, considering. "The whole thing would be"—he switches to a language that is blunt and prickly—"Come To Dinner, Bob, Ye Gurt Fool."

I nod. That sounds much more proper. I repeat it back to him until we are both pleased how well I can say all the sounds.

"How did you come by such a fine name?" I ask.

"Well, I am a cat," Bob answers. "I am always poking my nose through different doorways, and popping out in all kinds of interesting places."

"The doors through the Veil are intriguing indeed."

"Precisely. I've been through too many to recall. But one of my favorites... ah, what a place to land!" He twitches his tail in delight. "I had a little house to myself, with bags of grain to sleep on and mice going in and out the live-long day. Very pleasant. And there was a woman in the big house, and every evening she would make a fine meal with sausages and rashers of bacon. When it was ready, she would call out that name—'come to dinner, Bob, ye gurt fool.'"

I nod. That makes sense.

"So I would come racing from the little house, or sleeping in the sun, or whatever I was doing. She'd leave the doors open so I'd come right on in. She was a little silly, and always expected me to be taller, because she was looking up high in the doorway. But once I made some pretty noises, she would remember where I was, and say 'well, at least one fellow comes when I call, and aren't you the handsome one?'"

He pauses, and I sense this is my turn. "And very handsome you are, sir, for sure!"

He swishes his tail and wraps it around his feet. "Precisely. And then she would give me sausage and bacon. Ah! Mm! Ah!" He sighs. "That was the best meal I had, and every night she prepared it just for me! So I decided to keep that name through the rest of my travels, in honor of the best cook I ever met."

"A fitting tribute, indeed." I don't have access to the kitchen, but I'm sure I can save something from my plate in case he returns.

Bob continues on, telling me about meals that he has had in his many adventures. I manage to maintain my half of the conversation, asking how the fish was prepared and whether he prefers duck or pheasant, despite the oddity of the situation. Even when I have been in the Fae realms, I have never had a conversation with an animal! I am not even sure how he speaks, as his mouth does not move like a human.

"This is a pleasant room." Bob yawns, displaying his little teeth. "And the rumors are true; you are a pleasant girl. I could come back."

"You are always welcome." I may not know how to drive a bargain, but I know how to treat a guest, so I rise to arrange another blanket by the hearth. "Would you like a nap, Bob Ye Gurt Fool? I have no food, but I will share—"

"*What?* No food!" Bob's tail snaps and swishes.

"I'm sorry, I would give you anything if—"

"But how can you stay in this palace with no food?"

"They bring me a tray here, but take it away again, and I must have dinner downstairs. But I don't have a kitchen I can go to, or a pitcher of milk..."

"But this is terrible! Don't you wish for a kitchen?" His tail switches harder.

I bow I head in agreement. "I miss it greatly. In fact"—my emotions rise and the words tumble out—"I don't wish to be here at all!"

"Why don't you leave?" Bob glances at the window. "Well, of course you don't wish to leave just yet. But it will stop raining eventually."

"I'm not allowed to leave." I try to hold my feelings in my chest, but tears well in my eyes. "I am supposed to marry Lord Trencoss the day after tomorrow."

"Will he give you a kitchen?"

"I don't think so."

"Pah—no thinking this, thinking that. Has he ever given you a smoked fish? Or a rasher of bacon? One you can keep in your room, I mean, for nibbling at whenever you wish."

"No..."

"And he doesn't let you run about in the countryside, and explore different doorways, and meet new people?"

"No!"

"Then why are you marrying him?"

"Because...he caught me. And he tricked me."

"Aha!" Bob turns in a circle, then sits very upright with his tail swirled around himself. "Then we must trick him back. Won't that be entertaining?"

"I suppose." Freedom is more important to me, but at this rate we have neither. "But I tried, and he out-witted me."

"Aha!" Bob twitches the tip of his tail. "But now you have *me*."

"I am very glad to have you, Bob Ye Gurt Fool." Although I'm not sure how much good one more small fluffy creature can do, when I have an entire alphabet of dogs, a tree full of birds, and the shrubs full of rabbits and the walls of mice.

Bob blinks. "Tell me about this lord, who has trapped you with no freedom and no smoked eel. Then I will think of all the tricks I have ever played, and choose the best one."

Although I suppose Bob is a Fae, and can talk with me. He's more useful than anything else at the moment. I sit back down and describe everything I know about the sorcerer, starting with how he arrived at Fionn's castle just after Saba disappeared. I tell about how Fionn bargained all of us ladies-in-waiting into engagements, and Bob snorts cat-laughter as I describe the men's braggadocio.

"How did you escape? You don't have the smell of someone who knows the Veils."

"I only understood how they work because of—my friend." My heart pangs for Saba yet again.

"So back to this sorcerer fellow. I am highly entertained by your antics; go on."

I decide that it is better not to say too much about the dogs, but also foolish to lie by default and ignore them. "Trencoss owned a great black wolfhound, who escaped with me. And ever since then, Trencoss has pursued us both, using his sorcerous arts to find us no matter how far we run." There, that was honest but no more.

Bob purrs to celebrate our escape, head-butting my hand for some pets. After a moment, he pulls back and growls. "Could Trencoss not just find a new dog and a new woman? This is a nice house. If he offered plenty of fish, I'm sure someone would agree to stay here with him."

"He doesn't want someone else. He thinks….we are his lost property, and he deserves to fetch us back as he pleases."

The cat sneezes with disapproval. "I do not care for the sound of this fellow at all. I do not think you should marry him."

I almost laugh. "I don't think I should marry him, either. But what else can I do?"

Bob stares into the fire, tail twitching.

He says nothing at all for a long while, so I fold my hands and wait patiently.

"I am too small," Bob admits, finally.

"It's fine," I hasten to assure him. "I don't expect you to be able to help."

He yowls. "Don't *expect* me? Do you think I'm nothing but chopped liver, but less delicious?"

"I—no—"

"I am *very* useful," Bobs informs me.

"I am...sure you are."

"You are not sure at all. You are humoring me. Very well then, I will prove it to you!"

My head is spinning. This is the strangest argument I have ever had—and as the person in charge of staff at two separate castles, I have handled a great many strange arguments.

"I said I was *small*," continues Bob, lashing his tail. "Therefore, I will go and fetch someone larger. We must think of what sort of creature is good at dispatching powerful sorcerers."

"I don't know, I'm sure!"

"Then it's a good thing you have *me.*"

This is my cue to praise the little white cat, which I do. He extends his head, allowing me to rub behind both his ears, rumbling into a self-satisfied purr. I am tingling with impatience to hear his plans, but keep my demeanor appreciative.

Finally, he goes back to washing his paws. "I will fetch someone, but it might take a little time. Meanwhile, I will show you how useful I can be with my tricks! Just as good as yours, with poisoning the whole castle."

"I didn't do much harm," I add quickly.

"It was a *delightful* trick. I only wish I could have been there to watch. Now listen!"

Bob half-leaps, reaching up his front paws to bat at something in the air between us. There is nothing there—but there is! It sparkles blue, larger and brighter the longer he bats at it.

"Do you see this? Could you make something from it?" He holds it out, dangling from one claw.

I take the ball carefully. It fills both my palms, soft and light as feathers, sparkling like candlelight through colored glass.

"Why—yes. It's yarn, isn't it? Lightweight but fluffy, two-ply with a light twist.. I could...weave something..."

"It doesn't matter what you make."

"There are always criossana." Those seem terribly plebeian for such miraculous thread.

"That will do just fine." Bob licks his jaws. "Tomorrow, you will ask Trencoss for more...."

He spins his plans while I listen carefully. I must make another bargain, but this time I will do better!

While Bob is explaining, the gray day fades to black, and one of the faceless servants enters with a tray. I tuck the shimmering thread into my skirts, and Bob pretends to be nothing more than a cat washing his face. Once the servant leaves, I offer the best bits off my plate to Ye Gurt Fool, who climbs into my lap and nudges my arms so I can better concentrate on feeding him.

I steady the wine goblet he almost knocks over, smiling to myself. One bite for him, one for me, and we are sharing a plate. Food always seals a bargain.

"You are a good kitten." Bob sits up and washes his face, pushing me away from my own meal.

I wish I were as carefree as a kitten!

"You have fed me and sheltered me. I will come back, and I will make mischief for that sorcerer of yours. Pah!" Bob leaps off my lap, and I grit my teeth when his claws scrape my thighs. He trots across the room, and

I follow. "Open the window. Now then, you have been so good that I will give you a wish, as well. Merely unroll it when you are ready, and your desire will go into the world in a puff of smoke. But first"—he leaps onto the windowsill—"you have to catch it!"

Bob swings one white paw like a feline hurley stick, and bats a little ball—smooth leather with golden stitches. It bounces off the wall onto my dressing table, knocking over a bottle of scent, and I hurry to catch it. Of course he would want to do one more bit of trouble! But as I put out my hands for the ball, it skitters across my fingertips and flies against the other wall. Any normal ball would lose momentum, but this one rolls across my bed, bounces across the floor, and hits the door—which swings open, of all things!

"Watch out!" I call, hearing the scrabbling of enormous paws. "Get the ball!"

"Whoof!" a dog bellows, and by the time I get to the door, five wolfhounds are galumphing up and down the hallway, snapping at the ball, accidentally knocking it away from each other, falling over their own feet. I hesitate in my doorway, wanting to help but knowing one of those tumbles would do me an injury.

"Woof!" They growl and snap, all collapsing on one spot.

"Do you have it?" I hardly dare to hope. One wish—it is already clear in my mind.

"Woof," Omikron tells me, calmly, his tail wagging slowly.

But the ball rolls between Tau's legs.

"No!" I cry, lunging forward, but it is already gaining speed as it bounces down the stairs.

Two of the dogs follow, and the other three stand at the top, looking back at me and whining. Tau seems to move forward and jerk back.

"Oh dear, don't fight your collars for my sake," I tell them. "I don't really..."

Need it, I was going to say. But a tiny face pokes around the cabinet against the far wall, wiggling her whiskers at me while all the dogs are otherwise occupied.

I drop to my knees, extending my hands. "Mouseling friends, will you help me? Please, I do want that ball."

Three more sets of beady eyes appear, squeak, and vanish again.

"Thank you!" I call after them. "I am sure you will find it, too!"

I return to my tray, fetching the last crusts to crumble and toss under the cabinet, where the dogs' big noses cannot reach.

All the while, the cat is laughing and laughing. "I was right! You are so entertaining!"

I do not reply. I will thank him if he becomes useful, but just now I am a little annoyed with Bob Ye Gurt Fool.

Chapter Six

The morning after Bob's visit, I am determined to make the best of his plans, even though the wish is still missing. If they are naught but silly games, then at least I will have tried my best. I ask Alpha if he will be so kind to ask Lord Trencoss to meet me on the covered veranda overlooking rolling fields of wildflowers. Alpha pricks his ears, ducks into half of a play-bow, and bounds away. At least someone is enthusiastic! I am so nervous that I can hardly breathe, but I keep my hands relaxed and a small smile on my face.

Sigma looks at me, cocking his head in a question.

"Yes," I answer. "Your friends might want to come see."

Sigma nudges my hand and pads away.

The remaining dogs settle around the veranda or nose their way into the garden. Tau takes a sloppy drink from a shell-shaped marble fountain, and I smile as water drips off his beard-fur on his way to sleep under a table—the lazybones! I go out to examine the fountain, needing to do something besides worrying about attempting another bargain. Bob gave me advice, but it's not like Bodhbh Dearg, coaching his daughter Saba through years of practice.

I dip my fingers in the water when something catches my eye. A jay flutters its wings as it hops towards me, feathers dull pink against the emerald grass.

"Hello, little man," I say, kneeling on the grass. "Are you gathering acorns for the winter? Does winter even come here?" It's a funny thing, the way jays gather nuts.

It stretches its neck towards me, and I crouch to greet it.

"Is this acorn for me?" I laugh.

He hops closer, and I catch my breath at the golden glint. The ball! My wish! Carefully, I hold out my hands and cup the gift as soon as the jay drops it. He squawks.

"Thank you!" I exclaim, too shocked to move.

But then the jay hops back, and I remember my manners. "Wait! I have thanks for you in return!" My fingers stumble against my gúna, trying to remember how I am dressed today. The buttons are firmly attached, so I try my hair instead. The jay hops onto my knee, tilting his head back and forth as I fumble with my hairpins.

"Here you go. It's a nice shiny one, don't you think?"

He squawks and snatches the pin, hopping up and down before he flaps away.

I laugh with delight. "Thank you all, whoever helped! Thank you!"

A rabbit face pokes out from under a shrub, wiggles its nose and vanishes again.

"Hello and goodbye to you, too. I will bring you vegetables, tonight. And sing you a song. Thank you!"

I peel away one finger at a time, afraid the ball will leap out of my hands. But either it is finally out of momentum or it has been beaten half to death; it's nothing but a mess of tattered leather. I smile at the pinholes of different shapes and sizes, imagining mouse teeth and bird talons. Judging from its condition, even after my creatures caught the ball, they were good and annoyed with it.

There's movement in the castle behind me, so I slip the charm into my pocket. I don't want to explain it to Trencoss, and it will buoy my spirits while I face off with my fiancé; if he frightens me, I will just imagine all those little teeth and talons on his snow-white skin.

The man himself sweeps into the center of the veranda, perfectly framed between the marble columns, black cloak whisking behind him. I find the whole effect theatrical, and therefore absurd in a grown man with an audience of one.

Well, his audience is growing, but I don't think the wolfhounds strolling through the various doors and across the meadow appreciate Trencoss's grand gestures any more than I do. A flock of tits rustle in the bush behind me and a rook lands on the roof.

"My lord." I advance towards Trencoss, dropping into a low curtsey. My saffron-dyed léine bells around me like a flower, if we care about such things.

He crosses his arms. "Do you think to escape our engagement, Princess Ailbe? I warn you, it will go badly if you attempt to break your own word." He pauses, then continues as though I had spoken. "No, it is not me who will punish you. I am madly in love with you, and give you only the best! It is the rules of power itself. You should not violate promises when you are dependent on a magical place."

"Agreed, my lord." I have to interrupt quickly, before he argues with himself all day.

"You must—what, Ailbe?"

"I agree. I would—"

"This is much more pleasant, I must say."

I don't think Bodhbh Dearg ever had to deal with being interrupted so often. I take a slow breath and swallow my temper.

"Since you give me so much, my lord, I have—"

"You are asking for more?"

"I propose a bet."

Trencoss's eyebrows shoot up, and one side of his mouth cocks in a smile. "A bet? That is…interesting."

That is the point—he has so few chances to prove his manhood, being lord of all he surveys, etc etc.

"A gift for me," I murmur, keeping my eyes on the floor, "and a bargain for you."

"What do you desire? How do you challenge me?"

"I am sure you can accomplish something so small," I say. "A pretty little bauble has caught my eye, and I wish to weave the most beautiful crios to wear when I am your queen."

"I will give you whatever you desire!"

"You are so wise and powerful, I am sure you can," I reply, "even though this is difficult for mortal men to find."

"It is easy for me," he brags.

"Of course." I hold out the blue spool that Bob gave me yesterday, not allowing myself to wince when Trencoss leans close to examine it. He smells of perfume and sour sweat. "Isn't this pretty? I want three more just like this. One yellow, one red, and one white. Then I will weave the most beautiful cloth you have ever seen!"

"Isn't one enough?"

I open my eyes wide and helpless. "When is ever *one* color as beautiful as *four?*"

"True, true. What an unusual yarn, Princess. Where do you think I will find something matching?" He narrows his eyes. "This is the bet, isn't it?"

"Oh, it is not difficult to find!" I gesture beyond us. "You have such beautiful meadows! You merely gather the dew from the colorful flowers. Dew from yellow flowers for the yellow thread, white flowers for the white thread, and so forth."

"Is that what it is?"

"That, and spin it upon a rose thorn. Before the sun has risen above the Purple Mountains, of course, or the dew would evaporate."

He strokes his chin, studying me with narrowed eyes. "You think I cannot do this?"

"Of course you can! I could do it too." I smile gently. "But it will take me a dozen years, or perhaps a hundred. I assume we do not get old here, but you might be in a hurry for our wedding."

He eyes grow bright with avarice. "You are correct. I want you tomorrow, as we have bargained."

I hold back my fear and disgust, letting only sweetness show in my face. "Thus, I offer you this bet."

He paces around me, cloak fluttering. "What are your terms?"

"You will gather me the three balls of yarn that I ask for. As soon as I have them all, we will wed—that very afternoon, if you desire."

"That is what you want—a delay. What do I get?"

I open my eyes wide again. "I said it would be a dozen years if I gathered them. But how quickly can you work, my lord? You might give me the thread tomorrow?"

"So I might. Tell me, how is an Ailbe tomorrow with sparkling thread better than an Ailbe tomorrow with no thread? As you already agreed, princess." He pauses behind me, his nearness making the skin on my back twitch.

"I am not rescinding my bargain. I am improving it." I remain upright and calm.

"How so?" Trencoss places his hands on my shoulders, his long fingers sliding around the curves of my arms.

I shrug. "If you cannot give me the yarn, you withdraw our engagement."

"Ha! There is no danger that I cannot produce such a bauble!" He squeezes.

"Then name the terms you desire."

"Ahh, my lady."

I can hear the slithering smile in his voice. Bob told me that he would help me escape before Trencoss could gather the thread, and I have to trust him. I have to.

Trencoss slides his hands down my arms, holding my wrists. "I have a present for you, and I would have you wear it."

"What is it?"

Trencoss lifts my own hand and lays it against my throat. "A necklace, my beloved. Or some might say…"

My pulse beats under my fingertips.

Trencoss is not touching any part of me except my wrists, although his arms are a cage around me.

He leans closer, still not touching, and murmurs so close that his breath heats my ear. "Some might say…a collar."

"Very well." Not showing any of my emotions, I spin and step away, like a dancer. "If you are patient and bring me the yarn I desire, I will wear your necklace when we marry."

Trencoss chuckles, his eyes boring into me.

"But now we need a timeline, yes? Or the bet is not exciting." My heart thunders, but Bob told me this was important.

The sorcerer flicks his fingers. "Name your time. I will deliver it tomorrow, and get you in the necklace as soon as I wanted."

"A month."

He laughs harder. "A month? Of course."

"You will deliver in a month or you will let me go?"

"I agree. But Princess Ailbe"—Trencoss's voice drops low—"I will never let you go."

The threat terrifies me, but I pretend I am Saba, careless of my nobility. I nod my head, lift my chin, and sail away. Like a buttercup in the wind—if we are being theatrical.

CHAPTER SEVEN

For the whole day, I squeeze the tattered ball in my pocket, too scared to use my wish. What if Trencoss does just what he promised, and in the morning he waves his hand and collects all the thread for me? I might need a different wish then. After all, Ye Gurt Fool might have never bargained for anything more important than a smoked fish.

I might as well get to know the dogs better. No, that is selfish; I am making friends for their own sakes.

I invite the dogs to come with me (which feels much better than having them just stalk along wherever I go) and we explore another side of the vast gardens.

"And there's a wall here, too," I tell them, walking up to the stone. "Did you know about this one?"

Sigma whines and paws at it; Tau drops down for a nap.

Zeta, the one with gray in his muzzle, just watches me and sighs.

"I'm sure you did," I agree.

When we get back, I offer to brush anyone who wants it. Either the faceless servants or the magic itself does the basic grooming, but there is always more to be done. I lay out some old blankets by the fire in a work-room, and talk as they take turns being brushed. It is not like Bob, of course, who actually talks back. I have to hold both sides of the conversation, which I hope they don't mind like I do when Trencoss does it, but I watch their body language carefully, and try to only put into words the things that they are saying anyways.

While brushing the dogs, I try to examine their collars, but most won't let me. Sigma gives me a side-long glance and a gusty sigh, but lays down his head and doesn't pull away.

Carefully, I brush his fur away and look more closely.

"Ordinarily," I tell Sigma, "the dog-master would put these on before a hunt, and take them off when you are done work." I slide it back and forth across his fur. "These are locked tight and there's nothing I can do. I'm sorry."

Zeta scrambles to his feet, glaring at me.

"What have I done? I'm not hurting him, I promise!"

Zeta paces over and bats at Sigma's neck, lying on the ground. Sigma just blinks at him. Zeta growls, just a hint of a rumble, and then shoves my shoulder with his nose.

"Me? What is..." I put my hand on my neck, just gesturing with my words, but it reminds me. "Oh. Like Trencoss did this morning. You mean..."

Zeta glares at me, head lowered. It's rather frightening.

I drop my gaze. "When he spoke of putting a collar on me."

The room erupts with growls and snarls. I jump, my heart thundering, and Sigma lays a paw on my knee.

None of them are moving towards me; I am perfectly safe. I calm myself to try to read their body language. Alpha and Omikron paw the floor and show their teeth; Lambda whines; Gamma and Rho just keep up a steady rumbling growl.

They don't like the idea of a collar. Or me wearing a collar. Or Trencoss's collars.

I don't dare ask those things out loud. I don't know them well enough, and I don't dare make them angry.

So I murmur an apology and go back to brushing.

"You are very expressive," I tell Delta a little later, smoothing the hair away from his eyes. "I think you tell me everything with your face."

He thumps his tail.

"You're right, and the rest of your body too." I smooth the brush down his shoulder, and he leans in. It turns out that Delta loves being brushed, but not all of them do.

Theta leads me around the palace, shows his teeth if I disregard Trencoss's orders, and won't come close enough to touch. I wonder if he is actually loyal to Trencoss.

Xi is a loner. He is part of the guard rotation, but he doesn't seem to care about making friends with me or the other dogs.

Now that I am paying attention, it's clear they are assigned rotations. Like human squadrons, they work in sets of six. Theta is one of the captains, of course, but I watch carefully and learn the others. Zeta is my favorite, with a calm demeanor and gray in his muzzle. Rho is as steady and rule-abiding as Theta, but he manages to be more kind about it. And Upsilon is the largest of all the dogs—by just the tiniest amount, but it shows in his powerful walk. The squadrons are not fixed; the other dogs rotate whom they follow. Among humans, this is because during a battle things can change so quickly, they want the warriors comfortable working with anyone. My dog guardians have less onerous duties. Some to follow me; someone always laying in the hallway outside whichever room I am in; one set by the big front gate and another to patrol the castle. I strive for glimpses of the ones on outside duty often, and I think—

I can't hold back the smile that bubbles to my lips. I think that is my Acushla. He looks like all the others, but there was something in the way he moved. I am supposed to be sewing in the back garden and Theta won't let me go anywhere else, but...

I think Acushla was looking for me, too.

***

It's the morning that Trencoss will start on my bargain, and I am determined to see how he is going to do it. I wake before dawn, dressing by the fire in the barely-gray light of early morning. I swing a cloak around me and tuck up the hood, for the stone castle grows frigid at night.

I startle my dog guardians, who were sleeping in the hallway. Rho rises first, swinging his tail in a slow greeting, then checking the other dogs and returning to me. Omikron, Tau, Beta and Psi yawn and stretch, but it looks like Eta is assigned to stay at my room.

"Yes, we're going to go see what Trencoss is up to." I rub Rho's soft ears, and he does not actively protest. "Do you think he will gather the yarn quickly?"

Rho growls, a clear "no," and the others pad off down the stairs, ready to go.

I lead my squadron of six dogs up and down hallways, until we are at a little bedroom on the wing at right angles to the veranda. I marked the door from the outside when we examined the meadow yesterday, but did not dare go inside to confirm lest it alert Trencoss to my plans.

I hold my breath, hoping the room will suit my needs. The handle turns smoothly and the door swings open; everything in this room is velvet, in cream and dark red. I can't help but run my fingers across the tufted silk comforter and the sweeping carved back of the chaise lounge. Omikron sniffs around happily.

"Elegant, isn't it?" I smile.

Tau—the sleepyhead—drops onto a particularly fluffy rug.

"I know." I caress the velvet curtains as I push them aside. "It draws one in, doesn't it? But all this elegance doesn't make me a happier person. I'd rather have a tent by the river and a friend." Tears spring to my eyes. "What about you?"

Tau lifts his head, glares at me, and drops it again.

I chuckle and speak in a fake deep voice. "Don't be silly, Ailbe. Being comfortable makes life a great deal more pleasant."

Rho pushes past my knees, casting me a reproachful glare before examining the door that leads to the narrow balcony.

"Careful! This is the tricky part, because I don't want Trencoss to look up here."

Rho nudges the door handle again.

"I will go out," I tell him, "and you all can guard me from inside."

Rho lowers his head and flashes his teeth: I'm sorry, but you may not pass.

He doesn't want me to go outside alone, so we must negotiate. After a quick minute, where I discuss options and they approve or don't, Rho insists on checking the balcony before I go out, but is willing to wait just inside the door. Psi and Omikron creep onto the chaise lounge, the velvet curtain draped around them so they can see out but the light doesn't show. Beta is on duty in the hallway outside the room, and Tau is snoozing on the rug. He will be on his feet in a split second if there is a noise.

Holding my cloak tight, I slip out the door and close it quickly. The stone balustrade is right in front of me, space only to step once to the right or left. Hopefully this tiny space is still shadowed by the rest of the building as it was yesterday.

I don't know why it is so important that Trencoss not see me watching him, but the idea of being caught terrifies me. I don't know what would be worse, if he knew I was watching while he was unsuccessful, or if he could gloat in front of me.

Pah. I am used to being useful, not stuck with these foolish feelings. Maybe if I were an actual princess, I would know how to manage myself as well as Saba manages her ladies-in-waiting. I shake my head with the absurdity of the thought.

There is a flutter on the lawn below. I suck in my breath and press against the wall, nothing but a dark shape in the dark shadows.

But I am too intrigued to stay hidden, and gradually lean forward despite myself. By the time I can see Trencoss, he appears too busy to bother looking up.

But what is this in the air all around him? Dozens of little figures, zipping and darting. Sometimes I catch the movement of wings, but they might be fluttering like a sparrow or batting lazily like a moth. They are dull in places, but glint as their movement catches the early morning light. Even after a year of going in and out of Fae realms, I have never seen anything like them!

Causing Trencoss a great deal of difficulty—that is one thing. He strides further into the sopping wet grass, and I know he hates getting his boots wet, and he's so occupied with the air creatures that he can't even manage more than the occasional tug at his equally soggy cloak. I press fingers over my mouth, stifling a giggle. I can't make out all the words, but Trencoss's tone floats up to me, and he is frustrated. As far as I can tell, the little flyers will obey, but they take every excuse to slip out of his control.

One of the faceless servants brings a tray with a bits of undyed cloth. At Trencoss's orders the serving man holds it up, and with much shouting and waving of hands, Trencoss convinces the flyers to dart in and each grab something from the tray. I still can't make out who and what they are, but from the shape behind them, I deduce they must be collecting bags.

Ah...so Trencoss will make these tiny Fae collect my colored dewdrops for me? Perhaps they count as animals or are bound to this place. Can he command the Fae?

I would have guessed "no," especially after the antics of the last few minutes. But then Trencoss does—something else; it is obscured with his back to me, and too far to see clearly. But after this, each little flyer goes steadily where he points. I suppose they could all be abandoning him, but from Trencoss's apparent glee I assume there is no such good news.

As the sun creeps over the mountains, I lean on the balcony watching the distant fluttering. Rho squeezes out beside me, and I bury my fingers in his warm fur. Trencoss paces back and forth below us, shouting orders.

The sun rises higher, warming the breeze and drying the grass. The little flyers trickle back towards the veranda, where I assume Trencoss has set up another servant with a spindle made from rose thorns. He certainly shows no aptitude for doing anything himself. My throat goes dry as I watch the endless line of deliveries.

"How much do you think they collected?" I murmur.

Rho nudges my ribs, comforting.

"It always takes a great many flax plants to spin into linen. Hopefully this is not very much..."

Rho licks my hand.

"You're right. Trencoss would be acting happier if there were already enough to spin a whole ball."

We watch while Trencoss becomes grumpier and angrier, and some of the flyers buzz angrily or zip a wide circle around him. But there is nothing Trencoss can do; no matter how many assistants he can order around, the sun has dried up the dew.

I am safe...until tomorrow. Which does not seem very long.

Chapter Eight

I go another day without using my wish, in case I am more desperate later.

Or truly—I'm afraid to use my wish, because I know the Fae will twist and turn anything, and I haven't even done well with bargaining with a human.

But I'm also lonely. So lonely.

Several days pass. There is no real work for me here, although I embroider and warp a crios belt and mix up a few generic salves. I create a circuit of feeding the mice and rabbits and birds, bringing them seeds and cheese every morning. I learn which are the head-men and matriarchs, and I admire their babies and their nests—or in the case of the jays, their nuts. I enjoy these rounds, but I still have no idea what is the "magic of the animals." I wonder if it means I am supposed to take advantage of them in some way, like Trencoss with the little flyers—the magic is wasted on me if that is what it expects. I still haven't figured out if the dogs are hired warriors, or trapped like I am.

I've been listening to the stories from the "library" to keep my mind occupied. Gallant heroes, beautiful princesses, tall towers, brave voyages! But I know I am nothing like the heroines; I'm just the daughter of the dog-master and a maid. I'm not looking for love and I don't want anyone to sacrifice himself for me. I just want someone to talk to.

So that's my wish. I turn it over and over in my mind, trying to find all the ways it could be ruined, how it might become a weapon against the ones I love, which is why I won't wish to be with Saba or have my Acushla freed, or some such. If Bob's magic could sweep Saba here, it might give Trencoss the power to hold her hostage and make demands against Bodhbh Dearg. She was in the very early days of pregnancy when I last saw her, and the magic might rip her away from her babe—I cannot ask for the child by name, or even know if it exists. If I ask that Acushla is freed, then it will pit Bob's magic against Trencoss's, and I fear how that might play out.... Or my wish could be granted a hundred years from now. I have no desire to be buried together, whether or not a rose and a briar emerge from our graves.

But the only direction is forward, so I will take action. It's a warm sunny day, so I take my sewing box and my tattered ball to the central courtyard. I assume I must release the fluttering core, so I use tiny scissors to pull apart a few of the last remaining stitches in the leather, then pause. While I think through my entire wish yet again, trying to think of any way that either Trencoss or Bob could use it to trick me, I unpack the crios and tuck the loom bar under my foot. My fingers fall into pick and drop, shuttle back and forth, as my mind worries the wish-riddle yet again.

I pause to admire the crios as I stand. I think it's turning out rather nicely, if I do say so myself. I used horsehair for the warp, and keep the weft loose to show off the shimmering qualities of Bob's magical blue yarn.

Robins and tits flutter in the shrubbery and little noses appear below. Doves and rooks hop along the branches overhead. As always, a few dogs are flopped around me, but more appear in the courtyard, as though they all just happened to wander down the pathway to the same place.

"Interesting, is it?" I cut another thread on the wish-ball, and then push it back in my pocket. I'm not ready yet.

Their little noses twitch. The wee ones usually run once the dogs appear, so something must be calling them strongly that they stay despite the danger. Rooks hop down from the branches above, and when I glance up I catch a blurry glance of something with both legs and wings. Perhaps Trencoss's little flyers are curious about who is causing them all this work.

By the time my weaving reaches my knee, there are dozens of eyes on me—or carefully ignoring me.

Their pleasure, their anticipation thrumming around me—it makes me brave. I pull out the ball.

"I wish for a friend," I say clearly. "I want someone to talk with." I slide the broken stitching out of the tattered leather, revealing the glowing core. "Someone who is kind, and whose arrival at the Castle of a Thousand Doors will not harm themselves nor any creature who is already here, including me." The ball grows warm and I close my hand. Golden sparks fall between my fingers, pooling on the paving stones.

"So that is my wish—a friend to talk with." The ball fizzes, almost too hot, and I don't know how magic works so I toss it in the air.

It zooms above us all, like a comet into the bright blue sky, shedding a bright trail of sparkling gold. The birds launch themselves into the air, ignoring their roles of predator and prey in their eagerness to fly through the bright trail. Wings knock the glitter in all directions, sprinkling across the courtyard and lawns. The rabbits and mice shoot out from under the shrubbery and the red squirrels leap from the trees, all rushing to run and roll in the bounty. As for the dogs, they are so large they don't have to go anywhere; they stand and stretch and the gold dust accumulates on their black fur like snow.

"There's so much of it!" I cry, holding out my hands in the shimmering air. "It was just one tiny ball."

Sigma pads over and nudges my elbow.

"And me?" I answer. "I'm not a sorcerer or a druid. I didn't do anything."

Sigma snorts.

"Alpha, stop it!" I cry, as the young dog starts to bound onto the grass.

He turns to look at me, one paw still upraised. Luckily, these big dogs are so slow that there's usually time to talk with them.

"Let the little ones enjoy it first. You'll frighten them."

Alpha whines, and Omikron prances in place, begging me to let them play.

"Let everyone have a turn—"

Bossy Theta strides over and snaps at the frisky dogs, while gray-beard Zeta growls a warning. The youngsters subside immediately. Mu and Nu nuzzle the gold dust on each other.

I walk to the edge of the lawn, where I can best enjoy watching all the birds and animals in the courtyard and the herb garden and the lawn, frolicking. I lean against a tree trunk and let myself laugh at their antics as much as I want. After all, there are no chores to be done, and no one to expect me to be serious.

Eventually, the gold dust is scattered and the animals trickle away. Some of the birds swoop near me, and the furry creatures touch me with their noses. I crouch down.

"You're welcome," I say. "It's all right, you too. I know some of you are too shy to come closer. Stop that, little one." This to a squirrel who is trying to make off with a bead sewn into my léine. "Thank you for attending my wishing ceremony." I giggle at the absurdity of it. "Thank you for coming. Enjoy your gold dust!"

I get giddier and sillier, the way I never do with human company. I sweep over-deep curtsies, and call the creatures Lord this and Queen that. They seem to like it, and what's the harm in enjoying myself a bit?

The sun has sunk beneath the Purple Mountains when the courtyard has emptied, except for myself and the six wolfhounds on duty. I gather my weaving and cast one last glance around the gardens. The gold is all gone, every last sparkle affixed to fur and feathers, but—

Oh.

Deeper in the garden, a dark, dog-shaped shadow waits under the rowan trees. I just counted all twenty-four black wolfhounds. This is someone different.

And he is watching me as though he wants to come to me as much as I wish to run to him.

But his collar glints in the setting sun, and I know better than to flaunt Trencoss directly. Despite the risk, I lift my fingers, not even blowing a kiss, but knowing that if it is my Acushla, he will see. He will know.

***

By the time I return to my room after nerve-wracking dinner with Trencoss, my shoulders and neck ache and my mind is blurry with exhaustion. Tonight, the pies burst into song, and I was not even surprised by the absurdity. I find it ironic that I spend my days talking with the dogs, which involves me saying all the words, and the evenings wherein Trencoss says everything. Thus my wish.

I put away my headdress and hairpins, letting the braids tumble onto my shoulders while I rub my temples. I never feel my best this late at night, and—

"You should have asked for a fish."

I jump, my eyes flying to the little white cat sitting on my hearth.

"Sir Come to Dinner Bob Ye Gurt Fool." I curtsey, forming the strange words carefully.

He whips his tail back and forth. "I didn't design it for anything so complicated. You could have asked *me* to come back. Or pheasant. Cake, don't humans like cake?"

"I...I had cake and fish both. Trencoss gives me plenty to eat."

Bob sneezes in disapproval. "You could have asked for the key to the gates! A key I can do."

Did I waste my whole wish? I curtsey again.

"Put the whole castle to sleep for a hundred years! That would be complicated, but at least it's entertaining."

"But that would harm so many people!"

"I meant that you put everyone *else* to sleep. Then Trencoss wouldn't bother you any more."

I open my mouth, but close it again. I'm too tired to explain that I won't harm all the mice and blue tits and faceless servants, just to get back at Trencoss. I turn away to my dressing table. It feels indecent to unlace my gúna in front of a visitor, but I will brush my hair for bed.

"Principled, aren't you?"

I don't turn around.

"Well, you asked for someone to talk to. I was trying to find someone...are you even listening?"

He doesn't like being ignored, but I am very tired.

"Fine!" Bob yowls. "Fine. I'm doing my best. But next time, ask for a cake, you hear?"

He knocks over a spindle and two candlesticks on his way to the window. The leaves rustle as he leaps into the branches, and then silence.

I set down my hairbrush, glimmering silver in the candlelight. One of the many fine things given to me by an unkind man.

"I thought it was my own wish," I say to my own hands, tired and limp. "But I suppose that it never is. Not really."

I finish getting ready for bed, because that is what needs to be done.

***

Despite Bob's grumpiness, in the morning there are occasional glints sparkling at the edge of my vision, and I suspect that my wish is...doing something.

Since I can't tell what, exactly, I check on Trencoss and the winged people, like I do every morning. The celandine is blooming in a cheerful golden spill, but Trencoss has only a few yards of yellow thread. I have time.

Restless and unsettled, I go out with the dogs. All but one set come with me, and we make a circuit around the inside of the walls. It's not enough to wear out the dogs, but I'm pleasantly exhausted—and besides, they give me reason to smile, running in the bright grass and chasing each other through the trees.

When I return to my room to wash and change, the hallway is dense with sparkles, so I am on my guard for anything unexpected. I open the door carefully.

A man is sitting in the tree outside my window. That certainly qualifies.

I open the window and he smiles and crawls right in. I am a stuck for words, as I have never yet greeted an elegant young man climbing in my bedroom window.

He is tall and blond and handsome for a Celt; wearing fine linen garments, a large brooch on his cloak and a large sword on his back.

"Oh, you *are* beautiful!" he exclaims, and drops to his knees in front of me, which is especially startling given my wind-blown hair and muddy gown. "Bob was unable to tell me, but I suspected that you must be lovely, and you truly are!"

"I...am..." I am starting to deny any such thing—but that would be contradicting him.

He clasps his hands. "Hair like midnight, and eyes like the brightest stars!"

"My eyes are brown." Stars are... yellow? White? My eyes would be strange that way.

He already has a hand on his heart. "Your lips are the sweetest bow, and your rosy blush shows your maidenly modesty!"

My lips are hanging open in shock, that's what they're doing. And I am blushing, but most white men don't notice it.

"Bob sent you?" I manage to get out.

"Yes. My apologies." He half-bows from his position on the floor. "I am Fergus mac Finnbarr, second son of the King of Ó Fearghail. You must be Princess Ailbe of Dún Allaine?"

"Yes...but I'm not a princess—"

He is already talking again, rising to his feet as he reassures me of his heroic capabilities. I am familiar with the type of training he describes, including that the men are taught to tell tales of their own glory and prowess. Battles can be lost or won depending on the head warriors' swagger...although as I smile and insert the appropriate accolades, it occurs to me that Prince Fergus might not have matched wits with a sorcerer like Trencoss. My fiancé doesn't appear intimidated by much.

The prince concludes his recital and smiles hopefully at me.

I smile in return.

He bows with a flourish.

I drop a deep curtsey.

"Oh beautiful princess, you are so...serene."

What sort of compliment is that?

"And self-possessed. For a lady imprisoned and in distress, I mean."

Did he expect me to be sobbing and bewailing my fate? It is not possible to sob for two weeks straight; my throat would give out.

"Not to mention, you are very beautiful."

Now at least he is trying, although becoming somewhat repetitive. "Thank you. And you are very brave and strong."

He bows, then pauses.

"I am grateful that you have come to rescue me. Since it is daylight, I should not wish to detain you..."

"Exactly! I must be away on my mission, beloved princess..."

We both wait.

I smile and curtsey.

He smiles and bows.

"Fare thee well..." I suggest.

"Thank you. Oh."

And with that, he turns and crawls back out the window. It is quite an awkward size for a human being, and I look away lest I dwell on this un-heroic view. Finally, he detaches the hem of his léine from the window-frame and scuttles down the tree and out of view.

Was this supposed to be Bob's version of my wish, or the larger-than-cat size rescuer? I suppose I am a heroine now. And beloved.

I don't feel any different.

CHAPTER NINE

The sun is painting the Purple Mountains magenta when someone scratches at my door. It had better not be that blond prince back again; he's supposed to be off on his quest. It's Sigma, wagging his tail hopefully.

"Hello! But what are you—"

I break off, seeing something in his mouth. I put out my hands, and he drops in the rag.

I pull back the edge of the cloth. Flat, shiny, jagged, and dark.

"Oh. Thank you, Sigma." I smile, trying not to look confused.

He wags his tail again and pads away. Mu and Nu file behind him, and each lay something on the mat in front of my door. I crouch and find two more pieces. Is it glass?

"Did something break?" I ask.

Sigma wags his tail.

The hall is oddly full of dogs; far more than the usual six. Three more bring a rag-wrapped shard of glass, and I fetch a basket to collect them.

"What is it?" I ask, but none of them have words for an answer.

Zeta comes down the hall, staggering to the side under something long and twisted. I hurry forward to help him. It's a thin piece of wood, carved with whirls and gold paint mostly worn away.

Alpha bounds up, shouldering him aside. As he drops his piece, blood drips on the mat.

"Oh no! You're hurt! Come here, Alpha, and I'll see what I can do."

I move over to fetch the bandages and creams I keep handy, and out of the corner of my vision I see Alpha move forward—then Theta barrels into him with a snarl. I spin around as they roll and tumble into the hallway.

"Oh dear! Oh dear!" I hurry to the doorway.

The combatants scramble apart, Alpha's head hanging low as he gives me a submissive tail wag

"What happened? Theta, I know you're sensible, but you mustn't be..."

Sigma noses me, interrupting. He taps the mat with his paw, then the lintel, they raises his paw. He lowers his big head and steps back, panting. This is clearly "do you understand?"

"The mat...? The door...? Are you...not allowed in?"

Sigma stands and barks once, wagging his tail.

"That's the rule for all of you?" I look around, but that's clearly right. Eager, thoughtless Alpha almost accepted my invitation to enter, but now he's standing submissively and apologizing to grim Theta.

"But the collar didn't pull you back," I observe. "Is it Trencoss's rule?"

Sigma barks and wags his tail again.

Theta bares his teeth and turns aside.

I wonder what Trencoss did to him, and shiver, thinking of my Acushla under that man's sway—although lately, Trencoss has been perfectly kind to me.

"I wish you could explain things to me," I say. "Perhaps there's a good reason you tell me to obey him." Maybe Trencoss has his reasons and Bob is doing nothing more than making mischief. What with Fergus mac Finnbar, we now have a whole extra person in the middle of this mess. I sigh.

Upsilon brings another narrow piece of wood, and Zeta taps them both with his paw, giving me a significant look. The shards sparkle with gold dust and I look up, quickly. The hallway is growing darker, but yes, there is some gold sparkling in the corners. My heart rushes with excitement—is this my wish?

There's a tapping at my window, and I open it to find the rook, who hops in. As rooks are wont to do, he has something shiny in his beak, and he places it carefully in the middle of my rug.

More glass.

The dogs file back and forth with large pieces, and the rook and his mate flutter in and out with small ones. I lay the pieces out on the floor, trying to figure out what I am puzzling together.

The wooden pieces make a frame, and the glass with the dark backing…it must be a mirror, I realize slowly. The frame is half as tall as I am—I have never seen a mirror larger than my hand.

"There are all sorts of strange things in this castle," I tell the dogs peeking in the doorway. "Perhaps mirrors like this come from another time." I rearrange two pieces and see how the top made an arch. "Or perhaps large glass only exists among the Fae. Who knows."

Before I can finish sorting, the faceless maid comes to help me dress for dinner long before I can figure out how to assemble the dozens of jagged pieces.

Trencoss is unusually friendly at dinner, asking about the stories I have been listening to and actually waiting until I respond. I am fizzy with all the excitement of the day, and find myself speaking in an animated manner. I mention doves, and the conversation moves on to a dovecote he keeps. He has names for the birds, and speaks of them fondly. Instead of wrapping myself in silence, tonight I ask questions, which he seems almost cheerful to answer.

By the time I am headed to bed, exhausted and muddle-headed, I don't know what to think. I don't know why I am going to such trouble to avoid marrying him, and if he likes the doves that much he must treat his dogs well too. I have always done what I am supposed to do and I might as well continue.

Perhaps I will feel more clear in the morning, when I assemble my mirror.

***

I wake up with the birdsong, and a clear vision in my head. I know how to fix the mirror! I can barely wait, and when I go to put up my braids I find that I missed strands of hair, now trailing down my neck.

"That will teach you to act like a puppy, Ailbe." I laugh and cluck my tongue. "Now you just have to do it all over again."

I manage to dress properly, sipping my tea and eating bites of egg between my laces and hairpins. I hum, thinking through the rooms I've visited and where to find the supplies I need. I hurry off down the hallways, joking with the dogs on duty.

An hour later, I have gathered a thin board, a braided cord of wire, some herbs, a flat mat, a stiff paintbrush, and mixed up a large pot of glue with some saffron for color, and a new storebox, because this is liable to take a while.

Back in my room, I set the glue in a bowl of warm water to keep it soft while I set out my materials. Humming, I lay out glass pieces on the mat. I work from the curved top, occasionally finding a piece of glass broken into such an unusual shape that I can select the pieces that fit into it. Once I find several that fit together, I brush the correct section of board with the glue and set in the glass shards. I needed to start with the larger board, because the glass will never fit back together in exactly the same shape, but with the background and the glue I can adjust them as I work. Even if the mirror isn't perfect, the golden-dyed glue will be pretty.

I'm sure Trencoss won't mind me using expensive herbs in glue. After all, doesn't he make a fuss about giving me such nice materials?

It takes all day—really, all day. I pause to eat lunch and stretch my legs, my kneecaps throbbing from kneeling and crawling. Birds and squirrels come to the window to see what I'm up to, and I send them and the dogs to fetch more decorations. The rooks come up with some especially charming little additions, shells and pretty rocks and alder-cones. My braids come down and escaped curls tickle my neck, but I watching my artwork come together is thrilling.

I finish just before sundown, as the faceless servant enters my room. I ask if I can have a bath before dinner since I smell of sweat and glue, and a bath seems like a fitting celebration. I smile and chat with the maid, acting as though she is celebrating with me. My mirror is finished—as close to reconstructed as it can get, with shells and buttons in the missing parts, and gold braid around the edges where the frame didn't reach.

"Goodnight and thank you," I tell the rooks, making ready to close my window.

"Caw!" he snaps back, cocking his head to stare at the creation on my floor.

"I have to leave it there until morning," I tell him. "It will be ruined if I try to pick it up too soon."

The rook hops outside again, making little grumbling noises.

Tomorrow, I will see what this magic has done!

***

I wait until after breakfast— until after the little flyers have done their spinning, which is now half of one yellow ball.

I ask some of the servants for help, expecting that they won't respond, but two men follow me upstairs. They can't talk, but they follow my instructions, and lift the huge board-and-mirror-and-shells-and-beads creation to the top of the shelf which I cleared off. The gold dust goes wild around their hands, and maybe they are as excited as everyone else. It would be difficult to have no face.

I flutter about the room, trying to find the right way to thank them. They can't drink a cup of tea, they don't need a hairpin, their matching clothes are tidy...

"Thank you for your help," I say. "Would you like a design on your léine, in thanks? A flower, or knotwork...?"

The men turn to me. Their blankness frightens me in the same way that the dogs did when I couldn't tell them apart.

But then one goes to my sewing basket, picks out green thread, and points carefully to a pattern carved on my bedstead. The other almost drops the thread as he picks a deep russet. He prefers the symbol on the back of my brush.

"It is my pleasure," I tell them. "Just—um—have your friends deliver your léinte tonight, and I will decorate them."

The men bow, and I have to hope I have done them honor. Now...

Now, nothing. It's a mirror. Very large, very gluey, and—well, that's it.

I circle the mirror, I touch it, I sing to it. I go out the door (all six dogs stand up) and go back in (they lay back down). We all saw the gold dust, it must be something! I turn my back on the mirror, I ignore it, I peek out of the corners of my eye. Nothing.

I am a calm and sensible person, so I do not cry or yell, even when I want to. It's not like I have anything better to do, or anyone who expects me anywhere else, so I keep trying.

By midafternoon, I have to give up. My stomach rumbles and there's this queer prickling feeling in my throat. I put on my shoes and cloak and head out to find where the servants have brought lunch today.

Five dogs scramble to their feet, and Rho watches me warily. I have determined he is the head of this particular group. I am always glad to see him outside my room, because it means that Theta won't be on guard duty. Theta clearly thinks I am a fool who needs keeping in line.

"I know, I know," I tell Rho. "I keep going in and out. I'm going downstairs now."

Omikron does a little dance next to me.

"And then out for a walk?"

Bark! Bark!

"Very well. I will be useful to someone, I suppose." I turn towards the stairs, but the dogs move reluctantly.

"Prince Fergus will be back soon," I tell them. "And he's going to rescue me, and all of you too." Fergus didn't say anything about that, but I'm not going to leave the dogs behind. They don't belong here any more than I do. "The mirror is pretty," I continue. "It doesn't matter if it doesn't do anything, because I have my wish granted."

A deep bark splits the air behind me, and I turn around. Omikron is standing on the stairs, turning his gaze to my room, and then back at me. He barks again.

Sigma whines.

Guilt swamps me, that they did all this work for the mirror. Alpha even cut his tongue! And I have no idea how to finish the last step so it actually works.

"It's a wonderful mirror. Really nice! I've never had a mirror before, and I appreciate it so much. Thank you."

This is not what they want to hear. Sigma whines and paws the floor, and Omikron stares towards my bedroom and howls. The other dogs shift on their feet, looking between me and the door. They want me to go back.

"I don't know," I tell them. "I can't make it work. I'm sorry. I've tried."

Sigma comes over to me, nudging me towards my room with a slow wag of his tail.

"I can't." I rub his ears, fighting tears. "I've done my best, but I have to eat. Didn't you want that walk?"

I try to sound happy, but none of them are fooled.

***

I plead a headache after dinner, and Trencoss is surprisingly accommodating.

"Of course you must retire early, my dear." He strokes my hand with his long white fingers. "I will have a tisane sent to your room."

"Chamomile and willow-bark," I reply, having figured out the hard way that no one here knows their way around a still-room.

See, I will be of some use if I stay and marry Trencoss.

Upstairs, my new shift of dogs sprawls in the hallway, with the gray-beard Zeta in charge tonight. He is reserved, but something about him reminds me of my host's father in Lochan Uaine; the one who taught me how to camp. When Zeta is on duty, he always keeps his eyes on me, but rarely interferes. It is hard to imagine his half of the conversation, but he's one of those men who rarely speaks. I curtsey to him, and he inclines his head in a stately nod.

The maid helps me remove my fancy clothes and brush out my hair, and then a second arrives with the tea. She has one cup already steeped and sweetened, and chivvies me into a chair until I take a sip. The younger maid tucks a blanket around me, while the elder fills the iron kettle and swings it over the flame. She opens a little glazed jar to show me the herbs inside, then sets it on the hutch and taps the top. By now, instead of cosmetics my shelves hold a dozen different tisanes and three kinds of sweetener (for me), and jars of nuts and bells of cheese and butter (for the animals) and one tightly sealed container with extra smoked eel (in case Bob returns).

"I can make myself another cup of tea," I say. "I understand."

I thank both maids, hoping they will leave quickly, so I can have the cry I've decided to permit myself

But once I'm alone, I can't cry. I'm just hollow.

I pour the tea, stir in honey—one spoonful, two. In my old life, honey was limited so I always took the least amount. Here, it doesn't matter. I breathe in the steam, but instead of calm my body is antsy and impatient.

I circle the room and stop in front of the mirror, both hands curled around my mug.

"Cry, you foolish eyes." I lift the cup to my face as though the steam will loosen my emotions. The room wavers in front of my vision.

I blink, but it still wavers.

No, it's brightness. In front of me.

Green.

In the mirror.

It's the green of a meadow in the sunshine, and now I can make out a blonde woman bent over working. As I watch, the vision becomes clearer, as though I am walking towards her, although I am standing frozen with a cup in front of my mouth. The woman is leaning over a wash tub, and I can make out a little Black boy toddling on chubby legs, his easy smile just like Fionn mac Cumhaill's.

She twitches, as though noticing I am there. Pushing herself into standing, as though her limbs are aching, and turns to the mirror—to me—her eyes wide. Mine are as well.

Those bright blue eyes on stark white skin, clear jawline with an easy smile, blond hair tucked into her cap.

"Saba!" I cry. My cup crashes to the floor, splashing my feet with hot water, but I barely notice. "Saba, Saba..." I press my hands against the mirror, tears running down my face through my laughter.

"Ailbe," she is repeating. "Oh, to see you again!"

She places her own hands against whatever is in her world. I can feel nothing but the cold glass and lines of glue, but I can see her pale fingers against my dark ones, so familiar.

"You had the baby!" I exclaim.

"I have." Saba looks at the toddler, laughing and rueful through her tears. "I've kept him safe."

I recognize the shape of the steep hills beyond her. She's in Peaceful Valley, where I knew she would be.

"I couldn't find the door," I say. "I tried and tried—"

"I know," she is saying at the same time. "I can't find you either."

We can't do anything else that evening. We cry, and laugh, and reach out as though we could hold each other.

Saba, my Saba!

Chapter Ten

It takes another day to figure out how to make the mirror work every time. It turns out that it is not anything I am doing or wearing, nor the type of tea, but the steam itself. Once the steam shimmers between me and the mirror for long enough for Saba to appear clearly, then we can talk as long as we want and it doesn't matter what happens to the tea. It is, however, preferable not to drop it on my feet. Saba can see my mirror slightly and me clearly, as though she is looking through a window (she says), but she is completely unable to make the connection from her side first.

Over the next few days, we fall into a routine.

I greet her each morning, after the maid serves breakfast tea in my room. (That is the rich brown tisane, which Saba tells me is from India and called "right proper cuppa tae.") I always thank the maids and ask how they slept, even knowing they can't answer.

Saba is usually busy with household tasks and I want to check on how much thread the little flyers have gathered, so often our morning visits only last a minute or so, but it's amazing what a difference it makes to greet someone I love at the beginning of the day. Then, once Saba puts little Oisín down for a nap after lunch, we have a good long chat. We both have fireplaces and iron kettles, and have taken to planning what herbs we are going to use so we make the same tea and drink it at the same time. When I come back from dinner with Trencoss, I have the servants deliver a soothing tisane and I check on Saba again, just letting enough steam waft across the mirror that I can peek. Sometimes she is already asleep, curled around her boy's body in their bed. Other times she turns to me with tired eyes but her sparkling smile, and we say a few more words, or just sit together in silence.

It takes us a few days to work out what has happened since we parted! The Dark Man chased Saba and she took refuge in the Peaceful Valley, like I thought, but I didn't know she could come out in other times. She gave birth while staying in a library, and I am deeply relieved that someone was there to care for them both while she recovered from childbed, even though a bitter disloyal part of me fears this Mary Catherine has replaced me.

Before that, Saba visited another time or two, which were great fun (she tells me) but she didn't make friends close enough that she felt like she could stay longer.

I think it doesn't sound like much fun if she didn't have anyone to love. Never mind; I am not jealous of Mary Catherine, I am just glad Saba had someone. Anyone.

Oisín, her little child, is now twenty months old. She holds him up to the mirror and he babbles at me, waving his pudgy little hands. He looks more like his father, wide brown face and dense curls, but his cheerful attitude is all Saba. I sing songs with hand gestures for him, hoping that he learns to remember me even through the mirror. Saba explains to me that since we are both moving through time and worlds, we are growing older at different rates. In my life, I only left Fionn's castle a year ago, and Saba was only lost a couple weeks before that. In her life, though, well over two years have passed.

That is also why, when I found her, it was my night and her day. As long as we stay connected, Saba believes that we will coordinate the rhythms of our world. She teases that I probably don't need to check on her three times a day, but I would rather be certain. One day, one of our worlds will slip away, and I might never find her again.

"Take the mirror with you," Saba suggests.

"It's too large."

"Then take pieces." Saba sips her tea. "Like calls to like, which means that a small part of the mirror will remember how it behaves all together."

"Are you sure?"

She laughs. "Not at all. I just bumble along and figure things out."

I shake my head, smiling at her optimism.

"But it makes sense," Saba insists. "I promise, there are patterns. But Ailbe! Tell me more about this prince of yours."

"He's not mine," I reply automatically.

Saba raises her eyebrows and taps her playful smile. "He came in your window, called you beautiful, and now is off risking his life on your behalf? Come now, even you can't argue he's not interested!"

"Bob told him to come," I answer.

"But he thought you were beautiful."

I shrug.

"Which you are, by the way. And he liked you! He said you were... what was it, soothing?"

"What sort of woman is nothing better than soothing?" I laugh and wave away her comment, but secretly I enjoy her teasing. I hope she's right and someone actually likes me, for myself.

"Many men would go out of their way to find a wife who is soothing," Saba answers. "Oh, you're blushing! Don't tell me you haven't thought of marrying him, Ailbe!"

We both giggle, me so mortified I have to cover my face with my hands.

I don't really have much to say about Prince Fergus, given that I have only met him once, but she mentions him every day. That makes the whole thing start to feel more real. Maybe I do have an admirer.

"Ailbe, you are surrounded by admirers." She counts on her fingers. "Prince Fergus, off on a mission to rescue you. Lord Trencoss, who pursued you for an entire year, and now is going to great frustration with dewdrops, of all things. Then there is Bob"—she holds up three fingers—"who keeps coming around and sitting in your lap. And then twenty-four dogs! Ailbe, I have never seen someone so surrounded by males!"

I laugh, even though the dearest one is missing from her list, I've only told Saba the basics of how my Acushla and I traveled together, Trencoss searching for us both. My heart hurts too much to explain that night; how I didn't run when Acushla urged me to, and he wouldn't leave me. Trencoss flung Acushla in the dungeon and just put me in this pleasant room with birdsong in the trees, and I wish to every god that Acushla had run when he had the chance.

"Ailbe? Ailbe, dear..." Saba stretches out her hand, her expressive face melting into worry. "I didn't mean to tease. You are all right."

"You can tease." I take a swallow of tea, pushing down the lump in my throat. "I just.....don't know why they would care about me." That wasn't what I was going to say, but I don't have words for everything throbbing in me.

Saba shifts, sitting more upright. "Ailbe, you are very beautiful. And I don't actually mean that as a compliment." Her voice becomes bitter. "I've learned quite a bit in these months, and part of that is how men look at certain women as a conquest. You are petite and graceful, and you have those big eyes with the dramatic tilt."

"Like stars?" I ask, bitter.

Saba shrugs. "It's a compliment that springs easily to the tongue. But you're not listening to me. Men are entranced by you. They always have been, I just used to keep them away."

I stare into my tea, thinking of how Trencoss told me the first night that men want Fionn mac Cumhaill and they want Bodhbh Dearg, and they see me as a conduit to each. They saw me walking those hallways with the keys to the castle hanging at my waist, and do not believe that I am nothing but a servant.

***

There's a warm stretch of weather, so the dew dries up early and Trencoss loses his temper more often. Sheep's sorrel blooms on the heath beyond the meadows, and the little flyers gather red dew and spin red thread. I leave my window open at all hours, so the birds and squirrels can hop in and out, chirping when I fix my hair and checking to make sure I didn't leave any crumbs on the floor. Of course I put crumbs out for them, but only on the windowsill.

One night I am hanging up my cloak and hear a thump behind me. The creatures who come in and out of my window aren't large enough to make a noise like that. I spin around in time to see the laundry basket tilting.

Slowly, slowly, it angles towards the floor. Then—bang, it's down, and a white blur of fur shoots out and darts across the room.

I burst into laughter. Bob darts under the bed, then flies out and leaps across my dressing table onto the top of the wardrobe, skitters all the way across and lands on the floor in the far shadows, as though he has scared himself. I don't believe it.

"Bob, Ye Gurt Fool!" I crouch down, extending my hand. "Don't tell me you're too shy to talk. Not after I've been saving scraps from dinner!"

I wiggle my fingers, but he has to be a cat and prove he doesn't come just because I invite him. I tame my silliness, because I'm not laughing at *him*. I'm just joyful.

A long minute later, Bob saunters across the floor, his tail held straight up, twitching just the end. He deigns to sniff my fingers, all ten of them, then sits and washes his face.

"Fish or fowl?" he asks.

I laugh out loud. "Thin sliced beef and blood sausage. They didn't have fish tonight."

"I suppose that will do, if it's the best you've got," Bob grumbles. "Good thing I've sent that boy to get you out of here."

I rise to fetch it. I need it on hand for Bob, but a pair of short-eared owls stops by most nights, too. Trencoss can't help but notice that I pack up my leftovers, but he smiles with one half of his mouth and says nothing. We discuss animals most of the evening, now.

"I'm sorry it's not more, but the meat doesn't keep for long." I serve Bob on a saucer from the hutch, because he seems to deserve something more refined than the outdoors animals. I put away my headdress and over-gown while he is eating, and settle on the floor, nice and comfortable in my léine with my braids falling loose.

Bob twitches his tail, and pounces on my fingers.

"Ow!" I snatch my hand away. "That's not fair—you're sharp!"

Bob rolls onto his back, batting the fringe on my cloak. "Then get me something better to play with, princess!"

One of my socks has fallen on the floor, and I ball it up and toss it. Bob springs after it, throwing it in the air and batting it with his paws, and I burst into merriment, although I hop he will not rip it full of ladders that I must mend. Oh well; I haven't anything else to do. He fetches it back to me and I throw it again.

"For all the world like you're a terrier," I tease.

Bob drops the socks. "I've the softest coat of any terrier you've ever seen."

"So you do." I toss it again.

He skitters away, sliding on the stones into the corner of the room, and turns around as proud as punch. "And the most beautiful eyes."

"Very fine eyes, you have." I throw the sock.

"More clever than any terrier in Ireland," he warns me.

I laugh. "Than any terrier the whole world over."

We play and joke, and the night is soft around us, and I laugh more than I have in weeks. When I can't stifle my yawns, Bob orders me to get into bed, and once I am under the covers he paces up and down over the top of me, and eventually curls up behind my knees.

I used to feel guilty for any moment of happiness in this castle. I snuggle into the soft pillows, pulling the blanket up to my chin, and float away on the familiar warmth of a soft body at my back.

"Goodnight, my Acushla," I mumble.

"Goodnight, a stór."

It startles me like a nip to the heel. This is not my Acushla, and I don't deserve to be happy while my love is not.

***

My days are filled with unaccountable moments of joy—what with Saba to talk to, and getting to know the two dozen wolfhounds (plus various birds and small fuzzy creatures), and Trencoss becoming a pleasant dinner companion. Besides, the sun is shining and all kinds of blooms are coating the world in beauty. And now that cloth is given to me and I don't have to take my turn spinning and weaving, I am ever more intrigued by the detail work. I can make my gown into a work of art, and even experiment with weaving my criossana by mixing different fine silks and puffy wools in with the horsehair and magical threads. I have made six of them now, which is a ridiculous number with no sensible use. But I don't have to be sensible any more, right? I am a lady of leisure, and if I have a vision for a pretty crios then I might as well warp it.

Six…I stare at them, thinking how the magical numbers fit together, and wondering what the magical thread can do. I wonder if I could make four sets of six.

One afternoon in the back garden, I finish the embroidered border around the neckline of my finest wool gúna, and hold up the dress to imagine what else I will stitch. I reach for the gold wire, ready to couch a geometric pattern like I have done so many times before.

Overhead, a dove flutters from one branch to the next, and a soft gray feather falls into my embroidery box. My hand goes still.

Instead of the gold, I pick up the feather, and lay it on the dark green wool. I wouldn't actually stitch a feather into clothing, but I watch the down shift in the breeze and think about all the stitching I have ever done.

It is always for someone else. As a girl, I finished Saba's gowns when she was called away for her more important duties. As one of the highest ranking women in the household, I have sewn for Bodhbh Dearg and Fionn mac Cumhaill, and I've also chosen projects at will. Like making things for that nice knight, Rian of Kilkirk, who didn't have a wife to add prayers with her stitches. Even when I sew for myself, I am thinking about how to add consequence for Saba, or for her husband and father. I use gold and fine beads because it shows our household's wealth, and familiar patterns because that is what is done.

Yet only considering my own taste, I think the feather is prettier than the gold.

I am more like a dove than a princess. Fergus said that I am serene, and I suppose (the thought shocks me again) I have tamed Trencoss, in a way. At least taught him table manners.

"You have given me something very precious indeed, my friend dove," I say to the leaves above me. I rub the soft wool under my thumb, considering. "I think I will stitch a feather here, and across here, and a little one wafting here. I thank you."

I lay out the feather, to use as a model to create my design. It's the excuse I need, that my art will honor the dove—but I know I am honoring myself.

I think the dove wants me to do it.

Chapter Eleven

I take to leaving the laundry basket near the window for Bob. He slips in, jumps into the basket, and then slowly knocks it over to get my attention. I pretend I have no idea he's there until the basket clatters on the floor, and make an ever-bigger fuss about shrieking and clutching my cheeks in surprise. I can't tell whether Bob is fooled, but he certainly enjoys my histrionics. I have a whole repertoire of reactions, because Acushla used to play this game with me too. He would creep up and poke me with his cold nose, although in his case it was obvious that he wasn't invisible. He might be black, but he is distinctly large.

"You're not paying attention," Bob complains. "I told you I had something for you."

"Mm-hm, very nice." I finger the little bundle around his neck as he climbs on and off my lap. "Wait—it's for me?"

Bob yawns in frustration. "Silly kitten. I dragged it all this way so Fergus could send you a message. Come now, untie it, untie it!"

"I'm trying! If you will just hold still..."

Bob half-hisses and rolls on his back, putting the leather thong firmly out of my reach and kicking me with his back feet when I try to get it. I yank back, rubbing the thin red lines springing up on my hand.

This is not my Acushla. I'd do better not to forget it again.

I bow my head. "Good sir, Bob Ye Gurt Fool, if you will do me the honor of letting me untie your burden, and once you are comfortable may I offer you some trout cooked in wild garlic and wine?"

He rolls into his sphinx-like pose. "If you insist."

"Thank you for making such an effort on my behalf, you lovely little cat." I'm sure he has Doors everywhere, and thus didn't have to carry anything farther than up the tree, but it doesn't cost me anything to praise him.

I manage to untie the leather thong, and Bob rubs his cheeks against my hand, apparently mollified by the praise I keep murmuring. I give him a good thorough petting before paying any attention to the bundle on my knee.

"Well? Aren't you curious?" Bob pats it with one paw, and I assure him that I can hardly wait.

It's true, actually. As I work on the next set of knots, my heart pitter-patters faster, thinking of Fergus's sweet smile and—well, and Saba's teasing. I know I'm blushing by the time the linen rolls open.

The delicate purple flowers make me blush more. "Sailchuach chon," I say; the hedgerow violet. "It represents thoughtfulness and faithfulness."

Bob flicks his tail. "They are *romantic*, Ailbe. You are supposed to say things about *love*."

"It wouldn't be decent for me to say them," I answer primly.

"The lad had an entire speech for me to recite." He yawns, showing off his pointed little teeth. "You'll have to imagine, because I didn't bother to memorize it."

"Very well." Unfortunately, I can imagine too much. I only dared to long for a friend, but all these conversations are making me think of something else—someone to hold me in his arms, murmur gentle words, tell me that everything is all right. The little animals are all well, but I am lonely.

But I have to admit, I don't see Fergus's cheery face in my mind's-eye. I've only met him once.

I raise the next herb to my nose. Thyme.

"Constancy through adversity," Bob recites. "Meaning keep your spirits up even though you've got to have dinner with Trencoss every night, and he doesn't even feed you fish. Except tonight." He licks his lips. "You'll have no trouble keeping your spirits up, will you? You didn't even need—"

"Is that what Fergus sent you to say?"

Bob lashes his tail. "Fine. He didn't mention the fish. He wants you to know that you are very brave, just hold on a little bit longer, he'll see you again soon, yadda yadda meow meow."

"And this one? I don't recognize this leaf."

"It's from an orange tree."

I repeat the unfamiliar word.

"It's a fruit. That's his task, collect three different fruits from three different islands and bring them to you. That leaf is to demonstrate that he has arrived at his first location and is making progress."

"That's good…" I sniff the leaf. It's strange that Fergus is out there, doing all these things and having these adventures, all on my behalf. I'd rather just go to the island myself, although men like achieving the glory.

But what is very clear is that I'm supposed to entertain Bob right now. I serve him the fish and spend an hour tossing things around the room. I've collected a few little bits that he might like to chase—it took me two hours to mend that poor sock—and it turns out his favorite is a little spring. I make the spring jump until my eyes are like sandpaper and I can't hide my yawns any more.

"Very well. You have my permission to get into bed." Bob hops onto the comforter, washing his feet diligently.

I glance sidelong at the mirror as I do my evening wash and tidy. Unfortunately, Bob is now a purring pool of fuss in the middle of my bed, and clearly is not going anywhere, so I won't be able to call Saba. I'm sure she would be in bed by now, but I like to know she's safe.

All this about a prince trying to rescue me makes me unsettled, along with a wardrobe of silken dresses and days of leisure. Glib and excited, but also like I'm living a story about someone who is not me.

***

In the morning, I'm still jittery.

"It's just the way men talk," Saba says, stirring the porridge on her fire. "He's being encouraging and supportive, that's all."

"But he can't be in love with me already…" I wish I could give Saba and Oisín my plate of scones and bacon and honey.

Saba shrugs as she puts the spoon aside. "It means that he's ready to get to know you and fall in love."

My chest unclenches a little. "That would be all right. It would be nice to get to know him."

Saba shakes a finger at me and swings the pot hook. "See that you do! It's important to know a man before you marry him."

"How can I get to know anyone in this palace? I spend my whole days with the dogs."

"Look where I ended up." Saba shakes her head with a wry smile, wrapping her hands in rags. "A husband who isn't bothering to look for me, and who sold *you* into a slavery of marriage as well."

"It's not slavery," I protest. "Trencoss is treating me quite well."

"Huh." Saba thumps her pot onto the ground and shakes out her hands.

"I'm sorry I'm not there to help! I didn't find you either!" I reach out, then drop my hand, embarrassed how little I can do.

"Ailbe of Dún Allaine." Saba puts her hands on her hips, her face sterner than she ever used to look. "You searched for me. You tried! For a whole year you tried. It's more than anyone else has done."

"It isn't enough."

Saba rubs a hand over her face. "We don't get to make the choices, Ailbe. We just hold on to what we have and keep trying."

Behind her, Oisín wails.

"I'm coming, sweetie." She casts me an apologetic smile.

"I won't keep you." I try to smile back. "Give that baby a big kiss on his belly for me."

Saba turns, wiggling her fingers dramatically. "Watch out, a stór! Here comes a kiss from Auntie Ailbe! It's coming to get you! It's coming!"

She runs out of my vision, waving her arms and making Oisín dissolve in giggles. The mirror vision fades away and I imagine them, laughing and touching and kissing.

I wrap my arms around myself. It's time to start my day.

***

I invite the dogs to go walking with me, hoping the sunlight and exercise will burn off my mood like fog.

Theta, who is usually so strict, approaches slowly. He wags his tail, slowly. Not submissive, but welcoming.

"Good morning. I thank you for your company." I bow slightly, which feels a little absurd but I haven't figured out how to treat the more formal dogs. I certainly wouldn't rub his ears.

But when I try to head out towards the gardens, Theta blocks the door. Confused, I go back to the hallway towards another door. Theta bares his teeth—not at me, at Mu and Nu down the hallway. Quickly, the pair leave off grooming each other and stand in the next two doors.

"Where am I supposed to go, then?"

Apparently this was the correct thing to say. Theta perks his ears and trots ahead.

I guess he trusts me now, because he barely glances back as he leads me to the big front gates. The dogs on gate-duty greet us enthusiastically, bouncing on their front paws, and Upsilon pushes the gate open.

"I'm allowed to go out?" I glance at Theta. "No one will be in trouble?"

Theta nudges me forward, then passes the gate and looks back at me, proud and calm.

Sigma brushes my hand to get my attention. When I meet his eyes, he walks carefully out the gate, spins in a circle and makes a play bow, then trots back inside the gate and paws them slightly.

"So...we can go out, explore and play, and then we will come back, and they will close the gates again?"

Several of the dogs bark and wag their agreement.

"See, Trencoss is getting more reasonable..." I step through the gateway carefully, waiting for something to go wrong. "It's not so bad if I can leave to explore."

Alpha spins in a happy circle, but Delta growls his disapproval, and Zeta just sighs. I look between them and wish they could talk to me with words, because I don't know what to think. Most of the men I know have their moments of cruelty, and we women are just supposed to be their gentle half. Trencoss might not be worse than most.

Sigma nudges me, his body language gentle. He sees that I am distressed.

I rub his ears. "If you were a man, would you do terrible things sometimes? Or say a woman has won your heart when you only met her once? You are very large, so it would not be difficult to order around people who are smaller than you."

Sigma licks my hand, watching me intently.

I can't tell if that's a yes or a no or a "don't be silly, Ailbe," which is what my parents always said when I questioned my betters. "Fate gave you an opportunity, young miss," my mother would say. "Agree with the princess and her father, work hard, and your life will go better than mine."

Alpha darts ahead and barks, Mu and Nu nudge me from behind, and Theta trots forward with his purposeful, over-the-shoulder look.

"All right, I'm coming, I'm coming!" I laugh. I wish I didn't have to deal with the human men. "Where are we going today?"

The dogs gather momentum around me, and I half-run to keep up. It's not just a set of six today; almost all of them have come out. We left two at the gate, but the rest seem to be here—I keep glancing across, wondering if Acushla is kept at a distance, but here with me today.

Omikron howls with joy, Alpha pounces on Tau and they both go rolling in the grass, Mu and Nu put on speed and race down the path. We run through meadows and sweet-smelling ash groves, and over the play of the dogs I hear sea birds calling ahead. Sigma trots by my side, glancing up with his tongue lolling, and I keep my hand on his shoulders.

We crest a small rise and the lake spreads out below us, the water flickering and sparkling in the sun. We come to a stop in a half-moon of sand, and some black rocks to my left form a natural platform and jetty into the water. The dogs in the front barrel ahead, splashing into the water, playing and drinking. I laugh out loud and slow to a walk, pressing my hand against my stomach as I struggle to breathe.

"That was—a great deal of—running!" I gasp.

Sigma jumps to lick my face, knocking me over. My hands fling backwards to break my fall, but find wiry fur and solid muscles instead of sand. Zeta braces me up.

We walk down to the water together, and Omikron nudges me over to one of the flat black stones. I thank him and sit, looking over the water as my breath goes steady again. Thanks to all the walks I've been doing with the pack lately, not to mention the year of wandering before that, I'm in better shape than I've ever been before. Still, that was a lot of running!

My eyes find a familiar shape of hills and knolls, a beach—and there, that hollow in the trees must be where the little river runs down. And that soft pillow of green is where Acushla and I camped, within a couple miles of the Castle of a Thousand Doors.

"Just over there is a wonderful willow tree," I tell Delta, who has come for some pets. He nudges under my arm and I lean against him. "The canopy spreads as wide as a house—well, like a normal sized house, not like the one we live in now." I sigh. "There are so many leaves that it keeps off the rain, and they touch the water on the lake side, but there are some missing branches on the meadow side. So it is like a door, that we may go in and out. We set up our kitchen in the meadow." I rub his neck. "My Acushla pushed over logs for us to sit on, and I built the rocks together and made us a fireplace. It was the best one I ever did, because the riverbank had so many flat ones, I could pile them up like a stove. It was warm and toasty all night long, if we wished to sit out and tell stories."

Delta nudges me.

"Yes." I kiss his head. "I wish you could join us too. There would be room for all of us."

But first, Acushla and I need to be together again. I never knew I could miss a dog this much; maybe that is the magic in me.

To distract myself, I turn to the view in front of me. I laugh and watch the dogs romping and playing in the cove, running down the stones and leaping into the water. I rub Delta's back while he leans against us, both of us careful to avoid the points on his collar.

Far beyond, something glitters on the surface of the lake, and other forms cast shadows. Those must be islands, just as green as the far shore, but between the glare of the sun and the reflections I can't make out what the closest one might be. I narrow my eyes, trying to see more closely. Is that where Fergus is right now?

After a while, Theta gathers us together, and Sigma leads the way back to the castle.

This life isn't so bad if Trencoss lets me out occasionally. I'm sure it is not.

Chapter Twelve

The next afternoon, I am mixing herbs, singing to myself, getting ready to call Saba, when the tree branches shake violently. This is something larger than Bob! I set the teapot on the hearth and go to investigate.

"Fergus! Welcome!" I'm not sure if it's good news or bad that he is back so soon, but as I help him crawl through the window I get a bad feeling about the situation.

"My dear Princess Ailbe." He stumbles to his knees, leaning heavily on the windowsill.

I hurry to bring over a chair, then offer my own shoulders to help him to the hearth.

"Oh, you were making tea?" Fergus brightens.

I cast him a smile. "I had a feeling that someone might arrive today, so I was preparing a pot for two."

He drops into a deep chair, putting a hand on his chest. "Dare I hope...that you were waiting for me?"

It's a little self-centered, especially since I was not making tea for him at all. But I was the one who lied, and I *have* been thinking of him. Just not right now.

I smile warmly. "I dared not expect you to come, but I am always hoping."

He clasps my hand as I move back towards the hearth. "Dear Ailbe! You are always in my heart and mind! The thought of you shines in my eyes every day!"

I laugh nervously. What does he have to think about? He barely knows me.

"Your eyes...you are so beautiful!" Fergus pulls my hand to his lips.

I've heard that gesture in stories, and the thought of being the lovely lady gives me a twinkly feeling. But when he presses his lips to my hand, his mouth is warm and squishy, and his stubble scratches my fingers, and he smells of sweat and rain. It is all so very real and masculine, and I'm not sure I'm ready for that.

I pull away, trying to laugh, but I turn it into a curtsey instead.

Is Fergus any better than Trencoss? I know Trencoss's faults by now; Fergus could have terrible ones.

While I am pondering that, I move briskly. I put logs on the fire, close the window, bring a lap blanket for the prince, and add strengthening herbs to the pot.

"Thank you," Fergus says, quietly. "I know that I shouldn't have come back already. I was—I needed..." He shuffles his feet. "I thought it would help to see you again."

I'm not sure how to respond, so I get out cups and honey.

"I'm sorry," he adds, even more quietly. "I don't have the first fruit for you. The oranges."

"How many fruits do we need?"

"I am supposed to bring you three. Three islands, three challenges, three fruits."

I nod, and pour the boiling water. "I saw three islands on the lake." Plus the sparkling thing.

The scent of herbs tangs into the air. I perch on the other chair while the tisane steeps, watching the steam rise in the air.

I'm sorry, Saba, I think, twisting my hands in my lap. *I missed yesterday morning and now our good talk today.* She will forgive me as soon as she hears there is new gossip about Fergus, but it's harder to forgive myself.

"Oranges from the first island." Fergus ticks off one finger. "Plums from the second, and then starfruit."

"Starfruit?" I'm intrigued.

He smiles. It's a nice smile, not bold or flashy. I could be wrong, but it feels like it's in response to whatever expression is on my own face.

"I don't know what they are, either," he admits. "Something from the far East, I have heard. Perhaps it will be guarded by a phoenix."

He said starfruit using the words in our own language, star and fruit, but "phoenix" is just syllables to me.

"What is that? And what are the o-ran?" I pause to listen, but he glances away and shifts his feet. "Bob brought me the leaf of the o-ran, so have you seen them? I would love to see..."

I trail away in my own tangle. Have I just made his embarrassment worse, by saying I wanted to see what he failed to bring me?

And worse what if Bob made it all up? What if the package with the flowers was not from Fergus, but from Bob himself? I busy myself with the teapot, my heart thumping. I don't dare ask directly, because it would hurt too much if Fergus doesn't know about the message. Saba and I talked and laughed about that message; I've thought about it so much. I can feel the edge of pain at just the thought it might not be what I believed.

I hand Fergus the mug, not meeting his eyes.

"Don't worry," he blurts. "I can go back. I will go back! I'll go to the Island of the Oranges, and I will try again, and I will do it right! Never fear!"

I blink at him. I wasn't afraid. I wasn't even *thinking* about that, although now I can see I should have been.

"I am...sure you will...conquer the o-ran. I have faith in you."

He relaxes a little, so I guess that was the right thing to say. "I just didn't expect what I found. I had my sword and my weapons ready, and instead..." He shrugs.

I'm not sure which would be harder to live with, a husband with a flair for drama or one who can't even get from the beginning to the end of a story without trailing away.

"What did you find instead?"

"Do you really want to know? I don't want to bore you."

This is more promising. "Please, what is an o-ran?"

He perks up, like a puppeteer pulls the strings on his shoulders and the corners of his lips. "Orange. I know, it's a funny sound! It's about this big..."

He tells me about the trees, and then I ask about how he got to the island, and when I mention going down to the lake with the dogs, he asks me to describe it and his face lights up as he tells me it is the same lake—which of course I had already figured out, but I nod encouragement. He describes exactly where the coracle is storied, and I recognize the cluster of trees he describes. I try to not talk about myself, but he draws out the story of how I camped on the lake with Acushla. I tell him about the swans on the water and the rain on the willow tree, but not about the terrible ending.

We knew Trencoss was coming. We didn't have time to take everything with us; usually I packed everything neatly in a cart, which Acushla pulled with a harness. Acushla was worried, so I just bundled everything in our tent and put the cart upside-down over it all. I thought we would be coming back, but instead, we are both trapped here.

I shake my head and return my mind to Fergus's story. It really has become quite a pleasant conversation.

As the afternoon wears on, we both know he needs to leave. He asks about who watches me, and I explain the faceless servants and the dogs who are always on guard. I assume they both are forced to report to Trencoss in some way. We agree that if they happened to see a little white cat chasing a crumpled ball, they might think it was a bit peculiar but nothing more. But if they saw a grown man in my bedroom, with broad shoulders and strong thighs…

That was my thought. I look down at my empty cup, hiding my blush.

"I'm sorry, I would never mean to impinge your honor!" Fergus blurts at the same time.

"I wasn't—I wasn't thinking of that at all!" Now I am really blushing, thinking about both my honor and his manly attributes. At the same time. In my bedroom.

"I cannot think of another place to speak with you safely." Fergus, too, is turning ever-pinker. "Although I suppose I should not have come at all."

"You are quite safe here…"

"I meant, I should be out fetching oranges. You are waiting with patience, obedience, and faithfulness, and I am quite failing in everything…"

I am not sure about any of those qualities he has assigned me. It's not like I have any alternative to patience, and comparing my captor to my savior (and not coming up with a clear answer in my own head) doesn't feel very faithful. But Fergus is a nice fellow, and he has been very kind and respectful once he got over kissing my hand. Besides, he's quite handsome. And a Fae picked him out for me…or maybe traded him for some fish? I am confusing myself again.

"Maybe I can be helpful!" I leap to my feet.

"My lady, this task I must surmount on my own…"

"But isn't it terribly lonely to do things on your own?" I am already searching around the room. "I can't actually leave this palace, of course. But I could send something with you! So you can—um—know I'm—thinking of you." I almost stumbled into the word "love" there, and that is way too big to say casually.

"You're right! It is lonely." Fergus trails after me, peeking curiously at what I'm exploring. "Besides, if you give me something of your own, it might have powers we never imagined."

"What?"

He spins his hand. "The bond between you and I can create magic that neither of us ever imagined."

"The...bond?" I am blushing again.

"Yes—we are fated to be together."

I had been thinking of Acushla, and the collars and leashes that bind. That kind of *bond*. I'm so relieved that Fergus has something completely different in mind that the meaning of his words doesn't sink in, until it's too late to respond.

His statement feels much more romantic than I think this situation merits.

"What about this?" I hand him a beaded bracelet. "I have worn this at least a dozen times. Or these." I put some shells in his hand. "I used them"—in reconstructing my mirror, which I don't feel like mentioning—"to decorate my evening slippers. Can you take my cup? Is it too big?"

"Your lips have touched it every day. I will drink with my lips in the same place."

Now that sounds strange, but it's too late to take back the mug. I find several other trinkets around the room and press them into Fergus's hands. He continues to ask questions about my daily life, tucking my trinkets into his pockets like they are treasures.

The room is growing dim, when he startles and apologizes that it has gotten so late. I thank him for going to so much trouble, and he insists it isn't trouble, and we talk over each other until we both giggle nervously. He takes my hands in his and I look up at him. His hands are warm and strong, and his eyes are blue and smiling.

If we are fated to be together, then there will be someone with me for the times like yesterday, when I am feeling too worn out to keep going. Right? That's the point of love—and there's that embarrassing word again.

I look down, terrified he's going to try to kiss me.

He just bows over my hands, then presses our joined hands gently to his breast. The wool of his inar is rough beneath my knuckles, and if this were a romantic song I would feel the beat of his heart, but I can't.

"Good night, fair maiden," Prince Fergus says. "Let not your heart quail in fear, for I will return anon."

"Thank you," I mumble, and help him out the window.

Although frankly, I'm doing fine. I just wish I could get the collars off the dogs, and have my Acushla safe with me.

CHAPTER THIRTEEN

"But do you *like* him?" Saba repeats.

"Last time you were all excited about Prince Fergus!"

"Yes, but you're the one who's there, so do you *like* him?"

"He's my *hero*," I answer. "I'm *supposed* to like him."

"I know that!" Saba throws a turnip. She is so upset that she has turned our brief morning call into an hour-long argument. "But what do *you* think?"

"I've told you." I rub my eyes.

"You figure you are supposed to like everyone!"

"I just have to get through the world, Saba." At least, people like me have to. "I don't want to make a fuss."

"Not arguing with people is different than marrying them just because they happen to crawl in your window when you're in trouble. Drat. Now my porridge is burnt." She swings it off the fire.

"I'm sorry! I didn't mean to burn—"

"You didn't, you silly thing! I did! I burnt my own porridge, because I can't stop talking, and that's because I can't stop worrying, and that's because I actually want you to be happy!"

I rub my eyes again. "You're making me cry. And we're having a celebration this morning."

"You don't have to fuss around with looking good for Trencoss, and I doubt the dogs care."

"But I'm supposed to."

"Aaagh!" Saba wheels on me, waving her cooking spoon wildly. Bits of porridge fly off, but of course they don't touch me.

I think she's trying to make me laugh, and that does make me smile, just a little. Saba has abandoned her whole morning routine and is letting Oisín make mud pies with no pants on, because she thinks it's important to talk with me. She's infuriating, but at least she cares.

Saba puts her hands on her hips and stares at me through the mirror. "Ailbe, seriously. You don't have to dress up, and you don't have to fall in love with Fergus if you don't want to."

"I want to look proper. I feel better that way."

"And Fergus?"

"I never said that I didn't like him! I just don't know him very well yet!"

"And you said that his lips felt like soggy bread."

"Bread pudding is a delicious meal! I enjoy it! Especially with cinnamon!"

Saba blinks. Then chuckles. Then throws back her head and laughs and laughs.

"What?" I say. "What is it?" But Saba's moods are always infectious, and I start to laugh along even though I suspect the joke is on me.

Oisín runs into my mirror view, giggling and throwing his arms around his mother. She ruffles his hair and crouches down to hug and tickle him, unconcerned about getting mud all over both of them. I wish I could love someone like that.

"If you're given soggy men, make pudding out of them?" Saba wipes her eyes, streaking mud across her face. "It's the most ridiculous justification for falling in love I've ever heard in my life, but it's also so *you*, Ailbe."

Some of us have to be practical, I think.

Oisín buries his face in his mother's shoulder, grabbing at her bodice with chubby little hands.

"I know, I know, be patient, a chroí." Saba bounces her son on her hip. He settles, as happy as a trout, and she looks back at me. "If you're going to marry, I just want you to be happy, Ailbe. Not feel like the marriage is an obligation."

My look must show my skepticism, because Saba sighs.

"Once you have children, you will owe them your dutiful obedience. Children take so much energy! Your husband should be a support to you, not yet another thing to manage. Your husband should adore you!"

"Prince Fergus certainly—"

She waves her free hand. "Not just a string of generic platitudes, but you. The real Ailbe, who is creative and silly and careful about all the little details. And also"—she shakes her finger—"incredibly stubborn and bad at taking advice."

I almost scoff, but she deserves better than that. Our relationship has changed now—perhaps not equals, but two grown women with our own truths and struggles. I take a breath and try to formulate my thoughts.

Just then, Oisín points to a bird, and the gesture overbalances him in Saba's arms. He goes tumbling down, and she scrabbles and grabs as she spins them both away from the firepit. She keeps him safe, but he still hits the ground with a thump and a giant wail.

"I'm sorry, Ailbe—"

"You take care of your baby, I didn't mean to keep you."

"I did." Saba blows me a kiss and turns away.

I wipe the mirror with a soft cloth, which I have learned is the quickest way to close the connection, and turn to my dressing table. Trencoss said he had something special this forenoon.

The conversation has given me clarity, although it isn't what Saba intended. Fergus, Trencoss.... I will evaluate both, calmly and dispassionately. Saba is right, our true duty is to our children. I will marry the man who can provide a good home, and my own feelings do not enter into the matter in the slightest.

***

Trencoss had the servants decorate the front courtyard. Wreaths of flowers drape between the Greek columns, a long table is laid with fancy foods, and silver trees form a glittering walkway. The servants are gathered in a silent, expressionless row, dogs sprawl under tables loaded with cheese and fruits, the trees are full of little flyers, and I look for my Acushla. Is he still imprisoned? I hear the merry sounds of pipes and viols and I hope there are musicians, maybe even a bard.

But it is just one of the library boxes, set up with a trumpet-like appendage to carry the sound. I am irrationally disappointed, but I don't let it show. I adore the boxes, but they aren't the same as real people singing and telling stories. Having everything set up as though this would be a grand celebration makes it even more lonely, for it is still just Trencoss and myself. He won't let the dogs eat, and the servants can't. Maybe when we are married, he will let me go to villages again.

If. *If* I have to marry Trencoss.

I reach the center of the courtyard and curtsey.

"Greetings to the fair Princess Ailbe!" Trencoss rises from the throne, sweeps his cloak in a deep bow, and launches into a speech about my incomparable beauty and my illustrious history.

One is just as false as the other; I keep a smile on my lips and let the words wash past me. I am finding it difficult to see Trencoss in a positive light today, but after my argument with Saba I'm sure I would be grumpy about anything.

"I'm not a princess," I say quietly, when he is done.

Ignoring my words, he ushers me forward to a gilt-covered table.

"Let everyone see what I have prepared for my beloved!" He holds high a small basket, turning in a circle. "My beloved requested thread made from the morning dew, and the first skein is ready for her!" He sweeps another bow, then holds out the basket.

"Thank you." I take the thread, and despite what it means, I truly am delighted. It reminds me of the sunshine sparkling on the lake. I glance around, trying to catch Sigma's eye to smile at him, but in the noon sunlight and the among the absurd decorations, all the dogs merely look huge and black. That familiar panic collides into my heart. Why must they all look so similar in this light?

Trencoss is still smiling. "Although the other balls are not yet complete, my friends have been gathering all the colors you requested, my Mavourneen."

Wait—how does he know that is my special nickname? He has no right to use that!

"...so I conclude that we are halfway to our wedding. Let there be a cheer!"

I am too upset to pay attention. Yes, it's a usual endearment, but not a common one. Saba's mother used to call me Mavourneen, and I barely heard it again until I used the pair for us, my Acushla and his Mavourneen. It was ours.

I have not been listening, but Trencoss is presenting me with a wooden box, his face expectant. It is my turn to say something, and I paddle through the words hovering in my ears.

"Thank you," I echo. "You are always too kind to me."

"Nothing is too good for my beloved."

There is a strange glint in his dark eyes as I unlatch the gold clasp. In the edge of my vision, dogs are sitting up, some moving closer. The box balanced on Trencoss's arms is flat and two or three hand-spans square, but would be awkward to hold myself so I must come close to him. His perfume clings to my nostrils; frankincense and amber, I'm not sure exactly, for he wears imported scents with ceremonial significance. Saba only ever used herbs we could collect with our own hands.

I'm thinking about perfume as I open the lid, and have to blink to clear my eyes. Gold loops resting in red velvet.

Two of the dogs pace at the side of the courtyard, but I still can't see their faces. I don't know why they are worried; jewelry is an ordinary gift from a wealthy man to his betrothed.

"How pretty," I say, lifting the first one. A bracelet.

"Be quiet, dogs," Trencoss snaps, and the yard goes still. To me, his voice smooth—"As beautiful as you yourself. I hope you are pleased and will wear them every night to dinner."

There are two matching bracelets, heavy solid gold. These are neither flattering to my narrow bones nor to my taste, but they are a popular style. Fionn awards his warriors something similar after battles, and one of the other ladies-in-waiting even received such a pair as a courting gift. I force out something complimentary and nonsensical, examining the patterns. As I lift them, the velvet shifts and I can see a third loop underneath. Larger, and although it's half-covered I know what completes the set. Trencoss raises the box towards me, urging me to investigate.

"A necklace?" I reach forward, and everything happens at once.

A huge black form, all teeth and claws and earth-shaking growls, explodes between us.

I am knocked backwards by a warm body, and we land in a tangle of fur and linen.

The box flies into the air, gold loops flying, everything clashing and clattering on the stones.

My attacker lands on the ground and another wolfhound leaps on top of him, fangs flashing. More jump in from either side, pawing and biting at each other in a great melee. I push myself upright, blinking hard—I thought I saw—it was, it was my Acushla! He and Theta are arguing bitterly, snapping and tangling. I rub my eyes and check them again. They are angry, but not trying to hurt each other. Sigma must agree there is no danger, because he is steady behind me.

My elbow hurts terribly, terribly, and I am annoyed that it takes one tiniest part of my attention. I must get to Acushla! I fell on one hip and twisted my ankle as I fell, but it's the elbow that I can't bear. Pain yanks at me, my fear, my confusion. I clutch my elbow and try to roll to my feet. Sigma stands between me and the dogfight, and I thump his back.

Little flyers buzz around all of us, distracting the dogs and frightening me more. One zooms so close to my face that I trip against Sigma—this one is a wingless man with a pig's nose, riding a silver fork.

"Stop this!" From the sound, Trencoss has been knocked to the ground some distance away. "Stop—no fighting—get away! Get out of my face! Away!"

I moan, trying to crawl forward but tangled in my skirts. Acushla is among a mass of dogs, and I don't care if I am battered to a million pieces if I can get to him.

Trencoss is batting wildly at the little flyers, who circle him like a hive of bees. He knocks some to the ground, where they lay still, and I half-scream as though their pain splits my own body.

Other flyers zoom to the jewelry, surrounding the pieces in clouds of butterfly wings. Working several together, they lift the bracelets and lurch across the courtyards towards the forest. I assume the necklace must be inside the largest mass of them.

A necklace. A heavy, jeweled torc...like a collar.

And I almost put it on willingly, just because I wasn't thinking. My Acushla saved me.

Theta has won, and I can't there in time. Standing shoulder to shoulder with Zeta and Rho, he faces down my Acushla, who drops his head, panting hard. Theta bares his teeth and whips his tail, glancing back at where Trencoss is yelling and flailing. Alpha and Beta hurry over, and I'm terrified they will pile on Acushla. Instead, the three slip away with Acushla tucked in between the other two, melting into the shadows. Zeta, the graybeard, sighs and lets his head droop. Theta spins and trots over to watch Trencoss, tension in his every movement.

Trencoss finally staggers upright, pressing his hands outwards while shouting orders. The little flyers are knocked back, as though they have hit a wall of glass around him. The dogs go sailing away from each other, thumping on the ground as though someone lifted them by their collars and tossed them lightly away. They scramble to their feet, panting, heads dropped submissively.

I clutch my elbow and can't stop crying. I was so close to Acushla, and I have lost him again.

Trencoss points at me, and I gasp with terror—that he will issue orders that I cannot resist, or throw Sigma away from me.

"Assist her!" he bellows. "My princess is hurt! How dare you! Monsters all, monsters!"

A chorus of whines, one of the dogs drops to the ground. A flyer darts close and Trencoss knocks it down.

"Do not punish them, my lord!" I stagger to my feet, pulling my hurt arm against my body so I can use the other hand to push myself up.

"Monsters! How dare you harm my precious!"

One of the dogs—oh, how I wish I could see their faces clearly!—is lifted by the collar, shaking like a dolly.

I limp-run forward, grabbing Trencoss's arm with both my hands. "Please! No! Don't hurt them, please!"

Another dog yelps as he is flung in the air.

I shake his arm, gasping against the pain. "Don't hurt them! I beg you!"

"But they attacked you!" His face contorted with rage. "They all must be punished! Monsters!"

"As a boon for me, my lord, please, please!" I break off in a sob. "For a kiss! If I give you a kiss, will you leave them alone?"

Everything goes very quiet.

The dogs slide to the ground and regain their footing. Trencoss stares at me. Sigma supports me from behind, holding very still.

"I will accept a kiss," Trencoss says.

"And you won't hurt the dogs? You won't punish them any more?"

He rakes a glare around the courtyard. "Are you frightened of me yet?"

The dogs lower their heads.

"Do you remember to be obedient? Who is the leader of this pack? Who? I am, that's who!"

His yelling rattles my head, and I can hear the rough pant in his chest between words.

Theta approaches us, head and tail down. He drops to the ground, glancing side to side, licking his nose. Theta is always confident, and it makes my heart boil to see him like this—and I am mad at Theta too. He is the strongest, can't he stand up to Trencoss just a little bit? Obey, but not grovel?

I realize now why he scolded Acushla, whose rash action led to the other dogs being punished. Theta, stern and careful, would have thought there was a better way to take my necklace away. It is true enough; I love his passion, but Acushla does not always think before he leaps into action. He's gotten into trouble with it before.

Maybe Theta is Trencoss's lackey, or maybe he is like me...burying his true feelings deep below the decisions that are necessary.

With that thought, Trencoss takes the back of my head and presses his mouth against mine. It is not rough. It is not pleasant, either.

He releases me and I stagger back, but Sigma has me steady.

"The princess is hurt!" Trencoss bellows. "Take her away and tend to her!"

Faceless servants gather round, and I start to cry again. They wear the same gown and the same hairstyle, and some are shorter and some are older, but I cannot tell them apart and I cannot remember who was in my room yesterday and I cannot bear it. Two faceless men arrive with a chair they can carry, and I allow the maids' hands to settle me into position and bind a cloth loosely to keep my arm in place.

As my chair wobbles across the courtyard, I catch a glimpse of something else. Several other dogs—Mu, Nu, Upsilon, Beta, and Tau, I am delighted to recognize—are bunched together, looking apologetic and obedient.

But behind their huge bodies, completely hidden from Trencoss's view, the little flyers make their steady progress with the heavy gold circlet.

Chapter Fourteen

Once the fire takes the morning chill off my bedroom, I stir honey into my tea with one hand. I'm too tired to get dressed. I asked the maids to bring me more story-boxes, and I'm just going to crawl back in bed and listen to them all day long, like I did yesterday. Out of habit, I hold the teacup under the mirror.

"Ailbe!" Saba screams. "I've been worried! Where have you been? What's wrong? What happened?"

"Good morning to you, too." I manage a half-smile and a sip of tea.

"Oh, you look terrible!"

"Always nice to start the day with a compliment."

"Pffft!" Saba spins in frustration. "I wish I could just grab you, and hug the living daylights out of you!"

Oisín scampers into view, babbling enthusiastically.

Saba scoops him up. "Well, you too." She chucks him under the chin. "But I can hug you any time. I'm worried about Auntie Ailbe this morning."

"I'm here. I'm fine. Don't burn your porridge." Slowly, I move my left arm onto the table, wrapping both hands around the hot mug. I can move my elbow, so I know it's not broken. I'll just have to be patient, but it's not like I have any real work to do. No one cares if I spend all day in bed.

"I make porridge fine every day. Ailbe, are you still in your robe? Your hair isn't combed."

I grunt.

"Ailbe, you aren't going back to bed, are you? I've never seen you go to bed in the daytime!"

Oisín squeals.

"That's right," Saba tells him. "I have seen your Auntie Ailbe very sick, and she still always combs her hair."

"I miss calling on you for one day, and look what happens—"

"One? You call that one?" Saba holds up a finger. "Lunchtime, bedtime, then the morning, afternoon, and last night—look, I'm out of fingers or I'm going to have to drop this bundle of love." She pretends to drop Oisín, making him laugh as she catches him with a jolt.

It's just a game between them. But I stare into my tea, a lump choking my throat, and can't stop seeing the big dog shaking in the air.

"Ailbe? Oh, I wish I could touch you. I wish I could come. You've got to talk to me....just a minute." Saba secures Oisín on her hip, and my view follows her as she walks out of her front yard and around some berry bushes. The Peaceful Valley is set up like an ordinary country farm, except Saba and Oisín live in a cave instead of a thatched roundhouse. There's a fire-pit and kitchen area in the packed-dirt courtyard, with hoops and toys for Oisín, and a vegetable garden right off that. Now she goes farther, out into a mossy little grove. Someone has rolled logs around the edges to make a safe play-space for Oisín, and I realize that someone must be Saba. She never used to do physical labor like that.

She lays out a blanket and settles herself, checking that Oisín is content with some little wooden figures. "Now. Tell me everything."

I don't want to talk about it, but there's no resisting Saba in this mood. She wasn't trained for manual labor, but she *was* trained for managing people, and she does it well. She gets the whole story out of me, and makes me eat my breakfast, too.

"But I dealt with it," I conclude, playing with the drips of butter and egg yolk on my plate. "Trencoss lost his temper, but I kept him from hurting anyone. It is not so bad."

"Except you," she says.

I shrug. "I fell. That can happen to anyone." I would rather smash my elbow on the stones than wear that necklace.

Saba sighs. "I wish I could come put my hands on you. But I had a vision last night—no, the night before that. I was waiting up for you to call."

"I'm sorry—"

She waves my apology away. "I can't make the salve for you, but I can tell you what I saw. Do you have ingredients?"

"The stillroom is decent, but I haven't tried anything complicated."

"Very well. I begin."

This is what a mná feasa does; she examines the pain, then puts herself in a trance which will give her the vision to heal that exact injury or illness. Most of it is skills that any ordinary housewife can learn—myself, for instance—but only the ones the Forest Goddesses choose can go into the trances. I have seen what a difference these slight variations can make for the patient.

Saba recites the recipe for me, including the chant to sing while I mix the ingredients, and which herbs to stir widdershins for exactly fifteen turns. We repeat it back and forth until we are both sure I have memorized every detail correctly.

Saba nods, satisfied. Oisín crawls into her lap and she gives him her breast as they snuggle together. "Put that on your elbow and we will see what it does. It can't hurt, although I didn't see your injury in my vision."

"What then...what is it for?"

She strokes Oisín's cheek, thinking. "I'm not sure. Everything. I could see the Castle of a Thousand Doors quite clearly, shimmering with magic, both Fae and sorcerous. I saw shadows going in and out, representing the people who live there."

"Anyone?"

"Or animals," she adds, "given what your castle is like. But yes, I think it's for everyone." She considers for a little while farther. "Especially the magic, I think, because I saw that. So that's why I'm not positive it will heal your elbow, since you just hurt it in a very ordinary way. No one meant you any harm, and you didn't even touch anything magical at all."

"I had the bracelets."

"But the dog knocked them away?"

"Yes." It was my Acushla, and I'm not sure why I didn't tell her that. The words stick in my throat—that he saved me again. That I miss him so much.

Saba shakes her head. "I really haven't studied the way that sorcery works, but jewelry is meant to be worn so I think you would have to wear them to get the enchantment." She rocks Oisín, dark circles under her eyes.

The dogs. Sorcerous magic. Collars. Healing the mysteries that I can't figure out by myself—aha!

Whether or not my elbow hurts, I have work to do today. First, I need to braid my hair.

***

The next evening, I have just climbed into bed when my window bangs. It's cold tonight, so I have to get out of bed to unlatch it.

Prince Fergus tumbles into the room. I ought to be delighted, but given that my elbow and hip are still throbbing despite Saba's salve, I'm barely dressed, and I just spent hours having a polite dinner with Trencoss, so I would really rather deal with an owl or a mouse or something that won't try to talk to me.

"My lady, I have oranges!" Fergus gasps from the floor.

I suppress a strong wave of irritation. "Good. Let's get you warmed by the fire."

But Fergus won't do anything else until he finds a decorative bowl, sets the oranges inside, and then hides them in my armoire. His léine is torn and his arms are scratched and bruised, and my eyes dart to the jar of salve in the corner. My elbow has been healing much better with it, and I've used some on Rho and a tiny bit for a mouse who was singed in a candle-flame. I didn't make enough for Fergus, too.

Fergus builds up the fire and lights candles while I fill the kettle, and then he allows me to settle him in the comfortable chair with a blanket tucked around him. At least he helped out before he sat down.

"Do you want to hear how I got the oranges?" Without waiting for a reply, he tumbles into the story.

I am half-listening as I pull my cloak over my tunica. The gúna takes too long to lace, and a léine isn't indecent, it's just casual. If Fergus is going to come into my room this late, he had just better be happy however I am dressed. But I don't feel right, and spend the extra moments to pin up my hair.

By the time I finish, the kettle is boiling, and I start preparing the tisane.

"You are a sight for sore eyes!" Fergus exclaims. "So serene and always poised! I am thankful to have found you."

I don't feel serene, despite what he might think from the outside, so I ask him questions, almost at random, remembering whatever I can from his story. It seems like there are pieces missing—I don't understand why he was stuck on the island for all that time in the middle—but I probably wasn't paying attention. Fergus is especially eager to go into detail about his final escape, and the creatures who were chasing him. They sound like eels, but with legs and a lizard-like head. Out loud, I gasp and exclaim. Inside, I amuse myself that Bob would have liked to eat one.

Fergus thanks me profusely for the tea, which makes me feel a little better.

"Ahh..."

He settles back in the chair, and I fetch him another couple pillows, smiling to see his blissful expression. He really is quite handsome. I am not usually drawn to blond men, but the flecks of mud on his cheeks make him look more manly.

"A couple more days of this," he sighs, eyes closed, "and I will be ready to venture to Plum Island."

"What?" The protest bursts out of me.

He looks at me. "Oh, I know I can't stay here all this time. There's a village a couple miles north, and I'll—"

I make a noise of frustration.

"What is it? Oh dear...do you need something, my lady?"

I sink onto the hearth, letting my forehead sink into my hands. "I need you to—do your job!"

That sounded terrible. I don't talk to people this way.

Predictably, he is annoyed. "I've been working hard! I told you, I had to take the boat and the waves came up, and..."

Instead of asking me what has happened at the Castle of a Thousand Doors, he goes back into his own story. I don't know what to do, so I start to cry. Tears and frustration have been niggling at me for the last several days, and women have so few tools at their disposal, so I just let down the barriers and make a fuss.

"Gracious, what's wrong? Oh dear, oh dear..." Fergus insists that I take the other chair and pours me a cup of tea. "Don't cry, princess. Don't worry, I will take care of it. Don't cry."

"You don't understand!" I exclaim. "This isn't some sort of glory challenge for you, this is a race!"

"A race?" He is watching me carefully. Listening now.

"You have to get all three fruits before Trencoss gets the three skeins of thread. Because as soon as he hands me the third, we marry, and then..."

"Don't worry, I won't let him have you."

"Then we have to get the fruit! Oranges, plums, and starfruit, right?"

"Yes, and—"

I storm out of the chair, pushing past him to my workbasket. "Do you see this? Do you?" I hold up the yellow ball. Glimmers shake out in the firelight.

"Is that it? Can I—"

He reaches for it, and I pull back. I've already started to use it for more crios, and I don't want him to look too closely. Any sensible person would ask why I need eleven new crios belts when I have only one waist.

"One skein of thread, and one fruit, Ailbe. We'll make it."

"But you have to be *first*," I clarify. "And he's already most of the way through the next ball, and the third is started as well."

For the first time, Fergus looks uncertain.

What I am tempted to say is: *so fine! You go to the village and rest, with pretty girls asking how you escaped the walking eels. I'll stay here and marry Trencoss any day now, but it's all right, I'll just pay him with a kiss whenever he has a temper tantrum.*

But I didn't like the feel of that bargain, and once we're married my kisses will just be an expectation, not a gift. And I am fortunate enough to have the good regard of a Fae, who sent me Fergus, who so far has not shown any terrible characteristics. So I hold back my feelings and do not make him mad.

"I can tend your cuts," I say gently. "Then perhaps you will feel strong enough to go to Plum Island."

He bows. "I would be honored."

So he sits back down, and I get the basin and rags, and heat more water, and hide my sigh as I fetch the salve that Saba showed me how to make. He definitely is part of the rhythm of this castle, going in and out like the shadows Saba saw. It will help him finish his quest, and no one needs me to be healed quickly.

"What has happened here?" Fergus asks, as I settle at his feet. "I can see that you are limping. Did Trencoss hit you?"

I shake my head, but decide I should tell him the story. I stumble through the basics, unlike the way the thoughts and memories poured out when Saba asked questions.

I get to the end of the story as I finish washing all his scrapes and sores. The injuries aren't dangerous, but I can see why he would want to rest for a couple of days.

Well, we don't all get what we *want*. I dab the salve on his leg, trying to be sparing. Maybe if I don't use any more myself, there will be enough left for the dogs.

By the time I get to his second arm, Fergus is sprawled in bliss. "Ah, my lady, this helps so much! Did you make it yourself?"

"I did."

"You are brilliant. I feel much stronger already."

I finish in silence, debating how to explain about Saba, when I haven't the least idea how it works, myself. "A mná feasa gave me the recipe, once."

He stands, and I hold up the jar for him to see.

He takes it. "Thank you." He bows with his hand on his heart. "Your careful tending gives my heart strength, and your magical salve heals my body. The wind is calm, and I will get the coracle. I can make it to Plum Island, camp there, and begin my quest in the morning."

"That's...good." I'm watching the jar.

"You are right. I owe you only my very best effort, and you shall have it." He bows again, and then *tucks the jar into his pocket*.

"You are...it is..." I gesture, helplessly.

"With this, I will be able to heal any injuries overnight, so I am sure I will be back soon. I thank you from the bottom of my heart."

"Oh." Of course it's better that he heals quickly. Then he can save me, and the dogs, and it helps everyone. "You're welcome. I hope it works."

We walk over to the window, and he takes my hand.

"May I have a kiss? To speed me on my way?"

I pull away. Tears prickle behind my eyes, but I don't want to cry any more. I don't like crying.

"I'm sorry, that's too much after what you've just been through, isn't it?" Fergus squeezes my hand and sighs.

Immediately, I feel bad. "After the plums."

"The plums?"

"I'll give you a kiss when you bring the plums."

He chuckles. "With an incentive like that, I will be back tomorrow night."

I try to smile. "Fare thee well."

Fergus pushes open the window, wedging himself to get in the opening, but pulls back. "Which was the dog who stood behind you and kept you from falling?"

"Sigma."

He smiles. "That sounds like a good dog. When I get the starfruit and come back for you, we will take Sigma when we escape. You'll like that, won't you?"

He grins, waves, and clambers into the night.

I hold my breath. Hold my feelings. Hold my tongue.

Until the last bright flashes of his clothes are out of sight, and I bang closed the window, throw the latch, and pull the heavy curtains across.

"You think we'll take one dog, and leave twenty-four?" Now my tears spill out, hot and angry. "That's right, I haven't forgotten my Acushla, whether or not I can see him every day, because *I* don't forget my friends!" I pull out my hairpins and throw them across the room. "That's what you think, you fool little—little *pincushion* of a prince!" I bank the fire, slamming it with the poker to separate the logs. "I won't leave one single dog behind. I won't leave one single collar locked!" I tug my léine over my head and dive back into bed. So comfortable. So soft. My prison. I bury my face in the pillow, ready to sob, but my throat is hot and the tears won't come.

After a long minute, I flop onto my back, staring into the glowing coals in the fireplace.

"And if you plan to leave anyone behind," I conclude, "I will stay right here and marry Trencoss. Gladly."

CHAPTER FIFTEEN

Sunlight pours in the door of the stillroom. Bees buzz in the meadow outside, pollinating all those red and white flowers to seal my doom. I stare at the bundle of angelica in my hand. This one was tucked farther back, clearly from an older year that the stillroom worker did not yet dispose. Well, I have used the better bundles, and this is all I have left.

It has a bad smell. I bring it into the light and separate the leaves.

Mold. I wonder if there's enough if I take off the outer part—but no. Saba has warned me that it can turn the whole batch to poison.

The shells the recipe required are nearly out, too. There is nothing for it; I'll have to risk making what I can, because I wanted to try it for the dogs' collars. Before I started my first batch, I ran a test to see how much butter it would take to go around a collar, to see how much salve it would take. Omikron wagged his tail and allowed me to test on him, and later I tested a bit of the finished product on a sore on his paw as well. He leapt up and ran to the gate and back to show me that the paw was healed...but also, possibly, that the gate would open for us now?

I slam the shells and seeds with the mortar and pestle, weighing everything for a small batch, carefully selecting only the outermost leaves of angelica. My elbow throbs but it doesn't matter; I won't use any of this on myself. I mix it together, and spoon bits to the side as I squash, trying to figure how much there will be divided by twenty-five. Some. Perhaps a dash on their noses. One lick per dog, although their tongues are so big.

It's my only hope. I'm not a sorcerer, I'm not important. But I will weave the threads from Bob and mix the potions from Saba, and maybe it will be enough to free the dogs. My dogs, my friends.

But when I finish the batch, nothing happens. Last time, I could feel the warmth through the bowl, which crackled and shimmered and gave me visions of Saba. Today, it's just a glop.

A small amount of glop. Not nearly enough, and there will be no more.

Our days are running out, and neither Trencoss nor Fergus are going to save Acushla and all the dogs I love.

***

It starts to rain in the late morning, but too late to prevent the morning dew. As it is, the red ball is almost finished, and Trencoss has been gloating around the palace all morning, planning an even better celebration for tomorrow.

I have an idea, I'm just not clear on the details. Maybe if Bob or Fergus came back, I could ask them for help making my bargain, although if Fergus came back it would solve more than that. Once he manages his three fruits, I will manage him, and we will take the dogs.

I'm busy with the criosanna all morning, so when it's time to call Saba I just fetch some meat and bread to take to my room. I'm on the fourteenth crios, now, and Saba has been trying to go into another trance to see a different recipe might help dissolve the collars' power. It's difficult, since she can't touch us, and frankly I think she's afraid that becoming a mother has meant she can't use her powers as—

I open my bedroom door and pause. The fire is roaring and there's obviously someone here.

Not in the first chair, nor the second either. There's the tea tray the maid always leaves. I can't remember if I left the window ajar.

No one in my bed.

I spin slowly, my neck prickling, examining the corners of my room, and—no!

"No!" I drop everything in my hands, springing forward, but force myself to stop before I grab him.

Bob rolls over on his back, kicking his legs in the air. "You're waking me up, silly kitten."

I want to shake him, which would make me as terrible and mean as Trencoss with the dogs. Instead, I clutch my elbows, hoping the pain will ground me.

"Do I smell ham? Pheasant? Hm?" Bob spins upright, peeking around the edge of my basket and looking adorable.

My sewing basket. I put everything away neatly. I left it closed.

"What have you *done?*" I gasp.

"You know I like baskets," Bob tells me.

"But that basket was closed. And full of pins."

"I took care of them." Bob yawns.

That's one way to put it. There are needles and bobbins and the precious sharp little scissors all over the floor, and I can just see Bob pouncing and batting with abandon. But that isn't the worst of it.

I creep towards him, one step at a time. I don't want to see what has happened, but torn colorful threads poke out around the edges and I know. They are the colors from my dress, which was stored neatly in my sewing basket.

"Get out," I say, and my voice must be cold and vicious because Bob actually hops down. "Go. Just go."

"Ailbe, I was just having fun!" He edges closer to the ham on the floor.

"No!" I go to the window and bang it open. "Get out of my room, and don't come back! You're nothing but trouble!"

He sits upright, wrapping his tail around his feet. "You don't want to get rid of me. Not really."

"I do!" I take a deep breath, like glass shards in my lungs. "I know you're a Fae, and you're all-powerful and all-*everything*."

He puts back his ears as I say "fae" but I don't care. I tumble on.

"But I am just one woman in this whole big castle, and my Acushla is trapped and I have to get him out, and also I need to help the squadron of dogs. And I can't take care of everything by myself, and I can't even help Saba. So if you're just going to come here and want this from me and want that from me, I can't do it any more! You don't need me. You can get whatever you want! So out and do your Fae-cat thing, and leave me out of it!"

Bob flicks the tip of his tail. "I didn't know it mattered to you."

I take another painful breath. No one ever thinks of what matters to me. All these men, one after another. They just come by and think of what I can do for them.

"I'll get you a new one," Bob snaps. "Everything new. Much better."

I take a third breath. "Get out."

He prances across the floor, tail straight up except for the very tip. He leaps onto the windowsill and pauses. He butts my hand with his forehead, as though I will pet him.

I stand straight and tall, holding the window open.

He twitches his tail and hops out. The oak branch shakes with his weight, pelting my window with heavy droplets.

I close the window. Slowly. Properly. Because I take care of my belongings and do things properly. Then I close the curtains.

I go back to my sewing basket and gather up my dress in my arms. My beautiful dress, with the subtle beads and the embroidery of birds in flight, soft feathers fading into darker green wool. I used multiple shades of whites and grays, overlapping the threads to create a look of movement. The first thing I've ever made for myself because I wanted it. I only worked on it after I had done the other jobs, the criosanna and Saba and everything else. It was my treat, my treasure. Clearly, Bob rolled around in my sewing basket, kicking his legs and kneading his paws, so the embroidery is snarled, the beads have fallen off the ripped threads, and the fabric itself is full of puckers and pulls. I could make it wearable, but there is no way to make it beautiful ever again.

I curl up on the floor by the fireplace, pulling up my knees and wrapping my arms around them. Everyone is arguing over me, but in the end, it's not about me at all. None of them even knows who I am.

***

Fergus comes back that night. I'm hollow and exhausted, and his arrival means I can't even call Saba.

The prince's clothes are dirty and he's cold and wet, but he's full of good cheer and launches right into telling me all about his adventures. I still don't understand what took him so long, but I'm too tired to pay attention. I assume I should ask him about the bargain I plan to make with Trencoss. I hate making bargains; I've made stupid mistakes already.

Fergus shows me the plums, ceremoniously placing them in the bowl in the cupboard. I hand him his cup of strengthening tisane without comment.

He furrows his brow. "What's wrong, Princess Ailbe? You look a little..."

I pause. I don't want to burden him with my troubles. I don't want to be whiney. But I've been holding everything in all evening with Trencoss, and the story aches to burst out of me.

"Look at this!" I rush across the room and hold up the dress.

"Gracious!" Fergus touches a trailing strand of beadwork, missing its beads. "Did one of the dogs chew it?"

"No, it was Bob." I don't cry again, but my voice wobbles as I explain what happened.

"Gracious," Fergus repeats, fingering the battered dress. "But you know, Ailbe, this could be a good thing."

I wanted him to say the stitching had been beautiful. I needed him to say that he liked the idea of doves instead of gold-work. Something.

"Because now, you see, Bob owes you something." Fergus's voice is animated as he takes the dress from me and folds it. "He said he's going to bring you a new dress? That will have some new capability! And if you're still upset about it, then the debt isn't paid yet. You have one caught of the Good People in our debt. It worked out great, Ailbe!"

Our debt, really, as though Fergus made that dress. As though he loved it.

Fergus plops the dress into the sewing basket and holds out his hands to me.

Another debt. I promised him a kiss. I step forward obediently.

I don't feel like talking to him any more. I can't bear stumbling through the embarrassment of trying to explain my plan with Trencoss. I am all out of words, all out of feelings.

I let him kiss me, and wish him luck on Starfruit Island.

I am alone again.

Chapter Sixteen

I call Saba in the morning, holding my second cup of tea under the mirror.

Saba appears in a flurry of energy. "Good morning! Are you all right? You're already dressed—your braids are very elegant today."

"Thank you." I sip my tea, not sitting down. "I am fine. Are you—"

"You didn't call yesterday, not lunch or bedtime either." She puts her non-spoon hand on her hip. "I know something is up."

"Something *was* up, but it's fine now." I don't want to talk about the dress and get emotional again. "Today Trencoss is giving me the second skein of thread, I just wanted to let you know."

She furrows her brow. "Do you think your Acushla will be there again?"

"I'm sure he will be." We've already talked this over. "I think he's around all the time. That Trencoss makes him watch me, but won't let him near."

Saba's eyes bore into me. "This is important to you," she says quietly. "More than you've let on."

I glance away, then meet her eyes with a light smile. "Very much so. But I'm going to change it today."

"Change what?"

I laugh weakly. "We'll have to see, won't we?"

***

I enter the courtyard, wearing two of my magic-thread criosanna for luck and a gúna fit for a princess, wine red, with yards of fabric billowing out around me, the sleeves of my léine draping almost to the ground. I cross the courtyard, ignoring the reams of decorations and all the furry creatures watching me, pretending that I am the princess that people won't stop calling me. None of the dogs are sprawled; they are all upright and watching. Even the birds in the trees are quiet and cautious. The servants have decorated for an even grander party, but everyone is wary what might happen this time.

Trencoss bows. I curtsey.

He makes a speech: I am lovely, he is clever, red flowers, et cetera.

I curtsey again. My heart is fluttering like a bird's wings, but my ribs are as strong as the columns on the palace, holding everything in. Holding it together. It is almost time to say—whatever I am going to say.

"The red thread for my beloved!" Trencoss holds up his right palm. "Collected from the morning dewdrops, spun on a rose, woven with my love in every stitch!"

I curtsey again. From that mish-mash, it's clear he doesn't know much about women's arts, and he certainly hasn't spun any love into it—and I've been the only one doing any weaving.

Trencoss spins his left fingers and the little flyers sail out from around the corner. They are slower than they used to be—I think Trencoss has tightened his control—and I can see that they are mice with butterfly wings, little men with snake heads riding on spoons, giant moths with human faces and hands on the ends of all six legs. Despite the anxiety clawing in my chest, I can't help but smile to see their unique beauty.

"Put out your hands, and my servants will deliver your gift," Trencoss tells me.

I can feel their animosity at his words. I reach up. "Thank you," I say. "Thank you to you. And you. Thank you all. Your hair is so pretty, and

I love your beaded necklace. Thank you, little ones. What lovely wings! Thank you."

The red thread arcs from the sky, spooling through the air and landing in my outstretched hands. The loose thread floats like dandelion puff, sinking slowly as I reel it in.

"Thank you," I repeat, lifting my hand farewell to the whirlwind of magical flyers.

Something extra slithers over my fingers as they flutter around my head and away. Quickly, I close my hand, making an excuse to examine the red thread and tuck whatever-it-was out of sight in my dress.

"You're welcome," Trencoss answers. "Are you pleased? I see you are wearing my creations already."

I touch the fringe hanging down from my waist. I would dare say that the criosanna are *my* creation, but I'm not going to have that argument again.

"My lord," I say instead, not even sure what my next words are going to be, "when I arrived here, I was not alone."

My heart thumps, and Trencoss raises his eyebrows.

"I came with my companion, a big black dog," I say, forcing my voice to be strong. "You have hidden him. I want the chance to win him back."

"Have I not given you a big black dog?" Trencoss twitches his fingers, and Epsilon stands and shuffles over. Then Kappa. Omega. "How many do you need?" Another twitch, and Gamma and Nu join the others.

Mu raises his ears but doesn't follow, and I am suddenly enraged with Trencoss for compelling them to separate. It is such a petty cruelty.

"I love every single one of my beautiful guard dogs," I declare, "but none of them are the one that I came with. I want him back." Now, that's no way to make a bargain, Ailbe!

Trencoss folds his arms, one side of his thin mouth lifted. "You know what they say about wives...if you give them everything they ask for, their demands will never cease."

I set my jaw and do not answer.

"What will you give me in return?" Trencoss taunts.

"I am set to marry you," I reply. "You already have everything." That's really no way to make a bargain—I should have swallowed my pride and asked Fergus to help me make the deal.

But I don't think Fergus wants me to have what I'm asking for, either.

"But I am not offering you a trade." I am pretending to be a princess, cool and confident. "I am offering you a game. I just want a chance to win back my dog."

Trencoss's eyes light up at the word "game," but he just shrugs and says, "I believe I recall that he was my dog first."

"He probably was." I almost add *but we're both staying in your castle anyhow,* but I realize that could force my agreement, and I don't plan for us to stay here. So close to another mistake!

Kappa takes a couple more steps and nudges Trencoss's leg, looking up with a hopeful tail wag.

Trencoss looks at the dog. "I should give her a chance, then?" Then his eyes light. "Are you willing to risk it? Ah!" He claps his hands. "Who is willing to put themselves as stakes for this bet? Princess Ailbe can earn back her first dog, or she can lose you! Who will do it?"

Kappa blinks, but holds his ground.

"One dog for one dog," I say quickly. I don't want anyone to risk themselves ."That's fair."

"Not enough to be entertaining," Trencoss answers.

Lambda ambles over next to Kappa, his big shoulders rolling under his coat.

Trencoss laughs. "Who else?"

"No," I whisper to the dogs, glancing around the courtyard. "I'm not asking this of you. Please no. Please."

Phi walks over and sits in the line, perfectly composed. Delta—the sweetest cuddlebug—gives me a doggy grin as he trots past.

"That's enough!" I cry. "Four dogs for your bet!"

"Don't you think you can win?" Trencoss rubs his hands together.

I don't answer. I don't even know what the game is, but I shouldn't have risked a single one of them.

"Who thinks she can win?" Trencoss shouts. "Who trusts Princess Ailbe?"

There is a massive fluttering and shuffling. All the dogs are on their feet now, birds flapping between tree branches, the servants turning to each other and clasping their hands.

"Four is enough," I say helplessly, but Beta has already joined the others. "Five."

Everyone is moving but Theta leaps into the center of the courtyard and bares his teeth at the others. They pause.

Then Theta turns to Trencoss and I. His tail is high, the tip arching over his back, his head and ears upright. He looks straight at the row of dogs behind Trencoss, and gives a short low bark. Five times. Then he glares back at the two of us.

I want to apologize, but I don't dare disturb them.

"Fine," Trencoss says. "I understand. If Princess Ailbe loses too many dogs with her fool over-confidence, then you won't have enough manpower to guard the castle doors any longer. Or shall we say...dog-power?"

Theta stalks over and nudges Trencoss's hand. The birds in the trees call out, and several of the little flyers dart across the courtyard.

"I haven't forgotten," Trencoss snaps. "I will follow the rules of fair play when I make the challenge. It must be connected to Ailbe herself, I know."

His power is the animals, I remember. I wonder if they have a way to abandon him.

Trencoss swings back to me. "At high noon, princess. Meet me in the orchard and I will give you a way to win back the dog you entered with—*my* dog, remember."

I keep my head high and do not let emotion color my voice. "He will be my dog once I win the challenge, my lord."

The yard bursts into flutters and zips and yips, but I turn on my heel and walk away, my dress billowing behind me.

Chapter Seventeen

Only Theta is waiting outside my bedroom when I emerge, in plain sensible clothes, to head down to the orchard. Since I arrived at the Castle of a Thousand Doors, I have never seen one dog by himself.

He rises to his feet, looking me over.

"I'm sorry," I say. "I didn't mean to get the other dogs involved."

Theta paws the floor, just once, a controlled sign of frustration.

I kneel on the floor, my head at his level, and reach out my hands. I've never petted Theta, although he has touched me. "If I'd known it would have involved the other dogs, I would have asked for help to make the bargain, I promise. I'm not sure how it happened like that. I was just trying—I was trying—"

Theta sighs.

"I will never forgive myself if anything happens to them, but I know you worry about them even more than I do." He keeps his dogs in line to prevent their pain at Trencoss's hands, I realize. That was why he scolded Acushla on the day of the necklace. "You have worked together for so long. I'm sorry, and I will do everything in my power to keep them from harm. I'm sorry."

Theta sighs again, then strides over and bumps my shoulder with his nose. When I hang my head, he bumps harder. His meaning is clear: let's go, don't be a fool.

I get up.

But instead of trotting ahead, leading me forward, Theta pauses and leans against my legs. Lightly, for he could knock me to the ground if he chose. This is a gentle pressure like Sigma likes to give; a reminder that he's there. His strength is for me, too.

I reach out my hand, but pause before I touch him. A question of my own.

Theta wags his tail, once, crisply. I take that as permission and rub behind his ears, avoiding the spiked collar half-hidden under his fur.

One more brisk wag, and Theta sets off down the stairs. I gather my courage like a shield and follow.

***

Trencoss is waiting in a gazebo overlooking the orchards. Beyond him are grove after grove of neatly tended trees, separated by low hedgerows, and among them lay dozens of dogs. Hundreds. They are all sprawled on their right side, still and silent. I would be terrified, but Theta is calm next to me, his head high as he gazes across the gently rolling grass. They must be asleep, and he can hear their breathing.

They are neatly spaced, like onion bulbs ready for planting. If you planted wolfhounds, what would grow? What a ridiculous, macabre thought, but there are so many of them, so much the same!

I turn back to Trencoss, keeping all my feelings locked behind my ribs. "I am ready, my lord."

"Very well." He smiles, one side of his flat mouth. "Find your dog."

I wait. "What are the rules?"

He gestures casually. "You said you wanted one particular black wolfhound, and none of the other black wolfhounds would do. So here you go. Your one particular dog—that is, *my* dog—is here. If you can find him, you can keep him."

"What am I supposed to do when I find him?"

He holds out a hand, and the crow drops a ribbon into it, red as blood.

"Tie this around his neck and go back to your room," Trencoss tells me. "If you are right, I will send the dog to your room tonight, when the Arcturis Star rises."

My hope rises like a shooting star, because that reward would be so sweet—sleeping against his solid body, like we did for an entire year. "Will he be allowed past the threshold?"

Trencoss makes an impatient gesture. "If you want. I can't prevent it once he is yours."

I wonder if my bed is big enough. I could just pull off the blankets and make a nest on the floor, like we did in Lochan Uaine.

"Don't you want to know what will happen if you fail?" Trencoss snaps.

I don't, particularly.

Like usual, Trencoss takes over my part in the conversation. "You would? I will tell you, but first of all, I will warn you that I can see you, no matter how far you go in this orchard. You may not use magic of any type, and I will be careful that the dogs do not wake. You will have..." He steps backwards, uncovering a large hourglass. "One hour. When you are ready to begin, you pull this cord. The sand falls"—he wiggles his fingers—"and when the last grain falls, if you have not chosen the right dog"—he snaps his fingers—"those five dogs are gone. The ones you chose this morning are gone forever. You will never see them again."

"I did not choose them."

He shrugs. "You choose their fate."

I glance at Theta, trying to reassure him that I will keep his comrades safe.

Theta just looks out over the orchard at all the sleeping dogs.

At that moment, Trencoss's earlier words ring in my ears. *If you want—I can't prevent it.* And he had to make the challenge connected to me. So, although he is the master of this castle, he is not in control of everything. A little jolt of hope eases the vice in my chest.

"When you're ready, my lady." Trencoss bows, mocking, and hands me the ribbon.

"Thank you," I reply.

I examine the hourglass, half as tall as I am and glowing blue. Very well; there's nothing for it but to do the task in front of me. I pull the cord.

***

This one is Beta.

I stand and walk a half-dozen steps to the next dog. Crouch down, check his ears—worn fur on his left front paw; this is Rho. Stand. Walk to the next dog.

The hourglass is enchanted in some way that I can see it from anywhere I am in the orchards, and I try not to look but it draws my eye. At least a third of it is in the lower chamber, and it's spilling, spilling down.

Panic won't help, so I check the next dog. Eta. It would be faster if I could watch them move; both their personalities and their particular habits would be immediately obvious. But they are all fast asleep.

I have brushed each of these dogs, fed them, put salve on their paws and told them jokes. I know each and every one, and I will know my Acushla when I find him. But there are so many—Trencoss will use up my time just looking and looking. I've found several of each dog by now, and it's clear he has enchanted something else to take their forms. The constant repetition is surely supposed to upset me, but instead, it answers questions I have been asking for weeks.

I was right, it couldn't have been coincidence that I woke up in this castle and found myself guarded by a dozen dogs who looked almost exactly like my own. Trencoss found a squadron of human warriors, and transformed them to dogs based them off my Acushla, for the purpose of confusing me. If there are rules to this magic, maybe he couldn't separate me from my Acushla in body, so he separated us by making it impossible for me to find him.

But I will.

I will.

Another glance up, more sand has passed. If my eyes blur with tears, I will miss the subtle signals to identify which dog is which.

A blue tit chitters and sings from the apple branches above me.

"I know." I look up at him. "I am much too slow."

A dozen more tits descend around the first, all fluttering and hopping.

"You are so quick and clever," I agree, and then an idea bursts into my heart. "Would you—could you help me?"

"Ps-ps-ps-weee!" the first tit sings, and the rest flutter in an acrobatic cloud toward the next tree.

I gather my courage. It is a leap of faith to abandon my methodology, and risk losing the time I've spent so far.

I follow to their tree, checking the dog beneath. Chi, or possibly Psi. I stand, and the tits flitter to another tree.

Is it random? I follow them from tree to tree, finding dogs who are not the one I need, completely losing track of which dogs I have checked or not. Why would I even think that a flock of tiny birds would know which dog is which and where Acushla is?

We reach an open space with several dogs in a row, the tits waiting and singing. It will take two or three minutes to check all the dogs here, so I kneel to look at the first one. I have my hand on his shoulder when something tickles my foot.

A mouse. No, a dozen mice, scurrying right past me, all in the same direction. To the same dog.

I glance up at the front of the orchard, where I can still see Trencoss and the hourglass, even though by now we are far away. I haven't asked, but I'm quite sure he wouldn't like me getting help, so I pretend to look at several more dogs on my way to the one the mice have selected. I brush the fur away from his eyes.

Kappa. My chest fills with frustration—these little creatures don't know anything! What if we passed my Acushla ages ago?

I start to stand, but pause. I touch the dog on the other side, that the tits and mice ignore, and again the one they brought me to.

They're both Kappa, but I think—yes, I know—they brought me to the real Kappa! There is something different about the other Kappa next nearby...his heart is too fast for a wolfhound. There is a sensation of heartbeat, but below that, I can feel something else. The life-beat, maybe. The soul. It is a very small animal.

"Did he transform your friends and relations for my test?" I ask the mice at my feet. "I hope it doesn't hurt them."

One stands on his back feet, wiggling his nose and squeaking at me.

"Now we really must go!" I hurry towards the tree where the tits have gathered, now with a flock of song-wrens. The mouse squeaks at me, and I kneel and spread my skirt for them. Half a dozen mice clamber in.

The birds lead me from tree to tree. I let down the mice, who scurry about and show me which is the real dog in the area. Rho, this time. They can identify which are the true wolfhounds and which are the fakes, but they don't know which one dog is which. I scoop the mice back into my skirt and glance at the timer. Too slow! I am so much faster than these tiny creatures.

The mice squeal and the little birds chirp and spread in all directions. What now? A sharp shadow catches my eye, bursting from the hedgerow and circling the trees above me.

"Sparrowhawk? Are you here to help me, too, my friend?"

He circles one more time, and with the distinctive flap-flap-glide his stocky body shoots out towards the far side of the orchard. I gather my skirt snugly around the mice and run after him.

The sparrowhawk circles me, glides ahead, circles and glides ahead. I have to zig-zag to get to the openings in the hedgerows or cross a little stream, but even so, it takes only a minute or two until I am in the grove where he wants me. The sparrowhawk calls out, circles again, and then climbs high in the sky.

My breath is coming hard as I look around me, then stops altogether. Could it be?

I squeal in joy. My Acushla! And this one! And that. I am surrounded by a dozen of my beloved. I kneel to let the mice run, glancing at the time. From here, my regular eyes couldn't even see the gazebo where we started, Trencoss is nothing but a stick figure, yet the hourglass is still as clear as ever. Less than a quarter left, but there is still time, and the mice know how to find the real dog!

They scatter through our little garden room, running up one dog and then back down, squeaking at each other, switching dogs. A flock of finches darts out from the hedgerows, tipping their heads at me. But they are struggling to find the right one, and panic creeps up on me.

"Do you know which one is real? Which one is mine?" I'm checking each dog as I speak, rushing between them. Acushla. Acushla. Acushla. What do I do now?

The finches flit from tree to tree. The mice scurry around the sleeping dogs. A pair of red squirrels watches from a gnarled pear tree.

"I don't know!" I cry. "I've come all this way, and I'm going to lose him now?"

My foot hits a root and I go sprawling on the ground, knocking my knees and palms hard.

"Oh no! I didn't hit any of you, did I?" No little mouse bodies. "I can't fail now." I try to take a deep breath, but it turns into a shuddering sob. "Kappa! Lambda! Phi! Delta! Beta! You are depending on me. But look at the sand!"

Half of what was left is gone. I have only a handful of minutes, and fifteen identical Acushlas.

I lay my head in my arms. Not to rest, just to gather myself. I can't afford to be upset.

And in that moment, a little body hurtles towards me. I tense as sharp squirrel claws scrabble up my arms, and a little head rests for a moment on my chest. Then she sits up, looking at me, quirking her tall fluffy tail, and runs away again after she's certain she has my attention.

The other squirrel chirps from the nearby tree, almost like a question. I sit up, rubbing the places her little claws scratched, trying to figure out what they meant.

"A heartbeat?" I ask.

They chitter. The finches swoop and flutter.

"I have to try something," I reply. The animals have given me faith. I could recognize the fake dogs when I tried; obviously Trencoss has used extra layers of magic to disguise this set, but I will put my whole faith in my little friends.

I start over by the tree with the birds, and kneel beside each dog and lay my head on their heart. I try to let go of my fear and trust myself. I have rested like this so many days, slept like this so many nights. I *know* my Acushla's heartbeat.

This is it. It is him.

But I pause, suddenly unsure. The dog looks just like the others. What if I'm wrong? I should test all—

The squirrels chitter and the hawk screeches, becoming more agitated by the second.

Trust myself. Trust myself.

I pull the ribbon out of my pocket, fumbling with the fabric. How much time? Can't look. Quick—quick—his head is heavy.

There. It's done.

I lurch to my feet, staring up towards the hourglass. Despite the distance, it glows larger and clearer. All the animals are turned in the same direction, still.

Another minute passes. Maybe I should have checked the others—I'll start now and—

The last grain of sand falls, and fog pours out of the top of the hourglass. Within moments, it rolls over the entire orchard and I can barely see the next tree. The dozen Acushlas fade to four, and two, and none.

Trencoss said not until the star Arcturis rises tonight, so there is no reason to stay here for hours. I shiver, my head pounding and my legs trembling as I start the slog towards the castle. Little animals dart ahead, leading me to a hedgerow that I can follow through the fog.

How can I wait until tonight to know if I have saved my love, or killed five good dogs? Although Trencoss said I would never see them; perhaps he means only to send them away, but then they wouldn't...

I draw near the gazebo, and I have my answer.

Trencoss is in a rage. He paces back and forth, swinging a stick, letting out an occasional wordless bellow. He smacks the marble columns, he beats the bushes and the little animals flee. He sees me and raises the stick, and I wince although I'm still a dozen paces away.

I have won. I drop my head, trying to appear submissive, and press one hand against my heart. It is beating fast, and I tell myself this is joy. I will see my Acushla again! Trencoss promised! This is good!

But then the black fog rolls over the grass and Trencoss's face contorts with rage as he stares at me. Then he spins and beats the hourglass with his stick, which explodes in shards of glass and blue sparkling sand and clouds of strange-smelling fog. Trencoss hits it again and again, smashing the glass smaller and scattering the sand everywhere. It smells of ashes and vinegar, and none of the dogs move—not one.

I have won, but Trencoss's rage is dangerous. He is the ruler of this place, and can turn everything against us.

I turn and run.

CHAPTER EIGHTEEN

By the time I reach the palace, the fog is so thick that it might as well be night-time. Dark walls loom above me and I jog to the closest door, my breath fast and deep. I tug and nothing happens.

It takes me a moment to realize what happened; I really am pulling, but the door is locked. In this castle, I do not have keys at my belt.

They call it the Castle of a Thousand Doors; I must find another one. I follow the walls around, skirting bushes with drops coalescing on their dark leaves.

The next door is locked too.

And the next.

I hug my arms around myself, shivering. I've already searched this far wing, so I will try the main front doors.

Those are locked too, and now I'm really getting upset. Trencoss must deliver Acushla to my room, so now he is keeping me away from my room! Besides, I am becoming colder and colder, and don't even have my cloak. If I could get to the last camp that Acushla and I made, I would have our supplies, but it's more than twice as long as the outing with the dog-pack. I couldn't make it that far before true dark, even if I could pass the gates.

I tilt my head back and study the castle, as much as I can see in the skirling fog. Could I climb in a window? I'm not sure how they open, and they're much too precious to break.

I try anyhow, but it takes me several tries to find one that I can get close to. I'm no good at climbing trees, but there's a low twisty wych elm that I can use to scrabble up, right under one of the tall windows with a pointed top. Once balanced, I pull at the edge of the pane. Like in my room, only the lower part opens, but I can't get to the mechanism. What if I had a knife, or a spike of some kind? Where could I get one? I turn my head to see where to put my feet to climb down, but that twists my balance and I slip.

Crash! My head and shoulder knocks against the window as I slide down. I catch myself against the tree and the outer windowsill, but there's a terrible crackling above me. Cracks shatter up the glass—up and up and up—turning yards of glass into spears just waiting to break through and pierce me.

I leap free, landing hard in the dirt, bracing for the entire window to crash down on me and I will bleed out here, alone, in the dirt and the grass in the fog...

There's a dull clank, but nothing touches me.

I crawl to the side and dare to look back. Long cracks trace up the window into the blur of the fog, but the only pieces that fell must have been knocked inside.

Well, at least I don't need a knife to open it?

But I pace back and forth and still can't figure out what to do. If I break the window further, then broken pieces from the top will certainly fall on me. If I find a stick, then it will shatter widely and hit me. Even if I managed to break the window, I'd have to pull myself onto the windowsill on my belly, ripping myself on the jagged shards of glass. Frankly, I'm not sure what exactly would happen, because in my world we don't have big, smooth glass like this. If I'd broken that thick glass with my head, I would be knocked out and bleeding.

"I just want to get in," I say out loud. "Please, castle, can I come in?"

I turn around, looking through the fog, but there's no one. I've always had my guard dogs close in Trencoss's castle.

An owl hoots from above me, then flaps away. He perches and looks back, then flies again. I don't know what else to do, so I follow him. Down the pebbled paths, my feet aching, on and on, until we reach a small black door. There's something familiar about it.

The owl wheels away into the dark.

This is the entrance that Trencoss took us to *that* night. When my Acushla and I were bound in silver chains and thrown in the back of a cart, my body muffled in a blanket but Acushla's sliding back and forth with every lurch of the horses. *He* pulled us onto the ground here. Opened this little door. Lifted Acushla by his bonds and...

I don't remember. I woke up in bed the next morning, warm and cozy and miserably alone.

But now I will get my Acushla back, but I must get to my room. There's no other option, so I open the door.

On the narrow side table, a dancing flame lights the top of a candle. Does that mean there is someone nearby? I don't like that, but I don't like the dark, either, so I pick it up.

In front of me, dark narrow stairs go down and down.

No! I don't want to go to the cellar. Did the sorcerer drag my Acushla down there? Did he tie him up?

I can't marry Trencoss. I won't.

A musty draft floats up from below, and the fog floats in behind me. I close the door, being careful to not let the latch fall and lock me in. I just have to lock all those feelings away for a little while longer, so I lift up the candle and look around for another way out.

Around the other side of the wall, an equally dark staircase goes up. I'm disoriented, but I know my bedroom is up, and that's where I'll go. I start climbing, one hand trailing against the stone. I must be sensible. I must be there when Arcturis rises.

I unlatch the rough wooden door and shove it aside—I guess they aren't opening on their own tonight—and a long, dark hallway opens before me.

I step out, closing the door behind me, and hear the latch fall into place. I can feel thick carpet beneath my feet, and the air smells faintly of incense. I wait for my eyes to adjust to the dark.

For the first time in the Castle of a Thousand Doors, there are no torches and lamps flickering into brightness ahead of me.

For the first time in the Castle of a Thousand Doors, there are no dogs walking beside me.

I must be back in my bedroom before Arcturis rises. I begin walking.

Alone.

***

"I don't trust him." Saba leans towards the mirror, bouncing Oisín on her knees. He's pulling at her léine and fussing.

"I know not to trust him, but what can I do?" I'm wrapped in a blanket over my cloak, eating the last of the cold dinner that a faceless servant left on a tray outside my door. It was still there, because there are no dogs in the hallway. I've been in my room for hours, but none of them have come back. Even the mice will not come out of their hidey holes.

"He'll let the dog into your room, that's not the problem. Hush now, sweetie, hush."

"How do you know?"

Saba spins her hand, then grabs Oisín before he hurls himself off her lap. "In order to work magic, they have to set up a long chain of events, each one leading to the next, so when they start one thing going, it pulls over all the way back to the one they want. Ow, do you want a toy? Look, nice dolly."

"What on earth are you talking about?"

Saba pushes hair out of her face, tense and flushed. "This was why I never had any patience for learning sorcery, even though I was born as a

White Person and I could have done it. I mean, Trencoss would have had to connect his spells to you, and to the doors, and it sounds like he's looped in all the animals in the gardens, and then it tangles up with the dogs—please don't hit mama—"

Oisín wails, and I just want him to stop. Saba jiggles him, and I can barely stop from screaming with impatience.

She speaks in a rush. "So if he breaks his bargain with you, then it changes everything else he has set up. He stands to lose too much."

"Then we can trust him to give me Acushla?"

"Yes—no. The question is how he will change it, so he follows the letter of the bargain but you don't get what you want. He has all these hours between when the game ended and the star rises. Oh, get down then!"

Saba plops Oisín on the floor, whereupon he immediately starts bawling. She leans back in her chair and presses her hands against her face. Cheerful Saba has lost her temper, and it's probably my fault.

"I'm sorry, I shouldn't keep you. You've probably got to do dinner, or get him ready for bed..."

Saba gestures at the gray daylight. "It's not dinner time," she snaps. "He's been like this all day. Talking to you is the only interesting thing I've done. And look, he won't even let me do it!"

"I wish I could help. I'd take him for a walk, and even if he wouldn't stop grizzling you'd have a bit of peace."

She rubs her hands over her face. "I know you would. I wish I were with you, too."

We sit in silence, except for Oisín. Saba grates her teeth.

"Ailbe, that's it," Saba says quietly. "That's your power."

"The animals? That's what Trencoss said already." But it doesn't make sense in this context. "I'm not going to loop them into something dangerous, where they might get hurt."

"Of course not." Saba goes crisp. She swings Oisín back into her lap. "I'm talking about your own power."

I haven't got power, not like Saba and Trencoss and Fionn mac Cumhaill and even Theta.

I lean closer to the mirror, because there's one thing I can do right now. "Oisín. Oisín! Where's Auntie Ailbe? Where!" I cover my face with my hands, then pull away some of my fingers. Oisín watches warily. I pull back both hands, showing him a huge grin, and quickly hide again.

He giggles.

"Look at you." Saba strokes his springy curls, gazing into my eyes. "Your kindness, Ailbe."

I'm making silly noises for Oisín. "That's hardly a power," I sing-song.

Saba chuckles. "Call it true love, then."

I drop my hands, staring at her.

"You were searching for me for so long, and walked through Fae realms with no harm to you. That's love. That's power, Ailbe."

Oisín reaches out his little hands towards me. "Mo'. Mo'!"

I do another peek-a-boo face.

"It pulled you to Acushla today," Saba continues, while Oisín wiggles in her lap. "You have to trust that it will guide you forward."

"Through whatever Trencoss does next?" I wiggle my fingers in my ears and cross my eyes. "How does that work?"

Oisín claps and screams. We're all having trouble following the conversation.

Saba furrows her brow. "If we were sorcerers, we would have ways to test it, but the basic idea makes sense to me. So that means—oh! Oh *no*, baby!"

She swings Oisín off her lap, her mouth pressed tight. A wet spot grows on the front of Oisín's léine and pools on the floor around him. He giggles and dances in a circle, splashing in it.

"I guess I can't talk any more." Saba tries to smile, but rubs a tear off her cheek. "But what I was saying—" She bites her lip, watching Oisín make the mess worse and worse, then looks back up at me. "Hold on, Ailbe. No matter what. Hold on."

I put my hand against the mirror as Saba fades away.

I don't know what she expects me to do, but she thinks something bad is coming. I don't know any spells, and I won't try anything that could hurt someone else. So all I can think of is to take Saba literally.

I will hold on.

***

The evening creeps by. Arcturis rises after full dark, but before midnight.

My head is blurry with exhaustion, and I wish I could crawl in bed and rest before—whatever happens. But I don't want to miss anything, and I don't want to waste the time so I sit close to the fire, weaving a crios. The first red one is long enough to hold the bar under my foot, my fingers pick and drop, pick and drop. I've closed the window but left the curtains open so I can check the night sky. The fog has cleared and the moon sends a long pale rectangle creeping across my bedroom floor. The oak leaves block out most of the stars, but I keep checking as though I could see them.

Pick and drop, tuck my shuttle back and forth, the shimmering weft ball flattening as the weaving creeps up the warp.

My mind skitters around memories of traveling with my Acushla, playing hide-and-seek with Saba when we were little, the night when I ran away from Fionn's castle and abandoned everything I had worked for my whole life. I search for the earliest memories of my mother, but I can only remember Saba's mother. The queen was weak and spent most of her life on a couch, someone fetching her hot compresses and soothing teas, but she was the one who was kind to me. I remember her smile, the scent of her skin.

True love, Saba told me. Hold on.

If I am good at emotionally holding on, then the magic will expect me to physically hold on. Maybe I will have to nurse Acushla back to health, or he will race through my room only to jump out the window and fly away—either of those would be ways for Trencoss to uphold his bargain but not give me what I want, which is for Acushla to *stay*. I will just hold on to him with my hands just as firmly as I hold on to Saba with my heart, because now I think maybe that's what brought the mirror to me, too. Holding-on-ness. That pulled on one thing which pulled on another, and when Bob gave me the wish then it pulled on the dogs (who were full of magic, having been enchanted themselves), who pulled on the castle, who reflected back my true-love-of-Saba, and it all made the mirror.

Which I made with my hands, like I am making the criosanna with my hands, and then I will pull back through everything, and fix what I have caused to be broken.

I glance at the window. Not yet. If I check the stars every time I wonder the time, I will never finish this belt.

I glance at the floor. The shadows of oak leaves dance in the white patch of moonlight.

I look back at my hands, imagining his familiar face in the firelight. Calm eyes, ears pricked towards me, the left a little higher than the right. The exact angle he cocks his head when I am talking. Pick and drop, pick and drop, the magical red thread spooling across my fingers.

I keep my ribs tight, don't let my emotions burble up...but whatever happens afterward, I will treasure his presence even for a moment. I will hold on.

Chapter Nineteen

The door knocks back against the wall with a gust of wind, blowing out my candles and sending my threads swirling. I kick aside the loom and leap to my feet.

For just a moment, I see a large black dog in the doorway. But by the time I cross the room towards him, the shadow is lengthening and rising. I abandon rational thought and fling my arms around it—him.

I'm holding a sinuous curve of muscle and smooth scales. There's a hiss far above me, and I tilt my head and realize a giant serpent is filling my bedroom, its head curving down from the ceiling, its coils knocking my feet out from under me. I go down in a tangle, but it's as easy to hold as a tree trunk. I hold on.

Then the scales shift to pungent fur under my hands and face—not wolfhound curls but straight and coarse—I clutch my fingers tight and brace for whatever comes next. The creature lunges forward, dragging me with it, and rears to its hind legs with a roar. It's a bear, an enormous bear, and it swings me off the ground and then I tumble down as it lands on all fours. I cry out as it knocks me against the bed, galumphing back towards the door, its claws scattering my rugs. My fingers are slipping when heavy limbs slide into something narrow and sinous.

Something broad and heavy hits my face as my fingers slide past feathers. A raptor. But I have been falconing and I've tended poultry, so I know to lock my hands around its legs. It beats its wings, knocking my hair down and making me squeeze my eyes closed, and the talons flex with its movements but he doesn't claw at my face.

In that split second, I realize that the creature doesn't want to hurt me. It is caught in magic, but it is trying to be careful.

It changes again, pulling my hands apart with the force of the transformation. Another huge animal, its antlers knocking into the top of the wardrobe. It's a giant elk, the likes of which only exist in bones and legend. I stutter for just a second, fighting my instincts telling me to avoid those hooves. I leap upwards and grab onto the shaggy fur under its chest and shoulders, and at that moment it tries to rear. I'm flung upwards, my shoulders yanked against their sockets, but the elk crashes into the ceiling and loses the momentum that could have thrown me off. We come back to the floor, its front hooves slamming into the stone, and then my feet hitting—and we keep sliding down.

I'm on my knees with something small and wiggly in my hands. It's a stoat, scrabbling and writhing to escape. Its nails scratch my hands and I scream, not because of the pain, but because I have to hold it so hard. I'm going to hurt it, its back breaking under my hands—but if I relax my grip, it will dive under the furniture and be gone forever, so I scream and clutch and scream.

Then it's a fish and it does slip out of my hands. It flops on the floor with a sickening thud, and I dive after it, scrabbling as it bumps up against the lump of rug. I'm going to hurt it! No, now it's big and yanking me upwards—I'm too confused to even understand what's happened—my eyes squeezed shut, gamey smell in my face. My fingers spasm with clutching its fur, and as the thing knocks me back I throw my arms around it as the fur fades under my fingers. I squeeze something smooth and try to get my feet under me.

Is it the serpent again? It's not thrashing yet. My arms are locked around warm skin and my face pressed against heat, as I brace for it to shift into the next creature.

We're still.

Something touches my back and I shiver, waiting for it to throw me again.

"My Mavourneen," a voice rumbles. "My Mavourneen, it's me. I'm here."

***

I don't dare move. I hardly dare breathe.

Something spreads against my back, slow and warm. It could be a hand.

It could be breathing under my ear. Bare skin. A shoulder.

My arms could be around a waist. Not a serpent, but a man, although I am not certain, because I have never held a man in my arms before.

The might-be-a-hand strokes my hair away from my neck.

Without loosening my arms, I draw my head back just enough to peek at whatever is in front of me.

"You are not a dog," I tell him.

He smiles. "I am who I always have been. Your Acushla."

"You are *not* a *dog*." I'm starting to shake, but I don't let him go.

He strokes my hair again, as smooth and gentle as though I were the dog—and about to bite.

"I don't seem to be, am I? But I am myself. I promise, I'm the same."

"No." I'm shaking now, my legs barely holding me. My arms, however, retain their iron grip. "You're not. You are. I don't know!"

"Have I hurt you?" he asks. "I'm sorry—it was all a blur, but I was very large and I hope I didn't hurt you."

"I'm not hurt," I reply, though I have no idea if it's true. My teeth are chattering and my shoulder aches.

"Let's sit down." His voice is low and velvet and gentle. He tries to guide me, but I won't let go of him and can't figure out where to put my feet. He pauses, then simply leans forward and lifts me up.

He sits me on my bed, and he's stepping away—

"No!" I clutch at his arm.

"I'm not going anywhere," he tells me. "Let me get up next to you. I'm feeling a little run-down after all that, too."

I don't release him, but let him get the space to turn and climb next to me. He puts his hands on my shoulders, and just when I'm afraid he's pushing me away he tucks me close and tight against his chest. My forehead brushes the smooth edge of the torc resting against his collarbones.

I'm tense and careful, one hand clenched around his bicep, just in case he changes to something else or leaps away. But the man is steady and calm, and with each breath I relax a little. I'm leaning on him. He's holding me up. That much is like my Acushla. His hand strokes slow circles on my back, and my aching muscles unclench a little more.

"Who are you?" I manage to ask against his bare chest. This is shocking and horrifying, especially considering that I am officially engaged to Trencoss and unofficially engaged to Fergus, and this is *very* confusing.

"My name is Conall mac Dubhshláine, and my family has a small kingdom high in the mountains of Breifne." His voice is soothing, his hand still circling. "I went out to make my fortune, as young men are wont to do, and came afoul of a sorcerer. It seems that I spent several years as a dog, and the last one I spent with *you*, my Mavourneen."

I take a breath but can't find any words. Instead, I listen to his heartbeat. Do I recognize it? Is it the same?

"We helped find that cow with the red spots," he reminds me, "and they gave you an entire jug of oil in thanks. We stayed with the butcher who had eight daughters, who slept in one bed all lined up from biggest to smallest. We walked through a mushroom ring into the Fae world, where you found an injured wren-fae with terrible sharp teeth, and you made it a sling and put it back in the briar patch where it asked to go, and then it threw rotten berries at us."

I giggle, because that was a strange day indeed. "But it paid its debt when the storm came up—"

"Because our entire camp was washed away in the night, and our gear came back to us in the morning floating in a berry the size of a coracle—"

"Which fed us for a week."

"Mm. Ailbe, I have missed you bitterly."

"I have missed you too." Because it is him. It is.

After a long moment, I pull back and look at him again. It's different this time, because although I have never seen him I know he is not a stranger.

I reach out, brushing my fingers down his cheek before I think twice and snatch them away. "I'm sorry—I shouldn't..." I look down, confused. I'm still not releasing his arm, no matter what good manners dictate, but it's not polite to touch people's faces.

"It's all right." There's a smile in his voice. "May I?" He tucks my hair behind my ear. "As for me, you have already touched me just that way a hundred times. I know I look different, but it feels the same to me."

"I—"

He takes my hand, and with his eyes steady on mine, draws my fingers back to his cheek. I stroke the line of his jaw, across his high cheekbone, lay my hand against his warm skin.

It's dark in my room, lit only by the scattered moonlight through the oak tree, so my fingers tell me as much as my eyes. He is one of the Nemed people, more ancient even than my own race, with dark skin and midnight eyes and dense wooly curls. He has a high forehead, square jaw, and wide soft lips—not that I touch his lips. He is clean-shaven, but I can feel the prickle of stubble. Thankfully, he is not entirely naked, with a knee-length cloth cinched around his waist, and—well, I assume trews under that, as men usually wear, but that is another aspect I am not investigating. His silver torc glimmers with an intricate and intertwined pattern. His muscles are smooth and rolling, and I do run my hand down his arm and across his chest, because I need to understand the human-ness of him. I need to understand that he is human, exactly who my Acushla might be, but I can't help notice that he is beautiful and he is a man.

I leave my palm against his heartbeat, listening with my own bones. *Here, here, here,* they tell me. *Mine, mine, mine.*

I meet his eyes again, deep pools in the darkness. I shiver. "It is you."

"It is me." Studying me, he frowns. "You're cold. We need to build up the fire, and I know you're not happy with things knocked over like this. Let me—"

"No!"

He's already on his feet, my fingers around his wrist. "Mavourneen. I won't leave."

"But that's my job."

My tears start to flow again. He cups my face in his warm hands and wipes them away with his thumbs.

"I don't know what's wrong with me." I try to smile.

"You've had a long, hard day, and I don't know the half of it. I'm here now. Let me build the fire and get you a blanket."

If he's busy with practical things and won't let me help, I might as well comb my hair. It makes me feel lopsided and slovenly, hanging half-down like this. I don't take the time to braid it, letting it make a stormy cloud around me as I fill the kettle and fasten it on the fire hook.

"I'll make you tea," I say, since my own throat hurts. If I want tea, he must need it even more.

Instead of sitting in the two chairs in front of the fire, like I did with Bob and with Fergus, we go back to the bed while the fire catches and the water heats. This way we can be next to each other, our knees touching, holding hands. Mine is tight around his fingers, and his other hand is big and calm over mine. I'm still scared of what will happen if I let go.

"What are you now?" I ask. "I mean—will you stay as you are now? Where is the dog?"

He shakes his head. "I believe it is untangled, but not gone." He touches the torc, his voice bitter. "This is Trencoss's. But…"

He looks into the distance, watching the flames leap. I watch him and consider what Saba said, how I made one bargain and pulled out a thread of Trencoss's magic. If it is like sewing, now parts are loose and messy, but not free.

"So Trencoss has not released you. What else?" I squeeze his fingers.

"In the last few years, I have met a couple of people—or Fae—who could see who I really was. They told me…" He swallows. "I have been the dog for so long, I carry both inside me now. Even once I escape this"—he gestures to the castle, the torc, everything—"I will be able to switch back and forth."

"So you could be the dog if you wish?" I'm thinking of Saba, who can escape in her deer form, and survive when there isn't food for a human.

"I *never* wish!" he exclaims. "The hound form is nothing but a trap! I hope it wasn't a dog you wanted, because I will never go back to it."

"I don't care about the dog," I reply quickly, although in many ways I liked the dog. It's more important that my Acushla—Conall—can be what he wants.

He squeezes my hand back, a quick smile. "I suspect you will get it in the morning again."

"The man form at night, the dog in the day. Yes, there are many stories like that."

"So tell me how you have been, while we can still talk. That is—remember that I can listen any time, if you wish to say something. But it must feel good to hear a reply."

"Oh, it feels *so* good to hear your voice!" I exclaim. "I may be foolish, but…" I trail away, all those feelings I have been holding in bubbling up so large that I can barely speak.

"I always like listening to what you say." He runs the back of his knuckles down my cheek, and I put my hand over his, holding his warmth to my skin. "But it's good to speak to you, too."

My heart skitters and flutters, like a songbird bursting into the sky. I don't know what to make of this internal cacophony.

"The water is boiling." I stand up, not releasing his hand until the last moment. "Can you tell me more? About your family, or how you came..."

"I can." Conall follows me across the room. "But right now, I need to hear what has happened to you since we arrived here." He finds the spills and lights a candle, setting it on the shelf where I am preparing tea.

I murmur my thanks, suddenly shy in the light.

"Has Trencoss mistreated you?" Conall's voice is hard and sharp.

I look up at him, startled. His jaw is set and his stance is that of a warrior.

Conall has been so soothing and gentle, I have not thought about the other side to him. Those muscles are not just for show, and the casual comment that he went to "make his fortune" means he is from a wealthy family and either joined a fianna or led one of his own. In dog form, he once fought three wolves away from our campsite while I hid in the tent. In the morning, I packed immediately and we never spoke of it again, but of course that means that *I* did not choose to speak of it. Maybe *he* had more he wanted to tell me.

"If Trencoss has hurt you," my Acushla says, the words crisp and cold, "so may the gods help me, but I will kill him."

I look down. Drop a scoop of chamomile into the pot. I don't want them to fight.

"I have to escape this"—he touches the torc—"but then he will find that I may be patient, but I am not forgiving."

"He has not hurt me," I say. "He wants to marry me."

Conall growls.

Even if Trencoss has hurt me, I am not about to say it now. I don't want another display of masculine aggression that means I could lose my beloved as soon as I found him.

My beloved—the words feel different now that it is a man in front of me. I didn't mean it *that* way—I don't have time to sort through my thoughts, so I talk quickly. "Trencoss is trying to convince me that this is the best place in the world, that's all. He gives me fine cloth and beautiful thread and good meals. And the morning tea?" I am watching Conall's face carefully. "I don't have the leaves here, but it is wonderful. Saba says it is camellia sinensis, and it comes from China. Very energizing."

"Saba?" Conall glances away and then back to me, his body language softening. "Have you seen her at last?" He wraps his hand in a rag and pours the boiling water for me. Completely ordinary once again.

I put the lid on the teapot, then I take Conall's hand and lead him to the mirror, and he asks me questions, and that leads to explaining Bob and the balls of dew-drop thread and the bargain I made to delay the wedding.

"How long until the white thread is ready?" Conall asks.

"Some of the flyers have been finding white flowers all along." I take a sip of tea and pass him the cup, as is most respectful. "That skein is half-wound already, so I only have a few days left. A week at most."

Not that it matters, because Fergus left for Starfruit Island a few days ago, and it always takes him longer than he predicts, but he will surely be back before the white ball is done. I'm struck with a bolt of horror that if Fergus comes back and finds my Acushla like this, everything will become very, very complicated.

No man, least of all Fergus who fancies himself in love with me, would like finding a half-naked man in my bedroom, holding my hands and pouring my tea.

Conall is watching me closely I don't think he would like Fergus particularly, either.

"Thank you, my lady." Conall sips the tea in the formal way, and then touches my arm gently. "Do not worry about Trencoss, Ailbe. I am back. I will take care of things."

I smile, a little shakily. That sounds nice, to just trust him to manage everything.

We settle back on the bed, but this time Conall arranges the pillows and blankets so we can lean against the wall. I blow out the candle, since it is very late and my eyes are very tired. We have our mugs in one hand and are leaning together on the other side, my legs tucked over his and a blanket pulled over both of us, his arm behind me, my head and shoulders leaning against his chest, his heartbeat soothing me. It's rather like how we used to huddle together by the campfire, me leaning on him ever more as the evening wore on.

It's similar, just we have...different arms and legs now. And no fur. And...he's a man, and I'm very much aware of that.

"But what about you?" It's better to say something. "Trencoss has a reason to be nice to me, but I've been worried ever since he threw you down those terrible stairs." I shiver.

Conall sighs. "He has a reason to take care of me, too. He doesn't like me, but he needs warriors to defend the castle. As long as we are physically fit and he can force us to obey, he won't actually hurt any of us."

I had guessed that, but it's good to hear it clearly.

"What about when he lifts you by the collar and shakes?"

"It's disconcerting, but doesn't cause any harm. Wolfhounds can handle a lot of rough-housing."

"And he feeds you?"

I hear the smile in Conall's voice. "Plenty."

"You aren't locked up or anything?"

"Well..." He puts his cup aside and pulls me more comfortably into his lap. "We do live in the basement. But it is set up so it feels cozy and comfortable to us." He tenses. "Our dog bodies like being somewhere dark and hidden at night."

I sense he is ashamed, although I've known Saba my whole life and I know she has deer-cravings. "You mention the other dogs? So you're not alone?"

"No, I've been with them since I arrived. I'm assigned into the patrols like any other. I'm just never allowed next to you."

"Hm." I slide lower, just like I used to do by the campfire. "I saw you."

"I know. I was keeping watch over you, even when you couldn't see me. I've always been keeping you safe."

"Mmm." I want to stay awake, but it's so hard.

"Mavourneen?"

I manage a little sound in reply.

"Who is the other man in your room?"

"What?" I sit up, shocked and then confused. "Now? Where?"

"Not now. Settle back, I didn't mean to disturb you."

I lean against him, but now it's to avoid his eyes. Whatever he means, I need to plan this conversation out rather than just tumble in. I try to think, but he speaks first, his voice low and calm.

"The other dogs have told me they've heard you speaking with two different men. Relax, Mavourneen, it's fine! No one's being particular about your reputation, and no one can understand any of the words through the door. From your description, I can tell one must be Bob. But you haven't mentioned the second man. He's young, and he hasn't come often but he has stayed quite a while. Who is he?"

I run my fingers over Conall's fingers, trying to figure out what he wants me to say. I don't know, so I just use blunt words. "Bob sent him. His name is, um, Fergus, and he's...trying to rescue me." I explain about the islands and fruits.

"What have three fruits to do with Trencoss?" Conall asks.

"I...don't know, actually."

"There must be some magic tangled up with him, or the Fae have some way of unraveling Trencoss's magic if certain conditions are met. Well, I'll take that into consideration when I figure out how to get us out of here."

"All of us?"

"The twenty-four wolfhounds, and you and I. Do you know anyone else who needs to leave?"

"I'll ask. I wonder if the mice were really something else too?"

He chuckles. "I really am not sure I can take every mouse and nut-hatch in this place, but I'll do my best if you ask me. Now Ailbe..."

I've relaxed against him, wondering about all the birds and the rabbits and everything. Do the little flyers want to go, too? Can I release them?

"Are you going to marry him?" he asks.

I wasn't ready for that. I squeeze my eyes shut, which doesn't help. My Acushla just waits, not getting upset but not rescinding his question, either.

"I don't know," I mumble finally.

"Was that part of the bargain?"

"No one ever *said* it was."

He sighs. "Mavourneen. Is he here as your suitor or is he an old married man already?"

"He says he's in love with me," I mutter, curling into myself.

"Are you in love with him?" Conall keeps his voice very steady.

"I kissed him." I can't hold that away from Conall, even though he didn't ask.

"I see."

"I thought I was supposed to."

"I see."

"Was that wrong?"

He sighs. "Nothing you decide is wrong, Mavourneen. You have been alone and needed help, and your affections are yours to give away. I just think—ahem, I observe—"

For once, he is the one stumbling. "What?"

"I observe the way you are treating me tonight, which seems to indicate certain things, which don't match what you're saying."

This is true. "I...know. I didn't mean..."

He sighs. "I think you might be a little confused."

I make a faint sound of agreement. Some part of my mind tells me to pull away from him, because I'm embarrassed? Or not supposed to touch him. But I'm so comfortable. He's nice to touch. Can't think of why I need to move away.

So nice. Safe.

Something pulls at my hand, and I clutch my mug tight.

"I'm just taking it so you don't spill your tea on yourself," my Acushla says, his voice velvet. "You're almost asleep. I'm laying you down, too."

Strong arms lower me into my comfy, squishy, wonderful bed. Soft blankets nestle over my shoulder.

"Want talk. You."

"You can sleep. I'll be here again."

I'm drifting away when the weight on my bed shifts, rolls away.

"Wait!" I push myself half-upright, sharply awake. "Where are you going?"

He gestures. "I'll roll up a blanket and sleep outside your door. I'll keep a watch over you, don't worry."

"Acushla!" I throw off the blankets and stumble after him, grabbing for his arm. I ache for him in the same way that one thirsts after running in the sun; parched and clawing and painful, each breath excruciating. I need him to stay here. Need him!

"Aren't you going to stay with me? Sleep back-to-back, like we always did?"

He smiles gently. "Absolutely not."

"But you're here now." He can't leave. He can't. I'm lonely and scared and he's finally here. "I'm not asking for a kiss or anything. Just stay. Just next to me. That's all."

He turns me and leads me back across the room. "I'm still going to be here, but not *here*." He sets me on the bed.

"You always slept with me before!"

"Ailbe." He cups my face in his hands, makes me look up at him. "You are a beautiful young woman, and you may or may not be engaged to another man. I am not going to kiss you, and I am most certainly not going to sleep with you, until you decide what you want."

"What do *you* want?" I clutch his wrists, keeping his hands in place.

"I love you, and I have loved you for a long time." He brushes his thumb across my skin. "That means I respect your choices, and I'm giving you time to make a decision."

This means he is walking away. "Do you not want me?"

He sighs and drops his hands to my shoulders. "I think I've made my feelings for you pretty clear. But you've also had Trencoss making a fuss over you, and this Fergus fellow coming in and declaring undying love, and you've never even known that I was a man and you still don't know much about me. And furthermore, it's the middle of the night, and you're always muzzy-headed in the night-time. Mavourneen, I think you just need to go to sleep, and think things over in the morning."

I want him close to me, I know that. But my want is dark and deep and guttural—and completely irrational—and I'm confused about everything except how much I want him beside me right now.

"Goodnight, my Mavourneen." Conall lays me back down, his hands strong and confident, tucking the blanket over my shoulder. "I'll stay in here until you're asleep. You're safe. I promise."

Safe wasn't all I wanted, but it will do for a start. I wrap my arms around my pillow. The last thing I know is his breathing. In and out, in and out. I am not alone.

CHAPTER TWENTY

I wake with the sunlight across my room, and two faceless maids straightening out the rugs. We are alone—no dogs, no cat, most certainly no man. I roll on my side, trying to make sense of any of this.

I remember it all. I am not someone who wakes up confused—or rather, I don't wake up muzzy-headed. I am still very confused.

What do I owe to Fergus, who is risking life and limb for me? What do I owe to my parents, who gave up so much that I might better myself? They would expect that I honor my commitments, even the unspoken ones, and definitely expect me to marry a prince if one were available. That's what they dreamed for me, who was chosen by the Fates to be born the same day as a princess.

The maids pull the corners apart, struggling to manage the heavy rug. It is rumpled from the struggle with the elk and the bear and the fish; I have given them this extra work. They can't sing a song to keep their rhythm together, they can't grunt with surprise when the weight jerks. One shakes out her wrist and then grips the rug again. What do I owe them?

"Do you want to leave this castle?" I ask them. "Were you someone else..."

I was going to say "did you have faces, and voices, and wishes, and dreams?" But they both have turned to me, and they both are so stiff. It makes me pause, and then I wonder if they are loyal to Trencoss. I don't know whom I can trust.

I had imagined the mice were once people that Trencoss had transformed, but what if it is the other way around—the people were once mice.

I don't say any more. I don't know what to do about the faceless people or the mice either. And all of that is a distraction from my real problem, which is a triangle of men who all have the right to expect something from me.

***

After breakfast, I need a walk. I do not invite the dogs, but Eta and Iota and Psi follow me. I suppose they have to, but my mind is like a pie pan, scraped to the last crumb, and I cannot manage to talk with them. At first, my body protests any movement, stiff and aching from crouching so often yesterday, and I suppose the animals last night did bruise and scrape me. Have I hurt you, he asked—I said no and that wasn't even right.

He. My Acushla, the giant elk *and* the salmon *and* the wolfhound who saved my life *and* Conall, who is a man with feelings and opinions of his own. The Conall who rubbed my back and helped build up the fire is easy to figure out—after all, as a wolfhound, we worked together to set up camp and he comforted me when I was sad or hurt. But he's more than that, too, and I don't know what to do.

He said he'd manage Trencoss and the enchantment for me, which is a relief, but his anger and power was boiling just under the surface. I didn't know that was part of my dog.

I glance back at the three black wolfhounds following me, that gait that seems so plodding and uncoordinated until they burst into an explosion of power and motion.

My Acushla. It was a silly name for a dog. My heart is beating too fast, and I duck under a rowan tree and sit against the trunk, pulling my knees close.

Did I always know? That sweetness we had between us—the intensity of that emotion. He always knew who I was. I thought we were looking for Saba, but oh heavens, he was looking for the way out of his curse. He said it was a trap, the dog-form. We went in and out of Fae for a year. Of course he was looking.

But me...did I know all along, too? Because I've spent weeks with the twenty-four dogs, now. I know and trust them, some in particular. But it's not even a little bit the same as how I felt about my Acushla.

But even if I did know my Acushla wasn't just a dog...even if I was a little bit in love with him all along...

What do I do about Fergus?

***

"What are you even upset about?" Saba flings her hands up. "I don't understand you."

"I'm supposed to marry Fergus," I repeat. I've moved one of the fireplace-chairs in front of the mirror, and I'm tucked up with a blanket and pillow and pot of tea. I probably only got three hours of sleep, and now that it's afternoon I'm aching with exhaustion. I have the crios loom with me, but I can't keep my foot in place and my fingers are fat and clumsy.

"Did you promise?" Saba leans close, her blue eyes glimmering. "Did he give you anything? Jewelry, a sharing goblet?"

"He gave me an orange and a plum."

Saba sits back. "That is for the magic. It definitely does not bind you to an engagement."

I rub my hands over my face. "Then am I bound to Trencoss? He's given me lots of things."

Saba clucks her tongue. "Trencoss is the bad guy. He's not part of this equation."

"He's always part of the equation!" I think Saba over-simplifies. "He's not bad entirely—"

"He trapped you"—Saba counts on her fingers—"he loses his temper, he shakes the dogs, he swoops his cloak around in a silly over-dramatic way—"

"Think about the Morrígan," I tell her, tired. "Everything in the stories has a bad side and a good side. That is what we're supposed to learn." We're both quiet. "That it's not so simple."

Saba throws a turnip on her pile. She's supposedly cleaning vegetables while Oisín naps, but Saba uses her entire body to listen to me.

"The Dark Man chased me here and won't let me out," she says bitterly. "He's just plain bad."

"He is—"

"Fionn knew I was carrying his child, but he never made the effort to seek me out. And!" She holds up her finger. "As soon as I was gone, he arranged marriages for all of my ladies-in-waiting, and sold you off to an evil sorcerer! He's bad too!"

Fionn is definitely one of the complicated ones, but I'm not about to defend him to his wife.

Saba starts to say something more about Fionn, but interrupts herself. "No. For once, we were talking about you. We were talking about how you feel about this handsome, considerate, affectionate man appearing in your bedroom and how—"

"No." Heat washes over my heart and stomach. "We were talking about Fergus."

"It's the same conversation."

"It isn't!"

"My dear Ailbe." Saba stands, reaching out her hands as though she could touch me. "I don't even understand what you are saying. You have never felt particularly strongly about Fergus. Why do you insist on putting him first?"

"Because I owe it to him," I exclaim. "He's done work for me, and I'm supposed to be loyal to him." I press my palms against my cheeks, trying to breathe.

"You don't mention that you like him," Saba snaps. "Let alone that you've fallen in love."

I don't bother to answer.

"Ailbe!" Saba kicks her basket, spilling turnips all over the ground. "Listen!"

My hands twitch, wanting to help her with the mess. To be useful. Together.

Saba stares at me, her mouth set and her eyes serious. "No one else is going to care about your wishes. You have to fight for yourself, my beloved sister."

"My wishes don't matter if they are disloyal," I argue. My mind flashes back to the dinner in the throne room, when I said I didn't wish to marry Trencoss and he punished the dogs.

Saba shakes her head. "Your love is powerful."

"It's not. It's just"—I laugh bitterly—"one silly little woman, not anyone important."

"You don't understand! I'm not just flattering you. I'm talking about power, real power. Look at you! I can't escape from here, but your love for me opened up this way we can speak to each other. *You* did that, Ailbe. I cannot!"

"Yes, of course I would do anything for you, but this isn't—"
Saba stamps her foot and screeches in frustration.

"Hush!" I warn. "You'll wake the baby!"

We stare at each other for two heartbeats, and then Saba's face dissolves in laughter and I start to giggle. I laugh and she laughs, and the tears finally escape and bathe my cheeks. It's too absurd, me telling her not to wake the baby, when it's her baby and I'm not even anywhere nearby. Or maybe it's not that funny, but we can't stop laughing anyways. Every time one of us calms down, the other starts off and then we're both laughing.

Oisín sleeps through it all.

"Look around," Saba says once we are finally calm, spreading her hand to show me her courtyard. "I have my life here. It's not always easy, but I'm raising my child and making the life I want. I know you were raised to help me, and I love you so much. But you can't help me any more."

I put my hands over my face. Her words are a physical pain on my aching body.

"You are strong," Saba says. "I know what is hidden under your quiet expression and loyal heart."

I can't look at her.

"Don't give yourself away to some man who isn't worthy of you," Saba warns. "Use your own power. Love with all your strength. It's time to make your own life for yourself, Ailbe of Dún Allaine."

Chapter Twenty-One

I am stumbling through my weaving, refusing to check the position of the stars. Arcturis will rise when he rises.

I collapsed in my bed after speaking (arguing?) with Saba, and must have slept through dinner. The faceless servants brought me a generous tray of food, but I put half of it out for the birds and mice. The other half still taunts me, reminding me that I ought to be hungry, but I just sit and weave by firelight.

I know what I need to do, but the thought bowls me over like cold salty waves. I'm not sure I can.

Pick and drop, pick and drop. I keep my fingers going.

My Acushla is coming back soon! My heart soars.

What if he is a monster again? My heart goes cold.

His calm voice! His gentle smile! My heart flutters up.

I must tell him my decision. My heart crashes because whatever I do, someone will be hurt. Conall said I had the right to make my own choice, but I am not accustomed to being the one who chooses.

I let nothing show, keeping my fingers and my breathing steady. The warp is oddly tight and I pause, blinking to orient myself.

I have reached the end of the crios, that's all. Eighteen done. I bind off, shaking out my fingers as I glance out the window. I was looking for the stars, but wonder about Fergus instead. I yawn, and decide that if he were coming tonight he would be here by now.

I can't see the stars, so I start winding the next warp. I am just tightening the last strands when I hear noises in the hall.

I jerk upright, straining for any sound. I left my door ajar, but the servants closed it. Last I saw, six dogs were sprawled in the hall, but now I catch the tenor of words. A man's voice. A reply.

I tuck my loom away so the work is not wasted. I am calm. I am steady.

Except my heart lurches and tumbles.

My door opens, a man steps inside, then closes it carefully behind him. Waiting. He is in the deep shadows, but I see enough to know him—his graceful movements, careful hands, patient voice.

The frantic diving of my heart settles, and I know.

I know.

***

My feet fly across the floor of their own accord and my arms fling themselves around his neck.

"Conall mac Dubhshláine, I choose you." I laugh with the surprise or the sheer joy of saying it. "My Acushla."

His smile softens the dark, his hands steady on my waist. "Ailbe of Dún Allaine, will you marry me?"

I take a slow breath, letting the real-ness of him push away all the fear and doubt inside me. "Yes."

"You are sure, my Mavourneen?"

"You are the only one I ever wanted." The words are so big, so true, that they overwhelm me. I press my face into his shoulder.

Conall strokes his hand up and down my back, slowly, until I manage to soften a little.

"Don't be afraid, little Mavourneen," he murmurs. "I will keep you safe. I will not let Trencoss harm you."

"And what if Fergus comes back with the starfruit?" I mumble into his shoulder, which thankfully is clothed tonight. It's much easier to think that way.

"Then Fergus has simply been too slow," Conall answers crisply. "I can't help it if he's late, and it does no good to you."

I hadn't thought of it that way, and I relax more. That matches the stories—not that Fergus won me, but he entered a competition for me. Fergus was Bob's champion, but the dog-team is beating the cat-team. The thought is silly, and I smile.

"You are the one I choose to rescue me," I repeat, feeling like I have permission now. "You."

Conall strokes my hair, a smile in his voice. "If you look up at me, I will seal our bargain with a kiss."

I stiffen, but before I can obey he pauses me with a gentle finger on my cheek.

"What is wrong, Mavourneen?"

I study his face, my eyes adjusted to the shadows now. He is watching me, and my anxiousness fades under his familiar patience. He was the same as a dog; attentive to my moods and not allowing me to pretend something I didn't feel.

Except now, words are important. I stumble through finding the true ones. "I can look at you. And I don't mind...that is, you can kiss me. That's...fine. Of course."

"Is it?"

"Yes. Really." I am happy to know I can give him something. "It's just that I, myself...um, don't particularly like kissing." I mumble the last bit quickly against his shirt.

Something changes in the way he holds his body, although his voice is calm as he answers. "Well, then. Have you kissed so very many men?"

"Two," I reply. "Both this week, so I guess I would know by now."

"And it was...?"

"Boring," I answer, with great authority.

"I should not wish to bore you," he says, equally serious. "Let us go to the fire and talk, instead."

He takes my hand. I glance up at his face as we come back into the light, shy and eager to learn this version of him. I suspect he is hiding a smile, which surprises me. I thought our conversation was quite serious.

He helps me stoke the fire and fill the kettle, then glances at me. "Perhaps, if our conversation is interesting enough, you will permit me to attempt to change your mind about kissing."

That was definitely a mischievous smile.

"I don't mind if you kiss me," I repeat.

He laughs. "To be honest, I am hoping for more enthusiasm on the subject."

I don't get the joke, but it feels good to laugh along with him. We fall into easy conversation as I prepare the tisane. He prowls about and finds my dinner tray on the windowsill and lifts the covers without comment. When I pour the tea I find he has moved it between us. He breaks the roll in half, hands me part, and takes a bite from the other. Despite all the emotions churning in my stomach, I find that I can eat food when he hands it to me, and he feeds me the rest of the meal like this. One piece for me, one for him.

I do feel better once I have eaten.

I let my head rest against the back of the chair, my eyelids heavy as Conall clears the food and tea.

"I ought to do that," I tell him.

"You have cleaned up often enough while I did nothing," he replies, his tone curt.

I am learning he speaks this way whenever he mentions his dog form. He does not accept it, as Saba does.

"You did your part," I protest. "Men don't usually help with the cooking and cleaning."

He chuckles and shakes his head. "What do you think we do while we are on patrol or traveling? You sit, and I'll finish this."

It does feel good to be cared for, and it feels even better as he explains his plans for freeing me the Castle of a Thousand Doors. He has been investigating possibilities and conferring with the other animals, leaving me floating and light with nothing to worry about.

"The birds and mice and rabbits....?" I ask.

"Are happy here." He finishes washing the last dish and sets it upside-down on the towel. "This is their home, and they don't want to leave."

"But will Trencoss harm them? I hear about"—I can't bear to think of it—"the sacrifices, and blood, and..."

Conall puts out his hands, offering to help me to my feet. His gaze is steady. "Those stories are about the druids. Trencoss has the magic of the animals, so he will not harm them."

I put my hands in his. "Not at all?"

He sighs. "He is not like you, thoughtful for every creature's needs. But think how the logs fall in the forest, which makes rich dirt, which allows new trees to grow."

"What has that to do with the rabbits?" I let him pull me to my feet.

"His magic is a cycle like that. His heart is cold, but he does the right things for the animals and forest under his care, because it benefits himself."

I rest my hands on Conall's chest, breathing in the joy of being close to him. "How do you know so much? Are you a magician too?"

He laughs, short. "No, but I spent several years as Trencoss's favorite dog. Do you need to know anything else?"

I have a great many more things I wish to know, mostly about Conall himself, but the rest can wait. One day, we will talk about his time as a dog, and I will listen and give him space for his guilt and bitterness to fade. Not yet.

I shake my head. "So I will act ordinary tomorrow, and wait for your signal?"

"It will take a few days yet," he warns, "but the white ball of thread is still small. You have time."

"I want to finish the criossana before we try, anyhow." I let my head drop against his shoulder. We aren't sure what the criossana will do, but he agrees that I have woven magic into them.

His arm goes around my waist. Mm. Broad shoulders. Strong arms. Nice muscles. I sigh happily.

"If that's settled, then it's time for the second part of my campaign." The smile is back in Conall's voice. "If I don't get a move on, you're going to fall asleep."

"Not sleepy!" I try to protest, but yawn instead.

He moves back a few inches, taking my hand. "I do not intend to be bold, but since you appeared to be comfortable last night, we could...sit on the bed."

"Sit?" I look up at him. "I want you to hold me." I clasp my hand over my mouth, laughing because I didn't mean to be so forward. "All night," I add.

"Oh, Mavourneen." He is smiling. "Go and get comfortable. We have until dawn."

I slip behind the wooden screen for my night-time ablutions. The cool water hits my skin and my sleepiness dissolves into a thousand shooting stars. As girls, Saba and I used to compare our changing bodies and giggle hysterically about the absurdity of sharing ourselves with our husbands some day. Years later, Saba married and I thought her glee in her wedding bed was absurd. Not that this is my wedding bed—not yet—but my stomach is warm and I can't stop smiling.

In all these weeks of believing I was about to be married, I kept my mind firmly closed from the idea of actually touching either of the men. But with

Conall—he could hold me all night. He could hold me forever. I could never be afraid of Conall.

When I return, he is wearing just his loose léine and has piled up the pillows on my bed. He helps me into bed, staying himself on top of the covers while he tucks the blankets around me. Of course I could do these things for myself, but that makes his gesture even more sparkling and precious.

"Thank you," I say, sinking into the pillows and touching his face. "When we are wed, I will do pleasant things for you, too."

He chuckles. "You have already taken care of me so often."

I must look skeptical, for he continues, playing with my fingers. "Who has raked together soft leaves for my bed in every campsite? Who took splinters out of my paw, even though I could have licked them out myself? Who combed the burrs from my ears, and put a blanket over me on cold nights even though my fur is thick?"

I laugh, waving off his words. "I slept with you when it was cold, so you see I was merely selfish…"

I trail off, embarrassed. All that time, though I was so careless in my affection, he understood the intimacy we shared.

"Mavourneen." Conall runs his fingertips down my face, drawing my attention back to this moment. "You are never selfish." His deep voice is even darker and gentler, sending pleasant shivers down my spine.

I smile, and feel his gaze drop to my lips. Blushing, I turn aside, then remember I was going to look at him.

"May I try to persuade you to change your mind about kissing?" he asks.

"It doesn't matter what I think," I protest. "I told you I don't mind if you do."

He is still.

Finally, he says, "It matters what you think." He cups my face and turns my gaze back to his. "It matters to me."

I study his face in the moonlight; the angle of his lips, his short curled eyelashes. I study his expression, trying to read what he is thinking. What he wants.

Saba said to think about what I want.

"Yes," I answer. Not because I care about the kissing, but because I want to say yes to him. My Acushla, my beloved. The daytime is full of danger—a plotting sorcerer, a tricky Fae, two kind-of-engagements that I have now betrayed. If we have only a few hours, I want our night together to be full of yes. That's what I want.

I smile, my heart bubbling with happiness, and Conall smiles back.

"Close your eyes, Mavourneen," he murmurs.

I obey, breathing slowly and drinking in the warmth of his face lowering to mine. His shoulders are close and solid, and my fingertips slide around his bicep.

Then his lips brush mine. I brace for the flat squashiness of it, but instead he brushes my cheek and kisses lightly where his fingertips traced. Featherlight kisses—my temple, the hollow at the side of my cheekbone, the edge of my jaw.

Then he kisses the corner of my mouth.

My breath catches.

He pauses, then gently, slowly, his lips cover mine. His kiss is not demanding, but guides me as confidently as my Acushla led me through the woods. He nuzzles me, soft little kisses one after another, and my hand slides up to the back of his neck. He presses one more kiss, a little firmer, my lips half-parted so his breath mingles with mine. It warms me to my core.

He pulls back and my eyes open. He's checking my expression, his smile tender. "Well, Mavourneen?"

"That wasn't terrible," I admit.

He raises his eyebrows, then laughs. Full of yes-ness, I laugh too, lacing my fingers behind his neck. He is leaning on one elbow, warm and close and solid. His hand comes down, curling around my waist.

"Do you know what is terrible?" He is smiling, and I know he is teasing. "Your bedroom talk. That is no way to flatter an honest fellow."

I laugh. Who knew—my Acushla is playful—or perhaps I always knew.

The thought makes my stomach flutter, or perhaps it is the nearness of him. The soul that I know but his body is all man, and I don't know what I'm doing with a man in my bed even if he's laying on top of the covers.

I don't know, but my arms are around him, so I just kind of accidentally pull him closer. He is smiling as he kisses me again.

"I don't mind," I murmur as his kisses trail down my jaw, then up to my hairline. "You officially may kiss me all that you want."

He smiles into my eyes and kisses my mouth. I snuggle closer against his body, the blankets fluffy between us. I am all softness, all yes, and my mouth opens under his. I don't mind this kiss either, his lips as tenderly as moonlight. His tongue touches mine, and it gives me a shivery feeling that might be downright pleasant. His hand tightens on my waist, strokes the blankets smooth over my belly, and I certainly like that. Most definitely. Mm.

When Conall lifts his head, he is still smiling. "What do you want, my Mavourneen?"

"I want you to stay." The answer comes to me immediately. "Forever."

"Oh, my love." He lays his head on the pillow beside mine, tucking me into the curve of his body. "I will give you all the forevers that I have."

It's a gift more precious than all the silk and jewels in the world. My mind is blurry with contentment and exhaustion, but my fingers travel up his chest. Over solid curves of muscle, searching...I flatten my hand against his heartbeat. It thumps slow and hard against my palm.

My Acushla. Mine. Mine. Mine.

"I always knew it was you," I mumble, half-asleep. Even I don't know what that means, but Conall's arms tighten around me.

I sleep, warm and safe and beloved.

Chapter Twenty-Two

In the morning, I float through my routine on a zephyr of bliss. I have a sweetheart of my own! He loves me back! I'm allowed to choose my husband and we will find our own path in life! It turns out that kissing isn't so bad if you find the right person to kiss you, and he held me all night long, all night, all night!

When the maids arrive with my breakfast and to help me dress, I thank them and give them each hair-ribbons. They don't have mouths to eat or speak, but they do have hair, and every woman enjoys something pretty of her very own. They shuffle and turn to each other and to me, and the younger one touches her hand to her heart. Joy sparkles across my skin and I embrace her, which a real princess would never do, but she does not resist.

The castle mice may be mice and happy in their holes, but I should think of the servants. I wonder what I could ask them, when they have no speech to answer.

The sky is clear and blue and the little flyers are busy with their white dew before the sun gets hot, but for once it doesn't bother me. Instead of watching from the corners, I meander around the patio with Trencoss, peeking into the different baskets and asking him about the flyers and the yarn and sorcery and anything on my mind. He gives me one startled glance, but then seems pleased enough to answer my questions. Since I'm leaving soon, I might as well learn about magic while I'm here.

In the garden, I scatter seed for the doves, cheer on the squirrels' antics, and wait very still next to a shrub for a young rabbit to hop close enough for me to scritch his ears and chin. His mother rabbit sits nearby, her nose twitching as she watches us. She is the one I call White-foot, and she likes chin rubs.

I tease the dogs as they follow me around the castle. I offer to race Kappa to the fountain, laughing when he tears off ahead, and laughing harder when he pretends to take a nap ten strides from the finish line, letting me win. Omikron gives me a little nudge and a play bow. I throw apples that have fallen on the ground for him to catch, but Alpha pushes ahead and tries to nab them out of the air.

When I sit down, breathless and happy, Sigma settles behind me so I can lean back against him, his panting mouth in a loose smile. It's funny; I know they are men, now, and I am usually obedient and competent and polite around men. But I can't act that way around the dogs—or maybe I simply don't want to. I like them too much.

Delta flops down beside me, dropping his head into my lap. He is the one who always likes being brushed and petted, and I run my fingers through his soft curls without thinking twice.

"Wait—are you just here so you can get affection from another man's sweetheart?" I tease him just to say the words out loud. I am someone's sweetheart. Me!

Delta rolls his eyes to look up at me without moving his head. He heaves a gusty sigh, and I laugh.

"These are dog ears right now." I run them through my fingers, letting them flop back onto Delta's head. "I think Conall would have told me if I wasn't supposed to do this, wouldn't he?"

I'm suddenly uncertain. Sigma nudges my elbow, and when I glance down he flops his tail and licks his nose. Reassuring me.

"I would never want to be disloyal," I tell them.

Sigma licks my elbow, and I speak in my deep being-the-dog voice. "I'm a big black wolfhound, and Conall would have told you if anything were wrong. Don't worry, Ailbe." I switch to my regular voice. "Thank you,

Sigma." And I giggle with the absurdity and the joy of it all, closing my eyes and letting the sun warm my face.

I stand up to head back to the castle, nudging Tau with my foot.

"Lazybones, are you?" I tease. "You'll be the one who eats a second plate of stew and then falls asleep when it's time to wash the dishes."

Tau shakes his heavy head and sighs, but Alpha yips as though he is laughing.

"What about you two?" I shove between Mu and Nu, one hand on each of their shoulders. "In real life, are the two of you brothers or are you lovers?"

Mu plants his feet and blinks at me.

"You think I'm some prissy young maiden with my head in the clouds?" I put my hands on my hips, pretending to be insulted. "I take care of men when you come in from patrol, and I know what you get up to out there."

Nu nudges me to keep walking, saying as clear as daylight "it's not a big deal. No secrets here."

"Dogs like you, too," I add.

We walk together, the birds singing in the trees and the smell of cut grass and fallen apples all around us. I'm so happy it hurts, and it makes me want to cry that I've found such joy in a trap like this. Trencoss could close the jaws at any moment, and even if I escape my heart is too full of everyone here. All twenty-four dogs—I want hear their stories and laugh at their jokes. The soft bunnies and the wise owls and the hard-working, speechless maids...I am filled with so much love that my ribcage will burst, for I want every single one to be free.

***

I skip up the stairs to my room, so eager to talk with Saba. But when I burst through the door, a pair of green eyes blinks at me from the sunlight on my bed.

I stop singing, curtsey, and close the door behind me.

Bob yawns, showing all his pointy little teeth and his curling pink tongue. "What did you bring me to eat?"

I actually have a basket in my hand, because I was going to eat my lunch in front of the mirror with Saba. *No one else will care about your wishes,* I can hear her saying as I unpack my lunch for Bob's perusal.

It's just lunch. I let Bob have the cheese and the fish patty and pour the gravy on a saucer for him. I don't mind.

But I see what Saba means. I will hold onto what is truly important to me.

When we have finished eating—I get the plain bread and vegetables and tea—I clear the dishes and Bob washes his face with his paws.

"Look in that big box in the corner," he orders, licking vigorously under one arm.

"The wardrobe?" I glance at him for confirmation, and open the carven doors. My eyes go immediately to the basket on the third shelf—three oranges, three plums. Just like I left it, but my heart is pounding. "What?"

"Are you blind, silly kitten?"

"Oh!" I don't know how I could have missed this riot of fabric and color. "It is..." I take it down and lay it on the bed, which is the only surface big enough to hold this sunset of a dress. "It is something."

"Now you have a new dress. One without any holes in it." Bob wraps his tail around his front feet, pleased with himself.

My heart still twinges with the loss of all the work I loved, but I can't help but be amused about this very carefully-phrased apology—one without the slightest acknowledgement of culpability.

"Thank you," I reply automatically, running my hands over the fabric and lifting the sleeves. "It is...how do you wear it? What is this fabric?"

"It's very high quality," he answers. "It is taffeta on that poofy part there."

"Ta-fit," I repeat. "Look! How do you think they made this lace?"

"I'm a cat," he answers. "I don't really care."

"Oh." I don't know what else to say. This thing is a monstrosity.

"You have something to wear for your wedding!" he announces, tapping his tail. "Now let's play."

"Now?" The thought of weddings has distracted me again. I didn't want to think about all the people who think they're going to marry me. I return the dress to the wardrobe, just in case Bob feels the need to take another nap.

"Yes." Bob hops off my bed, ears pricked up cheerfully. "You throw the little crinkly thing, and I will hit it so it rolls. We will both have a great deal of fun, little kitten."

Obligingly, I sit on the floor and throw various things, ones that crinkle and ones that bounce. Somewhat to my surprise, I do have fun. Bob leaps and rolls and performs all sorts of tricks to make me laugh, then butts me with his little head and purrs like thunder when I rub his ears.

I settle my back against the bed and Bob crawls into my lap. I cover a yawn as I glance at the growing shadows. I want to talk with Saba so badly.

Bob curls into a purring fluff-ball, tilting so his belly shows. He is just impossibly adorable, especially for such a jerk.

I stroke his back, debating what to say. I don't want him to start thinking about Fergus, whom he has blessedly not yet mentioned, but I need some information. "What are the three fruits for?"

He purrs. "Plant by gate."

I give a few more pets, but he doesn't continue. "Which gate? And then what happens?"

"Back gate. Tree grow fast, mmm...."

I sigh. Half-asleep is better than discussing Fergus, I guess. I lift my hand, hoping he wakes up a little. "Three trees—a plum, an orange, and a starfruit? Yes? What do they do?"

"Keep petting. Very nice." Bob rolls so his tummy is all the way up. "Anyone who wants to leave. Eat a plum, gate open. Slice of orange, Trencoss can't see. Starfruit shines light."

I rub his belly, thinking. "So anyone who wants to leave this castle grounds can pick one of each fruit and escape?"

"Mm-hm." Purr, purr.

"Do they need all three? Could they just...take a plum and hope for the best?"

"Silly kitten." Bob opens one eye to glare at me. "Use the sense you were born with. All usual rules apply."

"Oh." I stroke him slowly, trying to think what 'usual rules' he didn't bother to tell me.

My head drops back against my bed and my eyes drift closed. My foot is going pins and needles. I wonder if Saba knows—wait!

I take a deep breath and dare to say what I need.

"Bob Ye Gurt Fool, I appreciate the dress and the game, but I need a nap this afternoon too."

I hold my breath, not sure how to reply if he demands to know why I want to sleep in the daytime. But Bob apparently accepts naps without comment, for he slinks off of my lap on and onto the windowsill, twitching his tail to show me he is irritated but not very irritated.

I open the window for him, stroking his back and thanking him again.

Bob pokes his nose out, then turns back to me with a blink. "Do you know the waterfall among the orchard trees? The one with the boy standing in the middle?"

"It's called a fountain, apparently." It's large enough to wash clothes, but Trencoss tells me that rich people use them for decoration, so I do not wash in it.

"Yes, that one." Bob switches his tail briskly. "There is a lever below the green stone that turns the water off."

I freeze, my sleepiness obliterated.

"Then the pool becomes still. Very still." Bob yawns, pretending to ignore me. "If you and your dress ever want to—"

He hops out the window. The oak branch shivers, the leaves clattering, and Bob trots away, the very tip of his tail twitching as though he is laughing at me.

Chapter Twenty-Three

That night, I finish the twentieth crios before Arcturis rises.

The starlight sparkles across my floor as my door opens, and I twirl into my Acushla's arms. He is dressed in a fine ionar and fringed cloak, and laughs as he bends to kiss me. I *really* don't mind at all.

"I have a surprise for you." Conall smiles into my eyes. "Put on something pretty and come with me."

"We can leave this room?"

He grins. "My Mavourneen, we can do so much in the moonlight. Come along."

"Something pretty, you said?" I wander over to my wardrobe, still holding Conall's hand. I open the doors and he rests his hands on my waist, bending to kiss my hair.

"What on *earth* is that?" he asks.

"Not pretty," I reply firmly, pushing Bob's dress to the side. It bounces back. "I like this blue one, but...is it all right if Trencoss gave it to me?"

Conall shrugs against my back, and I shiver in delight. I like the feel of him as a man.

"It doesn't matter. We know what Trencoss is. But will you wear your hair loose?" He touches my braids.

"If you want." I turn to him with the dress, smiling shyly.

"I want." He kisses me.

I can't stop smiling as I slip behind the wooden screen. All this time, I just have tried to look respectable, do honor to Bodhbh Dearg and then my Saba. I started putting my hair up years ago, because although I am not married I have an adult's responsibility. No one said anything. No one wanted my hair flowing free and beautiful, like a maiden.

I shake out the blue gúna and pause. It's easier to ask while I can't see him. "Conall? Is it wrong that I petted the other wolfhounds? Should I only touch them…with the respect I would give a man?" I hold my breath, not saying the part about the respect I would give my fiancé.

But Conall just laughs. "They're dogs, Mavourneen. When you see them as men, treat them as men."

"So it's not…and would you think…" I pull the pins out of my hair, my eyes filling with unexpected tears.

There is a moment's pause, then his voice is serious on the other side of the screen. "Ailbe, when we are in our dog form, there is nothing romantic or sexual about touching you—or each other. Touch is part of a dog's language, no more or less than kind words or pleasant stories between humans."

"Oh." I rub my eyes, irritated with this silly burst of feeling. "That's what I thought, but I didn't want to do anything wrong."

"Besides…" Now I can hear the smile in his voice. "The other dogs all know how I feel about you."

I pull the gúna over my léine and begin lacing. He can't see me, and it makes me brave. "And how is that?"

Conall chuckles. "When you and I first arrived here, I might have been…a wee bit upset. Made just a bit of a fuss, trying to get to you. Zeta and Rho calmed me down. Eventually. But they all knew…"

I pull the lacing taut my ribs. "What?"

His voice drops low and ragged. "That I would do anything to protect you. Anything."

My fingers still.

"I would kill for you," Conall says, his voice only inches away. "I would die for you."

I take a slow breath. I wanted togetherness, not for my brand-new sweetheart to immolate himself on my behalf. "I learned about the fruits today," I say instead.

Another pause. "Tell me about the fruit," Conall says, equally lightly.

I comb out my hair and practically dance around the edge of the screen. Conall laughs with delight and I twirl for my love, who drapes a cloak over my shoulders and kneels to help me with my boots. Imagine that! Instead of escorting me politely downstairs, he holds my hand. It feels so good, walking and talking with him, I put everything else out of my mind to treasure this moment.

Like Conall preparing himself for a battle that I don't want.

Fergus arriving with a starfruit and an expectation.

Trencoss's nearly-finished ball of white thread.

The rabbits and mice and maids, all trapped inside—oh. The fruits. Even if Conall gets me out with his plan, I can use them for everyone else! Trencoss won't be able to keep anyone against their will.

Maybe I do want Fergus to come back. Except I don't want to deal with Fergus himself.

Conall holds the outer door of the castle, letting me precede him. His eyes are dancing and his smile growing, the closer we get to this surprise of his. We wend through the garden, and I can see the sparks of a bonfire before we come around the hedge into the light.

"Here they are!"

"Our favorite lady!"

"Cheers for Ailbe and Conall!"

I gasp in delight as twenty-four laughing warriors surround us with whoops of joy. They thump Conall on the back and pass me between them, squeezing my shoulders and dropping rough kisses on my cheek. They are a motley mix, some in uniform and some in tatters; tall Celts, Fir Bolg like me with their quiet posture, Nemed with their teeth flashing white in their dark skin; some are gray-beards and a few barely past boyhood.

They all wear the same smooth torc, glimmering in the firelight against their collarbones.

As they move me between them, I recognize each one as I touch him. This is Omikron, playful but steady. Hands meet mine and I know Tau, his face calm but not at all sleepy. Someone spins me in the air and I know he is Alpha. I am laughing, steadying myself in their sea of arms, touching the scarred ear that remained in Gamma's dog-form.

"Your names!" I cry, laughing as Kappa swings me around and Sigma steadies me. "What should I call you?"

"We like your names," bellows a Celt with tumbling red curls. I called him Iota.

"Makes us feel like we belong together," Mu says from his seat by the fire.

"We're ready to leave what was in our lives before," Theta growls.

Several men clash their tankards together—agreeing with the sentiment, toasting me, just celebrating.

Conall makes his way around his own circle of congratulations, then wraps his arms around me. I snuggle against him, enjoying the steady warmth of him contrasted with the heat from the fire and the chill of the breeze. The men are talking at once, and I let their excitement wash over me. This must be the first time they have all been together, as humans, since Trencoss captured them.

"You are all here?" My voice is quiet, but Theta hears.

"Yes. The other nights, only the men on guard by your room took their true form. The others could not leave their patrol of the grounds, or the sleeping quarters."

I study the grim old soldier, whose eyes stay trained on his men. He glances to the path on either side of this courtyard, and I realize that despite the air of bonhomie, men are stationed at either side. Joking with their comrades, but also checking the dark. Their loyalty is so strong; it makes me feel like a foolish girl who has been nothing but trouble for them all.

Sigma comes up to us, holding out his fist for some sort of complicated bump-and-sign with Conall, then kissing my hand. "The bonds are loosening," he says. "You started that, Ailbe, when you made a bet with Trencoss and solved the riddle meant to bind you."

"Not by myself," I protest.

"That was the solution," Theta says, crisp. "To work together instead of alone."

"Are we ready?" Zeta calls from across the fire. He is the eldest, who as a dog had gray in his muzzle, calm and well-respected. "Conall, did you bring the things?"

Conall shuffles and holds something up, and I'm surprised to see a familiar red and yellow shimmer.

"My crios?" I ask.

Sigma grins. "Woven with love."

"Something else, besides," Conall adds. He passes away the crios and sweeps a deep bow onto his knees to me. When he raises his head, something is cupped in his hands.

I lift the figure, holding it to the firelight. The smooth alabaster nestles against my palm, carved into an intricate double spiral with a shining stone set in the middle. Conall rises gracefully, smiling gently as he puts the pendant over my head. He lifts my hair so the chain can settle cool against his neck, and the tender intimacy of his gesture melts my heart.

Then Kappa lights incense, Zeta lifts his voice in prayer, the men step aside, and I see the circle on the ground.

I gasp, covering my mouth with both hands. "My wedding? Tonight?"

The men cheer, but Conall pulls me close. "Only if you want, Mavourneen."

I can't manage to speak, but I throw my arms around him, and the men cheer louder.

Then my beloved leads me into the circle, through clouds of incense and song. Conall puts out his hands and I clasp his in the sacred way;

Zeta winds my crios around our wrists, and the five elder men each wrap it one more time while they each give their blessing. I have watched this ceremony so many times, long believing I would never be the one in the circle. Or if I were assigned to a political marriage, that it would be nothing but ceremony—not that I could look up into a face full of joy, centered entirely on me. Me, Ailbe, the daughter of servants and the helper of all.

Alpha knocks one log away from the fire, Sigma reminds me to hold up my skirts, Mu and Nu count together—and Conall and I leap over the flame and into our life together. I burst into laughter, reaching my fingers towards the sparkling stars, and Conall swoops me into his arms and kisses me thoroughly while everyone cheers.

Conall and I go around the circle of men, together this time. We are given more blessings, and buns and cheese and tankards of ale. Someone puts sticks of meat on the fire, and someone else takes out flute and drums, and Conall spins me out into a wild dance—then every other man has to take his turn. Even Theta laughs as he claps my hands and whirls me around.

I am not separate after all. I am in the middle of everything.

And these men—they like me for myself, for I have been my true self with them.

***

The darkness is not quite as heavy, the men's stories lingering and the laughter gentle. I am nestled into Conall's side, his arm around me. I am not asleep.

Booted feet stride into our circle, the bold tapping startling me. It's just Omikron, and my eyes drift closed again.

"It's ready," Omikron says. "We can hold it open for a few more minutes."

He tosses something and my husband catches it, jostling me.

"Time to go, then." Conall's voice rumbles below my ear.

"Just the right time before dawn," someone else agrees.

Go? I sit up, blinking in the gray. The fire is burning low, and only a dozen or so men are gathered round it.

"Where are the others?" My voice croaks. "Wait. Are you going? Don't go!"

"I told you, it will be fine. Trust me." Conall rises, dropping a kiss on my hair and steadying me.

"Where?" I stand with him. I want to ask him to take me, but I can't leave the others. I'm torn and confused.

"I'll be back, Mavourneen." He kisses my cheek. "I'm going to Starfruit Island to complete the spell."

"Don't leave!" I clutch his arm. "I wish I hadn't even told you about that silly fruit!"

"We all agreed it would be better to complete the spell," Omikron says, kindly. "Whatever it does or does not do, where magic is concerned it's better to finish what is begun."

"Then anyone can do it!" I glance around, desperate.

"The spell is bound to you, little princess," Sigma says.

"I will be back quickly." Conall kisses me, and I can feel the impatience in him. "I only need to row to the island and row home. Two days, at most."

"What about the ball of white yarn?"

"I will make it one day. You weave the last criossana and I will be home."

"Conall—"

"Goodbye." He steps away, firm and steady. "They cannot hold the gate beyond dawn. Trust me, Mavourneen." He swings the rucksack to his back as he and Omikron fall into a brisk step together. They both turn and bow just before they vanish into the gloaming.

"Did you all decide without me?" I ask.

"Conall told you he was taking care of you," Sigma replies, surprised. "We are doing our best."

"Making our battle plan," Delta adds. "You don't need to worry about it."

"Your only job is to be your ordinary self," Sigma says.

"I just found him. I didn't want him to go." I sink back to the bench.

"Do not be selfish, little princess," Theta rumbles, the commander's voice gravely. "Your husband has been helpless for too long. Give him this chance to be a man."

I pull my cloak in front of my face.

"Besides," Theta continues sternly, "if he escapes Trencoss's territory, he will be able to remain in his man form."

"By the time he returns, we will be ready for the next phase of the battle," Delta adds.

"We'll start at night, as men," Sigma explains.

"Out of all of us," Theta growls, "Conall hates his dog form the most. If this goes to plan, he never has to be a dog again. Let him have the kindness of that."

I sniffle into my cloak. I know they're right, but I'm cold. And lonely. And...tippy.

Thump.

"Good grief," says Delta.

"I'd better carry her back to her room while I still have arms," Sigma says.

Someone picks me up, and I'm asleep before we're inside the castle.

Chapter Twenty-Four

I wake in a pool of sunlight, a blanket tangled around me. Something is pounding. I push myself half upright, my mouth dry and fuzzy, my pretty dress wrinkled and making red creases on my skin.

Pounding. It's my door.

"Coming," I croak. I am muzzy-headed at night, but never in the morning—although from the warmth of the sun, it's not morning any more. I pause to gulp some water before I crack open the door.

It is my two maids. Flapping their hands, they push past me. The older one thumps a tray onto the table, and the younger points out the window, then at my dress.

"I know, I know, I slept too late." I rub my eyes, confused.

One shakes out my blanket. The other fetches a wet cloth for my face.

"What's the matter?" I ask. "Does Lord Trencoss want me?"

The younger one swoops one finger dramatically in front of where her lips would be. The elder checks out the window again, shaking her head.

Apparently, they decide to leave my gown but decide my hair is untenable. My head is jerked back and forth as they brush out the wild tangles.

"Thank—you—" I gasp.

The younger start to pin up the braids and my everyday veil while the elder pours tea. I reach for the cup, grateful, but she has turned away.

She holds it up to the mirror.

"Ailbe, at last!" Saba cries. "Thank the goddess! Oh, and good day to you as well, ma'am."

The faceless maid bows to the mirror.

"I see you are wearing Ailbe's hair ribbon," Saba says. "The red is very pretty in your hair."

The other maid abandons me to parade before the mirror, turning around and lifting her veil.

"And you! How absolutely charming! I adore them both!" Saba claps her hands. She is always good at being enthusiastic.

The maids hurry back to me, brushing out my poor wrinkled dress.

"If you'll pardon me—Ailbe, I need you before the herbs wear off," Saba says.

"What herbs?" I lean close, checking to see if her eyes are dilated or her hands shaking. "No! You mustn't—"

"Be quiet." Saba smiles to take the sting out of her order. "I told you yesterday, I was worried about you."

"I was married last night," I say all in a rush. Whatever she is planning, she should know that.

Her jaw drops. "Congratulations! Woman to woman, I'm delighted for you. In terms of the spells, that could make things very much better or very much worse."

"And Conall left before dawn," I add, the words making my body ache worse. "He is trying to go to Starfruit Island."

Saba knits her brows. "Where is Fergus?"

I spread my hands, helpless.

"Gracious." Saba shakes her head. "Must men always rush into things? Attack head-on before they even know who's what!"

"I think he was spoiling for a fight," I admit. Picking it with Fergus doesn't seem particularly useful, but he didn't ask me.

"To prove himself and his love," Saba says drily.

The younger maid shakes her head. The elder points to Saba.

Saba catches the hint immediately, straightening up briskly. "Speaking of Fergus, I think I have information."

"You think?"

She shrugs. "A vision. But it needs you."

"A *vision?*"

The elder maid passes me the tea, clearly thinking I am still asleep and incompetent. I have to agree.

"I went into the forest last night," Saba explains. "I drew the charms and went into a trance with your name on my lips. I told you, I was trying to do something!"

I sip my tea and wrack my brains. When we spoke yesterday, Oisín dancing around and playing peek-a-boo, I was giddy with new love and Saba was making a point to be happy for me, but...yes, there was something else. She said she was searching.

"I woke this morning knowing which herbs to take," Saba continues, "and that the forest promised me a vision about you. I keep catching glimpses of a fair-haired man and a coracle and fruit trees I have never seen before, so I know it has Fergus. But I need you to complete the vision, Ailbe."

"You don't usually go for visions," I protest. She's told me they are exhausting and the herbs make her stumble; much safer for the druids and sorcerers than the mná feasa like herself.

"I decided to," Saba answers, setting her jaw. "But we need to hurry, lest my herbs wear off before you are even ready. Not to mention, Oisín is taking his nap."

If she's going to have the after-effects, we might as well make them useful. I tip back the last of my right proper cuppa tae. "What do you need me to do?"

The elder maid refills my cup.

"You need a place to scry," Saba answers. "Still water, ideally."

I flutter around the room. We try my washbasin, the teapot, the water pitcher, dumping the fruit out of my breakfast bowl and pouring water in, then casting that aside and trying milk. None of it works.

"Is there anything connected to the earth?" Saba asks, trying to hide her anxiety. "Perhaps near trees. A sorcerer could use these items, but my power is the forest."

Still water. The orchard. Bob's words spring to my mind, and although I know it's a bad idea to mix magic, I repeat them to Saba.

"Perfect!" she says. "Go to the fountain, then."

I turn. "But you. I need the mirror."

"Then bring the mirror."

I tip my head back, staring at the heavy glued frame reaching high above my head. "I don't know...I can't possibly..."

The solution, Theta said, was not by myself.

I turn to the maids. "Will you help me?" I ask.

The elder points out the window and shrugs. When I describe how to get to the fountain, she shakes her head "no," miming her arms flopping.

The younger holds up one finger in the "wait" position, then runs out the door.

"Think what else you might need," Saba warns. "We only have one chance."

***

Half an hour later, our parade arrives at the fountain.

I am followed by two bulky, faceless man-servants carrying the mirror, the elder maid with a closed ewer of hot water, the younger maid with an embroidered cushion, nine dogs, and birds fluttering from tree to tree above me. I am not sure if they have a job to do, or interested in the bag of seeds in my hands. I have managed a castle for eight years, and in my experience feeding people always improves morale. I am still in my wrinkled dress, smelling of bonfire.

The servants arrange the mirror with a view of the fountain, the ewer underneath, and the cushion for me—I didn't ask for that, but the maid apparently thought it was necessary. They bob curtseys and bows and file away again, despite my protests. The dogs curl up in the shade with deep sighs. I search for the green brick, and indeed, there is a little switch. The fountain trickles to a dribble.

Rho watches the water, ears pricked forward.

"You tell me when it is completely still," I tell him, trying to sound ordinary.

He gives me one wag of his tail, not looking up.

I spread the seed, and birds and squirrels hop down from the trees, while rabbits creep out of the underbrush, eyeing the dogs warily. Except for Rho, they all look asleep, which sounds pleasant. I am hungry and my eyes ache in the sunlight, and I'm worried about Saba and even more worried about Conall.

In this state of internal distress, I have gone back to normal: calm and polite and poised.

Rho barks once, and I kneel on the pillow and remove the cover from the ewer. As the steam rises, Saba's face appears. She is in the forest now.

"Good, that's nice and dark—Ailbe, you have a doorway Between! Why didn't you and Conall take it ages ago?" She furrows her brow. "I don't think you could. It's locked, somehow."

"It's not just any door," I say slowly, figuring it out. "It belongs to someone."

She sighs. "And you know the doors. It might not have been there yesterday, and you can't take it without Conall."

The Fae doors, once used, vanish again. Although Saba could always open the door to Peaceful Valley, which belongs to her, so Bob...where does Bob's doorway lead?

I don't have time to consider, because Saba gasps and sways. The vision is overtaking her.

I always hate this part. It's losing the woman I love.

Saba drops into her story-telling voice. I stare at the water in the fountain and the murky scenes that appear to be floating below the surface, hearing slow footsteps pad closer. I can barely make sense of it, but Saba sees.

"The coracle draws nigh. The moonlight glitters on the water, but the island gleams with a gentle green, as though the trees themselves are happy. The prince's arms are tired, but he is yet careful. He paddles around, checking the island for danger. It is small. Nothing but the trees, with leathery dark half-moons of leaves. In the center of the island, the prince can make out a little castle made from pale stone.

Reassured that it is safe, the prince draws his boat onto the sand. He ties it safely, his sword ready at his hand. But there are no wolves, no warriors, no danger.

There are also no oranges.

Through the leaves, further inland, the prince can just make out something bright. Here is a path, pale in the moonlight. Holding his sword, he sets his feet towards the center of the little island.

Now we are walking with him. The way grows dark, but the trees themselves are comforting. Here is fruit, but it is yet hard and green. He tests this one, and that. This has a rosy blush, but his instructions were clear: Bring back one ripe fruit."

"That's all?" I interrupt. "He just has to row to a little island in the middle of a lake, and get one silly piece of fruit and come back?"

Saba is still in her trance, but Rho snorts and Omikron growls. I don't think they are any more impressed than I am.

"This tree! Here is ripe fruit! Oh, and this one! Now that our prince has reached the interior of the island, the trees are protected and they are filled with ripe oranges. He wanders from one to the next, smelling and examining. He must find the perfect one."

"No. Just a ripe one. He ought to leave already," I tell Rho, who nudges me in agreement.

"But lo! Behind him, the castle gate opens. A figure emerges."

Rho perks up his ears and Delta presses closer.
    "You fellows like this part." I sigh. "Thirsting for battle stories, you are."

Saba continues the story. The newcomer merely invites the prince to join them, and he accepts politely, only to find himself at a wonderful feast, seated across from a beautiful girl with a glittering crown. My heart clenches at the mention of a real princess, although I don't need to be jealous since Conall likes me just as I am.
    The prince asks if he may take an orange with him, and the king assents happily, but since it is so late he encourages the prince to stay the night. Saba tells every moment as she sees it, one night flickering into the next, but the simple fact is that Fergus stays because he's having such a good time.

He wakes one morning, shaking himself as he notices the sunlight. Saba sees a little white paw, but Fergus doesn't appear to notice. He washes himself, gathers his belongings and his orange, and makes his way back to his coracle on the beach.

"The king appears," Saba intones, "in a robe of glittering silver. We have never seen him in the daylight before.

'Do not leave, my friend,' he suggests. 'Stay and wed my daughter. Dance in the moonlight every night.'

The lovely maiden appears beside him. 'I will stroke your hair and sing you songs,' she offers. 'I will praise you the whole night long, except when you stop my lips with kisses.'

The prince waits. He glances at the orange in his hand, then back up at his gracious hosts. The king exhorts him to stay; the princess promises her adoration.

Our prince takes one step up the beach. Looks at the orange, appearing confused. One more step.

Ah! But there is a flash of white and a burst of fur and teeth. Tiny claws pierce our prince's trews, and when he looks down he finds the rope to his coracle in his hand. Shaking his head violently, our prince launches his boat. Shouting his thanks, he pushes into the water, not looking back until he has taken a dozen strong strokes into the lake.

A roar distracts him and he turns. On the shore, there is no king; there is no beautiful maiden. Instead, giant serpents coil and hiss, thrashing their tails and flicking their fiery tongues. They dart through the trees, diving towards him but stopping when they meet the water.

While the prince watches in horror, the larger serpent lowers his mouth and begins to suck at the lake. A current sweeps towards him. His belly swells while the smaller serpent gathers herself, ready to strike.

Just in time, the prince sees the waves reaching towards his boat. He plunges his oars into the water, rowing with all his manly strength. Finally, at nightfall, he lands on the shore...and ah, he fades away. I believe he is walking to you, Ailbe."

Saba's vision retreats and she blinks at me.

"Well, that's just fine and dandy!" I exclaim. "All this time I was waiting and worrying, Trencoss forcing those little flyers to exhaust themselves, while Fergus was having a grand old time being seduced by a different woman. One who was actually a snake, I might add!"

The dogs produce a low chorus of growls.

"It's just as well that Conall got to you first," Saba says, her voice rough, "and I dare say you needn't feel bad about betraying his trust. The way he was treating that princess, he was definitely untrue first."

"And he took all my salve!" I add. "I needed that."

Saba nods, but she is already falling into another trance.

This time, we are on Plum Island. Plums are native to Ireland, so this island is larger with more natural and varied topiary, which Saba (being an herb-woman rather than a sorcerer) describes in great detail. But the essential story is the same. Fergus searches for one ripe fruit and is about to leave, when a well-dressed messenger invites him to dine. This castle is larger and made of pink stone, and he has *two* princesses fussing over him. One morning, Bob jumps on his chest to wake him, and Fergus seems to remember what he is about. This time, he almost goes back with the lovely princesses until Bob trips him and scratches his face. Fergus announces he is leaving, and the princes and the king and the messenger all turn into slavering wolves and chase him through the brush, until Bob nudges the coracle in place and Fergus leaps off a low cliff into it and rows away.

"I guess he needed the salve that time," I admit. "He was properly scratched up."

Omikron blinks at me in disbelief, as if to say *all that and you care about the salve*.

"Which one came first, in real life?" I can't recall. "It doesn't matter. Once would be foolish. But how does he manage to fall for the same trick twice?!"

"Worse." Saba rubs her forehead. "He's not back yet."

Delta howls.

Sigma paces away, staring intently through the trees. Then he returns and bats my knee.

"Conall made it to Starfruit Island?" I suggest.

Sigma wags his tail in approval.

"Is he on his way? Can you hear him?"

The dogs all lower their heads; no. Rho glances up at the sun.

"You're right, he won't come back until nightfall." I put my arms around their sturdy necks, drawing in their comfort.

"Maybe they're saying that it's easy," Saba suggests. "He really just has to go out and back."

Rho yips in approval, and Sigma strikes a proud pose.

"He's an honorable warrior," I translate, or perhaps that's just my opinion. "He won't get caught by a trap with a pretty girl. Do you really think so?"

The dogs push close, licking my face and waving their tails. Despite everything, I manage to laugh.

"Starfruit Island," Saba mutters. "Starfruit, Starfruit…"

She drifts off, rocking back and forth. My eyes drop back to the fountain, and all the dogs watch with me.

These trees are taller and leggier, their leaves paler green on compound stems. Saba describes the colors as my gaze searches the little cliffs and rugged hills. This vision seems to be daytime, although the water itself is dark and it's hard for me to see—

I gasp. That shape, that man—we are looking at Conall this time.

We all go still, even Saba's enchanted intonation slowing to a stumble.

I can't see clearly, but Conall is clearly not rowing away. He sits on the cliff, yellow fruit by his side, turning something over and over in his hands.

Saba stops talking, so I can't tell who the figure is behind him.

But Conall stands, pauses, and follows him into the trees. To the gray castle in the center of the island.

Away from his boat, and away from me.

***

I do my work; I do my duty.

I stay with the mirror until Saba is safely home, dozing on her mat while Oisín cheerfully toddles around her. I cannot support Saba as she stumbles through the forest nor rub her back while she recovers, but I keep talking and remind Saba to change into her deer-form, where she is stronger and the herbs will influence her less. I wait until her blond hair and human face reemerge, and convince Oisín it is a game to bring her bread and water.

When I return to the castle, I find Upsilon and Xi waiting for me, blood on their paws and thorns tangled in their fur. I don't know what happened on guard duty, but I know how to fix them up.

I warp the twenty-first crios before I must dress for dinner with Trencoss. I let nothing show on my face; arrange my every sentence so it sounds ordinary to his ears. He must appreciate my facade, for he keeps me far too long; giving me specious compliments and telling long stories that don't interest me at all.

I must finish my crios belt. That is all I am thinking.

But when I finally am allowed to return to my room, I collapse in bed as soon as my hair is unpinned. I thought I needed to cry, but it turns out that I sleep all night.

CHAPTER TWENTY-FIVE

I have barely finished checking on Saba when the oak tree shakes.

Larger than a squirrel, larger than a cat—good gracious, there's a prince trying to climb in my window. It's a good thing I am naturally an early riser, properly dressed and my hair combed, even though the sun isn't yet over the hills.

Fergus has gotten his shoulders inside and one foot on my outer windowsill by the time I manage to block him.

"You can't come in!" I hiss.

He cocks his head in confusion. "Because it's daytime?" he guesses.

"Of course." Whatever makes him agree. As for myself, I am not letting any human-formed men into my bedroom now that I am a married woman.

He puts his foot back on the oak branch, which shakes. "Meet me in the garden, then?"

"Do you have the starfruit?"

He shakes his head, looking even more confused. "Bob told me to come right now. He said you needed me."

"But I don't—"

Fergus sets his jaw, looking somewhat warrior-like himself. "He said something is wrong. I dropped everything and hurried to you, Ailbe. I understand that I can't come in, but please meet me in the garden. I am trying my best."

I hesitate, twisting my fingers in my skirt. We could only see the outside in Saba's vision. Perhaps I owe it to Fergus to talk with him.

Besides, I want that starfruit.

I explain where he should meet me, choosing an area on the far side of the palace from where Trencoss will be working with the little flyers and the white dew. Fergus agrees and makes his way down the tree, and I pin up my veil and bolt my breakfast, hoping the right proper cuppa tae will sustain me. I pour the last of the kettle into my cup, and then on impulse, hold it in front of the mirror, which the burly servants left propped against the wall.

Saba is resting in the gloom of her cave, but she sits up. "What is it? You were just here. Remember, I'm fine."

"Good. Saba, I'm going down to the herb knot to meet Fergus. I thought you should know, in case..."

We used to tell each other where we were going, just to be safe, although now that I think of it I'm not sure what she could do. But the instinct is still strong in me.

Saba perks up. "Does he have the starfruit?"

I sigh. "No."

"And Conall didn't come back with it last night?"

"He's still gone."

Saba looks away from me. I hear Oisín chattering to himself, out of my sight but within hers.

Saba looks back at me, her face sad. "Ailbe...?"

I pull myself upright. "I choose faith," I tell her.

Saba nods, once, slowly. She raises her hand in the gesture of blessing, but Oisín howls in little-boy pain and she leaps to her feet.

We bid each other a quick goodbye as we rush off—to our separate lives, our lonely womanhoods.

***

The herb garden is not as far from the castle as I remembered. It doesn't matter; we will be quick, and light clouds are scuttling in, the air heavy with moist chill but no rain. It's the best weather to keep Trencoss in the meadows with the little flyers as long as possible. I ask my six guard dogs to wait just around the corner to give us some privacy, but Zeta fixes me with a stern look and patrols the entire herb garden before retreating.

Fergus is slumped on a stone bench, rising to give me a courtly bow when I approach. He really isn't a bad man. Is it so terrible that he was tempted by those pretty princesses, when his only "love" was because Bob told him to rescue me? I don't know.

It's not like I loved him, either.

I have brought him buttered rolls and cheese, thinking he might be hungry. He thanks me formally and rips into them like a starving man, so it is decent manners to wait until he is finished. I am consumed with an urge to tap my fingers and pace, but I repress it.

He brushes the crumbs off his hands.

"What about the starfruit?" I ask. "If you had to row all the way back, why not bring it along?"

"I was a guest of the king of the island," he says, choosing his words slowly.

"You just need one fruit!"

He takes a breath, measuring me and my impatience. "It seems, princess..." Another pause. "When I bring the fruit to my boat, that triggers their awareness that I am leaving. I judged that I would be able to make a smoother escape if I brought nothing."

"So you have learned something in repeating your mistakes over and over?" My words burst out, sharp and brittle. "Or did Bob tell you that?"

"I can go back for the starfruit," he tells me. "Yes, Bob is helping me, but only because he is determined to help you. All he told me this morning was that you are in danger, here."

Does Bob know something I do not? Or does he consider the danger to be my love for Conall, threatening the arrangement he chose with Fergus. I press my fingers to my temples, overwhelmed.

"Ailbe," Fergus says, gently, "tell me what happened."

"Are you a Fae?" I ask.

He shakes his head. "I am as ordinary and un-magical as you are yourself. I never spoke a word with Bob until he told me about you, a few weeks past. I realized then that I had seen him before, thinking he was just another cat in my parents' courtyard."

"I am—I am not sure we can trust Bob."

He smiles, very faintly. "We should never trust the Good People, and probably never trust a cat, either."

I pull in a breath. "Who are you? Why did you come here? There are too many mysteries!"

Fergus shrugs. "The third son of a minor king. My story is nothing in particular. When Bob showed me your image, I let him believe that he had enspelled me to love you. Really, I hoped that if I completed a quest then my father would consider me seriously, and if he did not choose me as his heir he would at least make me one of his generals."

That all makes sense, and it is also true that the Fae are known to become intrigued by a particular person. For whatever reason, Bob settled on me, and now he's determined to make my story come out how he wants it.

"I am married," I tell Fergus.

He bolts upright, stiff. "Since when?"

"The night before last." I feel him relax and realize he was worried that I had lied about it earlier, not that about whether I loved him. "When I last saw you, I knew nothing of the man who is now my husband. Trencoss had enspelled him, and I freed the enchantment without knowing what I did." I glare at Fergus, not wanting to deal with his scold. "You were gone a rather long time, just to fetch one fruit."

He runs a hand through his flowing blond hair. "I suppose I have. I think they put something in the wine, and the days all blend together. So where is your husband now?"

"He is fetching the starfruit."

Fergus's eyes widen. "Oh. Oh no."

"No? You have done so poorly yourself, can't you manage—"

He's shaking his head. "No, I mean I know who he is. I didn't speak to him, but I saw another prince on the other side of the castle. I wonder what they offered him?"

Conall isn't a prince, but that isn't important right now. "You were both there?"

Fergus nods. "His coracle was on the beach when I left. I didn't think imagine it had anything to do with us when I saw it, but now I realize it must have been him bargaining with the king late into the night."

Why, oh why, can't either of them just get the starfruit and leave? "We need that fruit! I don't care who brings it, but—"

"I know. The spell partway done is going to leave a tangle. If I have started the quest, and your husband has started the quest, then we are both wrapped up in it now. Trencoss and Bob will both have a hold on all of us until it is complete, in either tragedy or victory."

"How do you know all this? I thought you said you weren't a sorcerer!"

"I'm not! It's just basic knowledge!"

I draw myself upright. "It doesn't matter. Conall is getting the starfruit, so you can leave."

"I can't! I just explained, we're all tangled in it now."

Beyond the hedge, one of the dogs barks. Another bays. My heart goes cold.

"How can we finish the spell?" I say quickly. "Can you and Conall compete to bring the starfruit the quickest?"

Fergus paces, breathing quickly as he glances towards the dogs and back to his own thoughts. "Possibly. The problem is that you already married him, so the reward for the competition is gone."

"I'm sorry that my heart isn't available for your little chase—"

"Ailbe!" Fergus grips my shoulders, pushing me back and dropping his voice to a whisper. "If I knew what you were up to, I would have thrown the competition and let him win. We just have to finish what Bob set up, or..."

He looks up, and I realize he wasn't manhandling me. He has shifted me towards the protection of the hedge...

So when he draws his sword, he is between me and Trencoss.

***

"So, my little bride has decided to be untrue to me, hm?" Trencoss spreads his hands, a thin smile leaking across his pale face.

Behind him, the dogs writhe and snap their jaws. They are trying to leap, but their iron collars hold them in place.

"Don't worry, my dear." Trencoss takes a step towards me, but Fergus adjusts his stance and Trencoss clearly decides to stay on the far side of the herb knot. He smirks at me. "I never cared about your heart. Love whomever you please. But you will marry me."

"I am—"

Fergus interrupts me. "Why do you want Ailbe, then?"

Trencoss raises his eyebrows. "Wouldn't you agree she is beautiful? A delicious bed-mate?"

"I am already—"

Fergus speaks firmly. "There are other beautiful women. Why Ailbe?"

I begin to suspect that Fergus is warning me not to explain my marriage to Trencoss.

Trencoss ticks off a long white finger. "There is also Fionn mac Cumhaill, prophesied to be the greatest king Ireland has ever known."

Fergus turns as Trencoss paces, keeping his sword leveled at Trencoss as the sorcerer circles the herb knot. "True. My father would be pleased with that connection, too."

So that's what he wants to bring home—an alliance so powerful that his father will award him the status of heir.

Trencoss scoffs. "Her value would be wasted on a poor seaside kingdom like yours. I have been searching for years for a woman with the power of the animals, which joined to mine will give me the strength to build my kingdom in the human realm. Now stand aside and let me have my bride."

"You should ask what she wants," Fergus answers.

Trencoss twitches his finger, and I realize what he has done. By circling the garden and forcing Fergus to stand between myself and him, he has positioned his enemy closest to the dogs and with his back to the path.

The dogs leap towards Fergus, giant jaws snapping. For a split second, I am frozen in horror—but they are not leaping. They are half-dragged in lumpy bounds, their claws scraping the air as they twist away from the humans as much as they can.

The power of the animals. I have it too.

"Stop!" I cry. "Don't hurt Fergus!"

They drop to the ground.

Trencoss hisses some magical words, sketching a gesture in the air. "Wolfhounds who are bound to me, kill the man that here you see!"

They rise, slowly as though weighted with mud.

"Delta, Zeta, Psi, Beta, Xi, and Kappa!" I call. "By your love for me, do not harm Fergus."

Psi creeps forward a step and Kappa flings his head as though in pain, but they all manage to stop. I am impressed with Fergus, who has never relaxed his guard on Trencoss, although it means that he has had to keep his back to the six enormous beasts. Trencoss keeps darting glances at me, his hand flexing, and I have no doubt that if Fergus wavered the sorcerer would snatch me.

"We are at an impasse, then," Trencoss says.

"It seems so," Fergus answers, voice tight.

"I will leave you, then." Trencoss steps back, towards the path on the far side. "Frankly, I don't care what you do with the princess. Kiss her all day if you wish; I care neither for her heart nor her purity. She is unable to leave my estate, and at sunset we will be married."

"You cannot!" I gasp.

Trencoss's smile splits his face. "Ah, but Princess Ailbe, I can. You promised." He lifts his hand, and a tiny clattering sounds in the distance.

Closer to us.

And closer.

A little mouse-man riding a shuttle lurches over the top of the hedge, followed by a wobbly stream of butterfly-people and beetles with human faces. The ones with wings are sagging, and the ones riding can barely keep their tools upright. In the middle, a dozen of them strain with the strings to a tiny basket.

Trencoss spirals his finger. They circle my head, making me wince away lest their wings beat my face or my solid body knocks them out of the air.

"Hold out your hands," Trencoss tells me.

I obey, because I cannot bear to watch the little ones suffer longer than necessary.

Half the flyers yank their strings, and the basket spills into my hands.

A perfect, beautiful, fluffy ball of white thread. I grip it tight, gathering my strength, my love.

"I am already married," I tell him.

Trencoss cocks his eyebrow. "Princess Ailbe, did I not make myself clear?" He laughs, and flicks his hand, allowing the exhausted flyers to lurch away. "I know you betrayed me with my own dog, but I really don't care. Your promise binds you."

"I can't be married to two men."

Trencoss shrugs. "Then I'll have to kill him, won't I? Don't worry." He cups a hand over his eyes, checking the position of the sun. "We have a few hours yet. I will meet you at sunset, a free woman...except for your promise to me."

Chapter Twenty-Six

The sun is at its zenith when I bind off my twenty-first crios. Even with the loosest weave and simplest pattern, one belt takes about four hours to make.

I will weave faster, then, because I am not leaving three dogs behind. I see them, laughing as joshing as men or dozing back-to-back as dogs. Wherever they came from originally, their loyalty to each other is stronger than the mountains.

More fool I, that I slept at night when they might have spoken to me. At our wedding fire, the warriors explained that they had been pulling at the edges of Trencoss's spell—or that is how I envision the explanation, tugging at the loose bits after I pulled out the thread that bound Conall. Little acts of disobedience, Alpha explained, like waiting a moment after Trencoss tells them to do something, or mixing themselves up when he assigns their duties. Lambda said it was more like holding on to his memories of a man, and he could feel the spell loosening when he concentrated on his parents and the croft where he was raised. He described it all to me.

That night, Rho tested my crios, winding it around his torc until the metal didn't touch his skin at all. He reported back that he had been able to get out the gate.

"But what about when we went to the lake?" I asked.

"We can leave when he gives us the direct order," Rho answered. "We often patrol outside of the gates."

"That day was strengthening his own spell," Theta growled. "He sent us to the lake to set the pattern that we go and come back."

"But if you patrol...?"

"*You*, little princess," Sigma said. "He is proving to the spell that he can control you."

So, I think now, testing the tension on my new warp, when I leave I will not take that gate, where the spell remembers that I come back. It's a good thing that I didn't go to our camp and tangle that into everything, too.

The men weren't sure if the crios would still work on their dog-collars, so they were going to test it again the next night. But I slept through their time as humans and don't know what happened. In the stories with a night-time transformation, the characters never have trouble staying awake. I am like a bee, drifting off as soon as the sun goes down. I yank the weft over-hard, failing to ignore my frustration.

This is useless. I am supposed to be the reasonable one. I take a break to check out the window.

No one is coming. I open the wardrobe, batting aside layers of taf-fet as I glare at the fruits in the wooden bowl. Two. Back to the window.

As soon as Trencoss left, Fergus and I consulted hastily and he rushed away—since he has never been caught in Trencoss's chains, he can come and go like these are ordinary gates. We decided that the race to fetch the starfruit will have to complete Bob's spell, and Fergus added that perhaps it will help that now they are also racing against Trencoss, who is trying to kill Conall. I don't like that idea at all.

"I'll warn him if I can," Fergus told me, and gave me the salute of equals.

This morning, Fergus and I fought back-to-back. Fergus trusted me to keep him safe from the dogs, and I trusted him to keep me safe from Trencoss. This has changed something in me. Like a wave washing against the sand, it has revealed the strength that I never saw before.

When Conall comes back, I will let him see it too. I am small, but I don't need to be his little wife, protected and coddled.

If Conall comes back at all. He doesn't know that Trencoss is tracking him down, and he has no Bob to save him from whatever temptations they have on that island.

Tempting him away from me...and succeeding.

I choose faith. I press my fingers against my eyes, and return to my weaving.

***

The maids arrive with my lunch tray, but I wave them away.

The elder puts her hands on her hips.

"I can't stop to eat," I explain. "I have to finish this before dark. But thank you anyways."

The younger shakes the curtain and points to the sky, which is full and bright.

"I know, there's plenty of time to weave a belt this afternoon. But I have to finish before dark, actually." So I can get the criossana on the dogs and escape before...

The elder points to me and opens my wardrobe.

"Before you come to dress me. Right." The weft ball slips from my fingers, and my other hand seizes with pain. I shake it out, wincing.

The younger maid clatters my tray and stirs my tea violently.

"I can't stop to eat. I can't." What is an aching hand compared to what Conall faces, or my beloved dogs fighting their collars? Fergus too.

The elder maid bangs closed my wardrobe and holds something out for my inspection. At least, I assume it's the elder maid, because she is entirely hidden behind a giant poof of skirts and lace and beads.

Bob said it was my wedding dress, but he also told me about the doorway Between if me and my dress wanted to...well, I know exactly what I want to do, and if my dress wants to come along...

I jump to my feet, pushing the lace aside to look at the maid, as though I could meet her eyes. "Do you think I should put it on? Later this afternoon?"

She bobs her head enthusiastically. The younger maid taps my tray again.

I accept the mug of tea, but hesitate. The servants have been helpful so far, but I don't know what they really are or where their loyalties lie. Yesterday, between the conversation with Saba and bringing the mirror outside, they both left my room and could have reported everything to Trencoss. He has proven that he doesn't care what I do as long as my physical body is available for his plotting.

Therefore, I need to remove my physical self. Trencoss can block the outer gates against me, but what about Bob's doorway? Last I heard, the dog-warriors were still developing a plan to help me escape, but if I take care of myself and give them the criossana that will simplify everything.

I can't possibly weave three more criossana this afternoon. That's the truth.

I choose faith.

I take a deep breath, turn to the maids, and risk everything.

***

The sun is dipping behind the hills as the younger maid ties the last ribbons on my explosion of a dress. We are in the hills here, so we have about an hour until true sunset. The elder maid trims the edges of the warp on our criossana, fluffing them into a careful fringe and laying them with the last couple I still have left. The dogs have been creeping up, one at a time, all afternoon, and I wind a crios around each iron collar and fluff their fur over it all. Hopefully Trencoss is too busy to notice.

Busy hunting down my Acushla.

There's a scratching at the door. The younger maid drops Conall's charm over my head and I tuck it into my bodice as I go to open the door. I stare into the hallway. The usual torches are extinguished, and only a little light glistens from the windows at the far ends.

"Down here."

I turn, finding a man crouched against the wall next to my door. He is sitting like a dog, both hands clutching his collar, breathing hard.

"Sigma?" I guess. "But you already have your belt. Where are the others?"

He gasps, dropping his head in a gesture that is almost canine before he looks back up to me. If I hadn't spent a lifetime with Saba, I would be frightened, but I know what he is doing—pushing against the edges of the spell, using the desperation of his will to hold onto the form he needs. His man-transformation is allowed when it is dark, so he is trying to use the dimness and my crios-magic. I politely ignore his gasping and struggling, which is what Saba always preferred. She said it didn't hurt; was more like climbing a hill when your legs are already tired.

"You have done—all the ones—here," Sigma rasps.

"I have six belts remaining," I say, thinking.

He nods. "Couple hours—ago. Trencoss called—Rho's troop. Sent them—out."

"Out of the gates?" I suggest. "Into the forest?"

He nods. "Find Conall. Kill..."

"Can they resist? Those ways you have been pulling apart his control of you..."

But Sigma is already shaking his head. "Trencoss made—more magic—today. Refresh. Collar."

"Everyone's?"

Shakes his head.

"Just those six."

Nods. "Your belts—strong enough. But Trencoss ordered—can't—come back. Not allowed. Until dead."

"Conall is dead?"

"Or Rho's men. Every—one."

I stare into the dark, my heart beating harder and harder. Conall must die, or Rho and his five men. One or the other.

"Well then," I say lightly, "if they can't come to me, I'd better figure out how to get those criossana to them."

***

The maids have gone. Sunset is painting the sky over the darkening hills, and my windowpanes glow a deep gold. I have the six criossana laid out before me, my anger heating slow and dark. I will not trade Rho's men for Conall, nor Conall for the others—and not one of them shall be traded for me.

Neither the night-time birds nor the day-time ones can stay wakeful in this light, and they have no hands anyways. The rabbits and mice could not run so far, and any of the animals' instincts would keep them away from the hunting dogs. Time for a different bargain. I push open the window.

"Little flyers," I call, "little flyers, I have a favor to ask, and I have a price to pay. Come and treat with me, little winged ones."

I have drawn Trencoss into bragging about how he calls them. He doesn't tell me the price they ask, but I have eyes in my head.

A snake with moth wings flutters out of the tree. A tiny man with webbed hands riding a trowel follows, with two giggling purple girls in a ladle right behind. I keep repeating my words as they gather around, perching on the oak branches and my windowsill and hanging from the rough stone on the outside of the castle.

"You are so weary, working on my behalf," I say, when I judge that enough have arrived. "Please accept my food to strengthen you."

The maids always bring me more food than I can eat, and today I was too nervous to do more than nibble. They don't care about the seed that I offer to the doves and squirrels, but they fall on the baked goods, smoked meats, and cheeses—the things they cannot harvest nor catch themselves. I do not allow my fear to show as their teeth and claws flash in their feeding frenzy.

The mouse-man lands his fork on the sill in front of me. ::What do you want, human princess?::

He does not speak aloud, like Bob, but I can understand him clearly, unlike the true animals.

"I have these six belts, woven from my own hands." I hold them out, letting them see but not touch.

::Our thread! Our yarn!:: they cry.

"It is, O clever ones. I need you to find the six dogs who went into the forest, and bring them these criosanna."

The little flyers turn and chitter among themselves, and I can feel their skepticism.

"Only you can manage such a difficult feat!" I add. "Only you are strong flyers, with keen eyes and clever hands. Only you are brave enough to manage such a task!"

When it comes to the Fae, flattery never goes amiss. I can sense their satisfaction as clearly as hearing the words.

::You mentioned our hands, human princess. What do we do when we find these dogs of yours?::

I hold up one belt. "Wind this around their collar, one crios for each dog."

Their fear hits me like a wave.

"They will not harm you, I promise. Remember, they were in the garden when you came this morning? You were weak and tired, and they did not touch a feather on your precious wings."

They calm, reminding each other how it happened, how the dogs have never bothered them. They are curious how to wind the crios. They are excited, that they are allowed to touch the dogs. They laugh that they can tell the dogs what to do, and I promise the beasts will obey.

I have prepared a wooden hoop, and I demonstrate how to wind the belt around and around. Since I do not imagine that Rho's troop will ever return to the Castle of a Thousand Doors, there is no need to worry about hiding the belts. They will do what they do.

Finally, I sense excitement sparkling at me from dozens of tiny heads.

::Human princess, what will you pay?:: the mouse-man demands.

I smile. "I have so many beautiful things for you. Look—and look—and look."

I hold up silver needles and golden chains; the inlaid hairbrush and mother-of-pearl buttons; bronze drawer-pulls and shiny pins. The little flyers chitter, descending on the window with a clatter of silverware and hissing of little teeth, but my sparkly items vanish before the hoard is done. I pull the little scissors out from where they are stored on a ribbon in my pocket and cut the bead-work off my dress, finding the brightest and prettiest, and slide off my ear-bobs and bangles.

::We accept your price, little princess:: says the mouse-man—superfluously, since his compatriots have already seized my offerings—::but you must tell us how to find them. There are too many black dogs. There are too many trees. We don't know what to do.::

"Iota," I tell them. "He is taller than the others, he never complains when he is hurt, and his fur curls wildly in his eyes."

They chitter amongst each other, agreeing.

"Alpha," I continue, and I go through and describe each dog in detail. The more I can describe, the more I can sense their understanding.

Rho, Phi, Alpha, Iota, Mu and Nu. As I describe them, my love fills my chest and squeezes my lungs.

"We must find them," I announce. "I trust you. I thank you."

::So must it be. The bargain is made.:: Dozens of shades of the thought pepper me from all sides, as the little flyers swoop and cackle, lugging the criossana between them as they dive into the gloaming.

***

In the gloaming, the gloaming. Is there a specific moment that defines sunset? On instant that separates the day from the night?

If there is, I can't see it here—inside the castle, under an oak tree, nestled in the hills. I slide a few items in the capacious pockets of this birdcage-skirt—the plum and orange in one pocket, useful items one the other side, tea and thread and buns—wrap myself in my heavy cloak, and rush down the hall. Not too fast; I can't afford to trip.

Upsilon and his troop fall into formation behind me, their paws drumming a slow heartbeat on the stone.

Down the stairs. Around this corner, and I almost crash into a dark shape.

A candle flares into light, illuminating my two maids. They are wearing matching gúna and veils, and the elder juggles the candle with a vase of lilacs.

The younger has set down her vase in order to clutch my arm.

"What's the matter?" I ask, trying to sound calm despite my rush. "Of course I will help." Would they drag me to Trencoss? They spent the afternoon weaving for me, listening to the story-boxes and having a pleasant chin-wag with Saba (well, the maids have no chins, but they seemed happy enough to listen)—I trust them, but Trencoss might force them to act.

The younger maid mimes meticulously, the elder holding the candle near her hands.

"Balls?" I guess.

She makes to bite one.

"No, fruit."

They nod vigorously. The lilacs bounce.

The maid kneels, miming planting, then tracing the path of something growing. Two plants. Three. Standing on tiptoes, she traces an arch above her head, then mimes opening a gate.

"I understand. The three trees by the back gate—"

They both wave their hands, stopping me, putting a finger over where their mouths would be.

"I won't speak of it, but that's fine, of course I mean to get—the thing you mean."

The maid clasps her hands together and shakes them; the gesture for please. She points to me and then out towards the fountain, flutters her fingers like flying away, traces a smile on her face.

Points to me. Me again.

Then her hands go to her own heart. Point the direction of the back gate. More flying-away.

"You want to escape, too," I whisper. The rabbits and birds might be content here, the mice might prefer to stay, but someone needs that gate to open.

She clasps her hands again. Please, please, please.

"I'll do my best—the men were supposed to get the starfruit by now…"

The elder maid sets her vase on the floor. She brushes her hand against the place where she might have eyes, then tucks her arms together and swings them. Rocking a baby. She cradles the invisible body against her shoulder, pats the little back, then gestures to the height of a head beside her. This tall, and this, and this.

She points towards the back gate.

The younger maid makes the flying gesture.

"Your children. Your families." I find that I, too, am crying. "I will plant—those things. I will come back. I promise. I *promise*. But I have to leave now, my friends. If I don't make it out before sunset, I'm not sure he will ever let me leave."

They step aside immediately. The elder waves me forward, and the younger gestures again. Please.

"I won't forget."

Upsilon pushes me with his nose, hard. I run.

Down the hall, more stairs, another turn. The hallway leading to the front courtyard leads off the middle of this corridor, where Trencoss bellows about decorating for our wedding. A steady stream of servants passes with cloth of gold, waving plants, lanterns shining with colored glass. I pull my cloak across and keep to the wall, and Upsilon puts his own dark shadow between myself and the crowd. I dare not breathe until we turn into the next corridor.

The door at the far end is open, Tau waiting with perked ears.

I run.

Down the broad steps to the gravel path, still churned by the men carrying Saba's mirror yesterday. Tau nudges me onto the grass, and he's right; it's cold and growing damp, but my feet make no noise. The open air is growing dusky and blue but it is certainly still light. I have time before I break my own promise.

I spin back, checking the looming castle. Five dogs wait in the circular steps I just descended, arranging themselves neatly as I watch. I glance down. Only Upsilon and Tau remain with me.

"They are the rear guard, then?" I ask. "Our final distraction."

Tau nudges me forward; the sleepy dog is on high alert.

When we are in sight of the fountain, Upsilon stops, turning and baring his teeth towards the castle.

Just before the fountain, Tau sits in the center of the opening in the hedge, his back to me. Watching behind us.

I go on alone, my heart pounding so hard that the bile rises in my throat. Dusk drifts down like snowflakes, filling the air and making it difficult to find the correct brick.

Finally. I flip the little lever.

The fountain stops, but now I have to wait for the water to still. How long did it take yesterday? I count to twenty-four, say a prayer to Saba's forest goddess, press my eyes closed to hold back my impatience.

The last glowing embers of sunset are reflected in the ripples on the water. I tuck my cloak above my elbows so the fringe can't drag and disturb the surface, and grasping one stone pillar, pull myself up to stand on the edge of the fountain.

Ripples. Ripples.

The sunset colors of my dress sparkle in the water, blending in to the dusky red from the sky. A silver beam streaks across from the far side—the moon.

In the distance, I look up as Trencoss shouts my name—then a cacophony of barking, a yelp of canine pain. He holds their collars and Arcturis is hours from rising, so Trencoss will defeat my dogs easily. They are buying me these last moments with their own pain and embarrassment.

My eyes drop to my feet. One last glimmer of crimson. The water is still.

I step forward.

Chapter Twenty-Seven

This doorway is wetter than usual and feels more like falling. Several breaths pass before I tumble out into the world again, skittering onto my hands and knees with my birdcage-skirt swinging around me.

"My dear madam, what a fall you've taken! Let me assist you."

The voice is beside me, suave and calm and masculine. I catch my breath before I raise my head.

I have landed in the middle of a party, the likes of which I have never known. We are indoors, at night, but the rooms are bright and full of light. I stare around as the gentleman helps me to my feet. He is considerate about my enormous dress; he must be accustomed to such things, for all the women around me are wearing something similar. Skirts as wide as our hands might reach, entire curtains of lace wrapped about, pearls marching down fitted bodices, bows as large as their heads.

"Do you need something? Let me fetch you a drink, madam."

His language feels different, but I can understand him, unlike when Bob spoke the strange language in my room. My escort places my hand on his arm in a way that is unfamiliar to me. He is cheerful and grandfatherly, and I have never seen him before in my life. I follow, dumb, as he leads me through the milling crowd.

The room itself is all white marble, with dozens of pillars like a bizarre geometrical forest. Unfamiliar string instruments play in the distance. The people in their strange clothing are laughing and chatting, so I assume this is a genuine party, not political.

Servants pass through with trays. My escort snags me a tiny plate with something fluffy and red. I am not sure how to eat it, so I put it in my mouth all at once, while the gentleman procures a goblet of wine. Except this goblet is made of glass, imagine! I turn it in my fingers, impressed with how the light sparkles through.

"Hungry, are you?" The man chuckles.

It turns out I am. I eat four more tiny mystery foods that he procures as we walk through the marble room. By then, we have made our way to where the room opens out. This ceiling is high above us, and water flows down the far wall, splashing into a square pool on the floor.

"Is that a fountain, too?" I ask the man, and his language comes to me easily.

"Spectacular, isn't it? Here, madam, have you had a chance to greet our host?" He bows low to someone, and I automatically drop into a deep curtsey.

I rise, but my eyes must rise farther yet, to the top of a marble pillar cut off slightly above the height of my head.

A cat tucks his white tail around his front feet, twitching only the tip, and blinks his green eyes at me.

"Bob, Ye Gurt Fool!" I exclaim, and curtsey again.

"*What* did you say?" the man exclaims. A woman nearby gasps, holding her fan over her mouth.

Bob closes his eyes and lifts his chin, which I suspect is cat-ly laughter. "It means something different in this tongue," he tells me, winking.

"We call him Robert, the Great and Wise," the woman informs me from behind her fan.

"Or simply, Your Catness," my escort adds.

Bob just laughs.

Everyone around me bows and curtseys, so I join them again.

"Are you married yet?" he demands.

"I am," I answer, honestly enough.

"Good kitten," he replies. "If your dress has done its job, it should have pulled your husband over too. Check the room with the tower of oranges. Now then, *where's my tuuuu-naaaaa?*"

Since a dozen servants rush over, this is clearly not aimed at me.

"Thank you very much," I say, although no one is paying attention. "Just let me know if you need someone to throw crinkly balls for you."

Bob lifts his furry head from a tray of tiny snacks that a waiter holds up. "You see? She's a very good kitten."

"Yes, your Catness," everyone in earshot replies immediately.

How bizarre! I don't know what a great Fae lord like this would want with an ordinary woman like me, let alone why he would hang about in a woodshed waiting for dinner, like the story he had told me about his name. Oh well. Of all the people I am worried about tonight—and there are many—Bob can take care of his own blessed self. Cats do.

The rooms open, one to another. As I went through the crowd in the direction Bob indicated, I stop to look out the tall windows. These panes are even larger and smoother than the Castle of a Thousand Doors.

Outside, moonlight sparkles on a lake, but full dark has not quite fallen. Hills line the horizon.

I cross to a window on the next wall for a different angle. Yes. This is familiar. That is the dip where the river comes through, where Conall and I put up our last camp. There, where the hills rise taller, is where Trencoss's castle is surrounded by orchards.

Bob lives in the middle of the lake. This funny castle must have been the sparkling bit I saw.

No wonder he has an entire tower of oranges; they came from the island next door. Not sure what else to do, I wander into the next room, and there it is. The pyramid of fruit is taller than I could reach if I stood on the marble table next to it, although the table is covered in tiny plates with delicate servings of cut-up fruit.

And there—it takes no effort to recognize Fergus in the crowd. Although my heart plunges because I hoped for the correct "husband," it also thrums with relief to see someone I know.

"Fergus!" I cry, pushing towards him.

He spins around and puts up his arms, catching my elbows and laughing his greeting. After the fight this morning, we understand each other.

Unlike all the other men, he is dressed in ordinary clothes, léine and sturdy inar and linen trews, all looking considerably worse for wear than they were this morning.

"You made it!" he exclaims, as I say the same thing, and we both laugh again.

"Do you have the starfruit?" I ask.

He shakes his head. "Let me show you." He puts his hands in his pockets and draws them out, covered in mushy pulp and the occasional lump of yellow fruit.

"You didn't get distracted again?"

"Of course not! I wasted a little time looking for that husband of yours." He scrapes the mashed-up fruit onto a plate. "I saw him twice through the trees, but the damned island is all hills and brambles, and by the time I got close he was gone again." He wipes his hands with a napkin. "So I gave it up for a bad job and tried to get back to you. It's unfortunate I couldn't get to him, because if we could have worked together, one of us could have drawn the fake king aside while the other escaped with the fruit. As it was, he triggered them while I was two hills away, and when I got to the beach they appeared as soon as I touched my coracle. Right beside me." He holds up his thumb and finger with barely any space between.

"Did you fight?"

He presses his lips together. "Any other time, I would have. But you needed that fruit, and if they drugged me again it could have been days before I came to myself. I just ran."

I take a slow breath and bow my head. "I thank you. That took courage, to avoid fighting."

"It's not the way I've been trained, that's for sure." He's looking away, his jaw clenched.

I place my hand on his arm, in thanks and honor. "How did you get the fruit, then?"

He shrugs. "I played cat and mouse with the false king. Down to the coracle and back, a couple of times. Heard Conall try it, too, but I checked the lake and his boat didn't get away."

Drugged, I am thinking. So maybe Conall didn't betray me at all. Maybe he was forced to stay even though he knew better. Maybe he wasn't flirting with some other pretty girl; maybe he was laying in a dusky bedroom, barely awake.

I chose to trust him, but I can't choose away my fears. The worries shadow me even when I try to ignore them: I'm not enough for him; his love is as sweet but fickle as the baby bunnies.

"When did they drug you?" I interrupt Fergus's dramatic reenactment of his third escape from the king-turned-stoat.

He's startled, but gathers his thoughts. "At dinner, I think. I'm not sure. I felt normal, but it's queer that I slept the day away, and the ends of the feasts were always more bizarre and colorful than the beginnings."

So much for Conall laying in a room with no memories of me. I know the types of herbs he means; Saba used them when someone was recovering from an injury, to make them feel more sleepy and cheerful both. They wouldn't make someone forget the woman he truly loved.

"About the fruit," I say, more sharply than I meant.

"I was telling you, during that chase I managed to hide my coracle in a different cove. I thought if it got a little dark, I could jump off this wee bit of a cliff, and be away before they could transform, especially if I had the fruit in my pockets and didn't touch it nor the coracle with my hands. So there I was, tucked under a bush, clothes full of starfruit, when you must have gone through *your* door and it pulled *me* through the door, and it was an awfully bumpy one, and I rolled right out into this ballroom. I'm fine, but as you can see, the fruit didn't make it."

I sigh. "It's all right. You did your best."

"Is it all right, though?"

"No," I snap. "It's not. The servants have to get out. He took them away from their families." I press my fingers against my eyes.

"Maybe Conall had better luck," Fergus suggests. "That was the point, anyways—that he bring you the third fruit to complete the spell."

"But I've lost him! I don't know where he is!"

"Don't cry! Don't be upset, little princess! I'm sure he's around here somewhere."

I take this for pure hyperbole.

"Really. I'm sure he is." Fergus touches my arm. "He's tangled up in this spell as much as I am, and that door sure grabbed me hard."

"You think he's here? Really?" I take a deep breath and try to regain the calm, cool, reasonable Ailbe.

"Let's go looking for him." Fergus offers me his arm, and he's nice and solid about it, none of this fingers-barely-touching nonsense like the people in the impossible clothes.

We don't want to make any more of a fuss than we already do, so we weave slowly through the crowds, stopping to eat tiny meals when offered, returning salutations when greeted. We pause to listen to the music and examine the stringed instruments, which are delicately carved and lyrical, but not much good at making noise.

"No pipes or drums or anything," Fergus comments in disappointment, and I have to agree.

"Thank you," I say as we stroll across a bridge to the next area of the castle, the dark water beneath our feet twinkling with starlight. The castle is not built on any land; it is the island, itself, in the lake. "It must be strange to take the woman you thought you were going to marry to find her real husband. You've been very helpful, when you would have been perfectly justified in leaving once you knew you had lost my hand."

I hold my breath, afraid of what he will say next.

Fergus pauses, leaning on the marble railing. "It's been exciting," he admits. "Today has been the best part of this entire quest. I mean—I'm terribly sorry on your behalf. And I want to help those servants. The horror, the way he took their faces! To not be able to speak, to eat, to kiss—it's monstrous."

I can hear the anger in his voice, and I squeeze his arm in agreement. This is how a man should behave.

"But I mean...for the first time, I feel like I'm doing something useful. I'm using my training to help someone who needs it. For the first two islands, I had to keep pinching myself to remember that you were so pretty and helpless and have those big eyes. To be perfectly honest, I kept trying to remember about impressing my father with the alliance with Fionn. That kept me going, and it's not much, is it?"

"It's not." We continue down the bridge, light and noise spilling out from the room beyond. "I've liked you better today than the first two quests, too." I blush to say something so honest.

We pause as another group leaves the room, laughing and waving their fans. I touch the cool marble bannister behind me, my eyes caught by little coracles moored in the lee of the building. I suppose one would keep them on hand, living in the center of the lake like this.

The way clear, Fergus leads me into the room and we step to the side to let our eyes adjust to the light.

"That looks promising," Fergus says, his eyes trained on the far side of the room. "I see proper clothes."

Instead of rushing forward, I take a moment to compose myself. What was Conall doing on the island these last two days? Was he tempted to stay with a princess who wasn't me, before he learned she was a monstrous stoat?

"I've enjoyed getting to know you as well," Fergus said. "You are intelligent and brave and steady, which is really quite amazing because you've never been trained for anything at all. I admire you greatly." He heaves a great sigh. "But honestly, I'm happy to be your compatriot instead your lover. When I marry one day, I think I would suit better with a woman who is a little more...gentle and tender." He laughs. "I'd find you slightly intimidating."

My heart freezes. So that's all I am? He's right; my tenderness melted away years ago, seared away in the forges of adversity, shriveled in anger when the Dark Man chased Saba away from the life she deserved. I've learned to be practical and stubborn, and a year ago I didn't care that it also made me unfeminine.

But now I'm in love, and I hoped I was lovable.

A man in the far tableau turns and beckons to us. I can't make out his features, but he is wearing a flowing golden cloak and he has the dark skin of the Nemed.

Fergus waves back, and moves me forward before I realize that I dread seeing Conall again.

***

By the time we cross the long marble room (more fountains, more fruit, more quiet instruments) I can see that the man in the robe is older than my Acushla, although they have features in common. Beside him, a tall Nemed woman in a purple and gold-embroidered gúna watches me with a small smile. A dozen others surround them, in the dress of this place, but honoring the golden pair with attention and tiny foods.

Oh gracious. Who are these people? How has my dress brought them here?

When we are a dozen steps away, Conall turns around, a smile breaking across his face. He was speaking with the older couple, dressed as they are in rich clothes and heavy jewelry, in the proper Irish style.

Conall reaches out and Fergus drops into a low bow, one knee to the ground. "Your servant, Prince Fergus mac Finnbarr, second son of the King of Ó Fearghail."

I start to curtsey, but Conall catches my elbow, not allowing the obsequience. He gives Fergus nothing but a short nod, pulling me forward.

"Here she is! My wife, whom I was just telling you about! Ailbe, these are my parents, King Áed and Queen Gormflaith."

The queen holds out her hand, chin held high, permitting me to bow and kiss her ring.

The king nods at his son. "You have completed your quest, then."

Conall seems flustered. "I was off track for many years. But if you will forgive me, honored father—"

"The important thing is to achieve the goal in the end. I begin—the druids came to our castle!"

The king raises his voice in the story-telling fashion, and everyone in the area turns to him expectantly. I suppose that dealing with Bob has trained them well.

"Five druids made their way up our mountain, singing and beating drums all the way. Our kingdom, you see, is lodged in the ruins of the ancient City of Gold."

Around us, everyone gasps. The city fell to ruin some thousand years ago, but the entire area is still deeply steeped in magical protections. And, of course, in gold.

"I have five sons," King Áed continues, "and the druids spent five days in prayer and divination. They went into five trances, rolled five astragali each, and catalogued the flight of five flights of ducks and five schools of fish. They counted the points on the antlers of five stags, and each son spent one night in the sweat-house while the druids threw herbs on the fire. Then, at the moment the rising sun turned the distant ocean pink, each son took his turn to plunge into the pool in the center of our mountain, holding his breath so he could dive as deeply as man ever did go…since our mountain burst into flames and buried the world."

Beside me, Conall is tense, so I, too, am uncertain.

"On the sixth morning, while the world was still in deep shadow and the infant sun impaled on the pinnacle at the top of our mountain, the druids gave each son his own blessing, his prophecy…and his quest. Cheer!"

Startled, the crowd around us bursts into ragged applause.

"For today!" The king holds up his arms, his cloak swinging wide. "My eldest son!"

Everyone cheers.

"My beloved son!"

They stamp their feet and ululate.

"Has completed his quest!"

More cheering.

"And brought home—his bride—to me!"

Now the entire room has turned towards us, clapping and shouting with glee.

Queen Gormflaith glides over and pulls me forward. My hair is mussed from my fall through the Door and my silly gown snipped up where I gave the beads to the little flyers. Now Conall is several steps away, and for that matter, so is Fergus. I draw myself upright, wishing that I were wearing my own beautiful, peaceful, dark-colored gown with the embroidery of the doves in flight. I would still not be fashionable, but someone might admire me for who I am.

"Don't you want to know what the quest was?" the king asks the crowd.

Conall gives me a small, tight, smile. Knowing him, I suspect that he is ashamed of any quest where he spent most of it in a dog's body.

"What was Prince Conall's quest?" Fergus shouts obligingly.

"We thought it was simple enough, but the Fates provided our son with quite the challenge!" The king gives a deep belly laugh. "He was transformed! Unable to explain who he was! Unable to use our wealth or our name for his cause! Unable to even speak!"

King Áed laughs again, but Conall's smile is even tighter.

"What was the quest?" another man yells, and a dozen take up the shout. "What was it? What was the quest?"

"Simple enough." The king gestures to me, pointing from my head to my feet. "Conall must first earn her love, and then...*marry a princess!*"

Conall smiles at me.

My jaw drops in shock. "But I'm not a princess! I never was!"

The room goes absolutely quiet. Everyone—from the servants to the women in their ridiculous dresses to Conall himself—is staring at me in horror.

Chapter Twenty-Eight

King Áed takes a single pace towards me, his brow lowering. "My son told me you were," he says, as though that would change anything. "He said you were Princess Ailbe of Dún Allaine, lately the senior Lady-in-waiting for Queen Saba, wife of Fionn mac Cumhaill. Fionn is one of the greatest kings in all Ireland, and Bodhbh Dearg is even greater."

He sucks in his breath and draws himself up to his full height, towering over me. "Is that not true? Have you falsified who you are?"

I hold up my hands in helpless protest. "That is who I am. Ailbe, the Head-Woman of Dún Allaine and Senior Lady for King Fionn mac Cumhaill. I'm just..." I shouldn't have said anything at all. My voice fades into almost nothing. "...not a princess."

"Then you mustn't marry this one," QueenGormflaith tells her son, perfectly calm. "You aren't a dog any more. You can go find a new princess."

Conall just stares at me in confusion and horror. I can't bear it.

Fergus speaks up. "They already bound their hands with a crios and leapt over the burning log. He can't go and marry someone else." He glances about, rubbing his hands nervously. "It was a magical crios," he adds.

The queen flares her nostrils, as though I am a bug in her soup. I shrivel into myself, remembering what Trencoss planned to do about an inconvenient spouse.

"Son, why did you tell me she was a princess?" the king demands.

Conall spreads his hands, helpless. "That's what Trencoss always called her! That's what everyone called her—I never heard her introduced properly. Most of the time, I was a dog." He hangs his head. "I wouldn't expect her to go around announcing her name and title to a dog."

"Who are your parents, then?" the queen demands.

"At Dún Allaine, my father was master of the dogs and my mother was the second assistant to the cook," I explain. "I was born the same day as the princess, the same hour, and the queen took me under her personal protection. I was raised in a princess's room, with a princess's training, but I was there to be Saba's helpmeet. Everyone knew it. I never pretended otherwise."

"The child of the *dog-master?*" Queen Gormflaith says, pronouncing every syllable. She does not look at me.

"I'm sorry," I say. "I'm sorry. I'm sorry."

"You really have to marry someone else," the queen tells Conall.

"He can't," the king snaps.

"But King Fionn will honor his promises," I add, loudly. "Whoever I marry will have Fionn's full alliance and support. He has the best fianna in the land! He is—"

"We don't need an army," the queen interrupts. "We have enough power of our own."

"My son has failed his quest." The king shakes his head, still performing for the entire room. "Clear and simple. It was such a wonderful story, too! Foiled by an evil sorcerer, spending years as a dumb animal, he still manages to win the love of a..." He sighs dramatically. "A dog-master's daughter."

I can't bear it any more. I pull away from the queen, and find myself in front of Conall.

My Acushla. Just someone else who needed me to be someone who I am not.

"Did you get the starfruit?" I demand, because there is nothing else left.

"What? *What?* No—they were in my pockets but then my clothes transformed—"

"Five sons!" the king bellows. "Four completed their quests! Four earned their blessings! Four shall fulfill their destinies!"

"But you made it out," Conall says. "What does the starfruit matter any more?"

"But yet I have five sons!" the king wails.

"It matters to someone!" I cry. "And I promised!"

"Five!" The king beats his breast.

"He can try again," the queen says. "Look, this one is leaving."

It's true. I run, because I matter to someone—and they're not in this room.

***

I burst outside with little plan, gasping in the night air as I glance desperately around. Coracles! Remembering the bit from Fergus's story, I throw my cloak over the balcony and slide after it, not caring as my stomach of my dress catches on the railing and the coracle rocks wildly under me. I pull the scissors out of my pocket and desperately chip away at the hemp rope, which parts just as the ballroom door opens. I push off from the wall, and the little skin boat floats silently around the corner.

I need to catch my breath, because it's a long row to Starfruit Island. Besides, I seem to be crying. I pull my cloak around me and try to balance on the narrow bench so the boat stops spinning.

I can't find my faith any more. Conall was one more man who wanted me for my true self, not what I am. All those months, I thought we were happy together, working together, and he was just pleased for making me fall in love with him even though he couldn't speak. It was a prophecy. I was nothing more than a quest.

But it wasn't even *me*.

Feeling sorry won't do anyone any good. Who knows what trouble Trencoss is getting up to, and I promised the maids I would plant the three trees. At least one of us can keep their promises.

Women are allowed to divorce their husbands. If I must marry for my diplomatic connections, I at least want it to be bargained beforehand. None of that hand-holding in the dark, him washing the dishes and saying he wants to see my hair loose. Pah!

I pull on the oars, making the boat spin. Actually, I don't want to be married to someone who doesn't love me. I pull the oars and spin the other direction. Which way is the right island, anyhow? I don't need to be married at all. I hate men. All of them. One oar hits the water and the other doesn't and I lurch to the side, bobbing back up right before I'm afraid I'm going to the bottom of the lake.

Truth to be told, I usually let the man row my coracle.

Maybe always.

Well, I don't have a man any more, so I'll have to be creative. I hear someone call my name, but I'm still below the far side of the building, too close to be seen from the windows.

"Fishes," I call, gently so no one can hear me back at the bridge. "Will you bring me to Starfruit Island?"

It takes a minute, but there's a little thump below my feet, then another, and my boat starts to move. We're heading somewhere, but I have to clutch the sides as my round boat spins.

The beat of wings, and a bird flies low, circling me in confusion.

"Black-browed night heron!" I greet him. "Will you steady me on my way to Starfruit Island? Please? *Oh!*" As we tilt again.

The heron dips lower and I toss the ragged rope in the air. With the Night Heron holding the tow rope steady and the fishes pushing from below, soon I am gliding forward. Not knowing what else to give them, I sing them a song of thanks. Time passes; I pull my cloak tight and keep singing as the island grows closer. I tell them a story I learned from one of the library-boxes.

They leave as my boat floats into a little cove. My boat scrapes the sand, knocking me forward, but water still surrounds me.

Landing a boat is another thing I left the men to do. After three tries, where I'm afraid I'm going to tip myself full-length in the water, I have to admit that Fergus is right and I don't have proper training for this sort of thing. I finally manage to stumble out feet first, gasping as the frigid water goes through my soft boots and weights down my ridiculous skirt.

I grit my teeth and pull the coracle to shore. I tie it to a tree, briefly contemplating turning it on its side and taking a nap in its shelter. I probably would, but I'm not strong enough to drag the boat up to where the ground is dry, and I'll get too cold on the wet ground.

Starfruit, then. I wonder how hard they will be to find.

I wrap my cloak tight, trying to cover as much of the dress as I can. It's not that I care about keeping the dress nice, but the sturdy wool doesn't snag on all the bushes and the taf-fet and lace does.

The path is steep, but it isn't far until I am surrounded by the pale trees, the golden fruit hanging down like teats. That's a strange image, and I giggle, half on the verge of hysteria. I look around, frightened of what will happen next, but there is nothing.

I pick a fruit.

Still nothing.

Curious, I take a bite. This one is green, so I try again, testing until I know what the correct softness is against my hand. The instructions are for one ripe fruit, so I must be careful. I wander through the grove, pushing back the undergrowth to find the best ones. My skirt is good for something, for I push some of the fabric between the wooden hoops and tie other bits around it, making a basket in front of me. I move the other fruits from my pocket, making sure they are still unharmed. The dress came with capacious pockets, tied around my waist and accessed through slits in the fabric, but the basket will be more secure.

I yawn, but shake my head to keep myself awake. I just need to get back to land and I'll sleep all night. I don't trust these islands.

Just then, a soft voice calls my name, no more than a few steps away.

I spin around, startled.

It's a maiden about my age, dressed in a simple léine and serviceable gúna. Her loose hair shines golden in the moonlight, and her face is pale and beautiful beyond compare. I touch my dark skin and unruly braids, ashamed. Saba thought men wanted me because I am beautiful, but it turns out that I was just a valuable asset, what with my connection to Fionn and the magic of my ignoble father. Not to mention, I'm too brave and intimidating, when I'm supposed to be just a quest—

"Ailbe of Dún Allaine?" the girl says again.

"I am she," I answer, reminding myself not to ignore the Fae. "How can I help you?"

"Nay, it is I who can help you." The maiden ducks her head, glancing at me through her lashes.

"You are very pretty, but no thank you," I reply, with an awkward curtsey.

She laughs, like a shower of gold. "No thank you to what?"

I am embarrassed, but I know the pattern of this story. "I am not interested in women," I admit. "And if you think to offer me a brother, I have to confess that at this moment I dislike men even more."

The maiden laughs again. "Ailbe of Dún Allaine, do you think we offer the same dish to every guest?"

I am tired and confused, and would prefer not to think about her tricks at all.

"The handsome blond man"—she ticks off one finger—"he longed for tenderness and praise, not to mention someone soft and curvy in his lap.

I was happy to oblige. He was very handsome, Ailbe of Dún Allaine. You have missed out." She smiles, and I notice her teeth are pointed.

I curtsey, taking a step back as I rise.

"The handsome dark man"—she ticks her second finger—"could not have cared less about my feminine virtues." She giggles. "We had to offer him something else."

Despite myself, I am curious. I still will leave Conall, but it would be nice if he weren't flirting with someone else right after he married me.

"What did you offer? He—he really didn't want you at all?"

"I tried." She pouts, all adorable. "I don't even think he noticed. But a house and gardens—that made him perk up his ears. He kept testing to make sure it really belonged to my father, that he might bargain it away."

Conall wanted a house? That almost sounds like...I shake my head, not letting myself consider it.

"For you, Ailbe of Dún Allaine..." The maiden smiles again, all her stoat-like teeth shining in the moonlight. "I have something even better."

She holds out her hand, where two golden circlets dangle.

"These are yours for the asking." A smile creeps across the maiden's face, the gold sparkling in the moonlight. "Do you want to know what they are?"

I don't need to ask. I have lived next to those crowns my entire life.

Chapter Twenty-Nine

"Saba doesn't need them any more," the Fae maiden says. "They are yours."

I can't help but stare. It's true; there's the dent from where Saba fell, and the tarnished place where her fingers always touched. It's the sigil of Dún Allaine, and the other is marked with the symbol that Fionn designed for his wife's household. That was on my best brooch, to show I belonged to Saba.

"It's not just the crown, Ailbe of Dún Allaine," she says. "As soon as you take these, you will *become* the princess."

"Me? It doesn't work like that."

"Oh, yes it does, when the Fae make a bargain that it does." She steps closer, dangling the circlets towards me. "You have always wished to be a princess. You have always envied the princess, while you know you are a step beneath her. And tonight?" She raises her eyebrows, taunting me. "This would solve all your problems. You return to your husband, who loves you truly, and you are a princess."

I stare at her, and at the crowns, and back at the maiden.

She waves the circlets in front of my face.

"I am not jealous of Saba," I tell her, my voice rough in my throat. "She has her role, and I have mine."

"No," says the maiden, coming closer again. "Her role is lost. She is caught out of this world, leaving a space. An Ailbe-sized space."

"I don't want Fionn," I say firmly.

"You don't get him." She waves away my concern. "You get Conall, who you want despite all your fussing about *not liking men*." She laughs. "But you get Conall the way he needs, with honor to his father."

I touch the limb of the starfruit tree, grounding myself. I take a step back, my wet feet searching for the path.

"No," I tell her.

"You answer all of Conall's dreams," she hisses, leaning close. "I can make it so they all forget what happened tonight—wiped clear from every mind. You will be a true princess. His quest fulfilled. Just imagine his satisfaction with you! His delight in his wife! The verity of his love!"

I want Conall to love me, it's true. It was nonsense I was telling myself about men; Fergus and Sigma and Rho and all the others are true and honest and doing their best, and I'm madly, painfully, desperately in love with Conall. I want the warmth of his smile, the comfort of his arms. I want to learn the way he makes his jokes, and see his beautiful face in the sunshine. I want to serve him a right proper cuppa tae and have a conversation like humans, and I want to explore the woods and swim in the lake and doze in the sun together, like we did when he was a dog and I was myself. Myself, who was never a princess.

"Take them," the Fae maiden says. "Please your husband. Saba can't use her power, so you might as well have it. You have the speech of a princess, and the bearing of a princess, and skills of a princess. Everyone will believe you. Everyone will admire you. Princess Ailbe, Princess Ailbe..."

Packed dirt beneath my soles. The path.

"If you're not ready to decide," the maiden adds, "you can come back to my home to discuss it. My father is generous in his bargaining, and we have a soft bed waiting for you."

The bed, I regret.

"No," I say, and I run.

My feet pound down the path, but the maiden does not give chase—only her laughter follows.

Clutching my cloak with one hand and my makeshift fruit basket with the other, I leap and hobble as quickly as my dress will allow. I burst out into the moonlight—

In the wrong place. I am on a low cliff, water lapping the rock face. It's a little promontory, other rugged hills wrapping around the twisted shoreline. Starfruit Island is small, but there is no beach in sight, which means there is no boat in sight.

Splashing draws my gaze to the dark water. A little round face peers up at me, and once he has my attention, the otter curls and dives back into the lake. Moments later, my coracle comes bobbing around the next little spit.

I rub my temples while the otters push the boat into the tiny cove. The sweet tang of starfruit is on my lips, the night breeze a tender reminder of my connection with the world. I need to think clearly, but I'm so tired. The Fae woman is not following me right now, but in Fergus's stories and Saba's visions, the moment of escape triggered a transformation. Not escape, for Fergus left easily once... no, twice. Once without the fruit, and once without the boat.

The otter squeals from below.

I find my smiles. "You did a wonderful job. You are so clever and brave!"

He chirps with satisfaction, spinning happily in the water. But another otter nudges my boat.

"So clever, but I can't get into it. If I jump off the cliff, I will sink the boat." I am not sure I could jump at all. I stepped off the edge of the fountain, I squiggled on my stomach over the balcony, but this jump is too high and frightening. I'm not a hero.

One of the otters scrambles onto a tree branch, swings herself into the boat, and chitters at me hopefully.

"You're right," I agree, "there are plenty of trees. But I don't know how to swing by my hands like that."

The otters burst into a chorus of recriminations or explanations; I'm not sure, but I can't help but laugh at their antics. They are determined to teach me, so they climb up and down, slowly and quickly, shaking the best branches. I still don't think I can't swing down a cliff, but they scramble higher and higher to show me what to do.

They're going up a certain place, in a dark notch. Otters may be more agile than me, but they are not birds. They have to walk somewhere.

I creep closer to where they are climbing. One catches my meaning and pops up and down to show me where to go. I will have to drop a couple feet off the top, but once I make it that far, I think I can see a steep, muddy path to the water.

First, I set the starfruit carefully to the side. "Don't touch these," I warn the otters. "They're for someone else who wants to be with her family, like you are all together."

They clutch each other and hum in sympathy, and I caress their soft heads. The mere idea of being separated from family drives them to distraction. "I agree, little ones, I agree," I murmur. "So I have to figure this out."

First of all, instead of trying to leap like a warrior, I'm going to slither off this cliff like an otter. In order to do that, I have to break some of the hoops in this skirt. When they see what I am doing, the otters are delighted to bring me rocks, and then one sets up tapping wildly at the edge of one of the hoops.

I giggle. "Are you hoping there's oyster meat inside? Oh, aren't you the strong one! Look at it smash!"

It is refreshing to smash something to bits, and the otters are so funny and happy, so it is possible that we destroy the dress much more than strictly necessary. Finally, I sit on the edge of the cliff, my legs dangling down into empty air, and hike up my cloak so it is tucked over my shoulders and elbows.

"I can't outrun or outfight the stoat monsters," I tell the otters, who hum in agreement and fear. "So the boat and the fruit must not touch. You have done so much, my valiant little friends. Owls! Will any of you choose to help me?"

With a whisper of feathers, a short-eared owl drops beside me, cocking its head. The otters sit up tall, staring back, but they are much too large to be the prey of an owl like this one.

"My good friend owl, will you take this fruit and fly high on your strong wings? When I am in the boat and the otters push it away from shore, will you please drop the fruit to me? But only when I am safely away."

She hoots lightly.

"I won't go too far," I assure her, although of course she could be saying anything. "I know you are not a water bird. Just far enough to be safe from the Good Neighbors yonder."

The otters cover their faces and chitter with fear, and the owl blinks.

"Well, if you don't like them much, I have to say we're in agreement," I say. "Thank you for your assistance, and I had better get on with it, then."

I really don't want to drop off the ledge. I try to be brave, but I can feel myself sliding and knocking against trees and rocks all the way into the water and my stomach curls with fear.

It's not real. I just need to push off. That's all.

I can't.

The otters show me, again and again.

I think of Saba, who know matter how tired and discouraged she is, must keep going every day because Oisín needs her. She doesn't have the luxury of deciding something is too hard.

And that evil woman thought I was jealous; would desire her place. I push aside visions of redoing the scene with Conall's parents, except me bringing everyone honor instead of shame. I would be dressed neatly and properly, and present my new parents-in-law with a gift made by my own hands.

Never mind. Like Saba, this is the life I have to life, mud and chill and all. I open my eyes wide and push myself forward.

I land hard and slide in the mud, but I am in no danger of going off the cliff. The path is made by smaller creatures, the slope steep and muddy, but also filled with tree roots and boulders that hold everything together. I creep down, cold seeping through the seams of my wet boots. My skirt drags and would catch on everything, but the otters are having a grand time disentangling it and pulling it along. I'm sure they will all have bits of lace and bows by the time I leave.

I have to wade into the water again, but the otters show me a nice flat rock where I can crouch and then creep into the boat. I'm shaking with cold, but their joy makes me laugh. They remind me to be proud of myself.

The otters push the coracle just past the edge of the bluff. I thank them as they swirl around me and dive back towards shore.

The owl circles overhead. The first starfruit splats into oblivion, so I hold out my skirt and she swings lower to drop the second more carefully.

"It seems safe!" I tell her. "You did a wonderful job!"

She hoots a warning, then circles back with the third starfruit, and the fourth. Another? How many blessed starfruit did I think I needed to bring? I can't help but laugh. Two warriors couldn't get a single fruit between them, and I've fetched...six, it appears.

"Thank you!" I cry. "Thank you all! Thank you!"

The night heron swoops out from her hunting ground in a whirl of feathers, and the fish bump the boat from underneath. I hurry to fling the lead rope and tuck myself securely in the bottom of the boat, my cloak making a slight protection from the cold water, the starfruit carried in my skirt-basket.

"To the far shore, please," I tell them. "Just there, where you can see the two hills meet for the river to cut through."

We are off, gliding through the starlight on the dark water.

***

The night is beautiful, but I am cold and angry and helpless.

It was that easy.

All the things that were hard for me—rowing the boat and climbing the cliff and getting disoriented—were parts that would have been second nature for the men, but they failed the simplest part. They couldn't even hold on to what they said they loved.

Yes, everything the Fae maiden said about me was true. I have felt jealous and useless, and that I deserve to have the title that goes with my training. Yes, I love Conall and want to please him. I am raised to prepare everything in my power to do honor to my future in-laws, so their disappointment was a crushing mortification. Yes, envy and imbalance have always been part of my relationship with Saba.

But huddled in the boat, my rage burns through my belly and heats my limbs. Because that is not all that is true about me.

I love Saba with the deepest love I have ever known, and what is more, I have full faith that she loves me back. We have talked about that envy and imbalance, like we have talked about everything else, and I know she has envied me the simplicity of my life. I would rather be myself, plebeian daughter of the dog-minder, than a princess pursued by the Dark Man.

I want to do my parents-in-law honor, but I don't believe honor comes at the expense of truth. They will accept me for who I am, or they don't. As for Conall...maybe he was trying to find a home for us. He has been driven so powerfully by what he feels is the shame of being trapped as a dog. Unlike those first nights after I found him, I will not cling to him any more. I have learned that I am strong. But I will hold my half of the wedding vows if he holds onto his.

Even though he couldn't manage one silly little Fae trap. Men! All their ideas about honor and quests.

If that Short-eared Owl returned from her hunt with food in her claws for her hungry nestlings, but a beautiful Fae owl offered her a better nest—one day, somewhere—the owl would not give up her prey today. Her children need it.

If the mother otter is building a burrow in the bank, and a beautiful Fae otter offered her the most delicious clam ever—one day, somewhere—the mother otter would not leave her children in a half-dug burrow.

Saba has the spiritual power of the mná feasa, the political power of being a king's daughter, and her own power of being able to change to a deer. And yet every day, she wakes up and does all the boring and dirty work of raising a baby and cooking their food and cleaning their lowly cave-house, rather than take Oisín away to something that might be better—one day, somewhere—because by the work of her hands and the loneliness of her heart she can keep him safe. She will stay as long as that is best for him, as long as he is healthy and full of baby-smiles, and then she will risk everything to take him somewhere else that he needs.

"No, you beautiful trickster," I say across the water. "Even if I didn't know who you are, I would never trade a true gift for a promise. Not when real hearts need what I hold in my hands."

I slide down against the cold skin of the boat, closing my eyes against the tears.

I wish someone had done as much for me.

Chapter Thirty

The animals bring my coracle all the way up into the mouth of the river. I think it is otters, again, once we get close to shore, but these ones do not wish to talk and the dark is deep beneath the trees. I am pushed into rocky shallows, and I thank everyone, anyone, profusely. Cradling my skirt-basket with one arm and hiking my cloak over my shoulders, I am too stiff to get out of the coracle neatly. I accidentally roll it over, falling onto one hand and knee in the frigid water.

I manage to keep the fruit safe, and I am too tired to cry. I drag the boat behind me, sloshing through the water, and with one final heave manage to roll it onto a grassy patch. I'll come back and care for it in the morning. I am so very cold.

I trudge up the riverbank, trying to orient myself in the dark. Conall and I camped somewhere up here. Trencoss kidnapped us in the night, so I don't know what has happened to the tent or my sleeping roll. But I always tidied away everything before bed, so there should be a solid wooden chest with some supplies, and we had cached our food in a tree. Some oil, hard cheese, dried meat—that should last. If not, at least there is a fire-pit already built, and the willow tree was dense and dry. I had those tiny foods at the party, so I can last till morning, despite my growling stomach. I just need to find our willow tree, and I will be safe enough.

I try to pull up my skirt. Without the hoops the fabric is dragging, monstrously heavy with water and mud. But I must protect the starfruit, and the more I tug the more a different part slips away. I can't manage my floor-length cloak, too, so I keep it rolled up over my shoulders where it doesn't keep me warm, just flops around being another thing to manage. I'm so tired, and so cold, and the otters and the owls and the fish are gone and I'm alone in the dark.

In the morning, I will look for my twenty-four wolfhounds, who hopefully have all escaped into the woods and their human forms. Perhaps I will never know. And I will go back to Trencoss's palace and plant the three fruits. If the dogs escaped, Trencoss will not have his patrol, so I will just hope he doesn't notice me. But those are all problems for the morning, and now I must drag myself and my dress through these brambles.

Finally! I'm so relieved that I've found the right cut-off for our camp, that I don't even register that I am walking towards light. I push through the berry bushes, noting that they've grown back from where I cut a path, into the little clearing, and my sore eyes blink at the blazing fire.

Wait.

I pull my cloak tight against my shoulders, barely able to breathe, as a graceful figure rises from where he is tending the flames.

"My Mavourneen," he says, and reaches out his hands to me.

***

I drag my miserable dress the last few steps across the meadow, to where I can see Conall's face and feel the blessed warmth of the fire. I can't think of any of the right words, so I just stare at him.

He is watching me. Solemn.

Waiting for me.

I try to speak, but must first swallow, then cough. "Would you please put these somewhere safe?"

I show him the fruit.

"Of course." He glances down at my skirt-basket, moving smoothly to fetch a wooden bowl. I mixed so many meals in that bowl. He lines it with a cloth and holds it for me, and I carefully set the fruit inside. Orange, plum, starfruit—five starfruit. One is smashed, so I set it aside. Conall tucks the cloth over the top, then sets the whole bowl inside our wooden chest and closes the iron latches. I glance around, seeing that he has set up camp like I always did, even tying the ripped tent so it will cover us.

"Why are you here?" I ask, when he is done with the chest.

"Because I hoped you would come," he answers.

I don't know what I think of that.

Like me, Conall is still wearing his fine clothing from Bob's party, but his léine and jacket are much more practical, and he isn't covered with mud and brambles and mushed fruit. He is so handsome, and that reminds me that he is so wealthy, and I can't look at him any more.

I step past without looking at him, adjusting my cloak so it covers me, then holding out my hands to the fire. All my instincts remind me how I could fix this situation: praise his bravery, ask him to help me with something, step into his arms and offer my face for a kiss. I can sense that he would respond warmly to any of those overtures.

But I am hurting so badly, and for once, I don't put my feelings aside for someone else's comfort.

Conall puts another log on the fire and comes next to me, standing close but not touching me.

"Ailbe," he says, slowly, "I'm sorry for what happened back there. I never cared whether you are a princess or not."

"I never said I was!" My anger flares. They implied I'm a liar!

He shakes his head and sighs. "I suppose you didn't. I don't think about your formal name, so I just told my parents what I have heard Trencoss say."

I guess when I was still bothering to argue with Trencoss over my title, that was early days when Conall was still kept away from me, so he didn't hear me deny it.

"It certainly sounds like it matters to you," I point out.

Conall sighs. "It matters to my father. He was the one speaking. I—"

"And your quest? Was that, or was it not, your quest? I am nothing but a..." I break off in frustration, tugging my cloak tight.

"Mavourneen, I gave up on that foolish quest years ago," Conall says quietly.

I turn to him, surprised.

"It's nonsense." He gives an impatient shake. "A prince of one of the wealthiest kingdoms in Ireland, assigned a *quest* to marry a princess? It should have been simplicity itself. All my brothers had something similar—a quest with no real obstacles, something we had been directly trained to perform. The druids designed them not for us, but to stoke my father's ego, that he would pay extra tithes to the druid temple once he could brag that all his sons succeeded."

This all fits into the way the king told the story, and the goddess knows that I'm familiar with the way that powerful men love to brag. I watch Conall's face in the firelight, the tightness to his lips, the set of his shoulders. There is more to this story than I can understand tonight.

"Days ago, I told you that I left my home to seek my fortune," he continues, quietly. "That was the bald truth. The artifice of the quest gave me the permission I needed to escape the City of Gold. I have enough wealth of my own, and skill with my sword to be an asset to another king. I hoped to earn a place as a minor lord, with a small keep and a herd of cattle. And"—his voice drops low—"find a woman I loved."

I turn away sharply, my back to him. My chest hurts with the love I wanted so much, but cannot trust any more.

"My Mavourneen, I am sorry for the way I behaved in the ballroom," Conall says to my back. "I let my father do the talking, when it was my voice that should have been the loudest."

I take a breath but don't turn around.

"Ailbe, please talk with me." Gently, Conall puts his hand on my elbow. It's not a push, it's just a suggestion that I turn and face him.

I do. His touch settles me.

I even manage to look up. Something in my face softens something in Conall's expression, and he brushes his thumb down my cheek. His skin is warm and dry, and I want this to work. I dreamed that he loved me, and I want so desperately for those dreams to be real.

"I shamed them," I say, my voice wobbling. "In front of all those people, I was..." I shake my head, helpless.

"They shamed you, Mavourneen. And I am sorry because"—he looks up, swallows hard—"I had learned, over the years, that the best way to deal with my father is let him talk his bluster, and we all ignore what isn't true and get on with our lives. He loves to argue and I don't, so I can never win. But I should have realized"—he looks back at me, cups my cheek in his hand—"that it was *you* who needed me to speak. Even if I couldn't have convinced my parents, I needed to have spoken to you. To Fergus. To everyone else in the hall."

"I want to do honor to your parents," I manage to say.

He shakes his head. "They have very particular ideas, and you might never meet their standards. But you do honor to me."

That is more important, I suppose—if we are going to stay married.

"I could free you from your marriage vows," I say. "It is early enough that the magistrate won't order a payment. Probably."

Conall smiles, wistful. "Ailbe of Dún Allaine, you are tired and cold and there is nowhere else to go within miles. Since clearly you are stuck with me until morning, it is now my mission to use these hours to convince you to stay with me for the rest of our lives."

I am so surprised that I burst out laughing.

"I am cold," I admit, and my stomach growls.

"I made porridge," he replies. "Sit down and I will serve you."

All those months ago, I found a log half-smoothed by a woodsman's lathe, and dog-Conall dragged it to our campsite, where I made it into a flat bench. I spread and squash my skirts so I can sit there now, resting my cold feet on the stones around the fire, running my fingers across the familiar grooves in the wood. I can't believe I am back here, with my bench and the tent I had earned and the mixing bowl smoothed by my own hands. I can't believe it.

Conall fiddles with the kettle and the iron pot and all the accoutrements that made up our lives for so long. He passes me a bowl and settles next to me on the bench. The oats are slightly stale and there is no milk, but he added seeds and a touch of honey. I hadn't realized how hungry I was until I start eating.

"You didn't come back from Starfruit Island." I meant to make it a question, but anger tinges my voice.

"We all thought you had more time."

I put my bowl aside, too upset to swallow any more. "It doesn't matter why. You said you would come, and you didn't."

"I was coming. It was only a couple of days."

"You forgot me."

"Mavourneen." He takes my hand. "I didn't forget."

"We saw you in a vision." My fingers tighten around his, but my shoulders are crumpling into tears. "You went to a fine feast in the castle instead of coming back."

"Because I had the chance to do better for you."

"No!" The anger rips through me. "You risked everything for a promise they were never going to keep! I don't care about some silly house. You were trying to bargain up and play tricks instead of just finishing the job you promised!"

"It wasn't the house."

"The princess told me they offered you a house, and you came!"

"They did, but that wasn't why."

I sniffle, my shoulders shaking. I shiver. Conall's hands are still warm and steady around mine.

"I tried to have faith in you," I tell him, quietly. "When we saw the vision, it looked like the princess seduced you. All this time, I have tried to believe that surely wasn't true. I have tried and tried, but I don't understand."

He tensed when I mentioned the princess. "That blonde with the dramatic eyelashes? Mavourneen..." He laughs, weakly, and brushes his hand down my face. "I couldn't have cared less about her. Remember, I had just married you, mere hours before. We spent all night with our comrades, and I had not even had the chance to take you back to your bedroom. I wanted to, so badly. I had spent months with you as a dog, with a distant sense what romantic love was but no way to feel anything but canine comfort. You were all I could think about, but I wanted all the nights together. I wanted to be a man for you, forever."

He strokes my face again, and this time, I look up into his bright eyes. His fingers slip around to cradle my neck, his thumb brushing my jaw.

"Yes, the Starfruit King offered me a house, and I thought of you and wanted it. But then the very temptation of their offer made me suspicious; the way it was perfectly aligned to my own desires. So I went back to his palace to treat with him, because Mavourneen..." He shakes his head, blows out a slow breath. "I fear you underestimate Trencoss. Theta and the other soldiers do, too. You have only spent a few weeks with him, and I was forced to be his companion for years."

"So why bargain with a Fae?"

"Because they are the only thing more powerful than a sorcerer like Trencoss." He meets my eyes again, his gaze steady. "We were sent there by Robert, the Great and Wise—"

I snort.

Conall smiles in wry agreement. "Bob, then. Whoever he is, he took a fancy to you, and that made me think that whatever was on Starfruit Island might be a powerful ally when we needed to face Trencoss."

"I don't want to face him," I argue. "I just want to plant my fruit and go away."

Conall leans forward, lightly brushing my lips with his. "I will help you plant your fruit, and I will do everything in my power that we all go free. But I don't think that's what Trencoss has in mind."

I consider this all, fiddling with Conall's fingers at our joined hands. I still think attempting to bargain with the island Fae was unwise, but Conall didn't have the information we did. At least he had a plan, and wasn't just tumbling into their temptation. And the day when Trencoss finished the ball was the perfect weather for the dew, with neither sun nor rain nor wind. Driving the little flyers with all his power, he probably accomplished three or four ordinary days' of work. Conall thought that none of us were in danger yet.

"You are right," I admit. "Trencoss did fool me. Day after day, he was polite and ordinary, until I thought he wasn't so bad. Did he beat you? Was it terrible?"

Conall smiles sadly. "Since he has the power of the animals, it does him no good to harm us—*them*. But he has no natural reserves on his cruelty besides what is useful to himself."

"I feel foolish."

"You were very lonely. I am angry with myself that I could not be any more useful to you."

I suspect that Conall's anger with himself is driving him to impetuous action—marrying me without discussing the way it might change the magic; trying to bargain with unscrupulous Fae; even his own shame drove him to accept his father's criticism without protest.

I will be good for him. I sit up, thinking of the things I can do. I am so used to Saba and her transformations; eventually my acceptance of the animal form will sink into him. He needs to learn to express himself to someone who cares about his thoughts, and I am naturally a good listener. I think he likes to make me laugh, and laughter is good—

"Mavourneen," Conall says, a smile in his voice, "what are you thinking about? What else is worrying you tonight?"

I look up, smiling back. "I think I'm fine. Everything else can wait till morning. Oh! Wait." I start to giggle, embarrassed and frustrated and absurd. "Can you get this awful, awful dress off of me?"

"How does it unlace?"

"I don't even know!" And I dissolve into laughter.

"Let's see." He chuckles as he puts more wood on the fire, then folds my cloak and stands me up and spins me around while he studies the dress and I try to contain my hysteria. Here I am, asking my husband to undress me, and it's the least romantic thing anyone could imagine, all mud and goosebumps.

With the gentle, meticulous, care that I am realizing is the way Conall approaches the world, he unties the ties and unbuttons the buttons. Some parts are too worn or broken to do properly, and we use my little scissors on those, but the dress is too thick and heavy to cut it all off even if we wanted to.

I shiver, partly from the night air, and partly from the shame of the party and the fear on the island that is just now hitting me. Conall warms blankets by the fire and drapes them over the parts of me that have escaped from the dress, as he asks me about what happened on Starfruit Island. I start out saying as little as possible, ashamed of how my behavior made me unfeminine to Fergus. I want to be myself, but I also want Conall to see me as a woman. My selfish heart yearns to be beautiful, and I'm afraid these stories show the opposite. If he thought I was desirable, wouldn't he be kissing me right now, with my clothes half-off?

Conall just keeps working on the dress, and then the strange heavy layers under it, asking a question whenever I pause. I can tell he's making an effort to keep me talking so I don't get lost in my thoughts.

Very well. Conall is going to be good for me, too. I have been alone so long—well, alone except for the animals—that I've forgotten the way that I can fit with a partner. Saba and I were like this, before the Dark Man caught her for the first time, and she was a deer for three years while I managed her father's castle in her place.

Finally, Conall holds the stiff, broken layers of skirt while I step out of it, and I am in nothing but my own proper tunica, soft and loose from my shoulders to my knees. I take the pins out of my hair while Conall folds the last parts of the dress. He thinks it best to keep the clothing, given that it is connected to Bob, but we agree we have no idea what to do with it. It's not going back on a human body without weeks of mending.

Conall returns to me, with a worried expression and his own cloak.

"Thank you," I say, like I always do. "You have managed everything, from porridge to muddy buttons. You are so—"

"That's not what I was hoping to hear from you," he says, his voice a low rumble.

What did I do wrong?

He slides his cloak over my shoulder, then tugs the corners to pull me against his chest. Where did I put my hands the last time he did this? Do I smell like sweat and otters?

"My Mavourneen," he growls into my hair, "have you decided if you will stay with me? Because it's blisteringly obvious that I am full of flaws, but I love you with every beat of my heart. Please give me the chance to make you happy."

"Oh," I squeak. My hands find the solid warmth of his waist, his breath ragged under my ear. I slide my hand up his chest, under his jacket, to cup his heart.

I look up into his face. "This is how I found you, when Trencoss made a thousand dogs," I tell him. "Your heartbeat is always familiar to me."

"It's because it beats for you," he answers. "Man or dog, I am yours. Please keep me."

My answer is easy, because I know how to hold on.

"I will." I rise on my tiptoes and kiss his jaw. "Please stay."

Chapter Thirty-One

Conall and I wake with the first light, our breath making clouds in the air. We decide quickly to forgo lighting a fire; that exercise will warm us more effectively. Half our blankets had been ruined or vanished while we were in the Castle of a Thousand Doors, so it was a frigid night. We slept in our clothes—I had my spare set in the chest—too cold and exhausted to do anything more than huddle together. We pack up without speaking, our movements brisk and efficient, taking bites of cold porridge while sweeping and folding.

To my surprise, we find Theta and his squadron just over the rise. I am so amazed and delighted that I squeal and hug Delta and Chi, although I still find the grumpy commander a little intimidating.

"I thought you would be gone by now!" I exclaim. "You could have gotten a lot farther with all night to travel."

Theta gives me a disdainful snort. "We're not leaving until we all go together."

"You don't have to stay with me. It's all right!"

They all stare at me, skeptical. Someone laughs.

"Because I'm going back to the Castle of a Thousand Doors," I explain, blushing. They are more amenable in their dog forms. "I don't want to put anyone else in danger." I explain about the three fruits.

"We figured it was something like that," Delta replies. "We're going together."

"Hopefully we'll find the other three squadrons as we go," Chi adds.

"What happened to your torcs?" I reach towards Delta, but flinch back and touch my own chest instead. I am so comfortable with them, yet they are so different now. I have spent most of my life with women, treating men with formal respect, and I am not sure how to navigate this relationship.

Nor the one with Conall. I glance at my husband as the men gather.

Before we can start again, Zeta leads his squadron into the clearing, jogging and cheering. Now we have a dozen wolf-hound warriors! Everyone embraces and pounds each other's backs, and I'm in the middle of it. They make a big deal about being gentle lest someone squash me like a bug. It's silly and joyful, and I feel good.

All of a sudden, they remember my question about their torcs, pushing around to show me.

"Gone!" says Gamma, pulling back his collar to show his bare skin. "Did yours do it too?"

"Never thought I'd appreciate having my jewelry stolen!" laughs Omega.

In the chaos of checking each other's necks and asking about the other group, I conclude that the torcs and the criossana both just vanished while everyone slept. I peek at Conall, too shy to ask, but Omega grabs him in a wrestling move and dramatically checks his neck. Nothing.

"We're headed back to the castle, then?" Zeta asks, straightening his inar. He wears daggers on his belt, but the others are variously armed, several with swords sheathed against their backs, a few with axes or unstrung bows. Theta's entire squadron is wearing blue with a ram insignia, but Zeta's group is assorted. From what I can figure, in returning to their human forms, they also regained the clothes and tools they had with them at the time.

Conall's gear is long gone, and he is still in his formal wear from last night. When I asked about the sword across his back, feeling it was familiar somehow, he looked at me with an inscrutable expression.

"It's Fergus's," he answered.

"Do knights usually lend their..." I cut myself off, knowing the answer already. The two of them came to some sort of agreement.

Now, Theta stops the cheerful chaos with a sharp gesture.

"We need a plan," he grows, "and a backup plan, and one in case that doesn't work. But there are a few points that I won't hear argument about."

He raises his eyebrows and looks around the group, which has calmed instantly. Only Conall stands slightly apart, waiting. I am snugged between Delta and Omega.

Theta holds up one gnarled finger. "Ailbe wants to plant her fruits and get outta there, so that's plan number one, but we all know we've got to be prepared for Trencoss to ruin our day. Some of you aren't gonna like this, but you'll obey what I say or leave." Another glare. "No one makes a stand or goes after Trencoss, until Ailbe is completely out of the way. Got it? We run. Back rank distracts, and run."

"We don't take down Trencoss first?" Chi asks, surprised.

"Nope. Run."

This is mortifying for warriors! "Don't worry so much about me," I protest. "I can—"

"Shut up," Theta interrupts, not unkindly.

Zeta turns to me. "Little princess, all the rest of us are interchangeable to him. He wants strong bodies and can catch more any time. Do you remember in the garden, when he admitted everything? You have both a unique power and a particular connection to Fionn mac Cumhaill. He will stop at nothing in order to capture you."

"And we don't like to contemplate what happens after he gets his hands on you," Omega adds. "He doesn't need you strong and healthy, like he needs us."

"So that's settled, then," Theta growls. "Every hand and *every* blade is dedicated to protecting Ailbe. Once she's safe, we"—he pumps his fist—"will stand and fight."

The men cheer, and I shiver.

***

What defines keeping me safe, and what is the best way to arrange those blades? The men discuss these points as we walk to the castle. With the triplicate goal of avoiding detection, finding the other troops, and arriving at the back gate instead of the front, we loop up into the hills.

They are going to put me in the coracle and send me back to Bob's castle while they confront Trencoss. We can see across the lake and there's the palace, glimmering white, three little green islands in the distance beyond.

"As long as you don't expect me to row," I say. "I'm not very good at it."

"That's the rear guard," Theta growls. "One squadron at the lake."

"I want to be in the fighting group!" Chi says.

Theta looks grim. "We're all gonna do plenty of fighting."

They promise to put me in the boat, and someone will row me if at all possible. If not, they will defend the shoreline while my salmon friends help. Xi, who is the fastest runner, loops back down to check my coracle and put it in the water at the closest place to the Castle of a Thousand Doors. Fatherly Zeta helps me balance out onto a log overlooking the valley, then points over my shoulder so I understand where everything is. The Castle of a Thousand Doors, its front and back gate, the willow tree where we started this morning.

"There's the stones where we sat in the sun," I say, pointing to the dark line stretching into the water. "Do you remember?"

"I remember it all," he answers. "Xi is putting your boat just there. Now hop down."

Conall is standing below, and at that, he raises his arms and smiles up at me. He has said very little the whole morning. I am flustered and maybe a little afraid of the drop, but they both expect me to try, so when Zeta nudges me I go. Conall catches me, strong and steady, and holds me for an extra moment.

"Now you won't be afraid the next time you must jump," Zeta praises. "After last night, you have to do it again right away, little princess."

The men want to call me that, just like they want to be called by their Greek letters. They are glad to be quit of their old life, they tell me. They're lucky their old lord will have written them off for dead, and they can start fresh. I just hope we all survive to see what that life will be. Conall sets me down, already looking away. Zeta is training me like a warrior deserves—after the jump, he has other exercises to prepare us—and I fear it makes me ugly in husband's eyes.

As for the rest of their battle strategy, I don't really understand all the details, and I watch the forest instead. I raise my fingers to greet the birds, and peek under fallen logs to find rabbit dens. They twitter and twitch their noses at me, and I blow kisses.

It turns out that Upsilon was forced to order his squadron to disperse. We find them one by one. Everyone is tense that someone might be missing, but they keep turning up. By the time we catch up to Omikron, he has caught and roasted a brace of rabbits and a pile of mushrooms, and everyone is relieved to have a few bites of breakfast.

Theta forces the men to try to change back to their dog form, but no one can find it at all. I notice a flash of fancy clothing in the woods; Conall is fetching water and ignoring the others. I remember what he said about living in the dog form for so long that he will have it within him forever. Either Theta figures that the lack of collar has the same effect on Conall as all the others, or he simply doesn't have the authority to order Conall against his will, because he doesn't call him back.

We reach the back gates well before noon, but there is no sign of Rho and his group—the ones who were out scouting. As we make our way down the hillside towards the back of the castle gates, I brace for the very worst...that Trencoss called them home before the little flyers finished their work, they are back under his command...and that Trencoss will force one squadron to fight the others. I shake my head, trying to shake away thoughts of blade against dog; teeth against throat; one friend fighting his brother.

Chapter Thirty-Two

"Ailbe," says Tau, very softly, "don't look behind you, finish placing the dirt, and stand up. Keep your arms relaxed. I'm going to throw you."

I push the soft dirt over the plum, saying the world's fastest prayer for thanksgiving and safe growth, and rise to my feet, staying both as braced and relaxed as possible.

All at once, there's the clatter of chain, Trencoss laughs, and Tau seizes both my arms and flings me through the air. I didn't expect that—we had practiced that he would throw me over his shoulder—I half-scream before I land on a solid chest. Behind me, Tau yells a battle cry and there's a clang of metal on metal, and the man beneath me is already running. My stomach jolts against his shoulder, trying to stay loose and make it easy for him—Kappa.

When we discussed the plan, I said I could run as fast as a man could while carrying me, to which Theta simply replied "no."

"We can protect you better if we touch you, little princess," Sigma said, making peace.

As soon as I am hurling through the woods, my arms braced against Kappa's back as he takes great leaps, his feet steady and his breathing slow and deep, I know that Theta was right. Under the best of conditions, I could never run this fast, and conditions are about to get worse.

"Got her," calls another voice.

Kappa swings me to my feet, my head spinning as I go upright. Gamma was four paces behind, and he grabs me without breaking stride. He swings me to his back upright, and I cling on with my arms and legs. Behind us, there's yelling and howling and the clang of metal.

"Is he hurting them?" I ask, unable to ask if anyone is dead.

"Silver chains," Gamma answers in time with his beating feet. "We sleep."

That was how he captured Conall and I, all those months ago, although he and I could still fight against the enchantment. I remember jostling in the wagon between the campsite and the castle, screaming and banging my knees against the cart—since my hands were tied—but at the same time drifting in and out of unconsciousness.

Behind us, there's a nasty snarl and a shout of pain.

"That's not a silver chain," I say, completely uselessly.

"Also—wolves," Gamma gasps. "Pass!"

"Ready," answers Xi. He grabs me fast and rough, all wiry muscle and knobbly bones, but he is by far the fastest one yet. I cling tight to his back and his stride lengthens with incredible power.

Behind us, I hear Gamma shouting, more snarling, other men calling directions and support. They are holding the path behind us, giving Xi a few extra moments. I catch glimpses of the lake through the forest.

Trencoss shouts something I cannot hear through the rush of our run.

"Beware, princess," Xi says, not even gasping.

There's a screeching and fluttering behind, beside, all around us. Xi tries to shield his face as I cry "birds, leave us alone!"

Doves and sparrows, wood-tits and wrens, all in a a confused cloud. They try to veer away from me but most of them can't think quickly enough to escape Trencoss's command. With their hysterical beating wings and claws, they push Xi off the path. I drop from his back as his momentum takes him sailing into a ditch. He howls and clutches his leg, gasping.

"Go!" he yells at me. "Run, run!"

I look around but no one is near. At least we are on a path, now. Sobbing an apology to Xi, I take off with my best pace, which feels like a meandering hedgehog in comparison. The birds land on the path or flutter above my head, cheeping and screeching in confusion.

"I'm sorry," I gasp, "he must have pulled you from your dinners—oh!"

Around the bend, a wolf bounds after me, thin and patchy-furred, an iron collar around its neck.

"Make it stop, make it stop!" I cry, immediately hoping I don't harm the birds. But they descend in a quick and angry crowd. I stop running in the shock of watching them, all the little creatures diving at the slavering wolf.

Moments later, four men come around the bend. Eta catches the wolf, knocking it off the path and then bracing his sword as the creature leaps at him, while the other three keep running to me.

"Hup hup," Omikron warns me, grinning as he scoops me onto his back. The three run in steady formation until Chi drops and spins, raising his axe to defend the path. Omikron's bicep is bleeding slightly, his knife in his hand as he jogs.

I don't like this. I don't like their pain, I don't like the men falling behind.

Omikron stumbles and Lambda lifts me off his back while Omikron gets his feet under himself again. He, too, spins to defend the path, ululating his battle cry before we are even out of sight.

Conall, Theta, and Zeta had stayed back in a different position, to direct the battle and close in at the end. Upsilon is stationed with Beta down by the water. Lambda, who is carrying me, jogs into an open area and I check behind us, hoping to see a dozen familiar heads jogging down the hill in various positions.

I see nothing but a chariot, carrying a man with a black cloak flowing behind, and a horse who can run much faster than Lambda.

Trencoss yells, and Lambda heaves a burst of speed, cutting through bushes thrashing our legs. We burst into a clearing and something whips the air. Lambda yells and goes down, me flying over his shoulders.

I land hard and a tree lands on me, another chain clattering against the branches and stinging me. I snatch my feet away, but I feel nothing more; the magic does not work on me, or at least not quickly. Omega scoops me over his shoulder, still holding the branches in his other arm to deflect anything more that Trencoss throws. We can't get very fast like this—and besides, the men must be exhausted now—and his shoulder jabs my belly with each jolting stride.

Two wolves jump out at us. Omega hits them with his branches, which wouldn't do anything but the wolves seem as tired the men. Delta and Pi half-jog around the corner, back-to-back, each holding branches in one hand and their weapon in the other.

"We're the last ones standing," Delta gasps.

"You're almost to the lake," Pi says.

Omega drops me and pushes me aside while all three men fight the wolves. One lupine drops and the other flees, and Pi grabs me as Trencoss's chariot hurtles around the corner. He scoops me onto his hips like a mother carries her baby, so Trencoss's enchanted chains will hit him first.

In sight of the lake—and a blow hits us both, rattling and coiling. Pi's muscles relax and he goes down, trapping me underneath him. The chariot clatters towards us, but Conall rushes in with a battle cry, the horse whinnies, and the chariot tumbles and bangs. The wheels knock against Pi and I scream, but already the horse has zig-zagged away, his chariot empty. I push Pi's arm aside, trying to sit up.

We've made it close enough to reach the reinforcements.

Trencoss is fighting Conall only a few yards away, chains clattering against sword. Trencoss calls three wolves to him, and Zeta and Sigma come roaring in to help Conall. Beta, stationed by the lake, pulls me out from under Pi and carries me down to where Upsilon stands up to his knees in the water, holding the coracle with his massive arms. Beta splashes forward. Upsilon is grim, watching the battle on shore.

"We can't row you just now, little princess," he says, and gives my boat a giant push out into the lake before they both splash back to the others, grabbing their weapons that they left on the rock jetty.

Bobbing safely off shore, I grip the edge of my boat as I try to make sense of what is happening.

Conall is fighting hand-to-hand with Trencoss. The two commanders each have one man at their sides. There's no sign of Theta. Trencoss has a sword and swings chains in the other hand. He is not very graceful with the sword, but all the dog-men have to leap out of the way of a single touch of those chains. Three wolves leap and worry at the men, but their attacks are awkward and uncoordinated.

I suspect they were not wolves until very recently, and Trencoss's choice of animal is bitter and cruel. The wolves are quick and lithe and sharp-toothed, and the men have to keep their distance.

But in their former shape, this wouldn't have even been a fight. The wolfhounds each had twice the weight and reach of the wolves, their thick fur protecting them from teeth and those huge paws and heavy shoulders ready to pin the beast to the ground. I imagine the wolves must enrage my men in some deep guttural way, not quite entirely cleared of their dog instincts—for the dogs are bred and trained to kill wolves.

Beta, whose glaive has the longest reach, manages to take down a wolf, but Trencoss catches him with a chain and Beta drops to the ground, asleep. In that moment of distraction, Conall flicks his sword in some fancy maneuver that knocks Trencoss's sword to the ground.

Trencoss takes a chain in each hand.

"You don't want to come close now, my fellow?" he taunts, flicking the chains like snakes.

"Let Ailbe free," Conall answers.

"No, thank you kindly," Trencoss sneers. "I plan to marry her, but don't worry—I'll keep her alive for quite a while."

Then, in a whirl of black léine, Trencoss turns and runs, the wolves snapping to defend his back. He races down the natural stone jetty—now only a stone's throw from me and my boat. I remember Zeta joking about what a defensible position this would be, and that is what Trencoss has chosen. There is too-deep water on three sides of him, and the wolves on the fourth; one beside him and one at the beginning of the rocks. Upsilon paces closer, sword upheld.

"Let's make this interesting, shall we, boys?" Trencoss says. "You've become a little too dependent on those bits of metal. Soldier beetles! Come and shimmer bright!"

A clittering and clacking emerges from the meadow above us, as hundreds of chunky insects swirl all around. I try to bat them away, but they pay no attention, just bumping up and down and across me and my boat, then flying off again.

My cloak slides to the floor of the boat. I put my hand to where the simple brooch held it in place—nothing except tiny shards on the skin floor, like a pile of wood shavings.

On shore, the men yell. The beetles have swarmed over, disintegrating everything of iron. Their weapons are nothing but the last bits of leather or silver in their hands.

"What do you think of my furry friends, now?" Trencoss asks. "Want to dance?"

Upsilon braces himself. Before I can imagine how brave and foolish he is, he roars and attacks the wolf with his bare hands. They tumble and wrestle on the ground, Upsilon's hand around the wolf's muzzle as the animal kicks against his leather armor. Sigma and Conall are moving in when Trencoss tosses his silver chains, immobilizing both man and wolf.

Upsilon was the largest of the men. If he can't take down a wolf, none of them can do it.

"Interesting." Trencoss smirks at the remaining three men. "Do you want to just come home with me now? I've got nice beds for you down in the cellar."

"Never!" Conall cries.

"I will trade myself for Ailbe," Zeta says calmly. "I'll go back with you now, if you just let her go free."

"No!" I cry, but Zeta gives me a look and I stop.

"Come and prove it," Trencoss says.

"I have lived my life." Zeta takes a step. "Let her go free to live hers, too."

"You can be my personal guard," Trencoss sneers. "Sleep by my bed."

Zeta continues forward. "Let her go to Conall."

"I will," Trencoss says. "Come where I can see you."

The men have been so brave, standing their ground in a battle they know they cannot win. I try to be brave as well, watching the man who has been like my grandfather give himself away—not his life, but his pride.

That is worse. I want him to stop.

Zeta wades into the water, up to his knees, his thighs.

"Catch!" Trencoss shouts, and something flies through the air.

Betrayal! I gasp in horror as Zeta sinks to his knees, them tumbles forward into the lake.

Trencoss laughs. "How about I just take all of you? I will accept Ailbe too."

Sigma grabs a branch and runs forward, splashing into the lake. He hauls his leader up from the water. He's panting, struggling with Zeta's slippery body and holding the branch where it will shield them both. I couldn't carry Zeta, but I could help with the shielding. But I can't control my boat, don't have any oars, can't get any closer. Worse, I understand that I would put them all in worse danger.

Trencoss turns his back on the men, staring at me. It is the ultimate insult, to imply his enemies are so infantile that he does not even need to watch them. He is putting his trust in the mangy wolf at the shore side of the pier. I brace myself.

"Ducks," Trencoss says conversationally, "push this boat to me."

With apologetic quacks, a dozen ducks paddle around my little craft, giving it nudges to spin it towards shore. I have learned from the birds on the path that it does no good to give the same animals a different order. I look around for something new.

"Osprey," I call, "come chase away the ducks."

Out of the trees, two birds swoop upwards and plunge. I wince and catch my breath, and the ducks squawk and dive and flutter. Two sharp splashes, and the last of the ducks make their awkward run across the water as they gain the air. The falcons emerge, shaking their heads, and follow their prey.

"Friend fishes," I call quickly. "Come push my boat out into the lake."

Immediately, a splashing and whirling erupts under me, as though they were just waiting for the invitation.

"Otters," Trencoss snaps, "go and catch the fish."

We are getting farther from shore, but a dozen lithe bodies swim faster, surrounding my boat and chasing away the fish.

"Heron," I cry, "come and help with my rope."

A huge gray heron bats her heavy wings, reaching for the rope as I throw it. She struggles to gain altitude, much larger than the black-browed night heron.

Trencoss calls across the water, "Orca, great friend of the deep, splash your tail and send this boat back to me!"

Do orcas live in lakes? Do we have some access to the ocean, or can Trencoss call an animal who doesn't even live here? For a long minute I think it isn't going to work, and then a slow wave builds around me. Frantic, I drop to the bottom of the boat and brace myself under the wooden seat as the coracle spins faster.

I rock, then fly through the air. Well balanced, the coracle stays upright, and the wooden frame takes the brunt of the crash as we hit the water again—the skin splits and I am soaked, but at the same moment hands grip the shoulders of my gúna and haul me out of the water.

"My darling bride." Trencoss grins into my face. "So glad you have returned. I have a wedding present for you."

CHAPTER THIRTY-THREE

My knees are barely balanced on the end of the rock wall, and my boat is sinking behind me. I try to wriggle away, but can't fight too hard or I will knock myself into the rocks. Still smiling, Trencoss reaches into his pocket and pulls out a torc—intricate, beautiful, and heavily jeweled.

"A pretty trinket for a pretty girl," he purrs.

Behind him, Sigma roars a battle cry. Trencoss is startled and whirls around, giving me a little extra space to haul myself fully onto the jetty.

Sigma stands to the side, yelling and waving his branch. He throws a rock, which lands nowhere near. Trencoss scrambles for his chains, but I have seen what my men are doing.

It's a distraction. From the other direction, a huge black dog bounds out of the woods.

The last wolf is getting ready to pounce on Sigma, until giant black paws scramble on the black rocks. The wolf howls as he faces his mortal enemy.

Dog-Conall and the wolf meet halfway down the rock jetty, howling and snarling and snapping teeth. Trencoss holds a silver chain in each hand, only a few steps away from me.

The struggle is brief. The huge dog has every advantage and the wolf goes down, then goes still.

Dog-Conall knocks him into the water, then bounds towards me.

Trencoss is between us! The silver chains—but before Conall can even reach him, Trencoss dissolves into gray ash, his clothes unraveling to scraps of thread, skin and muscle disintegrating into powder, only his withered skeleton collapsing in a tumble of bones.

Conall's momentum takes him straight into the mess. As soon as they collide, the bones burst into an explosion of silver. I cover my eyes from the flash of light.

Silence.

I drop my hand and stare. There is no Trencoss, not even any bones....but there is a mass of silver chain, covering Conall's dog-body every which-way, like a sewing box tipped over and spilled unwound thread. Conall is trapped underneath.

He lays on the jetty. Still and quiet.

Crying out, I run towards him, pulling the chains away and dropping them in the water. They do not pain me, but leave faint white glowing marks criss-crossed against his dark fur. So many! So heavy! I yank and throw, yank and throw.

Conall is clear now, but still does not wake, does not move. I rub his neck, kiss his muzzle, tug his silky ears.

"Ailbe!" Sigma calls, and something in his voice jerks me to attention.

He is sprawled on the beach, bracing himself up with his hands, his head hanging and his breath coming hard and rough.

"Sigma! What's wrong!" I race down the jetty and throw myself to my knees beside him, placing a hand on his forehead to try to ease his breathing. "I didn't think he touched you."

He gives me the ghost of his usual insouciant grin. "It was when I picked up Zeta. His chains touched me, too, and I've felt myself weakening every since."

"But you—you just challenged him—"

"It was fake, little princess. I could barely stand."

"But Sigma—"

"Little princess, stop crying." He lurches forward, laying on the sand. His head rests in the crook of his arm, looking up at me. "Trencoss catches his prey with the silver chains, which put us to sleep." His eyes flutter, but he manages another ragged breath. "Usually, he comes back a few hours later and transforms us to animals. Then we wake up…after that." His eyelids droop closed. He pats my knee, fingers stumbling. "We will wake, little princess."

Pause.

"We will come back to you. Just keep…your faith."

***

I pace up and down the little beach, trying to hold my hysteria at bay. Just wait, Sigma says, but how long? Hours before the change, then hours after? I check the sky; an hour or two after noon, who knows. Will the men wake before dark? Where are they? Sprawled out all over between here and the castle? What if the crows get them? What if there are real wolves in the wood?

"Birds," I say, trying to control my voice, "please do me a kindness, and go watch the men who have fallen in the woods. Don't let them get hurt."

There are a few birds within sight, but they just cock their heads at me. Either I must be next to the animals to make requests, in which case I can't possibly be next to all eighteen fallen men, or I have run out of power.

There's a splash down the jetty. I run closer.

Conall is back in his human form, but he's still out cold. Worse, he wasn't balanced well to begin with, and now his legs swung into the water. That was the noise.

The water is probably waist-high below the rocks where he is laying. Not deep for a conscious person, but if he falls then he will drown. The men are wearing leather armor that pulls them down. I see Zeta vanishing into the water, over and over again. I press my hands against my eyes and try to make myself remember the next part; Sigma lifting him out, safe and sound.

But I can't lift Conall. I am too small.

So I run down the jetty and try to pull him back onto the rocks. I manage to drag him sideways a little, ripping his léine and probably his skin, but that's doing no good. I pull at his legs but can't get any traction.

So I go in the water and try to push him up from below. I get one of his legs up, but then an arm dangles over. Oh no! If his torso tips, that is much heavier, and if his head hits the rocks then it could smash him like a turnip.

I try from above, but I'm scaring myself that I'm going to nudge him over. His center of gravity is too far over, and he's too long and lanky. I run through all the available animals in my mind, but they are all small, and most frighten easily.

Zeta! Is he all right? I run back to shore and check on the others. Zeta is clammy and frigid, and there are crows hopping around Pi's body. I shoo them away, terrified for all the others. The crows won't do any damage to bodies that are still warm and twitching, but eventually, carrion animals will come. Certainly by dark. When will my men wake?

I run back. Zeta is blue with cold. Conall's arm is sagging off the rocks. I pull it back, and his foot tips.

"Help!" I wail. "Please. Who is out there? Please!"

My voice echoes off the water, the otters tilting their heads in question.

I sink into the sand and shiver.

Behind me, there's a crashing in the bush, as large a bear. Horrified, I leap to my feet and spin around—

And I face Rho, his sword upheld. Phi, Alpha, Iota, Mu and Nu are in steady formation behind him.

"Little princess!" Alpha calls, and I run to him.

CHAPTER THIRTY-FOUR

After searching for us all day, Rho and his men are angry that they missed standing beside their comrades in battle, but I am delighted that they showed up exactly when they did. They are fresh and strong, possessed of all their iron and entirely human. Rho has always been steady and logical, and he soon calms me down. He reminds me that nothing dangerous comes out until dark, which is still some hours away, and he sets all his men to tasks before I can even collect my thoughts.

They lay Conall on the grass above the beach, where the suns shines warm and gentle, and Zeta next to him, covering their still bodies with their own wool cloaks. They light a bonfire and tell me to tend to it. Already, another pair is headed up the hill to bring back the others, and bringing cloaks so they can carry the bodies without touching the chains. Rho makes me drink water from his flask and eat a handful of berries, then sends someone to my camp by the willow tree. Iota returns with porridge and blankets and dry clothes for me, and I am better with something useful to do.

Mu and Nu come back with Tau's wrapped body swaying between them.

"Went all the way back to the gates," Mu says.

"Better to get those ones first," Nu adds.

"Castle's falling," Mu reports.

"*What?*" I demand.

"Trencoss's castle?" Rho asks, calmer than I. When the men grunt agreement, he continues. "It figures. It was full of things that don't belong in this place, so it must've been held up with sorcerous magic. Without Trencoss, it's all coming down."

"What about the people inside?" I cry.

Mu and Nu look at each other and shrug.

"Aren't none," says Mu.

"Left ages ago," adds Nu.

"That's how we guessed you were here," Rho explains. "We saw a long line of servants streaming out the back gate, staggering under packs, their arms full of everything they could carry. We guessed that you had been there, drawn Trencoss out, and had some sort of confrontation."

"Definitely," says Mu.

"They're all gone," Nu concludes.

They both bob their heads and head back up for the next body.

By late afternoon, they've lined up all nineteen sleeping men on the grass. I've fed everyone, gotten Zeta and Conall warm and dry, and did my best to brace Xi's badly swollen leg and tend the few other minor injuries.

"Do you think they'll wake by nightfall?" I ask Rho.

He's staring at the long line while his men take a breather. "I think they've gotta have those chains off them. Trencoss did it as part of the changing ceremony. I never saw him do it, exactly, but we saw animals come in before and after."

The chains are delicate but strong, more the size of what a man would wear for a pendent than the chain on a gate.

"I've tried," I admit. "With Conall, they were just laying on top of him, but all the others, they've snaked around and bound themselves up tight. It's almost like they're alive."

Rho has Phi put on gloves and try, since he has the strongest hands, but he doesn't have any better luck than I do.

Alpha crouches by the line of men, rocking back on his heels. "What about those little flying guys? The one messing with my collar had a bit of silver that looked like this."

Iota laughs. "Mine was wearing pins and needles, all twisted into loops and—you're right!"

I'm already working on it. "Little flyers!" I cry. "I have a favor to ask, and I have a price to pay. Come and treat with me, little winged ones."

There is nothing; we are far from their home, after all. The men help me, wandering back and forth and calling the ritual words. I'm not sure if they can do it, but I can see they're all proud of themselves for being part of something important.

Finally, a sleepy-looking moth-woman emerges. She perches on a twig and glares at me.

::Your last task was too big:: she complains. ::We spent half the night searching the forest. And it was so dark!:: She shivers in disgust.

"Thank you so much for your help. You are truly the heroes of our tale."

She nods, apparently mollified. ::Fine. But we won't do something so difficult again.::

"I hope this will be easy for—"

::Unless you have lots of needles:: she adds. ::We liked your needles.::

"Ah—good. I haven't any needles just now. But look at this. Do you like these chains?"

Her eyes burst open wide, and she darts to perch on Delta's elbow and examine his chains. ::Very sparkly! Real silver! Very nice! We have, we have a little bit? How much you give us? Give give give!::

Half a dozen more little flyers emerge from the woods.

I spread my hands. "You may have all of it. All of the silver chain that is wrapped around all of these men."

::Nineteen? We count nineteen! How many chains? So many links of chain!::

"Yes, all the chain that is wrapped around their legs or feet or arms or wrists."

::Count men! Count men! Make bargain!::

::Wait.:: The moth-woman crosses her arms. ::For this, what favor we give? You ask big, big work?::

I shrug. "I just want you to take away the chain, and all of its magic if you know how. That's all I'm asking. You can have all the chain for that."

They swoop back and forth in giant happy clouds, and I feel their appreciation and loyalty pulsing around me. I formally touch each man they are allowed to divest of chains, and they sweep down with tiny tools.

When I return to Rho, he nudges my elbow. "You could have had them in your debt for years for that," he says. "Say you store up one favor against each man in chains. They want the silver; you're not making them do anything for it."

"I suppose so," I admit. "But if I stored favors, they would always be wary what would ask and when. This way, they will be eager to come back next time."

"That's the truth," he agrees. "You'll barely have to sneeze and have a dozen flyers demanding work."

I laugh, and we get back to work. The men rig a shelter, using some live trees and cutting some new ones, framing in a roof and walls with long strappy branches and returning with bundles of twigs and reeds to fill it in. By the time dusk is falling, we have a simple three-sided structure, open to the lake, with a hole so we can light a fire inside. The men bring supplies from the castle to supplement what was leftover from Conall's and my camp. Another group comes down from the castle.

"It's all for the taking." Iota shrugs, dropping a bundle of blankets wrapped around kitchenware. "The servants already took what they could, more blessings to them, and some of it is ruined as the walls fall in. But there's plenty enough to furnish a dozen houses for our little princess." He nods at me.

"I don't need a dozen houses," I protest, thinking about how Conall wanted one.

"It's a good point," Rho says. "With Trencoss gone, there's a change of power in this valley. Ailbe is well positioned to take it over, seeing as she can talk to all the animals. It seems to be mostly animals here."

"Since Trencoss has probably been in control for hundreds of years," Alpha agrees. "Wow, did those bones ever vanish fast! He was old!"

We found the skull and a tibia—or rather, the otters did. The state his body would be in, had it met a natural end.

"Talking to the animals isn't enough reason to be the lord of a whole valley," I protest, but I'm thinking of the little flyers, and the silver, and the islands on the lake with Fae who didn't trick me. I haven't done so badly.

"Better ally yourself with someone trained as a warrior and a diplomat, then." Rho nudges me with a wink.

"Maybe you could find a prince and marry him." Alpha laughs. "If he's handsome enough, eh?"

"Just make sure he's from a wealthy kingdom," Iota adds.

"I think you already know who Conall really is," I say, and the men all burst into laughter.

But it gives me an idea.

***

The sun sends streaks of red and orange across the lake, interrupted by black streaks where the ducks land on the water.

My body feels the same way. Each joint is throbbing with red and orange, black cords gripping my lungs. Each movement threatens to incinerate me, my head as heavy as the jetty's rocks.

But I stir the pot and swing it back over the fire, turn the fish on a stone glowing with heat. Phi and Iota return from their last trip to the ruined castle, handing me a stack of fine china bowls for our lumpy stew. Just seven, for Rho's troop and myself. The last little flyers coil up their bounty and vanish into the dusk, while the other nineteen men still sleep. My fear on their behalf pains me more than all the aches that besiege my body.

I brace a hand on my lower back before I bend to serve. The salmon has slid to the curved center of our grilling stone, and the pot bubbles ominously. Mu groans as he stands to help me pass the plates around.

"We'll assign night watches in pairs," Rho announces. "Who can manage the first shift?"

"You have forgotten my bowl," someone complains. "How can anyone work without food?"

"I'm sorry." I reach for the pile, but none are left. "I served all seven."

"I don't care how many you served, I want some of that fish."

We all stare into the shadows. Perched on a stump, twitching just the tip of his tail, sits Bob.

I slide the last of the fire-grilled fish onto my own bowl of stew and place it in front of him, gathering my composure as tightly as a cloak. "Of course. I am always pleased to welcome you to our fireside, Your Catness."

"Hmph." Bob's tail twitches faster. "I never told you to call me that."

I hide a smile. "Welcome, Bob Ye Gurt Fool."

"Better." He settles in front of the bowl, sniffing and then snatching his tongue back from the heat.

"You need to eat, too, little princess," Rho growls.

I settle on the bench, ignoring him. "Have you had a pleasant day?" I ask Bob.

Rho snorts.

"Kind of you to ask." Bob whips his tail. "I'm a bit strung out. You'll never believe what happened!"

"Dear me! What could it be?"

Bob whimpers. "My very favorite place to take a nap—it's gone! No more than a pile of rubble!"

"A pile…was it in that castle? Up there?" I gesture up the hill, because Bob has a perfectly fine castle in the middle of the lake.

"Alas!" Bob blinks in misery. "The foot of your bed! The kitchen windowsill! The soft red pillow warmed by the sunlight at approximately one hour and twelve minutes after noon! All gone, alas and alack."

I drop my eyes. "Do you happen to know why?"

Bob licks his nose, shifts his feet, and then speaks crisply. "Trencoss's power was tied into the animals. Once the last beast under his spell was gone, there was nothing to tether him. He would have died centuries ago if he didn't have them keeping him going."

"What about the poor transformed wolves? Did the men have families and—"

Bob sneezes. "Scoundrels and thieves, every one. Trencoss usually had better taste, but I suppose he was a bit desperate, what with all his dogs running off at once."

Rho chuckles, and Alpha high-fives the men on either side.

"It's nothing to laugh about," Bob scolds. "Now my napping places are ruined, and there's no one to cook me fish."

"I am cooking you fish," I remind him.

Bob humphs agreement, and hunches back down to eat.

"Iota caught it just this afternoon." I realize what needs to be done. "Would you like me to throw a ball for you, when you are done eating?"

"I'll build up the fire," Alpha adds, winking at me.

"Delightful, delightful," Bob mumbles through his mouthful.

I have not the slightest idea how our humble fire and burnt fish is better than Bob's marble castle, but I'll do whatever it takes to win him to our side. After he's devoured the last of the salmon and the men find items for me to toss, and Bob pounces and bats until he can barely stand, I finally dare ask the Fae for something in return.

"Bob, you sweet kitty"—I stroke his back as he kneads my lap—"do you happen to see these men all lined up on the grass?"

"Of course I do. My night vision is much better than yours."

"Your night vision is wonderful, just like your skill at dismembering dried leaves."

He purrs mightily.

"The thing is, they won't wake up. Bob, my delightful Catness, do you know how to awaken the men who were captured in Trencoss's chains?"

Bob hops off my lap and prances over to the closest sleeping warrior, tail held high. He sniffs Tau's ear, then walks down his body and bats the end of his crios.

"Haven't the foggiest idea." Bob sits down to wash his belly.

"But…" I'm so frustrated I struggle to contain myself. "Sir…"

Bob lifts a paw to lick under his arm more vigorously.

I bite my lip and try to breathe. The men sacrificed themselves for me, I must help them, I must find the right words—

"Good friend Bob!" Alpha swaggers between us, throwing himself on the grass beside Tau and Bob. "Look at Ailbe, there. Lovely girl, isn't she?"

Bob blinks his big eyes at me.

Alpha cups his hand as though he is telling secrets. "Let's take care of our Ailbe, shall we? So she can make us more dinners and brush our fur?"

"Mm, brush our fur!" Iota yells.

I blush and swat at him, and he grabs my hand and laughs. It helps. The worst of my anger bubbles away with his teasing.

When I look back up, Bob is accepting an ear-rub from Alpha, who is murmuring encouragement.

"What happened to the silver?" Bob suggests. "One or two of those enchanted chains. That's all it would take."

"Take for what?" Rho demands, swinging to his feet. "You can wake them after all?"

Bob butts his forehead against Alpha's shoulder. "I told you, I can't. But give me a chain and I'll do something else."

Rho turns to me.

"I haven't got a chain!" To my own horror, I stamp my foot and burst into tears.

All the men are horrified by my emotion, too. I cover my face, shoulders shaking with pure rage. I can just hear Rho saying *you shouldn't have given them away,* although he doesn't say any such thing.

"Look!" Phi shouts.

I lift my hands as a different emotion presses against me, from the outside this time. Frustration tinged with pity.

::You can have this one:: the mouse-man grumbles. ::You gave us more than the bargain required.::

::You owe us a favor later!:: a winged snake adds, as they both sweep through the clearing.

There's a clatter at my feet. I jump back as two silver chains hit the sizzling stone where the fish was cooking.

"Of course! Thank you!" I yell to the little flyers, staring at the chains. They leap and dance like cold butter in a pan, melting before my very eyes. Should I grab them? Before I know it, it's nothing but a pool of liquid silver.

"That's right," Bob says, perfectly calm. "Now pour it out. Best if it touches a tree."

I have no idea how to accomplish this, but the men are undaunted. Now that the instructions are clear, they are determined to find a solution. It takes them some time to manage the heavy, hot stone; full dark falls, while I flutter around nervously and Bob flicks his tail and enjoys the show. I expect the silver to sink into the ground, but it spreads into a smooth, wide puddle.

"Is it cool?" Bob paces closer, each paw in a careful line, tail held high. "Wait a minute. No, longer."

The men flop down, leaning against trees and shaking out their arms. Rho lights a torch and props it nearby.

We wait. And wait. I worry about all the sleeping men, and particularly about Conall. I was tired and unreasonable last night, and we have barely spoken today. What if I never have a chance to tell him how much I love him? Because after a day of fear, my feelings are as clear as glass and as strong as the mountains.

What's more, Conall proved his feelings for me, too. His pretty words last night were one thing, but this afternoon, he faced his worst fear to save me. For Conall, his dog form is the cruelest trap, but when he saw me in danger he chose his dog form in order to save me. I need to tell him that I saw, I know; I will never lose faith in him again.

"Now," Bob declares at last. "Ailbe, lean over and see what you can see."

The night presses against me. I never used to be afraid of the dark, or perhaps it was simply that I was always with Acushla, but I don't like it tonight. Rho adjusts the torch to shine onto the puddle, casting light into his tired face. I glance around, between the men and the cat and the silver smudge.

"Go ahead," Bob tells me. "It won't hurt. I have no idea whether it will help or not. That's up to you."

This makes no sense, but I will do anything for Conall and the men. Gathering my cloak closer, I creep towards the puddle and lean over.

"Tell us what you see," Rho says, after a long minute passes.

"It isn't anything," I report. "Just—well, my own face. My hair is messy. It's essentially a mirror, but on the ground."

I put my hand to my head, smoothing the mess...but there's something unusual about it. Almost glowing. As though my hair were golden.

And my eyes were blue.

And my hands were white.

"Saba!" I scream, and she steps out from the mirror, her little boy on her hip, and right into my arms.

CHAPTER THIRTY-FIVE

Whether or not Saba is still the princess or deserves to be the princess, she knows how to manage people.

Everyone needs to tell Saba what happened. Oisín needs to play peek-a-boo. Bob needs to go back to his marble palace and take a nap. Saba needs to examine the comatose men. According to Saba and Rho, I need to eat my dinner and get some rest. The whole scene is pure chaos for a while, but before I know it, I'm warm and full and in a proper bed in the little house, Oisín tucked up next to me; the men are taking their night shifts; and Saba has headed into the forest, singing and praying.

I try to pray, too, begging the goddesses of the forest and the hearth to return my love to me...

But before I know it, our hut is bright and Oisín is crawling on top of me.

"Go play?" he asks, his nose mere inches from mine. "Go auntie play?"

I squeeze his little body into my fluffy blankets, kissing his neck to make him giggle. I'm so delighted that he has learned who I am through our mirror conversations that I put aside all my other worries to focus on the toddler. We wash and dress, then find his mother sitting by the fire with Mu and Nu.

"They're waking," Saba tells me. Her eyes are shadowed and her shoulders slumped with exhaustion, but her smile is bright. "When they sit up, I'm giving them water and a little gruel."

"Then they sack out again," Mu says.

"Kip down," Nu adds.

"Hit the hay," Mu agrees.

"Anyways," Saba interrupts, with the tone of a woman who has been involved in a conversation like this for the entire guard shift, "this time the sleep is natural."

We prepare to switch off, as we have done so many times before. She shows me the remedies she has on hand and walks me down the line of patients, informing me who isn't allowed to put weight on their leg and who needs a dose for a fever. We fall into our rhythm easily, despite all the time apart and how much our lives have changed. This time, Saba has to add instructions for what Oisín likes for breakfast, and a whole litany of rules to keep him out of trouble, and especially out of the lake.

Rho is serving himself porridge with a nest of uncombed hair. "Don't you worry," he interrupts Saba. "I've raised four of the little buggers. No one drowned themselves yet."

"Maybe I should keep him with me..." Saba yawns.

"Nonsense. Lad's better off with all these eyes on him."

Oisín, though, is afraid of the big warriors. He's willing to come to me, but hides his face in my skirts whenever the men try to speak to him. Saba watches, her mouth tight, but goes to bed without another word.

The morning is wonderful. As the enchanted men awaken, we repeat the scene over and over—laughter, clapping backs, hugging and shouting. I prepare pot after pot of food and remedies, happy to care for each of my beloved friends. Everyone tells the story of defeating Trencoss over and over, sharing their own special part and demanding more details from others.

"That's how I had the extra moment to escape!" they shout, or "that's how Ailbe got down there!" They pound each other, enthusiastic in their mutual praise.

But Conall doesn't wake up.

"Everyone's on a different schedule," Saba reassures me, when she emerges around noon. "He had more chains than the others. Or the transformation to and from his dog form took more of his energy."

"He'll be back with us soon! Raring to go!" Alpha claps me on the shoulder.

"Ready to get a kiss from his pretty new wife." Delta gives me an exaggerated wink.

But he isn't. The hours pass, and Conall lays stiff and cold. Although Saba finds his pulse easily, his heartbeat is so faint that I can't hear it, and that unnerves me. I know he is alive. I understand that with my mind. But from the very first day that we tumbled Between together, when I had lost everything I had ever known and loved and he kept me warm all night—from that moment until now, his heart has always anchored me. *Because it beats for you,* my Acushla told me. *I am yours. Please keep me.*

I lay my head on his chest for the twentieth time this afternoon.

"He's still alive," Saba tells me.

"I know," I answer—but I've lost him.

"Come away." Saba pulls my hand gently. "Help me sort this load from the castle. We need to see what else they should bring."

I let Saba lead me, because of course I must do my share of the work, not just cling to Conall all day. While I've been trying to disenchant him, the men have been making decisions. The meadow where Conall and I camped is the best one, they tell me. I thought they're just setting up more tents, but when I arrive with an armload of clothes I find a dozen men humming around the framework for two houses. No, three.

"The others will be up there in the woods." Zeta loops an arm over my shoulders to show me. "Good look-out from that perspective."

"More privacy," Tau adds.

Iota emerges from the forest, leading a donkey with a cart full of blacksmithing materials.

"He knows how to run a forge," Zeta tells me proudly. "See, we have everything we need."

Except Conall.

***

I am determined to wake Conall. I must come up with the answer. I will do whatever it takes, even if I have to row a boat.

"Rowing a coracle won't help anything, little princess," Sigma tells me, fetching me from where I am spinning in useless circles in my mind.

"He can't hear you," Zeta reminds me, as I sing every song and say every prayer I can think over Conall's inert form

"He doesn't need to eat or drink," Saba tells me for the twentieth time. "It's an enchanted sleep. He will wake feeling just exactly as he fell asleep."

"She's right, you know," adds Beta, who remained enchanted for the longest. "It doesn't hurt. He doesn't feel hunger or pain."

I do. I have made it through so much pain, and this is what will break me.

They put him in the bed beside me, in the little three-sided house. I will keep him warm and beloved forever, but this is worse than being alone.

***

Whether or not Conall is awake or I am worried about him, everyone else is planning how to manage life in the valley without Trencoss.

Fergus comes by. He kisses my cheek and negotiates with Theta for supplies. He is going off to seek his fortune on some other quest, and offers to visit Fionn on my behalf. I stare at him in confusion.

"He made promises to your husband, didn't he?" Fergus reminds me. "You said he would make good on them."

"He sold you," Saba adds crisply. "You might as well claim your payment."

"We could use his help," Rho adds. "Sooner or later, someone with more than twenty-four soldiers is going to come into this valley and swallow us up."

"No one will swallow the ally of Fionn mac Cumhaill," Theta growls.

So I wish Fergus could stay, but I won't keep him away from his own destiny. I wish I could be excited about the village the men are building for me as Fergus is for his next adventure.

At mid-day, Zeta takes his troop up to the Castle of a Thousand Doors, and I must go too.

"You need to tell us what to do, little princess," he tells me.

"You need to visit the animals," Saba adds. "You can't ignore them any longer."

I'm not ignoring anyone! I'm watching over Conall. I'm assisting Saba with her remedies. I'm minding Oisín, who just got caught on a thorn-bush. Zeta ignores my protests and brings me along.

Everything looks normal at the front gate, and my heart clenches as we re-enter this gilded prison. I catch sight of a tower—is this a trick to catch me again?—but the connecting wall is tipped over, a pile of rubble where the entrance was. The next wing looks like a block tower after a child wandered away; not fully destroyed, but casually ruined.

"The working rooms are around the back," Phi says. "You'll need to check what we'll need for our kitchen and dairy."

"No, she needs to go to the throne rooms first," Beta argues. "She could feel if any of the royal objects are connected to the land."

"Or valuable in trade," Iota adds.

"Look sharp," Zeta interrupts, his voice low. "Formation."

The six men fall behind me. In my confusion, I draw myself up tall, my chin held high. It turns out to be the right thing to do, for the other group falls into respectful bows. They are six, a mix of elder men and younger ones bearing axes and knives. Their inari are dyed deep colors and well embroidered, but worn and faded, and their faces are pinched and lined. This is an honor delegation from the ordinary folk, the small villages—and they haven't being thriving lately.

I nod my head graciously. I understand the rules here.

The man in the center comes forward. He nods at Zeta and lifts his hands to show they are empty.

"You have defeated our liege," the headman announces. "Who do you send to replace Trencoss?"

"You behold our lady," Zeta answers. "She is wise and brave, and speaks for us all."

I merely incline my head again, not allowing my uncertainty to show.

The villagers mutter among themselves. "She is one who planted the Three Trees of Freedom?" one asks.

"We are inclined already to trust her," the headman explains. "For years, Trencoss has stolen our young people to work for him, and it is bitter to lose them."

The men all thump their chests, three rhythmic blows.

"I did plant the trees," I say.

They approve, and Zeta offers some kind of signal, which they all approve more. There is more thumping and kneeling and shouting, which I accept with cool graciousness.

It is all fake. Inside, I am alone and frightened.

"The Lady has the magic of this place," the headman says, once they have settled again, "but what about our villages? She cannot call her rabbits and owls to defend us from autumn raids and winter rains."

Iota howls and beats his breast, and I manage to avoid jumping out of my skin as Phi and Kappa follow suit.

"For that, she has ourselves," Zeta answers.

More howling. Gracious, this man stuff is peculiar.

"Furthermore," Zeta adds, "our Lady is married to the strongest warrior of us all."

"We were the wolfhounds who patrolled the grounds," Iota adds.

"You were very strong," the headman says in approval.

"We are still," Upsilon brags, and they're off on some sort of congratulatory clapping and grunting. My mind is still stuck on the husband part, but this seems to be enough for the villagers.

"Her husband was a prince in the north," Zeta half-shouts over the hubbub. "He knows what to do."

"We will prepare the fealty ceremony," says another villager, with the rings of a magistrate. "We have our list of requirements, and your Lady and her prince may make theirs."

What is supposed to go into a list of requirements? Taxes, men at arms, we're on a lake so they'll be boats—but I know that there can be dozens of points. I don't mind terms favorable to the villagers, who clearly have been barely surviving, but I know better than to promise something we can't deliver. Except I have no idea what that is.

I stand quietly, a little smile on my face, accepting any bows or salutes. They're sharing stories of the battle now, and what happened all over the valley when the castle crumbled.

The oldest man steps towards me, putting his hands out flat for silence. He receives it, immediately.

"This valley is not just our human villages," he says, his voice rasping with age. "We are the least among them."

Zeta gestures to me. "She is favored by Bob, His Catness."

"Has she attended a party in the palace in the middle of the lake?" asks the old man.

"She has," Iota answers proudly. "She ate the tiny foods and saw a waterfall on the wall."

The villagers nod and murmur, as though they expect this.

"His Catness is not the only Good Neighbor," the old man says. "Has she spoken with the people of the Fruit Islands?"

I curtsey. "I had a conversation with a princess, but I declined her gifts."

The villagers chuckle and elbow each other. "Clearly, she lived to tell the tale."

"They are the great ones, but what about the small?" the old man asks.

"We were animals in the castle," Zeta answers. "She remembered the mice in the walls and spoke with the birds in the trees."

"I was at the lake when she faced off against the sorcerer himself," Upsilon declares. "The fish and the herons did her bidding."

"And they come to her for the joy of it," Iota adds.

The old man nods. "It has been too long since they have had any joy of it. But I am nothing but a messenger; one small man with some small power of talking to the beasts of the field. Lady, you will have to bargain with the Dobhar-chú and the other guardians. They will feel the disturbance, and come to check on their little ones."

I have heard tales of the vengeance of the King Otter, but instead of being afraid, for the first time I am curious. I wonder what other Guardians will come to the lake.

I bow my head to the old man. "I would like to talk with the Dobhar-chú, and any other such who wishes to visit me."

"You are not afraid?" asks the headman.

"I have survived Trencoss. I am quite sure the Dobhar-Chú is more reasonable than many men I know."

The men laugh and cheer. We spend another hour or so walking about, the men giving each other challenges and promises, short discussions to resolve the more urgent of the questions around the fallen castle. We don't have time to do any of the things that my men wanted me to do, and I'm relieved to escape.

I shouldn't be so lazy. Everyone is working hard, and I have never shirked my part.

But I want to run all the way down the hill, straight into Conall's arms, where he will hold me and laugh and say everything will be all right.

When we finally get back, sweaty and my feet hurting, Conall is laying where we left him. On my bed in the lean-to, like a statue of my love. I still can't find his heartbeat.

***

"Will you be all right here by yourself?" Saba crouches beside me on the sand, watching the moonlight glisten on the water.

"Yes." My voice is sharp with exhaustion. "My animal friends are not large, but they will call the warriors before anything can go wrong."

The main camp is not far, and our feet have already worn a broad path. Oisín fell asleep listening to stories around the fire, and Alpha put him to bed in the one completed house, so of course Saba must go there for the night.

"You could come with us." Saba's tone says she knows I won't.

"Conall might wake in the night." I stretch my back, twisting to the side. "I won't leave."

"He might," Saba agrees.

Her optimism never wavers. I am not sure if she believes he will wake any moment, or just wants me to.

"The lake is beautiful." Saba sighs, settling into the sand. "I'll sit with you for another few minutes." She squeezes my hand.

"I only regret each minute I do not spend with you," I admit. "When do you—must you—when you go back?"

Saba is silent for a long time. "I am in such fear of bringing the Dark Man upon you, Ailbe. But I stayed in the Italian library for nearly a year before he found me."

"I *want* you to stay." I know that isn't the way we women make decisions, but I say it anyways.

"Oisín comes back in the tales, later. I learned that in the library. Fionn finds him in the woods when he is an older boy, and my child becomes a bard and a warrior."

"So you must keep him safe. So he can go back to Fionn and become a bard."

"Yes..." Her voice is heavy with uncertainty. "But I must raise him the right way. He is too shy, Ailbe. He has only been around women and old men for his whole life. Telling him stories about warriors isn't the same as living among them."

"So..." My heart rises like a kite on the warm breeze. "You will stay?"

"For a little while," she agrees. "While it's safe for—"

I throw my arms around her, making her gasp and we both giggle.

"I don't care if it's one week or a year! Any time you stay is better than if you leave. I will treasure every moment."

"I treasure you, too, Ailbe, my sister."

We cling for a minute, but then I sit back up, my mind whirling. "And if you stay—well, some of the dog-men are so nice, aren't they? Fionn has already remarried, so you are free and you could—"

Saba peals with laughter. "Ailbe, stop it. The men are for Oisín, not me."

"I know your first marriage wasn't perfect, but"—I can see it all, our lives stretching out together—"you could stay here, and these men would be loyal and defend you from the Dark Man. Sigma is always thoughtful, or I saw you looking at Omikron. He is fine and strong, isn't he?"

"I was looking to see if he limps," Saba answers. "He is handsome and Sigma is kind, but they are not for me."

"But they'd defend—"

Saba waves her hand, dismissing me. "As for the Dark Man, we will see what we will see. The stories only say what happens to Oisín, not to me."

And they say that he will return to his father. What a painful way to raise a child, knowing you will lose him.

"So you might find love."

"You are enough love for me." Saba squeezes my hand again. "Seriously, stop this! You are all full of excitement about your own marriage, and wanting the same feelings for everyone else. But I've been married."

"Not everyone is like Fionn," I protest.

"Of course not. I promise, Ailbe, I am happy without a man. I prefer my life this way."

"But if—"

"I prefer my life this way," Saba repeats firmly.

I take a slow breath of the night air. I know, really, that she can't stay forever. But we will have this time together, and then maybe we will find each other again.

"Maybe we will be old women together," I say.

"Once we have *both* raised our children," she agrees.

I need Conall if I am ever going to have children. I bid Saba goodnight, watching her pale léine vanish into the dark woods, and enter the lean-to. I undress slowly, dreading the next part. I have kissed Conall, wept over him, sung to him, made every enchantment of love and womanhood that any of us can imagine. I will treasure him to the end of my days, no matter what, but I want him to speak to me. His laughter. I need him.

In nothing but my tunica, my braids down my back, I slide beneath the soft sheets. I kiss him quickly, keeping all my emotions inside. I have so much to do, and there is no time for foolish hysterics.

I turn away and adjust my limbs so I am not touching his body, strangely cold and absolutely still. I pull the blankets up to my chin and stare at the lake, sparkling in the moonlight, until I fall asleep.

Chapter Thirty-Six

There's light against my eyelids.

Cold air on my nose.

A warm arm across my waist. I'm not sure it's possible, so I don't dare move or open my eyes in case it's all a dream. I think a body is curled around me, not laying stiff like a corpse. I think that's breathing tickling my hair. I think that's the smell of skin and the tang of masculine sweat.

Still without letting my eyes so much as flutter, I tuck my own hand under the blanket, so it drifts down towards my waist. I stretch just a little bit, a kind of half-asleep twitch.

There are definitely legs behind mine. My hands stumble the rest of the way down and settle over long fingers—not Saba's, not Oisín's—which give my waist a little squeeze in response.

"You're awake?"

His voice startles me, lower and smoother than I remembered. All the time we have spent together, and he has spoken so little. I manage a sort of strangled "hm" in reply.

"Did you *see* him explode like that? Wasn't it something?"

Apparently Conall is wide awake and full of enthusiasm. I blink rapidly, letting my eyes get used to the pale dawn across the lake, while he energetically describes his battle with the wolf and the explosion of the sorcerer. He's talking as though the whole thing concluded not five minutes ago, and although I watched the other men and understand that the enchantment makes them feel that way, the past three days roll over me like cold waves. Losing him. Fear. Alone, alone, alone.

"The wind was coming from the north-west"—he gestures so vigorously that our blanket flaps—"but the trees were blocking my view to the south, and I figured that the jetty was—"

I roll over in his arms and press my mouth against his. Hard.

For just a moment, he's still and I'm afraid he's upset that I wasn't listening to the story. But then his lips open and his arms encircle me, pulling me close, cradling my head. He is gentle, but everything is exploding inside of me and it's not enough. I'm angry and scared and amazed and confused, and I hook my knee over his leg and press into him. His arms are warm and hard under my fingers and I pull him so close I can feel his teeth under my lips, and none of it is what I want but I want everything.

Conall's hand goes steady against my face, and he shifts me in his arms and breaks the kiss.

"Mavourneen," he breathes, and before I have the chance to cry out in frustration he kisses me again. His kiss is firm and his mouth opens mine, and now as I lean into him he is hot and steady and strong. His breath is mine, his tongue touches mine, his fingers press into my back and weave into my hair.

It's enough to balance my desperation, this chaos pounding inside of me. We pull apart, staring at each other, faces inches apart. My lips are throbbing and my breath tumbles fast. I've memorized his every human feature in this last three days, mapping every inch of his face as though I am about to lose it forever, but everything is different now that it is lit from inside.

"Ailbe, my Mavourneen." Conall brushes hair back from my forehead. "I don't know how I ended up laying here beside you, but there is nowhere I would rather be."

I try to answer, but end up making a sad sort of squeak and pressing my face into his shoulder.

He cradles me, but at the same time rolls onto his back, and I feel the impatient energy twitching in him. After all, he's gotten plenty of rest.

"I must have been out all night. Don't know how that happened, but I know just the thing. Feeling musty."

Conall squeezes my shoulders and jumps out of bed. The cold air hits me as the blanket flaps away, and I gasp.

He laughs. "Rise and shine, my little beauty."

But I'm not beautiful, I'm unfeminine and *intimidating*. I open my mouth to ask him—something—but he chuckles and taps my nose.

"You like the mornings, Mavourneen. Come with me. Wait." His brow furrows in suspicion. "Are you hurt? Did he hurt you?"

"No—not at all." I swing my own feet onto the floor. "I'm just a little stiff—and so much happened at once."

The other men woke up ready for stories but Conall is all an explosion of action. I reach for my léine but he chuckles and grabs my hand, pulling me out the open side of our lean-to.

"Come on, Ailbe! Look at this beautiful day!" He swings his free hand, leading me towards the water. "No sorcerer, no dogs, no nonsense! Remember when we first got here? Our first view of the lake?" He turns, smiling at me, head cocked. "You said you could look at this view every morning for the rest of your life. Do you remember?"

I nod, oddly shy. I thought I was just chattering to a dog. I said so much that I wouldn't have shared with another person, and I can't even remember what he knows about me.

He leans down and kisses me lightly. "You were so happy, I wanted to tell you that I would give you this lake. I would make you the home of your dreams, right here."

"Under the willow," I whisper.

"I couldn't do any of it then." The hard edge comes into his voice. "But I can now. I'm glad I have fortune, so I can give you everything."

"We'll stay here—"

"Do you know what else I wanted to do?" He flashes a grin, drops my hand, and runs forward. "This! I always wanted to run and—"

He races down the shallow slope towards the jetty, hopping out of his trews and flinging off his shirt between strides. I trot after, laughing for the joy of the morning and his own bright enthusiasm.

Conall's bare feet hit the jetty and he runs forward in great leaps, soaring past all the remembered dangers. At the end, he arcs into the air, a parabola of masculine power and grace—then a distant splash.

Zeta told me to do the thing that had scared me. I follow my husband down the rocks, my breath ragged with fear. I can't help looking for scattered bones, scars that the enchanted chains burned into the stone. A bird splashes and I startle as though it is a wolf.

Nothing happens. The lake has healed itself. I shouldn't be afraid; I am the Lady of the Lake now, or the Lady of the Forest. I will serve the birds and animals here the way I served Bodhbh Dearg and Fionn. Remembering my duty makes me stronger, and I make it all the way to sit at the end of the pier, pulling my knees up to my chest.

Conall is bathing with a great deal of splashing. He rubs himself with handfuls of sand, darting under the water and leaping out like a whale, reaching his arms for powerful strokes into the lake and somersaulting underwater to return to me. I wrap my arms around my knees and smile at his antics.

"I feel awfully muddle-headed," he admits, sweeping his arms to get his feet under him. He shakes his head and droplets fly out of his curls, sparkling in the early morning sun. "And I was stinking! Never felt this strange after sleeping all night."

"It was longer," I say.

"So what happened? Tell me your story, Mavourneen."

The water goes up to the top of his chest when he is standing here, and I'm flustered watching him. Of course I have seen naked men before; the warriors wash in their courtyard and the head women manage the baths. But I've never been before one like this, nowhere for my eyes to go but the way the cords of his neck connect into his broad shoulders, the little waves plashing back and forth against his muscles.

It's the strangest way I've told the story to one of the disenchanted men, my own feelings swirling through me in joy and desire and confusion. The story has gotten longer, too, in the last couple of days. I try to get through what is needed, but not say too much. I don't want to brag.

No...I don't want to sound too important. Like another one of the men, tough and brave. I want to be feminine for Conall.

"So they are building our house. They want us to stay..." My voice trails into silence. I shiver, wearing nothing but my tunica. My feet are narrow and soft against the dark rock, and I rub my thumb across the arch.

Fergus implied that being feminine is the opposite of being brave, but what I want with Conall is more than desiring his attraction.

For all these years, I have done what needs to be done. I have been brisk and obedient and strong, and if I'm going to manage a kingdom here in this valley I will have to be all those things—even just a kingdom of birds and animals and little flyers and flowers that bloom in any season they want.

Conall could be my lord and master, stepping up to the role he was born into, and using my skills to advance his power. He could be my partner, each of us working tirelessly with our different strengths to lead and improve. But I want...I want...

I look up, surprised to find him standing right in front of me. His eyes are fixed on my face, his expression thoughtful.

I want to be vulnerable with him. When he went through those monster transformations and I was terrified, and he comforted me afterwords—when I leaned against him in the dark and he stroked my hair—that felt good. Not the way I felt, but sharing it with him.

It felt better than our last night in the campsite, when I was ashamed how his parents treated me and fearful that he had betrayed me with the pretty princess, but I held it all in because I wanted to be sensible and strong. Because it felt like giving him too much to admit how I felt.

"What's wrong, Mavourneen?" Conall rests his wet arms on the rock on either side of me.

I try to pull all this mess into words, but it feels like that first kiss—better than nothing, but frantic and unsatisfying.

He flattens his hand against the outside of my thigh. At first—the shock of his cold skin, wet going through my thin linen. But quickly, it's only the warmth of his skin against my body. The realness of him.

I pull in a breath and ready a statement about partnership, the vision for our valley going forward. But my mouth opens and the words tumble out like I'm talking to a dog, light and quick. "Do you even trust me? Or is this all—did you dream of falling in love, and think of all the ways you would be such a wonderful husband, and now I'm just"—I'm still thinking of being the object of his quest—"the woman who is here? Looking exactly like"—I clench my teeth—"the princess of your dreams?"

"Oh. Mavourneen."

He reaches out for me, but I hunch away.

"Do you remember how I fell in love with you?"

"Yes—I was the only woman you saw."

He clucks. "You were the woman who solved every problem. Who had been raised in physical comfort but learned to tie up a tent and cook over a campfire. You defeated all of Fionn's warriors in order to protect—"

"I made them vomit," I interrupt. "It was the most disgusting night of my life. And then I ran, and didn't even know where I was going, and everything went wrong. Don't make it sound glorious."

"You met my father." Conall props his forehead on his fist. "However briefly. It doesn't take long to see—to see why I value substance over style. You *do* things, Ailbe." He looks up at me, his gaze piercing.

I shrug. "And get them wrong. I made the wrong bargain with Trencoss and started it all out tangled, and he fooled me into almost trusting him, and I even *kissed* Fergus, which was—"

"You make mistakes because you take action."

"So does everyone here!"

"You're right; Theta and Sigma and Rho are all men of determination, although not all of them. But I don't want to fall in love with any of them!" Conall chuckles. "You're talking about women in dreams and reality. You're thinking about, oh, charming princesses and diplomatic marriages. Listen. Come here."

He puts his big hands around my ankles and tugs them forward, so my toes touch the water and I'm sitting flat on the rocks. I squeal at the shock of the water, and then because he's reaching up for me again.

"No—no, it's too cold!" But I'm laughing, because I love the morning and the lake and the expression on my Acushla's beautiful face.

"Come here!" Conall laughs. "I need to talk to you."

"It's too deep!" I protest. "I can't—*oh!*"

He pulls me off the stones and into the water, and it is so sudden and so cold! My back arches and my arms beat the water as though I am a duck who could fly away. I yelp as my own splashing hits me, but Conall just laughs and spins me, and his laughter is so rich and low and velvet that it warms me in spite of myself.

"It's not bad once you're used to it."

"That's what they always say!"

"I'll hold you up. Come here, Ailbe. Come here."

It's the truth; it's too deep for me to stand, and I was too surprised to swim, so Conall is just holding me. I would think I am here with him already, but his hands show me where to come closer. Closer. Settle in.

My legs go around his waist, my arms looped around his shoulders. He is naked and I am very aware of my skin against his, so I tuck my head under his chin so I don't have to meet his gaze. It's one sensation too many.

"Ailbe of Dún Allaine." Conall's voice rumbles beneath me. He pauses, rubbing slow circles on my back, his hand a warm contrast to the water eddying around us. "I chose you. I want you, with all your particular ways of being agreeable and quiet and contrary all at once—and as stubborn as this obsidian, Mavourneen!" He thumps the rock, making me bounce, and we both laugh.

Then I'm looking right into his eyes, my face next to his. He doesn't lean down or pull me in; we are already so close and our lips meet. The cold and the warmth, one after another. I shiver, and shiver again, and this time it is not from the chill, but his steady strong body under mine.

"You asked if I trust you."

I had forgotten my question; just the sense of raw gaping emotion I spilled out for him.

"I haven't shown it well. All those months of traveling together, and the guilt of everything you did for me rubbed me raw and ragged."

"But you took care of me, too!" I protest. "You caught us food, and pulled the cart, and kept me calm and led me to human villages and doors Between!"

His shrug rolls under my arms. "But I didn't help with your daily chores. I couldn't explain things when you were stuck, and I couldn't—I couldn't comfort you when you were sad. You wept, Mavourneen. You were sad and I couldn't—I didn't—"

I let him see me weep because I thought there was nothing he could do. I thought he was powerless and safe, so I let myself be open with him.

"So when I found myself a man again, I was determined to do too much. I planned our wedding without asking you to see what you could learn about the magic, because I thought that would prove how I felt. I thought it would untangle that foolish quest. Declare myself to the other men." He sighs. "I went to Starfruit Island determined to do more than you asked of me. Bringing back one fruit was too easy; I wanted to prove that I was useful. Make an alliance. Discover a clue. Earn our married home. I don't know, Mavourneen. It all seems foolish now."

I thought I could be vulnerable with dog-Conall, but now man-Conall is being vulnerable with me. That's more than I knew to expect...and maybe I can learn to talk freely with him, too. On purpose.

"I do trust you, Ailbe." Conall snuggles me close, his chest hot, his hand cradling my head. "I was thinking about it, yesterday—or whatever day it was—as we were making our way down to the castle. To plant your trees, or overthrow an ancient enemy." He chuckles. "I was watching you with all the men, and seeing..." He strokes my hair, struggling for words. "There is so much more to you than I had ever had a chance to know. The way the men respect you, and you seeing the woodland creatures that I've never noticed, and you're so small but so strong in yourself..."

"And pretty?" The demand leaks out of me, against his skin. I've spent so many years as Saba's helpmeet, nary a man giving me a second glance. Fergus's light-hearted comment stung deep.

"Planting? What did you say?"

I lift my face from his neck but can't manage to look at him. "All that jumping off logs and bargaining with the little flyers...am I just as tough as shoe leather and nine-day biscuits, or do you—are you—"

I pull back to examine his face.

He just stares back. As though my words didn't mean anything, which they probably didn't.

I bite my lip and try again. "Am I—beautiful to you?"

"Ailbe!" Conall laughs, which was not what I expected. "You are—goodness, you are a stunningly attractive woman."

"But to you? I'm not just like another man?"

Conall draws a slow breath, letting it out as he shakes his head slowly. "My Mavourneen." He kisses me. "Every breath of your bravery and determination makes you more irresistible." Another kiss. "I am happy to spend the rest of our lives proving how beautiful I find you, while you continue spectacular feats that only tangle me into loving you all the more."

I laugh, finally convinced. Besides, he keeps kissing me, and I want to be lost in it. "It's my own kind of spell," I tease, rubbing the wet curls at the base of his neck.

"That's the best kind of sorcery." He's smiling into my eyes, then leans forward to—

I pull away, circling my arm into the water.

"I really am very cold," I tell him, although I'm still not sure that's what is making me tremble. "Terribly cold. And wet."

"I ought to take you in?" He scoops me closer, smiling.

"You'd better." I lean against him.

He strides slowly, water sluicing off our shoulders. "I know where I can warm you up."

"They might have the fire going at the main camp."

He shakes his head. "You'd get too cold on the way to the main camp. I'd better keep you here."

"You keep me…" I grow heavier as we emerge from the water, my weight settling onto Conall's hips.

"Those were very warm blankets," he suggests. "I think I'd be taking proper care of you if I tucked you back in bed."

"I like you taking care of me." Even though I can take care of myself, it feels even better to know I can count on my Acushla.

"But to make sure you're warming up"—he hops me off his hips, setting me on my feet in front of him—"I'd better get in bed with you."

"I think you'd better," I agree, very solemnly indeed.

Then I burst into laughter, because I am just so happy. And we walk up the shore, hand and hand.

Chapter Thirty-Seven

By the time I am tucked in bed, I really am cold, and nervous too. Conall took off my wet tunica as though it were the most natural thing in the world. Maybe he is used to being practical about clothes, but I'm not. Not with a man.

"So these blankets came from the fallen castle?" Conall slips in bed behind me. He is warm and I shiver more. "You said the men are building a house in the meadow. Is it what you like? Tell me about it."

His big hands go to my shoulders, rub the tension away from my neck. Slowly, I begin to talk, waiting for him to interrupt me with kisses and...things that men want from their wives. He runs his hand down my arm and back to my shoulder, and asks me more about the plans here. I manage more detail than I did earlier, no longer trying to obscure my own role in what is happening. He sweeps slow strokes against my skin, like I am a cat.

I am not a cat at all. I am more and more distracted by his touch, the smell of his skin, the sturdy chest I know is inches away. I am not a naive girl; I know that bodies do this, but it has never been mine.

His hand finds the curve of my waist and I jerk, a shower of sparks shooting through me.

"I don't know *how* to be beautiful for you!" I wail, interrupting myself.

"Oh, my Mavourneen." He curls close around me, his chest against my back, his arm enfolding me. "I haven't been in this shape for years. I'm not sure what I'm doing, either." He chuckles. "We can take our time."

His forearm is across my chest and my breasts are naked. I rest my hand over his, cupped around my shoulder. "You are being rather distracting," I say.

I feel his smile. "Don't think of it as distracting, then. Think of it as directing your attention go to where it is most valuable."

I laugh. "To you?"

"To me." He kisses the back of my neck, and when I make a little squeak, his kisses trail down to the curve of my shoulder and up to my ear. I try to be rational, breathing evenly and not squirming around.

"Are you upset?" Conall pulls back to look at me, his arm still around me. "You stopped talking, but I can't tell what you're thinking."

I take a slow breath. "What do you want to know?"

"Ailbe, I want you to be yourself with me. Laugh, or push my hands away, or stroke my hair. Whatever you feel like."

For all these years, I have learned to be efficient and useful. He's asking for the opposite, and it doesn't feel fair.

"This morning"—he brushes hair back from my face—"you kissed me, and since then you've been so careful. I see flashes of Ailbe, with her quick thinking and deep feelings, but then you hold yourself in. You're letting me lead, and I don't mind, my Mavourneen, but I need to know where you want to go together."

"I want to be your wife," I mumble into the pillow.

"Yes, but there's a thousand ways to be together. I can't tell what you want when you're being so polite."

I push upright abruptly, pulling the sheet to keep myself covered. "You say polite like it's a bad thing."

"It's not helping us now—"

"How do you think I got through everything?" I pull the sheet tighter, glaring down at Conall. "I was fifteen when Saba was taken the first time, and no one talked about my wedding any more. The queen was dead and Saba was gone, and I knew how to do their work. So I did it." I rub a hand across my eyes, not even sure why I'm saying this. "And then, years later, Saba married and I went with her, but I never liked Fionn, and there were no ladies in the castle before we arrived so everyone looked at us. And how do you think I got by?"

He is just watching me. Listening.

"I tucked all those feelings away. I couldn't afford to flirt with any of the men. I couldn't risk Saba's honor by testing out my feelings with a kiss. No one asked what I wanted."

"I'm sorry that—"

"No!" I thump the blanket. "Don't be! My work is as honorable as any of you men with all your running and scheming and—and swinging sharp things around."

"It is." Conall sits up too, pulling me back into his lap. I don't resist. "But there's more to you than household management and being cordial to everyone, although I fully admit that's a skill that most people cannot manage."

"I don't know." I burrow against his chest. "I might have lost the rest by now."

I don't think I can do this. I don't think I can be a lover like he wants—I can lay still and be kissed, or I could get up and make breakfast.

"I know you can." He rubs his cheek against my hair. "I've felt your love and passion, and your laughter too. I love you for your playfulness."

"I don't play with people." I didn't realize it was true until I said it.

"Mavourneen—"

"Would you like me to throw a ball of dried leaves and moss? You can chase it. Would that make you happy?"

He bursts into laughter. "No, I want to make *you* happy, Ailbe."

"I don't really care about dried leaves," I admit, but I can see the absurdity of the situation. I turn and touch his face, his heart, trying to find who he is—or maybe, who I am with him. We are some sort of in-between world, where he holds the knowledge of all my chatty, silly self, but I can't get there with him in this form.

My hand grazes across his shoulder. I guess I need to learn something new, because this is what I wanted. To have the comfort of human love, I need to risk myself.

"I want you to hold me," I say, letting my thoughts burble out. "I want to be able to lean on you. I promise, I'll do my part too, but I want…"

I don't have words. When I was fifteen, I stopped imagining a marriage that was about what I wanted.

"Let's find out." Conall swings me around, laying me back on the bed. I squeak in surprise, and then he is over me, his mouth on mine. His tongue reaches for me, and I know what he's doing, but it's completely different from this morning. Without meaning to, I arch against him, and we are both naked and everything is—different. His kisses change, quick and brisk and strong, across my face and down my throat and nibbling my earlobe.

At that, my carefully constructed shell falls away like my cloak with the brooch gone. These three days of waiting and planning have made me both fragile and strong, pulled my own love and passion from the shelf where I keep it, throbbing whenever I looked at Conall laying cold and still. Today, he has been joyful and gentle and strong, and I can't hold myself back from this tumbling, wild, violent lovingness that beats in my heart—and now my heart beats against every inch of my skin.

Conall kisses me; his hands go from my hip to my breast to my face; and all the caution I ever had tumbles down like the castle, dissolves into dust like the sorcerer. Conall did it. Conall and I.

I pull him close and find his body with mine, and now we find a new path. A new way to love each other. A new joy.

This morning, he loves me as a husband loves his wife, with his hands and his mouth and his body. And I love him like a wife, because I am *his* wife. I open myself to him—not just my body, but even my feelings.

I didn't know I could feel these things, until he was here to give them to me. My heartbeat throbs in my face, in my belly, on my skin, and my Acushla—his heart beats for me. I know it.

***

We walk into the main camp as the morning sun grows warm—Conall and I, holding hands. I am laughing even before the men drop their tools and surround us, running in from the surrounding projects, beating their breasts and ululating. Oisín runs in wild loops, cheering and throwing wood chips in the air. The men clasp Conall's hands, and someone swings me in the air until I scream with laughter. Birds flutter and sing in the branches above us, and I see round furry faces peeking up from the trail to the river. The otters can't resist a commotion!

After a long time, Zeta builds up the fire to prepare a feast, and Beta and Tau get out their flute and drum. Some of the men go back to their projects, and others show Conall through what has already been built.

"What supplies are up at the old castle?" my husband is asking. "What other villages are in the valley? What did Trencoss tax them, and what support did he offer? Stores for the winter, perhaps? We'll have to do at least as well. Have we a grain silo?"

He knows what questions to ask, and the mood in the group shifts as he takes control. They were two dozen men of action, with good hearts and clever minds, but no one had been trained as a leader. No one understands the math that he spouts so easily, costs and advantages and percentages. We didn't know where to hire a magistrate or the proper messages to send to the nearby kings and landowners.

"They had a trading and defense relationship with Trencoss," Conall says with absolute certainty. "We can't let them find out he has died just through rumor and their own spies."

"Do they have spies?" Iota asks, worried.

"Of course. We will too."

"Can I be a spy?" Alpha asks, and Conall claps him on the shoulder.

"Can I send for my wife and children?" Kappa asks. Everyone turns and stares; I didn't know he was married, either. "They're in Ui Néill, but I promised to send for them when I had a place. We never imagined it would take so long."

"Would she wait?" Alpha asks, and I can hear the longing in his tone.

Kappa nods, as confident as Conall about trade routes and spies.

I put my hand to my throat, which has gone dry. Maybe it's what I just did with Conall, or the last three days of waiting, but Kappa's wife's dedication melts me entirely.

"The two of you will make this work." Saba has come up beside me, her low voice for my ears only. "For all of Zeta and Rho's good intentions, and all your speaking with the animals and good relations with your Good Neighbors, I knew you needed someone like him."

I take her hand, wanting to keep her close forever. I notice that she said *you* will make it. Not *we*. She is still caught in her own story; her own fate will pull her away.

I have a sudden suspicion. "Were you actually confident that he would wake?"

Saba smiles. "Mostly. Come, sit down, my friend."

We settle on the log bench, watching the men make their plans while keeping an eye on Oisín. He is perched on Rho's shoulders, hands buried in his unruly mane of hair, one fat little foot thumping while Rho holds him by the other foot and gestures to the men's conversation. Some of the warriors pay only slight heed to the wee lad, but several of them have taken the boy under their wing. He cannot be afraid of the men like he will one day become, they tell Saba, and I see the worry in her mouth but she lets him go. They are gentle but firm in a way that Saba and I are not, encouraging Oisín to carry his own tiny loads and bathe in the cold stream, and then chasing and tickling him until he squeals with joy.

I wonder what my own children will be like. My heart leaps at the thought of a baby in my own arms; to see what kind of father Conall will become.

Which reminds me—"I don't know what I did. This morning, he was just...awake."

Saba turns to me. "Does it matter?"

"Of course the important part is that he is back." I twist my hands in my léine. "But I need to know. I need to be able to be careful, and work things right."

"Do you want to become a sorcerer? Learning how all the tendrils of power—"

"No! No, of course not." I take a slow breath. "I just want to...do it right."

Saba asks what happened, and I describe everything about how he woke up, his mood, his vigor. "Maybe I wasn't important," I add. "Maybe the magic just wore off. It was just your herbs."

"Of course you were important," Saba says, perfectly calm. "Our very selves change the world around us. Every action touches something else, like those fine silver chains twisting."

"But what did I do?"

Saba turns back to the scene below us, watching in silence. Finally, she gestures to Oisín, who is now gingerly holding one corner of an oiled cloth while the men tack it in place.

"Sometimes," she says, "there is no more we can do. Right now, I can't teach my son to be a man. I can't teach him to be confident around strangers while keeping him always safe."

"No...of course, you are doing a wonderful job with him. But what about...how I am supposed to be a good wife?"

Saba looks at me, a smile playing on the edge of her lips. "You were asleep when his enchantment lifted. Perhaps this is a lesson for you."

I shrug, helpless.

Saba smiles. "Ailbe, maybe it is time for you to learn that you can do the best you can—and then, that is enough. There is nothing more to do. Just be yourself."

"Myself..." I watch the men, my heart melting with tenderness. There is Conall, who is working to figure out how to be my partner, leading our fledgling village with his meticulous care and attention. Zeta, who shares his wisdom freely. Tau, who is no longer lazy now that he has a purpose and direction. Alpha, eager to take on the world. Oisín, silly and chubby and full of unformed love. The songbirds and otters and mice and owls, the little flyers and Bob's marble castle, and somewhere in the distance, the servants who are faceless no longer, reunited with their families and ready to send us tribute in exchange for protection. All of that.

"Because you are part of the world," Saba concludes, "and your love has changed this corner of it."

"Ailbe!" Sigma calls. "Saba! Come tell us what you think!"

Conall jogs towards us, already smiling, holding out a hand for me. I smile back and he kisses my cheek.

I lay my hand in my Acushla's, take Saba's with the other, and we walk towards the others. Our new lives, together.

Author's Notes

Acushla and Mavourneen

A chuisle (uh KHUSH-leh): Pulse

Often used in the phrase: a chuisle mo chroí: the pulse of my heart, or the beat of my heart

A mhuirnín (ah woor-neen): Beloved

They are pronounced exactly how an English speaker would expect from reading "Acushla" and "Mavourneen." The first "a" included in the Irish is indicating the vocative case, and necessary when speaking *to* someone—however, it tends to be visually confusing for English speakers.

The English spellings, Acushla and Mavourneen*, date from the early 20th century, from a group of Irish writers and nationalists working to reclaim their heritage. These cross-lingual spellings were designed to make it easier for English-speakers to use Irish in their conversation or writing. It caught on, and the endearments were used especially broadly in the Irish-American diaspora as well.

I thought that Acushla and Mavourneen would "feel" like names to my English-speaking readers, but I am also especially delighted to include this nod towards the movement that did so much to reclaim Irish culture—which was also the movement that saved fairy tales, like this one.

* For those of you who, like me, grew up with Tamora Pierce and early feminist fantasy, this is also where the name Alanna comes from. It is the Irish nationalist Anglicization of *a leanbh*, my child, and used frequently

in Irish songs as well. The connection was coincidental, but I'm honored to use this connection to tip my hat to Pierce and Alanna!

Dún Allaine: doon AL-i-nuh
Bodhbh Dearg

Dún Allaine is the one of the great royal sites of early Ireland, similar to the hill of Tara, and in use from approx. 400 BCE-400 CE. For ease of reading, I have streamlined the conflicting references, but everything mentioned about Saba's family is taken from history. Bodhbh Dearg was indeed a great king, listed in both mythological and historical contexts, and Dún Allaine would have been one of the most spectacular palaces in Ireland at the time.

Bodhbh has a similar pronunciation to Saba (I chose to use the Anglicized version of her name for ease of reading), and difficult to transliterate to English. In both cases, the second half of the word is a lilt more than a strong syllable, and the middle consonant is between our /b/ and /v/.

That is why, in this book, Ailbe struggles with our English word "Bob," which ends with a hard crisp sound; as well as why in the "Irish Library in Kilkenny," the Italians struggle with the indistinct ending to "Saba." (That story, briefly referenced in this book, can be found in *Where Kindness Lives*.)

Léine/léinte
Inar
Gúna

The léine is the staple of traditional Irish clothing for both men and women. It was a loose gown with long, flowing sleeves, traditionally dyed with saffron.

A man would have tied his léine up at knee level, using their crios belt. He wore loose trousers underneath, and a wool inar over top. The inar is a square, boxy jacket, often with short or split sleeves so the léine sleeves came through.

A woman would have worn her léine more at ankle-length. In some cases, she would have worn a gúna—an overdress, probably sleeveless and laced under her bosom. She also wore a decorative cap.

It is important to note that a léine was complete clothing on its own, unlike French or English under-dresses. Although Ailbe was accustomed to having an elegant gúna to show off her protector's wealth, she considered herself fully dressed in only the léine and crios.

Léinte is the plural.

Crios/criossana

A crios is a woven belt, between 2-3 meters long, worn by both men and women, and wrapped several times around the waist with the ends hanging loose. Criossana is the plural.

I spend a wonderful amount of time researching how these belts would have been woven; there are many options. Often times, and implied in this book, the weaver would hold one end of the warp with her foot and the other in her hand or tied to a chair. Crios can be woven with almost no external loom at all, but an upper-class woman like Ailbe would have probably had a small shuttle for the weft, a specialized bar to hold with her foot, perhaps even with the capability to lift opposite threads like a rigid heddle. "Pick and drop" refers to choosing the warp threads to go over and under as the weaver creates her design.

Age of adulthood and succession

In Celtic society, women were considered adult at the age of 15, and men at the age of 18.

When this story begins, Ailbe has already been an adult for many years, although she is probably only in her early twenties.

Fergus and Conall would have both left their fathers' households soon after becoming adults. Among Celts, a king would have chosen his own successor—ideally from among his sons, but also potentially from his daughters or nephews. The oldest son usually had an advantage, but was not guaranteed the position.

Race in Heroic Ireland

The three races depicted in my books are historically accurate. I have chosen to depict them as overlapping in this period (we don't know this for sure), and used the mythological names for the early waves of immigration (Nemed and Fir Bolg).

We know the earliest Irish were Black, with long heads and sometimes blue eyes. In my interpretation, the Nemed are less common but still known in the older communities or most isolated regions. In this story, Fionn mac Cumhaill and Conall (and his family) are Nemed.

The next, long-lasting wave of Irish came from the area that is now Turkey and the middle east. Their features included medium-dark skin, dark hair, and slanted eyes. This race no longer lives in Turkey, but can be found in the Caucasus mountains and some of the regions in west Asia. In this story, Ailbe is Fir Bolg.

The Celts were still relatively recent in Ailbe's time, and had been trickling over for a couple hundred years. Fionn mac Cumhaill (and thus this story) is set in approximately 3rd Century Ireland, by which point the Celtic culture would have had firmly established itself, but not taken over the entire island. The references to magistrates, divorce, town structure, clothing, etc., are all taken from early Celtic culture.

Knowledge of Greek (and Egyptian)

Ireland was on direct trading routes going to the Mediterranean, and the diversity of artifacts in ancient Ireland makes it clear that there was active and profuse trading. The Irish kings had wine, olive oil, jewelry, precious stones, silk, and many other luxury goods from all over the world, via the Mediterranean.

Where there are goods traded, human beings and their knowledge goes along as well. It only makes sense that Ailbe—who was educated as a princess in one of the wealthiest households in Ireland—would have a working understanding of the Greek alphabet, Egyptian sphinxes, and anything else important in her broader world.

Wolf-hounds, cats, and all the furry and feathered creatures

All the information in this story is based on fact. Wolf-hounds were, indeed, strongly associated with kings, where they were treated with the same respect due to any other warrior. Wild wolf-packs were a grave danger in this period, but wolf-hounds also helped bring down game, protect the villages from other dangerous animals, and they were trained and armored to go into battle against other armies. They wore spiked iron collars to protect themselves.

I did, indeed, look up every plant and animal mentioned in this book, to ensure they were present in Ireland in this period (to the best of my research ability!). For my American readers—the Eurasian Jay does have pink feathers, not blue.

As for cats—there were, indeed, domestic cats. They were probably as sassy and demanding as cats are still today. As Fergus warned us... "...never trust the Good People, and probably never trust a cat, either."

The original fairy tale: The Little White Cat

The bones of this story are taken almost faithfully from the original story, "The Little White Cat," collected by Yeats in the 19th Century. That story gives us the name Trencoss and his Castle of a Thousand Doors. The princess is guarded by large dogs wearing iron collars. A cat comes in her window, gives her the challenge of the balls of thread made from dew, and sends a prince to rescue her. Trencoss uses magical servants to collect the dew, which annoys him because he thought it would be easy, and meanwhile the prince attempts to row to three islands to collect three fruits.

The prince, however, is an absolute knuckle-head. Unlike almost every other Irish fairy tale, he is terrible at following directions. On every island, he gets tricked by the Fae (whom he's not supposed to be talking with at all), stays longer than he's supposed to, and then when the cat finally reminds him what he's supposed to be doing, he escapes with the fruit and the supposedly-seductive Fae turn into monsters. Then he goes and does it again!

In the original story, after the prince fails repeatedly (while the princess valiantly fends off the evil sorcerer and all his dogs), the cat just whisks both the prince and princess to his palace in the middle of the lake and has them get married. I loved so many elements of this story, but the ending clearly needed to be adjusted—no one wants the knuckle-head to get the girl.

Being a fan of dogs, I leaned into the part of the story where the princess converts all the terrifying dog guardians to be her best friends. Being (apparently) unable to write one-dimensional characters, Fergus turned out to be less of a doofus and more just in over his head...but he still didn't deserve to marry the princess at the end!

Acknowledgements

Books don't exist in a vacuum, let along in one person's head, so I am thankful for my community that helps to bring these fairy tales out into the world.

First of all, any credit for a sharp and energetic story goes to my editor, Katie Tammen, who never fails to tell me when something is boring. I think I fixed it.

The beautiful object you are holding in your hands is thanks to Elaine Schroller, who manages the formatting and catches the final glitches. During the last hectic week when it's time to upload the many versions of the manuscript to the many different places with their oh-so-slightly different formatting requirements, I value so much having such a calm and capable professional working in my corner.

Karri Klawiter did an amazing job on the covers, and is a joy to work with.

Thank you to Beth Anne, Laura, Nicole, Roxanne, and all the other positive and thoughtful writers whom I am honored to call my friends.

I appreciate my newsletter subscribers and review team, who give me encouragement and feedback. After sharing so many pictures and stories about my own dogs, I hope you love this book!

I wrote a significant portion of this manuscript at the artist residency program at the Starry Night Inn, in Seaside, Oregon. I deeply appreciated the quiet and artistic space to write, and the endless supply of sandwiches and overnight oatmeal in the fridge downstairs allowed me to get in a couple thousand extra words each day! (Also, who knew you were supposed to eat overnight oats cold? Not me. I put them in the microwave, but upon returning home I learned that most people eat them...cold. Peculiar!)

Finally, I'm thankful to all the dogs and cats whom I have loved in throughout my entire life. You give me so much joy.

About the Author

Characters you connect with. Adventure. Love. Family... and endings that are more than a sugar rush.

When Christy Matheson is not throwing ordinary characters into fairy tales, she is busy raising five children. (Very busy.) She writes character-driven historical fiction with and without fantasy elements, and her "fresh, smart, and totally charming" stories have won multiple awards.

Christy is also an embroidery artist, classically trained pianist, and sews all of her own clothes. She lives in Oregon, on a country property that fondly reminds her of a Regency estate (except with a swing set instead of faux Greek ruins), with her husband, five children, three Shelties, one bunny, and an improbable quantity of art supplies.

Please join Christy in conversation about books and determined women throughout history.

Join her newsletter to get free stories, art giveaways, & puppy pictures. https://sendfox.com/ChristyMatheson

And you can always find her at: christymatheson.com

ALSO BY CHRISTY MATHESON

The Castle in Kilkenny: Fairy Tales
Book 1: *The Horned Women: A contemporary retelling of an Irish fairy tale*
Book 2: *The White Deer of Kildare*
Book 3: *The Knight of the Terrible Valley and Aiden of Florida*
Book 4: *The Squire and His Magical Library*
Book 5: *The Knight and His Magical Armlet*
Book 6: *Oona and the Swan*

The Horned Women and Other Stories: Castle of Kilkenny Fairy Tales Books 1, 2, and 3
The Knight and His Magical Library: Castle of Kilkenny Fairy Tales Books 4 and 5

Castle in Kilkenny: Romantic Fairy Tales
The Boat on the Lake of Regret
The Little White Cat & The Dog Who Wasn't

Available through The Sheltie Gazette (newsletter signup on website)
Book 0.5: *The Leprechaun and the Castle Magical Libraries*

Regency Romance, coming 2026
Book 1: *The Bonnet Brigade*
Book 2: *The Domestic Diplomat*
Book 3: *The Ambassador & the Architect*
Book 4: *The Musician & the Marquess*

Short Stories and Anthologies
In *Feisty Deeds: Historical Fictions of Daring Women*, "The Inner Good"
In *Feisty Deeds II: Historical Tales of Batches & Brews*, "Escape to Peaceful Valley"
In *Where Kindness Lives: A Women's Fiction Anthology*, "The Irish Library in Kilkenny"